Claiming CRUSHER
SAVAGE BROTHERS MC BOOK 4

By: Jordan Marie

Formatting Services: Paul Salvette & BB eBooks
Editing Services: Twin Sisters Rocking Book Reviews
Proofreading Services: Dessure Hutchins
Jen Wildner with: Prim and Wild
And Kathryn Jacoby with: My Book Angel Blog

Copyright © 2015
Print Edition

All rights reserved. No part of this publication may be reproduced, distributed, or transmitted in any form or by any means, including photocopying, recording, or other electronic or mechanical methods, without the prior written permission of the author.

WARNING: The unauthorized reproduction or distribution of this copyrighted work is illegal. No part of this book may be scanned, uploaded or distributed via the internet or any other means, electronic or print, without the publisher's/author's permission. Criminal copyright infringement, including infringement without monetary gain, is investigated by the FBI and is punishable by up to 5 years in federal prison and a fine of 250,000.00 (www.fbi.gov/ipr). Please purchase only authorized electronic or print editions and do not participate or encourage the electronic piracy of copyrighted material. Your respect of the author's rights is appreciated.

This book is a work of fiction and any resemblance to persons, living or dead, or places events or locales is purely coincidental. The characters are created from the author's imagination and used in a fictitious manner.

Cover:
Designer: Margreet Asselbergs – Rebel Edit Designs
Model: Ricky Alm
Photographer: Tristin Godsey of Trystram Photography Artistry
WebPage: Trystram Photography Web Page
Picture of Woman: Dollar Photo Club
(Stock Photo used on the back of paperback only)

Trademarks:

Any brands, titles, artists used in this book were mentioned purely for artistic purposes and are either used as a product of the author's imagination or used fictitiously. None of the herein mentioned products, artists etc., endorse this book whatsoever and the author acknowledges their trademarked status which has been used in this work of fiction.

Author acknowledges trademarked status or owners of various products and further acknowledges that said use is not authorized or endorsed by said owners. While some places in this book might mention actual areas or places, author acknowledges that it was purely for entertainment purposes and not endorsed by owners or has nothing to do with actual place and was mentioned to further reader's enjoyment only.

The Content in this book is intended for mature audiences only. 18+ and above.

Contains sexual violence, rape, sexual situations, multiple partner sex, violence, excessive profanity, and death. Reader should please read with that knowledge. Please do not read if any of the above offends you.

Previous Titles in the Series

Breaking Dragon Savage Brothers MC Book 1
Saving Dancer Savage Brothers MC Book 2
Loving Nicole Savage Brothers MC Book 3

Crusher

I see her. I see her clearer than anyone ever has—even her best friend.

There are secrets in those beautiful brown eyes. Secrets that have broken her.

She reminds me of someone else. Someone I loved. Someone I was unable to save.

I won't fail with her.

I want to claim her as my own and take away the ghosts that leave her haunted.

Dani

Little girl lost…

The woman I once was, is gone. All that remained of her were broken pieces lying ravaged and scattered by a storm.

I tried to piece her back together, to sift through the wreckage and re-create her.

It was impossible. She was too damaged. She died.

From her ashes I arose.

Untouchable, unfeeling, unworthy—the new me is not quite, right.

I don't even like me. Why would he?

One man destroyed me. Why would I ever claim another?

Two damaged souls—

One trying to re-live the past, one trying to forget it.

Can they heal each other?

TABLE OF CONTENTS

Previous Titles in the Series	iii
Dedication	vii
Foreword	ix
The Beginning of the End of Her	1
Chapter 1	19
Chapter 2	26
Chapter 3	33
Chapter 4	49
Chapter 5	54
Chapter 6	66
Chapter 7	72
Chapter 8	79
Chapter 9	83
Chapter 10	88
Chapter 11	93
Chapter 12	100
Chapter 13	108
Chapter 14	112
Chapter 15	118
Chapter 16	124
Chapter 17	131
Chapter 18	140
Chapter 19	145
Chapter 20	153
Chapter 21	158

Chapter 22	165
Chapter 23	174
Chapter 24	181
Chapter 25	188
Chapter 26	193
Chapter 27	203
Chapter 28	207
Chapter 29	213
Chapter 30	220
Chapter 31	224
Chapter 32	231
Chapter 33	237
Chapter 34	240
Chapter 35	245
Chapter 36	249
Chapter 37	254
Chapter 38	263
Chapter 39	269
Chapter 40	274
Chapter 41	277
Chapter 42	284
Chapter 43	288
Chapter 44	293
Chapter 45	297
Chapter 46	302
Epilogue	310
Trusting Bull	314
Exposed	321
Remember Me	332
Misled	347
Note from Author & Links	362
Links	363
Playlists	364

Dedication

I am a lover of words. They have saved my life, help me to escape and brought solace when it felt as if I was drowning. It's still hard for me to believe that I get to write words and that people want to read it. I can never express what a gift that is, because I honestly don't think words are invented that adequately describe it. So, first and foremost, thank you readers for not only letting me live my dream, but encouraging me. I am forever in your debt.

Thank you as always to my friend Kurt Gangluff, may life always find you filled with joy and peace and dreams of Rooster.

Tammie Smith, you are my wonder twin. You save my life daily and there's no way I can repay you for everything you do. I love you boo thang. I love you beyond words.

Dessure Hutchins, you didn't know me but you had my back. That blows me away. From that, I gained one of the best friends and confidants a girl could have. Thank you for all your hard work and for always making me laugh and sharing your misadventures with Grady. You're a light in my day woman.

Grady 'G6' Hutchins, thank you for becoming what I must now measure every book boyfriend I write by. Keep our DD happy or I shall have to write you in a book and do something evil to you. Sorry, not sorry.

Tami Czenkus, I don't need to say anything, you know. I love you beyond words.

To my crew who helped me like crazy with this book, LaVida Briscoe, Michelle McGinty, Jen Wildner, Tammie S., Dessure, and Tami C. Thanks for holding my hand and telling me when I sucked.

To the Badass Betas who provided great feedback as well as helped encourage me, I love you ladies big, Tamra Simons, Andrea Florkowski, and Melody Bruce Miller.

Neringa, I don't think you get how much you mean to me. I shall tell you as often as I can so that maybe someday you will grasp it. Thank you woman, you are AMAZING.

Melissa Anne Allen, I hope you like your rendezvous with Bull. Thank you for the support lady. Happy Reading.

Angel Dust, my friend, I just love the hell out of you. That's all I got. You are amazing.

Fran and CJ as always thanks for putting up with me missing deadlines and working in a panic. I truly love you ladies.

To my street team, which really are just some of the most amazing women I have ever had the chance to get to know. I love each and every one of you. I have signings piled up next year and I hope I get the chance to meet all of you. If I get so lucky we must make it a point to get together and get *chocolate wasted*. My treat. #BadassBitches4Life

Foreword

Readers as always I've tried really hard to write this book so that you don't have to read the whole series. For the most part, I do believe I have achieved that goal. The heroine in this book was first written in Breaking Dragon and at first she was a throw-away character I had every intention of writing off and never hearing from again. Then she spoke.

There are scenes in this book that contain **graphic violence**. Her story is not pretty. Do not read if you can't handle the violence she endured. However, I hope you do follow her journey and see the strength it took to get to the other side. That said, along with the violence and rape scenes there are consensual sex scenes that involve multiple partners and all that entails. This was your warning.

For those that remain, enjoy! (Hopefully)

J

The Beginning of the End of Her

MELINDA

I DON'T KNOW what set him off this time. I honestly don't. I'm always so careful—the past year has taught me to be careful. I don't argue, I don't question. I make sure everything he could possibly want or ask from me is within reach. The cook knows the menu a solid week in advance. All meals are approved by Michael. In fact, *everything* is approved by Michael right down to the color of my hair (red) and the pale, pink lip gloss I wear. I do not make a move unless it is approved by him.

I've been doing this for so long now, it has become second nature. I'm almost robotic with it all. So, I honestly have no idea why I'm being summoned to his office. My hands are shaking and a cold, clammy sweat pops out over my body. My stomach flutters nervously and I'm glad I haven't eaten. I'm standing outside Michael's office in our home and I'm terrified to knock, because I know what will happen. If I don't knock? If I try to run away? Michael will make me pay. I know, because I've done it in the past. I've learned not to run now—it hurts less. I stiffen my backbone and knock gently. I send up a prayer that he will be asleep or gone. As usual, the prayer goes unanswered. God forgot about me a long time ago. I'm not sure he ever remembered me.

"Come in, Melinda." Michael says through the closed door. His voice sounds bored, tired even. I know better. The monster inside of him is pacing quickly, back and forth, waiting to pounce.

I come in without a word. I still the shaking in my hands, so I can gently shut the door. I walk to the chair in front of his desk, keeping my head down and avoiding eye contact. When I sit down and notice the green silk slip dress I have on, I panic. Michael doesn't like green. He prefers me to wear light pastels. I have closets full of pink, lavender, and yellow. Those are acceptable colors. I have on the green dress because Michael was supposed to be gone today. Is that what upset him? I'm so stupid! Why do I even keep this dress?

"It would appear we have a problem, Melinda," he states calmly. Then again, Michael is always calm. Even when he is doling out punishment, his voice never raises. It stays clipped, concise, and in a proper tone. That somehow makes him scarier to me.

"I'm sorry," I say by reflex. I don't know what I've done, it doesn't matter what I've done.

"I'm afraid that's not good enough considering your crime."

My crime. He always uses that term, as if he is the judge, jury, and executioner in charge, and I'm the repeat offender. I want to ask what I did. It's on the tip of my tongue to question. I don't, I bite my tongue and concentrate on the pain instead. When I make no move to question him further, Michael lets out a loud sigh. The sound is one of annoyance. Annoyance from Michael and directed at me, only means bad things. I can't stop the way my heart kicks into overdrive, or the apologies which immediately spring up and rest on my lips. I don't give them voice, I beat them back. You can't show the monster weakness, he can smell it and he will devour you. I pull my eyes from my shoes, to look out the window. I search for the sun outside. I'm not free, but if I can concentrate on the warm glare of the sun it will help—another lesson I've learned over the last year. I try to focus my breathing and that's when I see it.

On his desk is a tube of carnal, red lipstick. I love it and I put it on when I'm alone. I dream of a day when I can wear this color all the time. I'm not brave enough to buy it. No, I'm not sure I have any bravery left in me. It was a gift from Nicole. I try to keep nothing out in the open of Nicole or my time at Three Oaks. Nicole might have hated the place, but I loved every minute of it. If only because it allowed me to stay away from Michael. When his lawyers found a judge they could buy and had that portion of my father's will overturned, hell truly began for me. I had no choice but to marry Michael and move in with him. I tried running. I tried and failed. I have the scars to prove it.

So, I stored away the good memories I had. Most of which, admittedly, revolve around Nicole. I risk a lot just to remain in contact with Nic, but she's my lifeline. If I don't hear her voice at least once a week, I feel hopeless. I can't let hope fade. If I give in…I'll never survive. Then, Michael will truly win.

How did he find the lipstick? I'm always so careful. I rack my brain trying to remember where I could have left it. Then I see it. The small, wooden box I keep hidden in the air conditioning vent in my closet. Inside are my most prized possessions. I may have been the Marinetti Shipping heir, but I had nothing unless Michael provided it. No, my most prized possessions would bring you nothing at an auction. They consist of four things. Four things that mean everything to me.

First was the lipstick Nicole gave me. Next was a note from my father. The very last note I ever got from him. I don't know why I keep it. I hate him for what he did to me. There's a picture of me and Nicole in one of those silly photo booths at a town fair. It was probably the best day I've ever had in my life. Finally, there is the one thing in this world that I need to survive. The one thing I touch every night. My mother's medallion. She gave it to me before she died. It's my last connection to my mother. I can't lose it. I can't.

My heart stops. The monster has them. I know he won't give them back. He will destroy them, just to prove a point. He will relish in the fact that he is hurting me. A hundred words come to my lips, words I could use to beg him to give back my things. I clench my hands in tight fists, letting my nails bite into my skin. I can't beg. Begging him only incites him to go further, to be meaner. I remain quiet, waiting.

"Have you nothing to say, Melinda?"

"I am sorry, Michael."

"Is there some reason you have kept these things hidden from me, my darling wife?"

The fake sugary-sweetness he uses when calling me his wife causes the acid in my stomach to boil. How much hate can one person hold in their body? There are times, when I think I have nothing left but hate.

How do I answer? Do I tell him I didn't want him touching them? That if he did, he would somehow taint them? Do I lie and say they are unimportant? I'm honestly at a loss on how to answer.

In the end, I shrug and try playing down the whole thing.

"They are just memories of my childhood. Nothing that important, Michael," I answer, trying to inject sincerity into my words.

Michael comes around in front of me leaning on his desk. His arms are crossed and he looks so relaxed. I know what's coming though. I know what always happens when I do something to displease the monster. The sick feeling inside of me floods through my bloodstream. Will he kill me this time? He's come close before. Will tonight be the final end of it all? I think I'd be okay if it was. I need it to end. I can't keep going on like this. *I'm tired.*

"Very well Melinda, you may leave. I shall dispose of your trinkets."

Two main emotions flood me at the same time. Relief that I have escaped his punishment this time and then agony. He will dispose…my gaze lands, one last time on my mother's medallion and I can't stop the small tear that falls on my cheek. I know it's a mistake. I know I should be quiet, but I can't. That necklace is all I have of my mom. There are no pictures, everything else has been ripped away from me, save for that one lone trinket. So, even knowing I should hold it back, I can't. I know before I say the words I shouldn't. I do. I just can't stop myself.

"Something you would like to say, Melinda?

"Please, Michael, please."

"Please what, wife?"

I hate that term. I am barely eighteen. I shouldn't be married. I should be dating and I would never date anyone like Michael Kavanagh. Just hearing the words and knowing that it links the two of us together causes bile to rise into my throat. I fight it back down.

"Don't destroy the necklace. It was my mothers. It's all I have left of her…"

I hate begging. I feel so *weak*, so inferior. Yet, I know if I approach this any other way, there will be no saving any of my belongings. The chance is small even with me begging.

I watch as he picks up the chain and lets it slide between his cruel hands. I see it now. The smug darkness in his eyes. I've given the monster power. It is all he needs. It is what he has been waiting for. Perhaps I am as stupid as Michael keeps insisting I am.

"Is the necklace important to you, wife?"

Again that word…the term that makes my stomach roll.

"Yes, Michael."

"Do you know what I can't understand, Melinda?"

I want to answer, but fear has paralyzed me and my vocal chords are frozen as well.

"Well, wife? Do you?"

I try to talk, I open my mouth, but all that comes out is a squeaky half syllable. I quickly clear my throat and start again.

"What, Michael?"

"How my darling wife could keep something so obviously important hidden from me. Can you understand that, Melinda?"

I say nothing, by this time the look in his eyes has rendered me speechless. It's too late. It's much too late.

"Furthermore, if a small ratty necklace that is far beneath your station in life is important, I can't begin to imagine what the other items you've kept hidden means."

He reaches over and slides the medallion over my head. The cold medal lies against my breast and I have a moment of relief. Is he going to allow me to keep it? That's the only thought I have before he grabs the hair at the back of my head and fists it so tightly, so painfully, my eyes water. I gasp at the hurt. He drags me from the chair, so I am standing in front of him, my head is forced back, and tears are streaming down my face. I have to strain to keep my eyes on him. I need to know what is coming. My time with Michael has taught me nothing—if not survival.

"Tell me Melinda, what does the lipstick mean to you? Besides coloring your lips so that you look like some two-bit whore."

He doesn't give me time to answer, not that I could with the way he has my neck twisted. The pain is bad, nowhere near what he's capable of, but bad nonetheless. He takes the lipstick and paints it hard on my lips, to the point it cracks and twists to the side and I can feel the metal rim of the container biting into my lip and cutting as it goes. I try to pull away, but the pain only intensifies and his grip is so tight there is no breaking free. He then pushes the lipstick itself through my teeth and into my mouth. The sick, faintly plastic taste mingles with the coppery taste of blood and I choke. This only serves to piss him off and he back hands me on the side of the face, *hard*.

The impact is jarring and I would scream, but my mouth is clogged and the force of the slap leaves me stunned.

"Swallow the fucking stuff, Melinda! If you want to be a whore then by god, I shall treat you like one!" He lets go of my hair, but only to use his hand to bite down on my chin and imprison me so I can do nothing but look into his hateful, cold, blue eyes. *Ice*. Frozen and so unfeeling, they send terror into my soul.

I choke the lipstick down my throat, doing my best not to gag. The problem is the fear of losing my connection with my mother, of knowing the pain I will soon endure, and the half of a grapefruit Michael allotted me for breakfast this morning, all roll together and combine to tear my insides up and I vomit. I try to clamp my lips and teeth together, but the force is too strong. Michael growls and pushes me away from him so hard and fast that I can't even begin to stop myself. I fall back into the chair and it slides when my weight impacts it. I feel my back scrape along the metal of the arms as I fall to the floor. The chair continues to slide until my head hits the floor.

"Fucking cunt. You will pay for that." He growls, wiping the small amount of lipstick-tinted bile that sprayed on his chin. It's then that he kicks my stomach. I curl to try and prevent it, but I'm too dazed, too slow and I can't. One…two…three…the impact of his booted foot slams into my stomach over and over—until it *finally* stops.

I'm gasping trying to catch my breath, thankful for the small reprieve when his foot comes at my face. I see a flash of black, feel the forceful hit land on my mouth and taste copper again, only this time a lot more. Another hit, this time on the upper part of my head, it leaves me lightheaded. I pray I will lose consciousness. If I do, maybe he will leave me alone, and even if he doesn't, I won't know. Again, my prayers are unanswered. He pulls me up by the collar of my dress. I hear the tearing of the fabric and even in my pained, fearful state, I mourn it. There was a time I adored dressing up and feeling pretty. I vow if I survive this, the only thing I will adore is being cold. I need to be as cold as Michael to survive. Then again, I'm not even sure why I want to survive.

The dress must rip even more, because as quick as he begins pulling me up, I fall back against the cold tile. I feel the cold air of the room hit my chest and down my side. Michael grabs my head and pulls me by my hair. He drags me through the office chairs, but I barely notice the way they rake over my body with their metal legs. He throws me on the couch and my stomach revolts. If I had anything left inside, I would vomit again. *I know where this will end.* I know *how* it will end. I don't want it. Everything in me is screaming out at the injustice, the unfairness of it all. I close my eyes and try to remember something...anything to take my mind away from what is about to happen. Nicole's face dances in front of me and intermingles with Ray. My only friends in the world. They have no idea how bad my life is here. If they interfered, Michael would kill them. I can't let that happen. I vow no one will ever touch my friends the way that Michael does me. It's a weak vow, but still a *vow*.

"You want to be a whore my darling wife, I will treat you like one."

How can his voice sound so calm? It's as if he's talking about the weather. What kind of monster can do that? Again, he pulls me by my hair until he has my face pushed into the top of the sofa. My knees sink into the cushions and I try to reach back to stop him. It's no use, he grabs my wrist and I feel immense pain as I hear a bone snap. I scream out and he pushes my face harder into the wood on the Queen Anne sofa. I try to move my face to the side, I can feel the teeth in my mouth and they are loose and at least one is chipped. There's so much blood in my mouth, I almost choke on it. The ripping of my clothes continue, but it doesn't matter anymore. He grabs the necklace at the back of my neck and pulls. It's a thick chain and in this instance that is bad, because he pulls tighter and tighter until my head is snapped back and my air is restricted.

He plunges inside of me. Tearing as he goes, *as he always does*. My vision starts to dim, the room goes gray and I'm ready for it. I'm ready for death. Anything so I no longer have to endure this...

As he finishes, the hold on my neck loosens and I gulp in breath. I want to refuse it. If I don't breathe, I die. It's a reflex though and I can't stop myself. He crushes me underneath him and his vile stench is even more prevalent over the scent of blood. I remain quiet, waiting for him to get up and forget about me—as he always does. Only, this time I sadly underestimate him.

"Look at you, Melinda." He says as if disgusted. I can hear the sound of his zipper. This time he grabs the back of my leg and pulls me from the couch I use my hands to try and stop myself from being slammed around but one hand is completely useless, and I end up trying to hold it tight to my chest wrapped against the other one to stop it from hurting more. He brings me to the wall that has three large mirrors hanging on them, and pushes my face against the glass. My vision is blurry, my eyes are swollen from the kicks he gave me and being ground into the hard wood of the couch. I make out my form through the mirror. The reflection makes me sick. Not because of the way I look, more for the weakness I see. I hate that word and how often it relates to me... *Weak*.

"Look at you! You think you can hide things from me, Melinda? Will you never learn? Do you think you could paint yourself up and people won't see how ugly you are? You're lucky I agreed to your father's request and kept you from being on the streets. The least you could do is know your place and be grateful—instead of being a sneaky, conniving, cold bitch. Your cunt is so fucking dry it's no wonder I have to fuck other women. You'd freeze a man's dick off. Then again, maybe you just need more practice. You want to be a whore?" He asks, and his face goes close to my ear and his voice drops down. "I'll give you exactly what you want, dear wife...DONALD!" He screams and it's in that moment I know, if this happens, I won't survive. I won't even retain a piece of me. He's been slowly killing me since I married him, but this...this will destroy me.

Donald comes in like the ever faithful dog he is. I can see him through the mirror.

"Melinda wants to be a whore Donald, so I've decided we will teach her. You may fuck her face while I continue to teach my wife how a woman accepts her man."

"Yes, sir." He says and the eagerness in his voice awakens what fight I have left.

I can't do this. I can't. I know I will never be able to stop them, but I have to try. I have to. Donald comes around to the side of me. Michael, uses my hair to pull me onto my knees. He bends down and whispers into my ear.

"Open for him and suck his cock all the way in. Show us what a whore does, Melinda—since you wish to be one so badly."

He pushes my face towards Donald's hard member and I refuse to open my mouth. Donald yanks hard on my hair and I yell out and he pushes my mouth down on him. It's vile. I promise myself that I will never taste a man's cock again. Never have them in my mouth, and never feel powerless around them again. With the last ounce of rebellion I have, I pull away, releasing him, then I look Donald in the eye and *bite*. I bite so hard on the head of his cock, I know that it's his blood filling my mouth now, not my own. *I don't let up*. Michael is pulling at my head and my shoulders, but I don't let go. *I bite*. I bite and I hold on with every ounce of anger I have inside of me.

Donald is screaming. That just makes me clench my teeth together even firmer. I know there will be hell to pay. I don't care anymore. *I just don't care*. That's the last thought I have before I see from my peripheral vision a large bottle of liquor slam into the side of my head. I don't want to stop biting, but the world goes dark.

I DON'T KNOW how long I've been out. It could have been hours or even days. I am in my room. I'm lying on the bed, and I'm not wearing anything. There's a stale smell of smoke in the room. For a minute, I'm afraid that he has set my bed on fire, but there is no heat. I can barely see. My face is even more swollen and I feel…heavy and drugged. They've continued beating me, even while I was unconscious. My sides are sore, I figure I have some cracked ribs. It's a feeling I can recognize, because it's happened one too many times. I try to sit up, but I can't.

Michael enjoys hurting me, but it has never been this bad…it has never been like this. I know if I don't get away soon, he will kill me. I drag myself with my good hand up the bed, pulling on the sheets beneath me. I reach the edge and look down and there's a waste basket with the burnt remnants of my box. My things are gone… on top of them is the medallion. It's unrecognizable now and is charred from the fire. I've been out awhile, because the metal is no longer hot. I stare at the medallion. I stare at the charred, unrecognizable medal of Saint Alexander. The patron saint of bachelors, victims of betrayal and *torture*. If that is not irony, I don't know what is. I grasp it in my hand and pledge to get away. I don't know how long it will take, but I will get away from Michael Kavanagh. It's the last thought I have before I go under again and lose myself in the darkness.

MELINDA

Six Months Later

SIX MONTHS...I have tried to get away for the last six months. I haven't stopped trying since my rape. Every time...every damn time...he finds me. You would think in a city as big as Manhattan and in a state as populated as New York, I could find safety. It makes me feel stupid that I haven't. The truth is, living with Michael and listening to him talk about me, I've not felt smart in a long time. I've not felt...able? I feel *alone*. I have no one, save Nicole and Ray who are friends left over from TOA days. It hasn't been that long since I was at Three Oaks, but it feels like another lifetime. I'm not that person anymore. I will never be that person again. The name Melinda makes me physically sick. *I hate her.* She is *weak*. She is *stupid*.

Melinda is a failure. Melinda tried to run away again, got to Maine and...got caught. Michael owns the police. He owns....everyone. I know this for sure now, because he carted me back to New York and I'm currently locked in the basement of Michael's house. It has never been our house, or my house. Everything belongs to Michael...even me. I've decided this after a week of being beaten, and having him show me over and over just exactly how stupid I was. Those were his words. Melinda is too stupid to know when she has it made. Melinda is too stupid to know when she has everything other women would kill for. Melinda is too stupid to live.

My bloody hands reach up to touch the leather dog collar around my neck and move it around just a little to get air on my neck.

If you're going to act like a dumb animal Melinda, I shall chain you like one.

My hands are raw from trying to protect my body against Michael's and Donald's blows. My eyes are swollen shut and my lips are busted and cracked, from both the abuse and the fact that Michael hasn't really been feeding me or giving me water regularly. I'm having trouble breathing and I'm pretty sure I'm running a fever.

I hear the door at the top of the stairs open and I know I must be really sick, because I can't drum up the courage to care. The creaking noise of the wood can be heard with each heavy footstep. I can't see, so I don't bother raising my head off of the cold cement floor. I prepare myself for more abuse. That is all I can do. Because Michael is right, I am stupid. No smart person would be trapped like this—would be living in this hell.

"Oh honey! What has he done to you?"

I hear a woman's voice from somewhere above my head. I know the voice. It's Mrs. Marten's voice, from next door. I don't know her that well. She's an odd bird in her fifties, with purple hair, who wears yoga pants and tank tops with in your face sayings like *'Sucking Cock since 1959'*. I have always liked her, Michael refused to talk to her. He would have forced her to move years ago, but she has more money than him.

I want to talk, but I can't make my throat work. It's so dry and sore…

"Don't you worry honey, we'll get you help. I knew when I hadn't heard from you this past month that fucker was up to something. Someone needs to cut off his balls and shove them down his throat. Yes, indeed…Hello? I need an ambulance and the police right away at 103 Pleasant Hill Drive. Yes! It is an emergency! If it wasn't, I wouldn't have called!"

I want to warn her, to tell her to stop. The minute the police are contacted, they will let Michael know. I can't manage it though. I hear some noise and I wish I could see, but the room is black to me. There's so much pain and my head is too foggy to make anything out. Hell, maybe she's not really here. Wouldn't it suck if I am dying and my last dream is of Ms. Martens? *Jesus, couldn't I at least have Johnny Depp save me?*

I don't know how much time passes. I feel someone brushing my hair along the side of my face. I want to scream at them to stop, because even that faint touch... *hurts*. Eventually there are more footsteps and voices. I want to try and stay awake to find out what is happening. I can't, no matter how much I fight it, darkness beckons.

IT IS DAYS later when I wake up in the hospital. I don't know how Michael explained things, but somehow he managed to. I know, because his face is the first I see when I come through. I look around the room for help, but it's empty. I reach out for the nurse-call button and Michael grabs my hand, exerting so much pressure I feel like he may re-break the fingers which are already splinted.

"I wouldn't do that, darling wife of mine."

I lick my lips and try to speak. At this point, I don't know how long it's been since I've spoken, but obviously awhile, because my voice comes out dry and cracked.

"I didn't Michael, I wouldn't..."

He leans down closer to me, so that his lips are beside my ear. He's wearing some expensive cologne, which might smell great on another man, but the scent is what I associate with

Michael and it makes my stomach burn in revulsion.

"I must play nice while you're in here my dear, but I thought you would need a reminder of why you shouldn't try to upset me."

"A reminder?" The fear is thick in my voice. *I hate it.*

"Oh yes, Melinda."

He holds his phone in front of me. I'm relieved, because I thought he was getting ready to beat me again. I honestly don't think I can survive another beating. Then he pushes a button and a video plays on his phone.

Ms. Martens is tied and in a porcelain bathtub, gagged. Her large, eyes are wide with fear. I know, because it is an expression that is permanently worn by me. My heart kicks up in denial and a moan of sadness escapes me. My hand goes to my mouth to keep from screaming, as I watch Donald place her fingers in this metal tool and with one push of a lever a finger is cut off. Donald continues, one by one with such a perfect, cold precision until all that is left is her hand from the knuckle down and blood is everywhere. I gag and try to turn away, but Michael grabs my hair and pulls my face back around and it gets *worse*. I watch as he stabs her, slowly and shallowly at first and then with more vehemence. I watch as the life drains from her eyes. I don't cry. *I want to.* I don't scream. *I need to.* Instead, I let the weight and truth settle upon my shoulders. *I am the reason this woman died.*

Michael says more words. I have no idea what they are. I am in shock. I don't even react when he puts pressure on my chin and forces my lips and gives me his cold kiss. He leaves and I'm sitting in the bed, listening to the beeps of the machines around me and crying. That's how I am when the orderly comes in. His voice works through the haze surrounding my brain.

"He'll kill you next time. You need to leave."

I look at him. He's older, late forties maybe? His dark hair is definitely more salt than pepper and he has kind green eyes. But, then what do I know of kind?

"I know." I whisper, because I do. I just don't care anymore.

"You have to get away."

"I've tried. He always finds me."

"Do you have any friends to help you? To help you leave the state?"

"I've left the state, he finds me," I answer, tired of this conversation already.

"What about friends he doesn't know you talk to? Is there somewhere you can go that he'd never suspect you would pick? A way for you to get lost?"

My mind immediately goes to the only two friends I really have in the world, Ray and Nicole. I don't want to get them involved. I couldn't live with getting them hurt…or worse. I just couldn't…*Could I?*

"He wouldn't stop hunting me down…"

"Unless he thought you were dead."

I look up at this stranger's words. They give me hope. It's a strange feeling…an *odd* feeling.

"How? He would never believe it."

"Make him think you died trying to get away from him."

My mind goes over his words. Ray would be able to help. He was bragging just last month about dating a hacker. He could help me…*Can I do this?* Can I risk my friends and put them in danger to do this? Would they be in danger if we succeed in making Michael think I am dead?

My palms are sweaty, my heart rate is crazy and I feel like I'm on the edge of a cliff. The orderly hands me his cell phone.

Briefly, I worry he is setting me up. Then I stare at the phone like it might bite me. I have two choices. I can stay here and die—let Michael kill me. Or, I can call Ray and get his and Nic's help. I hesitate and can feel fear crawl all around me—surrounding me. I can't let it win…*not this time.*

I wrap my hands around the phone, dial Ray's number and pray I'm doing the right thing.

Chapter 1

DANI

Arrival in London, Kentucky

I'VE NOT HAD much happiness in my life, but the last year I have managed it. Living with Nicole and Ray was the best thing to ever happen to me. They helped me rebuild my life. Ray helped me burn down the house Michael made my prison. Then, with his help and that of the orderly, we got a Jane Doe from the hospital morgue. We made it appear I had been released from the hospital, came home against doctor's orders, only to perish in a fire. They did it all, I couldn't help. I was in such bad shape, I couldn't even walk. I had to finish my recovery in Ray's tiny apartment while his boyfriend fixed up my new identity. With a camera, some major league hacking and forged documents, Dani Smith was born.

I'm not sure who Dani is just yet. I'm still trying to live up to the image I have of her in my head, but I know she's loud, outrageous, and unafraid. She will *never* bow down to a man. She will *never* let anyone control her life. She will embrace being a woman, but be the strongest one that ever walked and the only thing Dani and Melinda will ever have in common is their love of Ray and Nic. Regardless of my name, I will always put those two first in *everything*.

That's the plan, and I live up to it mostly. There are days I forget. Days when parts of Melinda and the fear that helped to destroy her creeps in and I have to fight and push it back. Today is not one of those days. Today I'm driving down the road with my girl Nic, in her Mercedes convertible, the wind in my hair, and feeling like I'm taking another step *into* Dani…at least the Dani I want to be.

I hold my hands up letting the wind flow through my hair and yell out.

"Whoooooooo…."

It's a fake sound to my ears, but as I look to the side, I notice that Nicole is smiling. So my mission is achieved. If she honestly knew how I felt right now, it would hurt her. I'm excited to be moving with her, but I wish it was out West. I tried to talk her into it, I figure the more mileage between me and Michael the better. Nicole insisted we didn't have the money to do that. I suggested we use his money. She said no, that I might need it in the future. She didn't say it, but I knew what she meant. She thought he might find me someday and we would have to run. Just the thought of that causes me to get dizzy, making black spots fill my vision and I want to pass out. *Panic attacks*…I fucking hate them! They kick in without warning and they get such a strong hold on me, it's hard to breathe.

I look down and see my hands shake. *Shit*. I can't do this right now. I fight to keep Nic and Ray clueless to the things I deal with. They've done enough and seriously, I don't want their pity. I can't handle that.

"Hey, I'm thirsty!" I call out to Nic. I'm not. We're only about fifteen or twenty minutes from the house we've rented. Yet, if I don't get a drink and one of my pills, this panic attack will go from zero to sixty and I'm going to let all my crazy hang out. I can't do that. I can't…I won't.

We're just thirty minutes away!" She yells back, and you can tell she's not excited about stopping.

"Big damn deal, let's get some drinks and chocolate, girl!" I yell back, the music is annoying me and grating on my nerves. Panic attacks and loud noises do not mix, but this song, this speaker thumping sounds like something Dani would want.

Nic flips on her turn signal to get over and takes the upcoming exit.

I wrap a band in my hair, attaching a messy bun at the back of my neck. I need to keep my hands busy and hide the shaking.

"Whatcha' want, bitch?" I ask, yelling over the music. Ludacris is blasting through the speakers. There's this pain behind my eyes and the blinding black spots are still floating in my vision. I need to get out of here quick. There are people everywhere and it feels like all of their eyes are on me. Goosebumps skitter across my skin and a blast of cold...*stark cold* fear, chills me to the bone.

"Pepsi, fountain if they have it," she says back, her attention landing on a bunch of bikers to the side of the parking lot. I nod and try not to run into the gas station. I manage, barely. It is definitely a fast pace, with my head down. I'm counting backwards from a hundred in my head, trying to stave off the attack. My eyes are glued to my feet as I say a number in my mind with each footstep, making them smooth and rhythmic to try and slow my thoughts and heart rate down. I really should have looked up, because I run into a solid steel wall—of muscle.

I look up to see the sexiest man I have ever laid eyes on in my life. Skin tanned and warmed lovingly by the sun, beautiful dark hair scattered in different directions with the wind, a leather biker cut over his chest with a black, sleeveless tank under that and tattoos, lots of tattoos. Praise Jesus, this man has gorgeous ink and he looks like a piece of art. In another life, this man would have made Melinda pray he noticed her. Would he notice Melinda? In her retro-styled dresses and perfectly pulled back pony tail and looking like she belonged on the set of 'Leave It to Beaver'?

Somehow I doubt it. This guy is a charmer, I can just tell by the look in his eyes. He's probably been in more pants than he will ever remember. He likes *Dani*. I'm wearing my cut-to-your-ass jean shorts. They look worn and frayed, but I just bought them last week. I have on a hot pink tank that reads, *'Smooth As Tennessee Whiskey'*, Jimmy Choo stiletto heels that are too fucking tight and silver bangles on one arm that jingle when I walk. My hair is a mess despite pulling it back and my face has no makeup on, save for Dani's signature red lipstick. Yeah, he likes what he sees. My heart kicks up yet again, whether it's because the panic attack is getting closer to the point of no return, or the way the man in front of me makes my body tingle—I'm not sure. I shouldn't like the way he is looking at me, I shouldn't take pride in it. I find *I do*, and that's just weird. What would the biker think if he knew I'd rather be home wearing a sweater and sweat pants? What would he think if I did what I really wanted to do with these fuck-me shoes and throw them in the garbage?

He puts his hand on my shoulders to steady me, which wasn't needed. I might be tall, and these shoes might be dangerous and very conducive to falling, but I'm not going to. Shit, I dance in shoes higher than this. The only thing surprising me at this moment is how tall the man is. He's taller than me—even in my heels.

His touch sends heat through me and immediately my body coils in fear. I stiffen my back to hide that reaction and do what I trained myself to do when I created Dani, *show no fear and be a badass.*

"You going to let me go so I can get in the store stud, or stand there and eye-fuck me all day?" I ask, full of attitude. I want to cringe, but I ignore the impulse, Dani wouldn't give a fuck and this is who I am now. So I disregard everything, including the sweat trickling down my back and the wave of nausea in my stomach.

"Sorry, Darlin', didn't mean to mow you down," he says and that country boy accent and good ole' southern boy charm oozes off of him.

I like it. I like it *too much*. I shake my head, more at myself than at Biker-Cowboy. Then, I move around him. He lets me go and I'm through the door and scanning for the restroom area when his voice stops me again.

"What's your name, sweetheart?"

For a minute I don't turn around, instead I close my eyes and try to still the thoughts spinning in my head. I've got to get away. I look over my shoulder, but even as I do, I'm aware that part of my mask has slipped. I'm too close to the edge.

"Today, I'm not even sure," I reply, hating how sad my answer comes out. I push through the store, ignoring the small crowd of people and hunt out the restroom.

Thankfully it's one of those single restrooms and completely empty. I lock the door and lean against it for a minute. I need to catch my breath. I count quietly and get to fifty before my pulse begins to slow. I reach in the pocket of my jeans and pull out a small pill case. I cup water out of the sink, using it to wash down the pill.

I'm not sure how long I'm in there, but it's nowhere near as long as I want it to be. I force myself to come out of hiding and get the items that Nicole asked for. When I make it back outside, Nic is talking to one of the bikers. He is definitely delicious eye candy, and very busy looking at my girl. He's staring at her like she's an all-night taco bar and he's the stoner who smoked blunt after blunt and has a serious case of the munchies. Normally, I'd be all for Nic letting her hair down, but this guy screams danger—even more so because he's starting to look like he's going to strip and bang her right here in broad daylight against the gas pumps. Time for Dani to move in, divert, make them laugh and get us the hell out of dodge.

"Damn, Nic! When I said I wanted chocolate, you didn't have to go all out, bitch." I say it loud and my body instantly wants to crawl away and hide as eyes shift to me. I hate it, but I stay the course. "Hello there, Tall Dark and Do-me-all-over." The biker pulls his eyes briefly away from Nic and looks me over, but I see the lack of heat when he looks at me. He really is wound up over my girl. *I like that.* If he didn't have this look that said, I-kill-people-eat-them-for-dinner-and-spit-out-their-bones, I'd even encourage Nic. Trouble is, he *has* that look.

"Dani meet Stud, Stud meet Dani. I popped his cherry while you were in the store," Nic says walking around to the driver's side of the car.

The guy I should no longer be thinking about and his crew have been watching it all and laugh loudly. I look over towards them and he isn't joining in the laughter. He is watching me...*closely*. For a brief space in time, our eyes lock. Everyone and everything fades away. I could get lost in the way he's looking at me even from across a damned parking lot. *This cannot happen.* I laugh, open the car door, trying to be careful not to hit Nic's boy toy and get in. He closes my door, but his eyes are zeroed in on Nic. Shit, I can almost feel the heat coming off of him, he is seriously in lust over Nic. I spare a glance at her. As usual, Nic doesn't see it—she's oblivious. Her parents have worked her over so much she doesn't think any man would want her.

The man and Nicole banter back and forth as he leans on my car door. I don't pay any attention. In my head, I'm still counting backwards. I try to concentrate on the sunshine, the color of my fingernail polish, anything but the panic I can still feel inside. It's better and subsiding. Still, I wish we could just get out of here.

I feel sparks of awareness flash over my body and look across the parking lot. Cowboy-biker now has his shades on, so I can't really see if his eyes are still on me, but he's staring straight at me and my mouth goes dry. I am at war with myself. I want his attention, but at the same time *I don't*. He screams danger. He chooses that moment to smile. It's a good smile. It's a sexy smile. *I hate it.* I shake it off and turn back to Nicole.

I've apparently missed their whole conversation because by the time I snap out of the trance the cowboy put me in, the other guy is tapping the hood and walking away.

"Be seeing you soon," he calls, but Nic drowns him out by cranking our music back up.

The music tenses me up again. I can't handle it right now…I need to give the pills more time to work their magic. I have it down to a science—relaxation in t-minus ten minutes.

"Who the hell was that?" I ask Nic when we get on the road, turning the music back down.

"I have no idea. Thought he was sexy, but he seemed to be getting his jollies off messing with me while his buddies laughed."

I don't say anything, because I didn't see it that way at all, but she'd be better off if she stayed away from him.

Chapter 2

CRUSHER

*I*T'S BEEN *A hell of a day*. There are no other words for it. We've been traveling non-stop back from Alabama, after checking on a shipment that was fucked up. We hadn't got control over it when it was stolen, but the fact that it was reported and intercepted at all, reflects badly on our club. It is unacceptable and Dragon is fit to be tied. I don't blame him. Hell, as his VP, a lot of the blame is on my shoulders as well. I'm pretty fucking sure we have a narc somewhere in our group, whether from a hanger-on, prospect, or fuck, even a member, I don't know. Something is going to have to be done and done soon though. That much is clear. The only bright spot of my day so far, is seeing that fuck-me brunette with killer legs, a flawless face, and dark haunted eyes that call to me. I can tell they are haunted and they remind me of a girl from long ago…a girl I can't ever let go of. All of that combined with those damn shoes she had on, makes me want to slam her against a wall, and fuck her hard enough that I can feel those damn heels dig into my ass with every thrust.

She has a body made for sin and I have the raging cock stand to prove it. *Fuck*. It's been a good ten minutes since she shot my ass down, and I'm *still* hard. I tried to watch as Dragon hit on the brunette's friend and it was probably an enjoyable show, but I couldn't tell you. I was too busy looking at the hot little piece of ass who's making my dick ache.

Apparently the blonde had the same effect on my brother, because instead of heading straight home to the club, we're following the two women to a house the club rents. We pull in the driveway behind them. *Shit!* The place looks bad. Irish is in charge of renting it and having it looked after. Apparently, he dropped the ball. I can tell by the look on Dragon's face he's not happy. It's probably a good thing Irish is working at the club and didn't go with us to Alabama. There's enough tension between those two lately.

"Nice place, Twinkie," I hear Dragon say and watch as he climbs off his bike and makes his way to the women. I follow suit a little behind him. I notice Gunner and Freak do the same.

My attention goes to the brunette, who doesn't bother to hide her laughter at the way my brother and her girl are going at it. She's got on designer sunglasses and her nails are perfectly done. She's high maintenance and probably a bitch. She's everything I should stay away from, but I keep remembering her words to me at the gas station when I asked her name. *Today, I'm not even sure.* In that moment she looked so haunted...so sad. She reminded me of Melly and it hurt. It hurt like a motherfucker. I drag my attention away from the babe's lips and listen to the blonde yell when Dragon picks her up.

"Wait! What on earth are you doing?"

"Mama, those things on your feet are cute as hell, but they aren't going to protect you from snakes."

It's an enjoyable exchange until I hear other laughter, *deeper laughter.* The brunette's voice is deeper and huskier. It reminds me of an old country song and an aged glass of bourbon. Something that burns going down, but settles in your gut and warms you. I watch as she climbs on Freak's back and he hauls her to the porch of the rental.

I don't get jealous. *Fuck,* I have never been jealous a day in my life. Yet, in that moment, when I see Freak's tattooed fingers wrap around the brunette's tanned, silky-smooth, legs, *I feel it.* I feel it deep and I want to deck my brother for touching her. I shake my head because that is stupid. I don't know the bitch and she sure didn't warm up to me like she seems to have with Freak. *I need to forget her.* Maybe Dragon will strike out with the blonde and I can bury myself in her. *Fire…*I need someone with fire. I stomp back to my bike, mad at the little brunette with the fucking sexy legs. I have a feeling her fire might burn me for a long damn time.

BACK AT THE club, I'm on edge. I had a shower and grabbed some chow, but I have this restless energy. The memories of Mel are threatening to come out to play and I can't handle that shit. I enter the main room looking for two things, a bottle and pussy. Maybe I can get drunk and fuck myself into oblivion.

The Twinkies are out playing, but none of them grab a hold of my cock like the brunette did. *Junior just lays there.* I see Dragon at the bar and decide to join him instead. I know what's on his mind, so I decide to add a little fuel to the fire. I'm a bastard most days, what can I say?

"She's a hot little piece," I say as a prospect puts a glass down in front of me and I grab Dragon's bottle and pour myself a drink.

He doesn't respond, unless you count grunting at me.

"You gonna push it?"

"Fuck if I know." Dragon answers, and it's almost enough to make me stop. He's apparently more than mildly interested in the blonde. I should back away and let it go, because honestly my interest is not there. Then I look around the club and realize it's not there for the free pussy either. *Fire*. I need fire—something to keep the memories at bay. I don't know why the memories are so bad lately, but I need them to *stop*.

"Let me know if you don't," I tell him, only half meaning it. He gives me a look that would make a lesser man quake. "Hey, she's damned fine."

"She's got trouble written all over her," Dragon replies.

"Yeah, but what a trip. Some things are worth the trouble man," I answer, but it's an image of the brunette that flashes in my mind.

We talk for a few more minutes when I notice Tash walking towards us. She's trouble. She has her sights set on Dragon and becoming his main bitch. I don't see it happening. I hope like fuck it doesn't happen. She's weak and I don't trust her. She could spell nothing but trouble for my brother.

"Hey Dragon, you looking for some company?"

"Nah, Tash, why don't you see to my brother here. I got things on my mind, girl," Dragon replies.

I cock my eyebrow up and laugh before I can stop myself. I know Dragon's game. If he thinks a cold piece of snatch like Tash will derail me, he's a stupid mother-fucker. Tash walks over to me and slams her lips down on mine. Her tongue pushes in my mouth like a cobra getting ready to devour a baby rabbit. Her breath is thick with smoke and alcohol and it feels *wrong*. Still, I take her kiss and move my hand under the barely there mini dress she's wearing. The skin on her naked ass feels leathery in places. She keeps her ass in the tanning bed too much. The club keeps one for the girls to use, but if this is what it does, Dragon should take that shit out.

I stand up and slap my brother on his shoulder.

"She starts work next week at the club man, let me know before then or she's free game."

Dragon growls again. I'm pretty sure I'm not going to get my shot at the blonde. It's just as well, I'm not positive I want it anyway. I motion at one of the new girls, who isn't quite a Twinkie yet. She's more of a hanger-on. She doesn't really appeal to me, except for two things. One, she's a brunette with long hair that waves and curls on the edges. Two, she has big, doe eyes. It's no coincidence that I'm picking her because she reminds me of the girl from the gas station, but I don't really care. There's also the added bonus that by using her and Tash, I might be able to get through the night without memories of Mel.

She slides up beside me and I ignore Tash's grunt of disapproval. Bitch is fronting. She fucking loves to eat pussy and I'd much rather she do that shit instead of kissing me again.

"Want some company, Bro?" Freak asks, as we round the corner to the hall which leads to the private rooms. He and I tag team sometimes, so it's cool, but his ass is sticking his dick in Tash, I don't want to go there tonight—*most nights really.*

We make it into my room and I immediately grab the brunette by the hair and pull her to me. Tash takes the hint and goes to Freak and begins undressing him.

"Bambi…" I mumble, giving her a nickname, as she pulls my shirt up over my chest. I help her take it the rest of the way off and she looks up at me with a grin.

"I like that," she answers and her voice is *wrong*, so I decide to give her something to do with that mouth of hers instead.

"I feel like making sure these girls ride the train tonight brother, what about you?"

"Fuck yeah," Freak answers, already naked.

He goes to the opposite end of the bed as me and yanks

out a box of condoms from my night stand drawer. He tosses them over to me, but I don't bother with them, I won't need them right now.

"Get up on the bed, Tash and lay that ass down and get ready," I order. My voice has the hard edge it always gets during sex. I like control. *I like to fuck and I like it a lot.*

Tash strips, lies on the bed, opens her legs and bends them at the knee, watching Freak. She knows the drill. Fuck, she should. There's not a brother here that hasn't had her this way. She's good at it. It's one of the reasons we've let her stay even if she is annoying as fuck. Freak grabs her legs and pulls her so her ass is closer to the edge of the bed. Bambi is watching with interest. Why do I get the feeling this little club girl might be new to multiple partners? *Oh, this could be fun.*

I pull her to me, so her back is against my stomach and she watches as Freak slides his dick into Tash. Freak is not small, not by any means and the latex is tight. I look to the side of Bambi's face and smile as she watches my boy start fucking Tash. I yank Bambi's shirt over her head and throw it to the ground, enjoying the way her bare skin feels against mine. She's soft and warm…so warm, but I'm about to make her hot. I lean down and whisper in her ear.

"You like watching how eager Tash is for Freak's dick?" I ask the useless question. I already know, because her nipples are so fucking hard they could cut glass. My fingers move down to her center. She's trimmed, but her muff is covered by dark curls and I like the way my fingers disappear as they sink into her. I don't bother testing, I thrust two fingers in and immediately Bambi gasps in pleasure. My fingers push in and out in a rhythm perfectly matched with Freak's thrusts.

"Tash is a greedy little whore. I wonder Bambi? Are you too?" I ask, twisting one of her nipples hard, as I continue finger-fucking her. Bambi doesn't talk, but her breathing is erratic and loud. "I know something about Tash, I don't think you do yet, Bambi…"

"What's that?" She gasps, clenching and riding my fingers.

"She loves to eat pussy. Now get up on the bed and straddle her face and let her eat your juicy little cunt," I order, slapping her hard on the ass. She starts to turn towards Freak and at last minute I direct her so she's facing me. I pull her up so I can watch as Tash's tongue flicks into the lips of her pussy. It's fucking hot watching Bambi getting tongue fucked. Tash grabs her by the hips and pulls her down on her face. "That's it baby, ride her face, make yourself come." I encourage, as Bambi starts grinding hard and wild against Tash's face. *Fuck, I doubt the bitch can breathe underneath her.* I look up when I hear Freak groaning, and we grin at each other. Fuck yeah we're both going to have fun with little Bambi. I push Bambi's shoulders until she gets on all fours and her mouth is even with my cock. I grab the hair on her head in my hand and grin down at her. "Open wide baby, because I'm going to fuck that pretty face, hard."

She does as told and her groan falls against my aching cock as I stretch her mouth. Her big brown eyes look at me and I watch as her lips slowly slide down my dick. I find myself wishing her lips were dark red…

Fuck.

It's messed up that's for sure. Still, when I jerk out of Bambi's mouth and shoot my load all over her face, it is in that moment I make myself a promise. One day, I am going to have that brunette in my bed. Just the thought of it, makes me hard again.

It's going to be a long night.

Chapter 3

DANI

WE'VE BARELY SETTLED in London and I can already see the writing on the wall. Nicole is totally hung up on the biker called Dragon. I'm worried about her. He seems nice enough, but I see the darkness, the *hardness* about him, that he beats down around my girl. He gets a coldness in his eyes sometimes that remind me too much of Michael. The problem is that Nic is *really* into him, in a way that I think if she doesn't have him—it will hurt her. So I've encouraged her to go for it, but inside I'm screaming no.

It's water under the bridge now however, because Dragon has made it in with my girl and they're going at it like rabbits. Bright side, she is happy. Hell, she seems ecstatic and even though inside I'm screaming don't do this—a part of me is glad for her. I wonder if I let loose and get laid, if I would be giddy. *Is that what it takes to be normal?* Would that stop the nightmares and the visions that drag me into hell every night? If I had someone strong around, would he be able to keep the ghost of Michael away? Would someone strong be able to protect me from Michael if he found me? A picture of Dragon's friend, Crusher, comes to mind, the semi-cowboy from the gas station. I instantly shut that forbidden thought down. *I am being weak for even thinking that.* Dani should be able to stand on her own two feet. I can't afford to be weak like Melinda. I'm not her anymore. *I can't be her.*

Dragon is taking Nic upstairs for another round, when the doorbell rings. I go to the door trying to ignore the way my heart picks up speed and fear swamps me. I look carefully out the window and though I'm freaking ecstatic my past isn't catching up with me, the fact that it's Crusher at the door, does not fill me with joy. He hangs around the club where I work, but I've been doing my best to avoid him. *He's danger.* He makes me want things that I *shouldn't want.* The way he watches me sometimes…it excites me and *that* terrifies me.

"Stud," I say, leaning on the front door and looking at Crusher through the screen. His eyes rake over me and warms me. No, they *burn* me. Still, I do my best to appear unaffected.

"You gonna let me in, darlin'?"

"Haven't decided."

"You're looking damn good tonight and as much as I'd love to just stand here and enjoy the view, I need to talk to my boy," he says and I begin to notice he's more tense than normal.

I stand back so he can come in, trying to ignore the way being next to him sends electricity through my body. I've never been attracted to a man before—*not like this.* I had boyfriends before Michael came along, but nothing serious and after Michael…well…I'm surprised I even want to look at a man. *That's why Crusher is dangerous.*

"That right there," Crusher says, and I look up at him in confusion.

"What?"

"When you get that look in your eyes, I want to pull you in my arms and kiss you until it leaves."

"You've barely seen me. You might save that line for a woman who will buy it. It's a good one," I respond, turning my back on him. *It is a good line.* Too good, because I wish he could do that. I instinctively know that Crusher would do more damage than any man before or after him, if he hurt me. When you have my scars, that's saying something. It's just not worth the risk.

"Believe me gorgeous, I've seen you and I'm not going to give up until you let me all the way in."

My breath stops. I know it's a game for him, a chase. Just once though, I think I might like a man to look at me and see the real me. I don't think anyone has, except maybe Ray. I even manage to keep most of my shit hidden from Nic. I do wonder what Crusher would think of the *real* me. It doesn't matter. Crusher makes me *weak*. I can't be weak again. I have to get rid of him. I have to find some reason to make him leave me alone so I am off his radar. The thought makes me sad.

"Hey D-Man, you got company!" I call out, trying to ignore the way my palms are sweating. I definitely need to medicate, if I'm going to survive tonight.

"Yo! Dragon, we got trouble man," Crusher adds, as Nicole and Dragon come down the stairs. Dragon is carrying Nicole yet again, the man sure seems to like to cart her around.

"I can walk you know." Nicole grumbles, but the flush on her face tells me that she likes his attention.

Dragon waits until they get to the bottom of the stairs to let her down. Then he takes her by the hand, walking over to where we're standing. It's as if he can't stand to be away from her touch.

"Sorry man, didn't mean to interrupt. Hey Darlin'," Crush tells Nicole. I can't help but notice how he takes in every detail of Nicole's body, and my stomach turns. This is just another reason why I can't even contemplate letting Crusher anywhere near me. He's eye fucking Nicole, after feeding me lines about wanting me.

He's wearing a black muscle shirt and showing off his gorgeous ink. He really is too beautiful to believe. Nicole and Dragon start bickering and it pulls my attention away from Crusher, which is good—since he's still panting after Nicole.

"Hey," Nicole mutters, as Dragon yanks her to his side.

"Quit checking Crush out before I have to kill him," Dragon complains.

I listen to Dragon's words and I can't help but be annoyed with all three of them. I walk off into the kitchen pretending to be uninterested. In reality it's time I take some pills.

"Hey boss? Man, we got shit going on. Need you out at Pussy's now."

"OH MY GOD! YOU HAVE A PLACE CALLED PUSSY'S!?!?!?!"

"It's a strip joint. That's where I was a couple nights ago, Nic. Some hot looking women there." I supply without looking over my shoulder.

"Of course it's a strip joint! Dear Lord, I bet you even picked out the name, didn't you, Dragon?"

"Shut it, Mama."

I tune them out after that. Those two fuss, fight, and then fuck. I've only seen it up close twice, but I know the drill.

I grab a wine cooler and find the cabinet I stash my meds in. Nicole has never mentioned them. I don't know if she has investigated to see what I'm taking or if she just figures she knows and lets it slide.

I'm sitting at the table, trying to calm my heart and vaguely listening to the conversation in the living room. What I hear, doesn't help my anxiety. Crusher is telling Dragon about some woman named Jess who was beaten. Dragon's reply hits my stomach...sour.

"Pissed off man?" Dragon asks.

Is there any other kind? I sit there and replay Dragon's question in my mind and it pisses me off that he says it so *calmly*. Is this the shit he deals with every day in his world? *Is that why he sets off my warning bells?*

"That's just it, Boss...she had a note taped to her chest." Crush reaches inside his jacket pocket and hands Dragon a piece of folded white paper.

Dragon opens the paper and you can see it's covered with blood. My panic inches up another notch as I swallow down a large drink of the wine cooler. This woman they are discussing...was beaten... beaten and bloody. Was she dying...or dead? Why is Crusher here telling Dragon? Shouldn't he be at the hospital? Did anyone call the police? Is this Jess some dirty little secret they are going to keep hidden?

I tune them out again, but not by choice. My head is full of memories. Of my last beating, of the injuries that are too many to count. How I was hidden and chained like a dog. If not for Ms. Martens....my hand shakes at her memory...at all the memories. I can't be around Dragon and his men. *I can't be around Crusher.* I don't want to be around men who can act so calmly about a woman being hurt. I don't want to be around men who come to each other to talk about things instead of calling from a hospital or calling the cops! *Something!*

I force my attention back on the three in the room and stand up. I need to get out of the house. It feels like air is being withheld from me. *I need to breathe.* I look up at Crusher and he looks over my body again. This time I don't feel excitement though. No, this time it is *bone-deep fear* I feel. Time for kick-ass Dani to come out and give the world a fuck you. I grab a bottle of vodka, stuff it in the inside pocket of my leather jacket, carefully hiding what I'm doing behind the opened refrigerator door.

Nicole has this idea that going to counseling will help me. It's making things worse. It's bringing up all the shit I've fought to bury. One of their main rules is to not use alcohol to deal with your problems. *Fuck that!* They don't live in my brain. I need the alcohol. So, I hide how bad my drinking has become from Nicole. *I hide a lot from her.* I couldn't handle it if she knew how pathetic I truly am. I go to stand in the far corner, watching everyone and waiting for my chance to escape. Dragon lays a kiss on Nicole that *almost* melts my panties. What would it be like to have a man so crazy into you that he sets you on fire just saying goodbye? I immediately look at Crusher, because I'm stupid. I assumed he would be watching Dragon and Nic play tonsil hockey, but his eyes are glued on me. There's a heat in those dark eyes that…if I had been a *stronger* person…a *different* person, I might have investigated. I am not a different person though, and all I can see right now when I look at either of them is how they dealt with a woman who was beaten and hurt. Worse, neither one of them seem in a hurry to go check on her—*even now.* They are more concerned with what happened instead of her and what she's going through now…*that's wrong.* So I give him a look that conveys my distaste for him and study my nails instead. When they finally leave, I look up at my friend and there's so much I want to warn her about, but the words are frozen.

"Damn, Nic girl. You might have a problem," I lamely say and I know she doesn't understand why I said that. I can't find the courage to have a serious talk, so I laugh it off.

WE DECIDED TO spend the day shopping, hanging out and

getting away from men in general. It was Nic's idea and I agreed, as long as I didn't have to watch some totally lame romantic sappy-crap movie. Nic loves them, but to me they're stupid. I know better than anyone, that those movies are garbage. *There are no happy endings.*

It's been a pretty good day and I have a great buzz going on. *Buzz hell!* I'm actually pretty fucking drunk and I don't really give a damn because my brain isn't bombarding me with images of the past. Screw what the counselors are saying. I'll take tonight's feeling over the constant fear and pain I've been dealing with.

"Seriously Dani, what kind of twisted freak could come up with this in their head?" Nic asks.

"Quit your bitching, girl. Your ass made me watch four fucking hours of Julia Freaking Roberts. Thought I was going to go into barf mode on that last one. I'm just a girl, standing in front of a boy, blah, blah, blah," I respond and it's not really a lie. I hate that damn movie. It makes you *want* to believe in fairytales.

"Shhh…" the lady behind us says, and it's only because I'm drunk and took a second happy pill on top of that shit, that I'm able to not slap the shit out of her. She should consider herself lucky.

The nightmares have been so bad lately, I don't think I've managed an hour's sleep. Last night I woke up after dreaming about the last time Michael beat me and I swore he was standing over me, swinging Ms. Marten's head back and forth like a pendulum. I can't believe I moved closer to Michael. I should be in Mexico or something. The problem is, that's not where Nic is, that's not where Ray is and I'm terrified of being on my own. *I'm still weak.*

Nic thinks I have this hard shell around me. She thinks I'm

a party girl, going to strip joints and getting laid every night. What would she say if she knew the truth? I go to the strip joints to watch the dancers. I need to be good at my job, learn the dances because if I go on the run, completely on my own, I will need to get a job quickly, that pays in cash and has great tips.

I don't get laid every night. I haven't had sex since Michael. *I don't even want sex.* I'm afraid I may never want it again. I bullshit my way around men and then find some way to bow out. It's worked so far, but it pisses me off. The whole world around me is having sex. I'm young damn it, even if I do feel like I'm eighty. I should be having sex. I picture Crusher immediately. *Shit.*

I take another drink of water. I wonder if Nicole knows I laced it with vodka after we left the concession area. Good thing she's driving.

"Amante' Nicole, is that you?"

I look over to see yet another, sexy-off-his-ass man looking at Nicole like he wants to eat her alive. Hell, if I still had an ego, this town would crush it.

"Well fuck me Nic, did you start a freaking harem when we moved?" I ask, when it doesn't appear the latest Nicole victim is going to move along. *Great.*

"No, just finding I'm in the wrong place, at the wrong time, way too much since we moved," Nicole answers, and boy could I give her a high-five on that one.

"Do you people mind? We're trying to watch a movie here." Ms. Huffy-phone-woman demands.

"Mamacita, does Dragon know you are in my town?" The man asks Nicole.

I tilt my head to the side to watch him for a minute.

"Your town? Odd, you don't look like a mayor."

He looks over at me and flashes a smile. It does nothing for me, but he *is* pretty.

"Yes well, appearances can be deceiving. Can they not, querida?" he asks. I start to respond, interested. Does he and the people with him have *this much* power? *Could they protect me from Michael? If I'm right and Dragon and Crusher are just as dangerous, could they protect me and Nic?* He's speaking Spanish…could he help me make it to Mexico? I could pay him…I have the money from Michael that I've barely touched…

"You want to go?" Nicole asks, grabbing my attention again. I don't really want to…but hell, I could use another water. Actually it is more vodka than water. *Whatever.*

"Yeah, sure."

Before we can leave, the guy fixes it so Nicole can't get out. I look away, still wondering how to get in with his club. If they could offer Nic and I safety, or better yet, if they could help us get away…*Nic doesn't understand.* She hasn't dealt with men like Michael or Dragon. *I have.* I need to look out for her.

"Excuse me, I was going to the restroom," I hear Nicole respond.

"No you weren't, querida. You were ditching me, but I am not ready to let you escape."

"Dear Lord Nic, can't you find any normal men?" I interject, my eyes glued on the movie scree, but in my mind I am making plans.

"Apparently not," she sighs.

"Skull baby, I thought you and I had a date? The woman who came in with, apparently *Skull*, whines.

Skull? That sounds mean. *Mean enough to kill the Devil?* Maybe not, but he seems to have firepower with him. Hell, there's at least ten with him now. Some giant of a man picks a woman up, lifting her over the top of the seat and into the next aisle.

He repeats the action until he clears a whole row for his buddies. I laugh out loud as women go running out of the theater.

I throw popcorn at the man in question. He's big and apparently doesn't talk much, but I do notice how *careful* he was with each woman as he moved them. I may be drunk, but I take this as a *good* sign.

"What's your name, big boy?" I ask as the popcorn bounces off his head.

"Why you asking?" He asks and his voice is hoarse like he doesn't use it much.

"I want to know whose name I'm calling out tonight," I say only half joking. Maybe if I have sex it will loosen Michael's hold on me?

"That's Beast," Skull says helpfully, while the big guy turns back around ignoring me.

"You're shitting me? Well fuck my ass and pull my hair, I think I'm going to be his Beauty at least for a night or two. Yo! Beast! Turn back around here and let me see those baby blues."

"They're brown." Some man beside Beast joins in.

"Well hell, I don't care, can't see them anyway, I just want to look at him some more." Beast keeps ignoring me and that kind of ticks me off.

Now, normally I run from men, but whether it's the alcohol and narcotics in my system, or just the lure of being safe, *I don't know*. Before I can question myself any further, I climb down in the man's lap beside Beast. I would have sat in Beast's, but he's making that impossible.

"C'mon give me some attention here. I promise not to bite."

"That's too bad."

His monotone, bored-sounding voice is *not* encouraging.

Still, his eyes…

"I think you're playing hard to get. Why is that do you suppose?"

"Babe, you looking for dick, you can get it from any man here, why don't you put your efforts into choosing and leave me the alone."

Boom. I'm not sure you can get slammed more than that.

"You don't find me attractive?" I ask and he studies me for a minute. Can he tell that I would totally understand that? I feel like the *ugliest* person around. Maybe that's why his words sting.

"Beast here lost his old lady a bit ago, but me and the boys can show you a good time," the other guy chimes in and despite being on his lap, I ignore him.

I can see pain flash through the Beast's eyes. He *cared* about his woman. I *grieve* with him and find myself jealous of this unknown woman at the same time. She may be gone, but at least she had someone who truly cared about her. My hand goes over to Beast's and I squeeze it. I thought he would push me away, he doesn't. He lets me hold his hand and then eventually pulls me onto his lap. There's nothing sexual in the way we're sitting. It's the first time I've relaxed in months.

I'm feeling good and even half-way safe around Beast. Skull and his crew might be the answer to my problems. Beast is definitely safer than Crusher or Dragon. I can say that unequivocally. After the movie we are walking with the crew, discussing going to a bar. I don't really want to. Although, more alcohol might help at this point, I don't know. That is put to an end when Dragon arrives upset, because Skull is putting the moves on Nicole.

Guns are drawn, knives…Instantly I am transported back into the past. Dragon is no longer Dragon. *He is Michael wielding a knife. Michael holding it towards me. Michael grabbing me, threatening to end me. It is Michael stabbing me in the stomach repeatedly.* I scream out in terror. I can't stop the sound or the tears that gather, though I do my best to fight them back. My entire body starts shaking and that's when Beast covers me. He stands in front of me. *Protecting me.* He pulls me tight against his back, not letting my hand go. It stops my screams, though the tears refuse to end. I can't stop the shaking, but he doesn't seem to mind. Over his shoulder I see Crusher and he's holding a gun and pointing it in Beast's direction. *In my direction.*

I *have* to get away from Dragon, Crusher and that whole crew. *I need to get Nic away.* Dragon will turn his anger on her someday. I can't let what happened to me, happen to Nic. *I can't.* I feel like I can't breathe and the memories try to swallow me. I don't even notice that the confrontation has ended. I'm lost in the past. That's when Beast grabs my face and forces my eyes to him.

"You're okay, little hummingbird. You're okay."

I don't know where the ridiculous nickname comes from, but something about this gruff man who could snap men like twigs being soft, pulls me out of the darkness. I still can't quit shaking and I feel so cold.

"I…I…can't stay here." I gasp, my voice winded, broken, and weak. *God, it's so weak.* Beast nods and begins to pull me away from the crowd. Crusher puts his hand on my shoulder and stops us. I look up into his dark eyes. I see concern there and I *want* to believe it's real. Then I remember how he held a gun on us…*on me.* I can't trust him. I can't trust Dragon. I know their types.

"Don't do this, darlin'."

His hand warms me. There's so much heat coming off of him, through our connection. I want to embrace the warmth, because I feel so cold, but I pull away. Instead, I look at Beast.

Who has been nothing but kind and even now is holding onto me. If he wasn't, I would fall to the ground. *Beast protected me. No one ever has before.*

"Can...can you get me out of here?" I look up at Beast, begging him silently.

"Let's go, hummingbird."

"You're making the wrong choice, sweetheart," Crusher says.

"My life is full of them. At least this one isn't holding a gun on me," I tell him before I can stop myself, then let Beast lead me away.

They decide not to go to the club after all the excitement. I'm glad. The world is buzzing around me and I can't seem to grasp it. My stomach is in knots. I keep thinking back to Crusher and our last exchange. What is it about that man that makes me...*want?* That's it really. He makes me *want* and for someone who has never even looked at a man in that way? *It's terrifying.*

I go with Beast to Skull's compound without talking. Right now I need *three* things. *Nicole, safe. Michael, dead. Me, somewhere warm with my toes in the sand, far away from anything and anyone.* I doubt Beast can make that happen, but he's big, he's warm and he's looking out for me. *That's more than I've ever had.*

When we get inside, he leads me back into a small room with a bed and a dresser in it. I look at the room a little lost. I wrap my arms around myself, trying to stop my body from shaking. Tiny comes to the door, but Beast stops him.

"Hey man! I thought we were going to party! The bitch has been begging for it all night. Surely you're going to share."

"Go find one of the club girls, I'm flying solo with this one tonight," he says and I pull myself up to a sitting position on the bed and hug my knees. I thought I wanted sex and I know

Beast has been nice to me and all, but I don't think I can do it. Shit. I don't have a contingency plan either. I always do, I always have some way to extract myself out of any situation. I didn't tonight and I have no idea what I'm going to do.

"She's mine tonight. Now get the fuck out of here, so I can get my cock sucked on for the first time in a year."

"Hey okay man, I get you dog, you want some privacy for your first time since your old lady. I get it, but tomorrow you're going to have to share, because that's some sweet ass in there and I want to tap it."

Beast closes the door—more like slams it on Tiny and while I'm glad about that, I have no idea what to do here.

"Listen…I know I offered and everything, but I've been thinking…"

"Relax Hummingbird, I ain't about to give you my dick."

I freeze. I mean that's good, but still, shit could he at least *act* like he's tempted?

"Hummingbird?" I ask putting my head down against my knees wishing the room would stop spinning.

"If there was ever a woman with a broken wing, it'd be you."

Well, he has me pegged.

"I'm sorry about your family."

"Life's fucked up," he says, staring off into space.

"Amen."

He turns back around and looks at me.

"Do yourself a favor hummingbird, drink yourself to sleep tonight and then get the hell out of here in the morning. This life ain't for you."

"I've never really had a life," I say, taking a bottle of Jack he hands me from his dresser. I take a drink, wincing at the burn and pass it back to him. He sits down and we pass the bottle back and forth for what seems like hours, not talking.

When it's empty I lay back on a pillow and Beast lays beside me. He makes no move to touch me and as odd as it sounds, this is the best night of my life. Lying in bed with a complete stranger drunk as a skunk is calm, relaxing, and wonderful. Of course maybe I just feel relaxed because I am drunk. Who knows?

"How long were you and your woman together?"

"Not long. Should have never knocked her up, but it happened and I wanted our child more than anything. Annabelle was all that was good in the world. Without her the place is just cold and dark."

My heart turns over for Beast and the loss he has to have suffered. My hand goes to my stomach and I rub it absently.

"I can never have a child," I whisper, my words slurring.

"Sorry, hummingbird."

"The world is fucked up," I say staring off in the darkness, ignoring the tears sliding silently down my face.

"Amen." Beast says.

"Can I hide out here for a couple days?" I ask, before I can talk myself out of it. I don't think I've ever felt safe like I do around Beast.

"You can't run away forever hummingbird," he says and he doesn't know he just whispered the words I fear the most.

"I just need to catch my breath," I whisper.

"Then breathe, I'll make sure the demons stay away until you can fight them," he vows, and I suddenly wish with everything I have that he was Crusher. It physically *hurts* that he isn't.

In a little while, I hear Beast snore and I know he's sleeping. I'm close to going there myself, I'm just fighting it. The nightmares are always waiting for me. Michael is always there, I hate sleep. Just as my eyes close, Beast curls into me and hugs me close. I let him and his warmth soothes me. I hope it's enough to keep the nightmares at bay. I surrender to sleep and it's not Michael's face I see first in my dreams. *It's Crusher's.*

Chapter 4

CRUSHER

IT'S HER DAMNED doe-like, deep brown, eyes. *They haunt me.* Something about Dani calls to me. Even when I know she's going to shoot me down, I can't stay away. I don't understand it. Women usually eat out of the palm of my hand and this one...*Motherfucker!* This one runs from me.

I'm pissed off about how the situation unraveled outside the theater. There was only one way to handle things, because at that point no one could control Dragon. You'd have to be a damned fool not to see how hung up he is on Nicole. She has his balls tied in a fucking bow. All us brothers could do when he went off was make sure we protected his ass. So I did. What did it get me?

At least this one isn't pointing a gun at me.

Her words *wound* me. I have never hurt a woman, and this one well, you'd have to be a fool not to see the pain in her eyes, or to miss the fear that came off of her in waves tonight. *She's broken.* Some fucker shattered her and left her bleeding. When I see her, I'm reminded of another girl. *Melly.* A girl I loved with all my heart. A girl I wasn't able to save...a girl, I failed. Losing her has always hurt me. It changed me, but Melly is not why I am drawn to Dani.

No, if it was just Melly and their similarities, I wouldn't be lying here in bed with my dick semi-hard thinking about Dani.

I wouldn't be jealous that she went off with some overgrown, over-haired, half-wit... *Beast?* I mean c'mon, I've heard some fucked up road names in my life, but Beast? The fact that his dick is probably where I want mine to be right now—fucking pisses me off.

I think back to Melly. It was such a long time ago. Another lifetime really, before I grew up, before I met my brothers, before the army...*all of it.* We were kids, just trying to figure out life. Melly was innocent and pure and I had never been exposed to that in life. Her laugh could fill in any dark space in the world. She was full of life—until her mom remarried. I grew up hard, mostly on the streets, in and out of different foster homes, so I saw the signs quickly. The bruises Melly would come to school sporting, the circles gathering under her eyes, the broken bones. I knew it was happening, but fuck I was little more than a kid myself. Melly didn't trust me to be able to take care of her. How many times did I beg and plead for her to let me take her away? How many times did I lay down at night worried, wondering what was happening to her? Maybe Melly was right not to believe I could save her? I tried once and ended up in the hospital. A kid is no match for a grown ass man. Still, if she had gone away with me, I could have kept her safe, *I know I could have.*

This shit is going to get me in trouble. When my memories are this close to the surface, I don't rest. The pictures haunt me. *You don't see the things I saw that night and remain unscathed.* I need to shut them down and lock the door, but seeing how bad Jess had been beat, together with Dani and that mess. *I can't.*

I thought about searching Bambi out, but the truth was she was a disappointment, a pale substitute for what I really want. *What I really want is a county over getting fucked in another club, by another man.* That shit burns my gut more than the bottle of whiskey I'm drinking. I want to go get her and drag her ass back here, but I can't. She made her decision. I need to forget her.

At least this one isn't pointing a gun at me.

Fuck, am *I* the reason she chose another club? Should I have grabbed her and then covered my boy? Did I choose wrong? *Did I fuck up, when the decision mattered the most?*

"Hey man, you busy?" Freak asks knocking on my door.

"Nah man, c'mon in. What's up?"

Freak opens the door and pulls in his latest bitch, Nikki something-another. She's damn pretty, her hair a mixture of colors ranging from a chestnut pony to warm sunlight. Her eyes are green and sparkle, but I instantly miss the dark color of Dani's and the secrets swimming in them. I take another drink.

"My woman here wants to play a little. I ain't about to let those other motherfuckers around her. You game?"

Freak and I have shared women a lot through the years. We both enjoy it and we work well together. When you do this, you need trust or shit can go wrong, real quick. I'm not really in the mood, not for Nikki anyways. This bitch means something to my brother. He just met her a couple days ago, but he's already pushed Bambi away and been keeping his shit under wraps, except for Nikki. Still Freak likes to share, so I expected this. Me? I ever find a bitch I want to claim, she's *only* getting my dick. That's just the truth, I may like to play, but *I'm a possessive motherfucker.*

I take another drink as a vision of Dani flashes in my mind. Then I remember she's probably knee deep in cock at Skull's place. *Fuck it.*

"Hello there darlin' you want to play?"

Nikki looks back at Freak and then to me, she smiles a

dirty little smile and I have to say, I like her spirit.

"Oh, yeah," she says and you can hear the excitement in her voice.

"What do I get, Freak-man?" I ask, looking down my eyes traveling over her sexy ass body and tats that are mostly hidden by her clothes. I wonder if Dani has any tats?

"My girl loves being fucked in the ass. I'm feeling generous, you can take her ass while I drill her hungry little pussy."

I think on it. It's fucked up a thousand ways to Sunday, but I don't want my dick in her. The next woman who gets my cock will be Dani. I don't know why I feel that way, I just do. Half of me wants to put an end to this now. If Dani wasn't off being fucked, I would tell them to leave. My head is messed up. *Jesus.*

"Strip for me, sweetheart," I order Nikki.

Her eyes go back to Freak, she might be his girl, but I can't allow that.

"Eyes right here, sweet Nikki. You want me to give you a good time you need to mind me. Now fucking strip."

She turns her attention back on me and smiles while sliding out of her skin tight jeans and tank top. The woman is built, no doubt about that. Her ass bubbles out and I *almost* regret not sinking my dick into it. I maneuver so I'm lying sideways on the bed, and slide my sweat pants down easily, kicking them to the ground. My dick springs out, more than ready for attention.

"Climb up here and ride my face darlin' and if you suck my cock good enough, Freak will fuck that ass of yours at the same time."

"You sure man?" Freak asks, because though it's not new to us, it's not my usual preference.

"Yeah man, just make sure you keep your balls out of my face," I joke.

Freak flips me off and I laugh.

Nikki lays a hot as fuck kiss on her man and my dick jerks as I watch him slide his fingers inside the valley of her ass. When the kiss ends she climbs up on the bed, takes one long, slow lick of my cock and lets her tongue swirl in the pre-cum, her eyes are locked on mine the entire time. I have to admit, she has my dick throbbing. She crawls up to my face and gives me her mouth. I can taste myself on her and decide to pull on her pierced nipples as a reward. She groans into my mouth and then turns to straddle my face.

I lose myself in her snatch, while Freak gets ready above me to take her ass. I hope I stay busy enough to stop thinking, but since I have the taste of Nikki on my tongue, and Dani is still in my mind, I'm not hopeful.

Chapter 5

DANI

I NEED TO *give up drinking.*

The thought registers as my body catches up with my brain and protests waking up. Everything is sore but nothing hurts more than my head. I squint against the sunshine that's in this damn room. I look around and realize there are no curtains on the windows. *Jesus.* You would have thought I would have noticed that before.

I've been with Beast for a few days now…three, I guess. It all runs together. I haven't spoken with Nic besides being a bitch to her in some text messages. I need to fix that, but thinking of her makes me think of Crusher and I can't go there. So I'm hiding out with Beast. It's not healthy for either of us, but it is what it is. *Escaping.* There is no sex, not even a hint of attraction. We're…*friends*…or maybe just lost souls searching. Every day is the same we fall asleep drinking, trying to fill the holes that life has gutted us with. *Each day we fail.*

"About time your sweet ass woke up."

My body feels like dead weight as a man's voice grinds over my exposed nerves. Never drinking again.

I look around and spot Tiny, who is leaning against the door. I don't know how I feel about him. He's Beast's friend and I feel safe with Beast. I kind of understand him. Tiny is a different thing entirely. I don't like him, but I couldn't begin to tell you why. Maybe, I'm just jaded against men in general? Lord knows I have my reasons. Regardless, I've spent my time here avoiding him. Seeing him here, doesn't make me happy.

"Where's Beast?" I ask.

"He had some club errands to do, he sent me to look after you. He said you were too innocent to go wandering around here by yourself."

I remember Beast telling me that same thing my first night here. This makes me relax some. The fact that Beast sent Tiny and is worried about me warms me. Has anyone besides Nic or Ray ever worried about me?

"I should get going," I say, my voice hoarse and quiet. I need to go talk with Nic and face the world today. I've been overdoing it on the pills and booze. I don't want to live what time I have left like this.

"You know Dragon's old lady pretty good?" Tiny asks out of the blue. The question startles me and something about it instantly puts me on alert.

"Pretty good. Why do you care?"

"Dragon is a dangerous man."

"I've never known one who wasn't," I answer honestly.

"Listen, I'm not supposed to tell you this shit, but Beast he took a liking to you, so he told me to warn you. Our club has some dealings with Dragon, but there's been rumors of bad shit going down and Skull asked me to check into it."

"I don't think I want to hear this. Honestly, I don't know you any more than I know Dragon." Yeah, I'm ready to get the heck out of here. I don't want to be in a pissing match between men and clubs trying to proclaim who has the bigger dick. I'm here because I want Beast and Skull to help me and Nic get to Mexico. Of course *if* Nic knows how dangerous Dragon and his buddies are, Mexico would look better to her, right? The thought makes me pause and listen further.

"I get that, but I have proof that I'm telling the truth," he says calmly and I freeze.

Proof? Do I dare check this shit out? If something is bad, would Nic even believe me? Maybe if I had something to back me up? One of the things I am the most ashamed of, the thing that I keep hidden away, down deep inside, is the fact that once upon a time, I liked Michael. I liked him a lot. I didn't fight the marriage because he was rich, powerful, and sexy. He was all of the things that a stupid girl who had no experience in the world could want. I *liked* him. I *wanted* him. Eventually I woke up and I tried to run, but even then I had no idea how bad he *truly* was. It took him beating me, basically raping me while taking my virginity, to show me the monster I said 'I do' to. What if Nicole is just like I was? What if I don't talk to her and ignore Tiny. *Will Nicole turn a blind eye to all of the red flags, just like I did?*

I beat down the panic I feel at just the small remembrances of Michael and my past. I look Tiny in the eye and do my best to act like I don't have a fuck to give.

"Show me," I tell him, hoping the so-called proof he has is nothing to worry about. I'm concerned though, because Tiny looks way too cocky.

Creepy. The description fits Tiny completely. He even has the cliché beady eyes and greasy hair. Suddenly I am even more thankful for Beast this strange friendship I have with Beast. Tiny gives a whole new meaning to your judgment may be impaired when mixing medication and alcohol. He walks over beside me and gives me his phone.

On it are pictures, not great quality, but I can still see Dragon torturing some man. My world tilts and the vision changes in my mind. I'm not seeing the photos at all now. Suddenly I'm transported back into my hospital room. Michael is standing beside me and it's *his* phone I'm holding. *His* phone showing me a video of Ms. Martens. *Michael* killing someone who cared about me, just because she tried to help save me.

It takes me a minute to breathe and even longer before I realize it isn't Michael I'm looking at in these pictures. Still, I make my mind up immediately. I have to show Nic. I have to get us away and into safety. She needs to see what Dragon is capable of before it's too late for her. *Like it was for me.* With that in mind I text her and head out with Tiny on a mission.

OKAY SO I may have jumped into the fire without thought. Tiny had a member of Skull's crew drop us off at the house Nicole and I shared. He didn't want to drive—in case we partied later. Yeah, I hated to be the one to break it to him, but that was *not* happening.

"Maybe you and your girl will party after this. You owe me, Beast kept you to himself and didn't share," he says and his voice and words make me want to hurl. *Definitely need to watch the meds and alcohol mixing.*

"I don't party with other women, Tiny." Or men...*or you*...like ever, I add silently.

He doesn't respond and a few minutes later we pull up to mine and Nic's place. My beat up old car is in the driveway and I'm glad. I'll use it to get away from Tiny later, because seriously his creep-o vibe is registering off the charts. Our ride drives off and leaves me with Tiny. I fight the urge to plead for the guy to stay. Instead, I walk to the front door and reach in my pocket to get my keys to let us in. Tiny immediately grabs the keys out of my hand and unlocks the door—then pockets them. I start to demand he give them back, but it's not worth the hassle. Nic will have hers, so we can easily get away from Tiny. All these thoughts settle me, I like having contingency plans—*a safety net.*

When we get inside Tiny's quiet and I'm good with that. I do nothing to invite conversation. He goes into the kitchen and talks on his cell phone. He's whispering and I can't make out what he's saying, but I don't really care. I'm here for one reason and as soon as that's done, Tiny will be a bad memory. *He will pale in comparison to the nightmares I pack around.* I just have to get Nicole to listen to me. Then we can work out the rest together. My eyes stayed glued to the clock, and eventually we hear a car pull up. Tiny cusses when he looks out the window.

"Your girl brought a friend," he says and my heart kicks up in speed.

If Dragon is with her, there is no way I will be able to talk to her and she *needs* to know. Tiny goes and stands behind the door and pulls out a gun. A sick feeling of heat from the inside covers me, and I seriously might hurl. *I don't want this.* I need to get control here. Badass Dani needs to take over.

"What the fuck are you doing?"

Oh, but that doesn't sound badass at all. That sounds full of fear, which is what I am now. I need to warn Nic, but I don't want a showdown with Dragon and Tiny. I know Dragon will win, and then he'll turn his anger on me and Nic. Fuck, why didn't I demand we find Beast and take him with us?

"Cool your jets, I'm not going to shoot him, at least not yet. I just need to put her guy out of commission if you're going to talk to her," he says calmly and the smile on his face unnerves me.

It's not like I trust him to begin with, but I'm starting to think there is more behind Tiny's offer to help than I realized.

Shit. It doesn't matter, I'll show Nic the pictures, and together we'll ditch Tiny and get the fuck out of this town. Screw getting Beast and Skull's help, I can use Michael's money to get us to Mexico and set us up somewhere safe. *Safe.* God, I need safe.

Seconds later the door opens and Tiny immediately uses the butt of his gun to hit the guy with Nic on the head. Nailer, I think he's called. I've seen him when I dance. I wince, wishing he hadn't gotten hurt, but glad it's him there instead of Dragon. I don't think Dragon would have gone down so easily. Nailer *does* however, with a horrible thud. Nic screams and Tiny pulls her into the house, trying to muffle the sound with his arm. She looks over at me and my stomach lurches. I do my best to remain even-keeled. I need to calm Nic down and get her to listen and then we both need to get the fuck away from Tiny and out of here.

"Calm down, Nic. It's not what you think. Tiny and I are trying to save you. Girl, you just don't know what that man you are with has done."

Nic is elbowing Tiny and I look at him in frustration. He finally let's her go.

"Are you crazy?" She asks, getting down on her hands and knees to check on Nailer.

She probably has a valid point. I've been crazy for so long, I don't know any other way. I need to make her understand. If Dragon, turns his anger on her like Michael did me…if she has to endure the things I did….I can't let that happen to Nic. *I just can't let that happen to anyone else.*

"Nic, I had to get you away from that club. You don't know what they're doing!" I say walking to her and trying to pull her away from Nailer. We need to get out of here.

"Have you lost your freaking mind?" She asks again. My

panic is increasing, this is not working out like I had it planned in my head.

"Nic!"

"Dani! How the fuck do you know anything is going on? You spent what? A couple nights with this asshole and decide everything he's telling you is the fucking truth?"

"He has pictures, Nic. You need to see what Dragon did to his own man! Here look at them! You can't stay with him Nic, he'll *hurt* you!"

I can't keep the panic out of my voice. *I'm saving Nic, right? I'm giving her a lifeline I never got. Why is it not working?* She takes the camera out of my hands and starts looking at it. I step back. It'll get better now. She'll see him killing Ms. Martens…no that's not right. She'll see him killing one of his own and she'll see that we have to get away. *We need to make ourselves safe.*

"Why do you have these pictures?" Nic asks, so calm. She gives me this look of disgust and my soul feels…*wounded*. Nic is my best friend. Her and Ray are my only friends in the world. How can she see those pictures, be calm and look at me like I'm the piece of shit? What am I missing? Is the whole world okay with men killing and hurting others? Why does it feel like Nicole is betraying…*me?*

"Tiny is in charge of following Dragon and his crew when they're in Skull's city to make sure they don't do shit like this! Nic, you can't be so far gone over Dragon that you don't see how wrong this is!"

"Get the fuck out of my house!" She yells, throwing the phone across the room.

"Not going to happen, bitch," Tiny says smugly. When I see the look on his face, I feel my panic nearly drown me. *No!* This is not how it is supposed to go down.

"What do you want from me?" Nic growls at Tiny.

"To play with you, sweet cheeks. Maybe I'll do you and your girl at the same time. Dani here likes to party. The more the merrier, right baby?"

I try to concentrate on what they are saying. I know it's not good, but a panic attack has me in its sites. The room is starting to tilt and swirl and the noise around me is distorted. I can't hear what they are saying, but the anger in Nic's face is clear. I try to concentrate on it and use that to ground me and keep the fear at bay.

"...Now enough of this shit. Strip before I decide your fat ass is more trouble than it's worth."

"Tiny baby stop it, you're going to scare Nic. Besides, I told you I don't party with other women," I argue, when I hear the shit he is spouting. I'm starting to think I underestimated Tiny, and how truly vile he is. I need to distract him so Nic can get out of here. I try to let her know that with my eyes. I never meant to put her in more danger. I just needed her to see what Dragon does. I want her safe, but right now the main threat to both of us is Tiny.

I count backwards from one hundred in my mind and promise to wash my mouth out with soap and shower a thousand times as I kiss, Tiny. I do the fake movements Michael always seemed to like. Pulling my leg up against his hip and unbuttoning his shirt.

80, 79, 78, 77...

Tiny pushes me away, but I see the sick look in his eyes. I'll kill myself before he ever touches me. I never want another man near my body. The only time I ever think of sex is when I'm drunk and high on meds, we've seen how well that works out. *I ignore the name Crusher that drifts through my thoughts.*

"Come on over here. Let me see what you got," Tiny orders Nicole.

She walks towards us and if looks could kill, I'd be dead right now. I can't blame her. I try to keep the tears away, but I know I'm failing. I only wanted to save Nic from the life I have and it's going horribly wrong and worse, Nic doesn't even seem to want to leave Dragon.

"Take off your shirt. I want to see the merchandise."

I can't let Nic do this. I'm about to push her away and jump on Tiny with my nails, my fists, my legs, my teeth anything and everything I can and let her run, when I see she is palming a knife. I hope she goes for his jugular. If she can stab him in the neck he'll go down and we can run.

We need to run—preferably to Mexico.

"Oh yeah, look at those big-ass tits. I'm definitely going to bury my cock in those fuckers. I think you're starting to grow on me, puta."

I want to kill him. If Nic doesn't kill him, *I will*. I have a lot of pent up rage, maybe I should let that out for a change.

"I've never done anything like this…"

I grab my hands to keep them from shaking. I need to be ready to help Nic and then to make sure she gets away.

"That's okay puta, lucky for you I have."

As Nic gets closer to him, I take a step back to give her more room to swing, giving me more room to get a running start to attack him in case she fails.

"Should I…take my bra off?" She asks, and I want to scream. *Can't she just attack already?* There are black dots swirling in front of my eyes and I'm trying to breathe through them. The last thing Nic or I need is for me to pass out, it doesn't happen often, but it can during my panic attacks.

"Oh yeah, show ole' Tiny what you got for him."

Nicole screams as she stabs him. She didn't go for the

neck, but it seems to work, because Tiny falls back on the couch cussing. Nic and I look at each other and we both yell for the other to run. When we discover that neither of us have keys, my heart flips in my chest.

"We have to hit the hills. We'll circle around and come back out on the main road by Dragon's compound!" She says.

I don't agree but I can't keep arguing, so we run. I don't know how long we go. I know it's been awhile, but it feels like forever. We're walking in circles and mostly in silence now. Nic is pissed. I feel horrible about the mess I created. It's just another sign of how fucked up I am. Maybe Michael is right and I am nothing but a worthless waste of air? How many times did he tell me the world would be a better place if I would fucking end myself? Maybe I should listen to him?

I've tried to defend myself with Nic. I've tried warning her further about Dragon. She's not listening. She said they were taking revenge for what was done to that girl who was beaten. I find it hard to believe. Why would they care? They were so callous about her that night at the house. In my experience men don't care about anything if it doesn't pertain to them. I'm so tired. I thought escaping Michael would give me a life, a chance to be...*normal*. That hasn't worked out. I've only managed to hold on because of Nic and Ray and now Nic is so upset with me. *If I lose her...*

"I'm sorry, Nic," I say again, because without Nic, I don't think I could go on.

"Forget it. I understand, but you've got to trust me when I tell you Dragon is nothing like Michael," she responds.

I hope she's right. I really do.

"Should we try getting off the trail and sliding down the mountain to see if it might end up near the road?" I ask, trying to keep my voice steady, knowing we're so high up, sliding might be more dangerous than facing Tiny and whatever goons he's called for help. I think of Beast and the betrayal I feel in my gut...it hurts. *Why did I trust him?*

"Hell if I know at this point, Dani. You know my parent's. Our trips to Lexington and Louisville were their idea of hiking. I don't know shit about climbing hills—or directions apparently."

"Did you hear that?" I ask. Someone is following us and they're closer than they've ever been. I stare at Nicole. I can't panic. *I can't.* I show Nicole a big rock behind me, we'll have to hide behind there. It's not much, but it's better than being out in the open. We crouch down behind it and I grab her hand hard. God never hears me pray, but I pray that he makes sure Nicole makes it through this.

"Alright bitch it's time for you two to come out. I know you're here, Irish tells me I don't have time to watch you squirm anymore. It's time we finish the game," a strange voice calls from in front of the rock.

As further proof God hates me, my prayers are not only unanswered—my boss, the man who offered us an escape to London, Kentucky, is now standing behind us while the other guy had us distracted. He's pointing a gun at us. *Shit.*

"Irish?" Nicole questions.

"Sorry Nic, just business. You got caught up in it. It's time Dragon is brought down and sadly girl, you are a sure way to keep him so wrapped up in his head he has no idea what's going on." He says, pulling her away from me.

He grabs me by my hair at the same time, pointing the gun at my temple walking us around the rock and making sure Nicole leads the way. I don't fight or scream. I'm trying to figure out a way to save Nicole.

"How can you betray Dragon like this? He thinks of you as his brother?" Nic asks. In a lot of ways she's naïve. Men don't need a reason to be cruel. *They just are.* The two of them go back and forth and I tune them out. I need to find a way out of this.

"Fucking shut it. What are you doing telling this whore our business?" The first voice we heard yells. I had forgot about him.

I swing around to look at who it is and see....*evil*. I see the same anger and hate in him that has been in Michael's eyes every time he hit me. Irish is a dumbass, he won't survive this. This guy will kill him, easily.

"What does it matter anyway? She'll be dead and we'll be long gone by the time Dragon finds her or her friend," Irish maintains.

They argue back and forth a little longer and I can hear Nicole's voice but I can't concentrate. They're discussing mine and Nicole's death. I can't let her die. I need to get them focused on me and give her a chance to get away. If they aim their anger at me she might have a little more time to get away. I fucked up so bad. Nicole would never be in this situation if not for me. I was trying to save her and instead...I've killed both of us.

"Well since you're doing the world a favor and ridding it of morons, maybe you could turn the gun on yourself," I say, trying to sound cocky. I need to draw them away from Nic. I have to.

The man doesn't react like I thought he would though. In my experience men enjoy hitting and beating up their trophies first. Apparently not this guy, because he shoots me. I feel the sharp pain in my leg in unison with the sound of the gun going off. Nic is screaming as I go down, again I want to focus, but I can't. All I can feel is the white-hot agony of Nic pushing at my wound and the warm liquid pouring against my skin. I want to look and see the wound, but everything is going black.

Chapter 6

CRUSHER

HOW DO YOU know when your ass is sewn up over a woman? You see her lying in a pool of blood. *That's it.* That's all there is to it. My world stops for the space of a minute and my heart actually hurts. I'm in deep and I haven't even had my goddamned tongue in her mouth.

When I got to the top of the mountain to find Irish, an original member of our club, had shot not only Dani, but Nicole too, I thought it was a nightmare. I was afraid the club had a traitor but a brother who helped create the Savage MC? Never. A brother who fought with us overseas betraying the club cut so fucking deep, there just wasn't words. It still hasn't fully sunk in. I haven't had time to think about it, because we had to rush both women to the hospital.

One of the bullets that lodged in Dani's leg, nicked an artery. If not for Nicole trying to stall the blood and having a compress wedged against it, I would have lost her. She's undergoing emergency surgery. I stayed close, waiting for word that she'll be okay. The other brothers are with Dragon, because Nicole is in bad shape. I'm worried about her too, don't get me wrong. Still, it just didn't seem right that everyone turned their backs on Dani and left her alone. I get the feeling the girl has been left alone a lot in her life.

"Mr. Dawson?" A nurse asks, coming out of the surgical

room door.

"Yes, Ma'am?"

"Ms. Smith did fine with everything...but..."

"But?" I question, trying to ignore the way my heart kicks against my chest.

"I'm afraid she's disoriented. She had a panic attack and the doctor ordered a sedative, but first we were hoping if she saw you, it might help. We hate to give her more medicine so soon after coming out of the recovery ward. However, we can't allow her to hurt herself."

"Take me to her."

I follow the nurse down the hall, more anxious than I can ever remember.

"Ms. Smith? Look we told you it would be okay. See who I've got with me? It's your step-brother."

I had to tell the staff that I was Dani's step-brother before they would give me information on her, or let me near her in general. I was afraid she would ruin the set up by denying our involvement. She doesn't and I'm glad, but I think it has more to do with the fact that the girl is in the middle of a full blown hissy-fit.

She is holding one of those big huge thermal cups and aiming it at an orderly. I take in the mess on the floor, a couple boxes of Kleenex, a plastic pan like they give you to wash in, toothpaste, generic deodorant, a phone... Hell, she must have thrown everything at them she could get her hands on. Just as I'm about to speak to her, the cup she was holding comes sailing at my head. I duck, but it hits me in the chest and ice scatters over me, the nurse, and the floor.

"I told you I don't want to talk to anyone but Nicole! Take me to Nicole!"

She looks brave, lying in the bed in a faded blue hospital

gown and her hair a tangled mess around her head. She's pale though, *too pale*. Her lips which are normally adorned in bright red lipstick are a pale pink and dry. The black circles under her eyes are so dark, it gives her a haunted look. I can also see the shaking in her hands. She may be fighting like an alley-cat but she's scared shitless.

"Nicole is in surgery, Hellcat, and you're in no shape to go see her. I can take you down there when she comes through." I don't add that she might not, it's not something that Dani needs to hear right now. It'd take a fool not to tell that she's close to a nervous breakdown.

She looks at me like she just now realizes it's me.

"Crusher…it's me…I mean, my fault.…"

"Leave the room!" I growl. The nurses and doctors stare at me like I'm insane. I cross my hands over my chest and wait. They look back at Dani and then to me, before finally leaving.

"Don't talk about this shit in public, Hellcat," I caution her.

She looks down at the covers she's holding in her lap. She's gripped the edges so tight that her fingers are white from her hold. Before I can stop myself I walk over to her bedside and sit down putting my hand over hers.

"I thought I was saving her… I was scared…there were pictures. Dragon was…he was torturing…"

"Ours is a world of its own, Hellcat. We play by a different set of rules. What Twist and Irish did…that can't go unpunished."

"When a man is that dark it spills over, Crusher."

"My name is Alexander," I say before I can stop myself. I want her to use my name. I want her to say it often.

She doesn't give me what I want. She continues just looking at me, I finally give up and answer her as honestly as I can.

"Doesn't matter how dark the man or the world, a real man

doesn't hurt a woman, Hellcat."

"And Dragon?"

"He'd die for your girl. I have no doubt about that and I know for a fact he'd never hurt her. Hell, if my guess is right he'll spend his life making sure she has everything she could ever want."

Dani's dark eyes are opened wide and she looks at me with so much concentration, it unnerves me. It's almost like she's trying to see straight through me. I stare back at her calmly. I got nothing to hide and everything to gain if Dani can trust me, even a little bit.

"If you're lying to me Zander, I'll hunt you down and cut off your balls with a dull potato peeler."

I laugh. Just when I start thinking she looked helpless there in that bed, with that gown swallowing her small, frail body she shocks the hell out of me. What is it about this woman that keeps my head spinning? I wish I knew.

"Point taken, Hellcat, and since I'm partial to my balls, I'll make sure not to lie to you."

"You will. Men always lie. It's what they do." She says looking out the window this time instead of at me. I find I don't like that. I want her attention on me. I put my index finger under her chin and pull her face back around to me.

"I will never lie to you, Dani. You may not always like what I tell you, but I will make a vow to you right now, to never lie."

"Will Nicole be okay?" She asks quickly, and damn I should have seen that one coming.

I take a breath and look down at the floor.

"That's what I thought," she whispers brokenly.

"Hey Hellcat, I didn't say she wouldn't. She's in surgery. That's about all I know right now."

"I need to go be with her," she says and there are tears in

her eyes, but somehow she keeps them from falling. I don't know why, because I don't like women crying, but the fact that she is trying to hide her tears, *hurts* me.

"Hellcat, I'm not sure of everything that's going on, but I've heard things…"

"But…"

"Sweetheart, I don't think Dragon would want you there right now," I say honestly.

Her face has been pale as a ghost and it still is, but I can see the hint of color that enters her cheeks at my words. I hate it, this can't be a shock to her. Right?

"I thought…I was…it doesn't matter."

We sit there in silence for a little while longer. It's not awkward, but it *is* strained. I feel like I should be finding words to make her feel better. Hell, other than sticking my dick in a woman, I've not had many dealings with them. Unless you count Melly, but then again, Melly was special.

"Zander, will you go sit with them…and find out about Nicole for me? Please?"

"Everyone calls me Crusher or Alex," I respond, watching those big dark eyes of hers.

"I'm not them. I like Zander, it suits you."

"What's a Zander look like?"

"Like someone who does what a friend asks him to, when she can't do it on her own."

The girl is determined, you have to give her that. I stare at her for a few more minutes. She doesn't dodge my eyes, but I notice the longer I stare at her, the tighter she grips the bedsheet. It wouldn't surprise me if it rips any moment.

"She has plenty of company, Hellcat," I answer, thinking she was the one who was all alone here.

"Nic is all I have in the world besides Ray. I want…I need

to know she's okay."

"Are we friends, Hellcat?" I ask. I get up to head to the surgery waiting room.

"Time will tell I guess. I'm not exactly bosom buddy material these days," she answers holding her head down. She looks kind of defeated and I hate it.

"I don't know Hellcat, I kind of like your bosom."

She doesn't laugh, which is what I wanted, but she kind of half smiles before lying back against her pillow. *She's worn out.* I leave without any further words and close the door quietly behind me.

Chapter 7

DANI

*T*HE BLACK PLAGUE.

Did you know another name for the Black Plague is death? I feel about as welcomed as that, so it fits. I understand it—*I do*. I don't really like myself right now. I add it up as just another mistake in a long line of them. Everyone has given me the cold shoulder, and if looks could kill, then Dragon and Bull's death glare would definitely have done me in.

I've gone and seen Nicole, but she hasn't regained consciousness. She developed an infection. When I first came through and the nurse told me Nic was shot too...it felt as if my world was ending. All I ever wanted was to protect Nicole and I'm the reason she's clinging to life.

I'm supposed to be getting out of the hospital today. Crusher says I need to come home to the club. The club isn't home—especially with everyone hating me. I don't want to leave Nicole either, I'd rather stay at the hospital until I know she's going to be okay. I've said some prayers for her but it's been well established that God doesn't answer my prayers.

I'm sitting on my hospital bed, wearing the bloody jeans and a hospital scrub shirt the nurse gave me. The jeans have been cut up on one side, but they're all I have. One of the nurses offered pants too, but I declined. I'm just thankful they didn't cut the pants off of me for some reason. I don't want charity if I can get away from it. I'm used to having no one looking out for me. It's less risky, and better not to depend on people.

Still today, I'm feeling...*lonely*. I'm feeling...*isolated*. Part of it is the way the club is treating me, part of it is fear over Nic and still some is...being tired. Deep inside I'm disappointed I didn't die. It would have been easier and better for everyone if it was me fighting for my life instead of Nicole. She has everything to live for. Me? Hell, I wouldn't fight for life...not even a little bit.

"Those look like deep thoughts, hummingbird."

My body jerks as I look up to see Beast standing there and I instantly want to scream for help. I don't trust him, he sent Tiny to me... he...

"Stop the looks, I had nothing to do with Tiny. When I woke up you were sleeping I went to find us breakfast, when I came back you were gone. I'd hoped that meant you felt like you could tackle things now. I sure as hell didn't expect you to go off with Tiny—never did like that asshole."

I'm not sure I believe him, but his words do have a ring of truth in them. Then again, what have I ever known about a man being truthful? There's also the fact he's holding a vase full of yellow daises. The flowers are big, but in his large hands they look small and awkward.

I clear my throat, trying to tread slowly here.

"He said you sent him. He mentioned things we talked about while I was there."

"Little weasel probably listened through the door. I'm sorry," he says taking another step in.

I keep my body from retreating further. I've been in the hospital for four days now and that's four days without pills. I wanted to tell the doctor that I needed some sort of anxiety medicine, but it felt like a weakness. What if Crusher or one of the club members found out? Would they label me as Nicole's unstable friend who is completely crazy that got her...almost got her killed?

"Pretty flowers," I say trying to sound tough, but I have a feeling it's going to take a bit to find that voice again. It'll at least be after I get out of here. Being in a hospital brings back memories. Memories I shouldn't have. Memories that are slowly cutting holes inside of me, and that's bad because I already have craters the size of football fields.

"You look like a daisy kind of girl instead of roses," Beast says as he puts the vase down beside my bed.

I touch the petals slowly. They are beautiful. Bright, soft petals the color of sunshine with warm dark brown centers.

"Why do I look like daisies?" I ask before I can stop myself.

"Daises are strong. They can grow in the middle of a desert with little water. They bend and flow with the wind and still remain standing. Their stems are strong."

My finger moves over the stem thinking on his words.

"The stem looks like a weed to me," It's probably not the nicest thing to say. They're pretty, I don't mean that. It's just once...couldn't I be like something beautiful...instead of something *less*...

"Looks can be deceiving," he says bringing his hand under my chin and pulling my eyes from the flower to his face. "You have your own beauty, hummingbird."

"What the fuck is going on here?" Crusher asks from the door and I can feel the anger vibrating off of him. He's staring Beast down and I bite my lip. You can feel the testosterone fill the room.

Beast turns around to face Crusher. I get there is probably

hostility between the clubs, because of what happened and with Nicole right now, but I can't handle any more fighting...*not now*. I'm on a razor's edge as it is.

"How's Nicole?" I ask Crusher, trying to redirect the conversation.

I stand up and wince as a flash of pain enters my bad leg, Beast places his large hand on mine and offers me his support. I push down using his arm almost like a cane. Once I get my balance and shift my weight to my good leg, I look up at Crusher waiting for his answer. His dark eyes are glowing...some anger yes, but something else I can't really decipher.

"She's showing signs of coming out of it. They're monitoring her closely. You can go see her before I take you home if you want," Crusher says.

I swallow and think about what he says, before I answer.

"I don't think it would be good for me to go to the club..."

"Why the fuck not?" Crusher growls and Beast blocks me from his path. It's sweet, but even without my pills I don't really fear Crusher...I don't know why.

"I'm not exactly the most loved person around the Savage Brother's MC right now. I just think it would be better for everyone if I stay at the house that Nicole and I rent."

"No. You're coming to the club, where I can take care of you."

"It doesn't appear you're taking care of her now," Beast says, folding his huge arms at his chest and making his biceps pop so much, I think they might need their own zip code.

"What would you know about it?"

"I have eyes," Beast shrugs "You're more than welcome to come back to the club with me hummingbird, my club will take care of you."

"You're the fuck-ups that got her in this mess to begin with."

"Funny, I'd say that'd be your president pissing off the wrong people," Beast responds to Crusher.

*Four…three…two…one…*please let me hold on to my sanity long enough to get out of here, get to the house, swallow some pills and regroup.

"I can take care of myself. Can you two stop your pissing match over your clubs until I get out of here, please?"

I feel them looking at me, but avoid them. Instead, I choose to busy myself with packing up the hospital toiletries they gave me in a plastic bag the nurse gave me.

"I have your discharge papers, Miss Smith."

The hospital nurse comes in with her clipboard and papers, oblivious to the tension in the room. Me? I breathe a little easier having her in here with me until she looks at me and I see the disdain there.

"Thank you," I answer trying to ignore the dull ache of pain that is slowly increasing the longer I remain standing.

As she goes over the care of the bandages and things, I feel Crusher standing close to my back. I look over my shoulder to see he's standing right behind me, so close I can feel his breath against my skin. Beast is standing by the door watching us.

"Do you mind?" I ask Crusher, annoyed.

"I need to know how to take care of you, Hellcat."

"I told you I will take care of myself, been doing it for a while now."

"You need someone to help you until you're better, and that's me," he answers.

"Doesn't look like you're doing such a great job right now," Beast speaks up from across the room.

"Did someone ask what you thought?" Crusher asks.

"No, but she's standing there in pain and instead of helping her, you're yelling at me."

Crusher's body goes rigid at the rebuke, I know, because suddenly he pulls me back against him and takes my weight. His warm body slowly heats my back and I find myself relaxing against my will.

"Why don't you fuck off? No one wants you here." Crusher responds to Beast and the nurse looks up at me and shakes her head. She's judging me, but I shake it off. Everyone does. I learned a long time ago that people will think what they want. The key is to pretend you either don't give a fuck, or pretend you earned their dislike and enjoy it—for that reason alone I give her my fuck off smile.

"You're treating her like your woman," Beast starts again. This time my heart kicks in with fear and I pull away from Crusher...*no*.

"Not my woman, but definitely property of the Savage MC, fucker."

I ignore the way the distinction makes my heart feel as if it's being squeezed in a fist. I don't want to be any man's property. I don't even know why his reply should hurt, but it does.

"Will you two..." I begin only to have Beast interrupt me.

"Why doesn't she have clean clothes then? Are the Savage pussies too busy to make sure their property doesn't have to go home in clothes they've been shot in? Where's her flowers or balloons, something to show she's at least a good piece of club pussy?" Beast asks and I flinch.

The nurse shakes her head and gives me *that look*. The look I've gotten my whole life. The look that broadcasts one word. *Whore*. I got it when I married Michael with the whispered word *gold-digger* thrown around. I got it in the emergency rooms the few times Michael allowed me there for treatment. He took great pleasure in telling the doctors how I had a drug problem and he would find me on the streets having been beat up by some john. He loved weaving lies that put him in the best light. I got *that* look every time I climbed up on the stage to dance and take my clothes off. None of those times hurt as much though as the nurse's.

"Do you want to start something with me, motherfucker?" Crusher asks, but really I've kind of had it by then. I grab my papers the nurse thrust at me, I take the small bag of items I saved from the hospital supplies, and put my papers down in it. I hold the bag in one hand and the flowers in the other and hobble out. A wheel chair would have been nice, but Nurse Ratchet hasn't mentioned one yet and I'm tired of waiting.

"Woah, Hellcat…"

"Thank you for the flowers, Beast." I say stiffly as I pass him.

"You can come back with me hummingbird, you'll be welcomed there."

Crusher growls and picks me up before I can respond. It's all I can do to hold onto my flowers and not drop them to the floor. He shoots Beast a look and stomps out with me in his arms.

Chapter 8

CRUSHER

I TAKE HOLD of Dani, pulling her into my arms and stomp out. If I don't, I'm going to kill that mother-fucking-son-of-a-bitch. When I walked in and he was touching Dani's face, I wanted to break his hand. It's bad enough that she chose him over me that night. It fucking pisses me off that he's had his dick anywhere near her. It sure as fuck ain't happening again. It sits sour in my stomach that she let him anywhere near her.

"What the fuck were you thinking letting that son of a bitch touch you? If you need dick that bad, I can give you mine..." I break off my tirade when I hear a large crash. I look down at her, then down to the floor. I see a broken vase, scattered flowers, and water all along the hall in front of us.

Dani's elbow swings into my throat, it's not powerful because of the angle, since she's in my arms, but it is hard enough that my hands lower her quickly to the ground.

"What the..." I gasp and massage my Adams-apple before continuing. "What the fuck?" My voice sounds like freaking Mickey Mouse, while I catch my breath.

"You don't get to talk to me like that. *You don't know me.* We are nothing to each other, so stick your condescending attitude up your ass. If I want to fuck the whole Green-Bay Packers team, I'll fuck them." She growls hobbling away from me.

I watch her for a minute. I can admit it's mostly to admire the way those jeans are molded to her ass. Then I look at the mess she left behind her. I take pleasure in seeing the fucking flowers broken and scattered on the floor. I would be lying if I didn't confess I like the way she doesn't even seem to want to take one with her. I kick them with the toe of my boot and smile as I think about Beast coming out and finding that shit. Then I jog down the hall to catch up with Hop-a-long.

"You need to let me carry you to the cage," I say when I notice how much pain and discomfort she is in.

"I need for you to leave me the fuck alone. I can take care of myself."

"Doesn't appear you do such a good job of it, if you make choices like Beast and Tiny," I return before I can stop my mouth.

She stops and turns to face me, putting her hands on her hips, the bag with her belongings swaying at her side.

"Maybe if *you* weren't so busy holding a *gun* on me, I wouldn't have!"

"Will you keep your voice down? And it wasn't at you, Hellcat. I think you know that. You're the one who fucked up here."

"Are you always such a self-righteous prick, Zander?"

I look at her and that's when it hits me. She's pale—really pale. Her face is tight indicating her pain and she's playing the hard ass, but those dark eyes of hers show…fear. I'm an ass. I pick her up and ignore the way she protests and beats on my chest. Instead, I lean down and kiss the top of her head. I'm not sure why, but that seems to calm her.

"I'm sorry Hellcat, I got my nose out of joint because Beast was right. I should have brought you some clothes and your own stuff."

At my words the fight goes completely out of her and she rests her head against my shoulder. I continue down the hallway towards the exit, oblivious to the stares we receive. It feels good, having Dani in my arms. It feels...*right*. Which is a scary, fucking thing to admit.

"I don't know why. I'm nothing to you. It shouldn't have bothered you," she says quietly.

I look down and her eyes are closed. She looks so sad and more than a little haunted. Again, she reminds me of Melly. Maybe it's her sadness? Or the way she tries so hard to be tough as nails, yet still looks so fragile. I honestly don't know why the two of them are linked in my mind, but they are. Except, the emotions that Dani brings out of me are much more volatile. I don't say anything while I carry her outside to the cage. I let her slide to her feet, gently but keep my hands on her ass and can't help but squeeze. I pull her close, knowing she can feel the hard ridge of my cock. I'm not about to hide it from her, Dani and I both have been around the block. She's going to know that I want to fuck her and I'm not going to hide it. I plan to show her, and show her often.

Her face raises to mine and those eyes of hers...eyes that hold a million secrets pin me in their gaze, and I can't look away from the interest and the excitement flaring in them.

"That's where you're wrong, Hellcat. That's where you're wrong," I whisper.

I expect her to question me, to accuse me of trying to get into her pants, which admittedly I do want. She doesn't however, and I'm glad. Truthfully, I don't know how I would have answered her. I don't know what she is to me, but I know she has potential to be more and I don't want to leave her alone. That's probably why I can't stop myself. As I gently place her inside the vehicle, I lean down on the running boards and look up at her. My fingers slide under her hair. My thumb gently massages the skin at the corner of her lips.

"Zander?" She questions, confused.

Hell, I am too. I'm absolutely confused, but I can't stop myself. I bring my lips against hers, tasting her, and swallowing the soft sigh of air that escapes. The kiss is gentle and sweet, not at all what I planned to give her. My tongue brushes along the top of her lip and slowly enters into her waiting mouth. At first I'm confused, and take the fact that she's not participating as rejection, but gradually her tongue comes up and dances against mine. It's a sweet kiss. A kiss from another time. Chaste almost, but it soothes an empty spot inside of me I didn't know was there. So, I don't push it. I slowly break away, leaving our foreheads connected. She closes her eyes and lets me hold her. Dani, who is always fighting, lets me hold her outside in front of everyone and doesn't protest. No, if I can read her body's reaction right, she is just like me at the moment. *Wishing we could stay like this and not move.*

Have I ever savored an innocent kiss? Have I ever given one? Have I ever enjoyed just holding someone before?

I honestly don't think so. *What the hell do I do with that?*

Chapter 9

DANI

WOW. NO, SERIOUSLY *wow*. What the hell was that? What the hell just happened? I can't help but touch my lips, once Zander closes the door. I started calling him that because I thought it might irritate him, but now I like it. I like that I'm the only one who uses it and I know I'm getting too drawn into him. I think about him way too much. I'm curious about him in ways I haven't been with other men. He's dangerous. I planned on retreating and ignoring him completely, but that kiss...

Before Michael and sadly even at the beginning with Michael, I enjoyed kissing. I had. I loved the feel of lips sliding against each other, the taste of another person's tongue and the pleasure that could come from a good long, slow kiss. I loved all of that. Still, that one small, sweet kiss with Zander blew away any other kiss I ever had out of the water. I fight down the nausea at what this means. There's no reason to panic. It wasn't even a sexual kiss. Zander's a man who has a different woman every time he wants one. This meant nothing to him. He's probably just feeling sorry for me. He's trying to make me move into the club and we both know I'm not wanted there.

With that worked out in my brain, I feel slightly better. The last thing I need is to be pursued by a man. Especially a man like Zander. He's too potent... too consuming... I look over at him as he climbs into the truck and take in his dark hair which is messy and going in different directions, either by the wind, his fingers, or a combination of the two. He has on faded jeans and a plain white t-shirt under his Savage MC cut. His beautiful skin hints at a Latin heritage, but has been bronzed by the sun into this utter perfection that makes any woman, myself included, curious to see more. He is danger, definitely danger. Have I reminded myself of that enough yet?

I turn away to look out the window, as Zander pulls out of the parking area. The cab of the truck is quiet and I feel awkward, but I have no idea what to say.

"Do you need to go to your place and pack before we go to the club?"

"I'm not going to the club but if you could take me to the house, I would appreciate it."

"Hellcat, we've been through this."

"I know, that's why we shouldn't re-hash it again."

Out of the corner of my eye I can see Zander shake his head, but he doesn't say anything else.

We drive the rest of the way in silence, the sound of the radio in the background is the only noise. I feel bad, I should find something to say, because he's been really good to me and though I've dialed back my bitch meter towards him, I'm never going to be like the other girls. I don't have that in me anymore. No one grieves that loss more than I do, but it's true.

When the vehicle comes to a stop, I jump out, wincing at the pressure it puts on my leg. I ignore it and don't give Zander time to react. I look through the open window at him.

"Thanks for the ride Zander, stay cool." I walk off. *Dismissed*. I must keep him dismissed.

I'm at the front door and have it opened before I realize he is standing behind me.

"What are you doing?"

"Hellcat, until we make sure everything is locked down and the danger is gone, you can't stay by yourself. That leaves two routes this can take. You either come back to the club, or I can stay here. If you're going to insist on being a stubborn ass, then I'm here."

"No fucking way."

"Not open for debate. Now I'd rather be at the club, but baby you want to play it this way, I'm down."

I shake my head, this is *not* going to happen. I cannot be anywhere near Zander.

I go inside, ignoring him. He follows, as I knew he would, but I want to change. I want my own damn deodorant, clean clothes not covered in blood and my hair washed in my own shampoo. Once I have all that done and I'm back to myself, I can deal with Zander. Right now, I feel...too raw.

I look over my shoulder, as he follows me.

"Take your damn boots off so you don't track mud in the house."

I catch him giving me a mock salute out of the corner of my eye as I leave him behind and go to my bedroom. Once I escape to the adjoining bathroom, I lock the door and relax my weight against it. I've held it together, but that's come to an abrupt end. The shaking starts and the tears slide down my cheeks. I go to the sink and turn the water on. Hoping the noise will drown out my tears.

I've fucked up. I've fucked up so bad. I want nothing more than to jump in the shower and let the water rinse me clean and hide my weak-ass tears. I can't do that though, because of my damn leg. So instead, I rip my shirt over my head and push my pants off, cursing Tiny, my stupidity, Michael, and the stupid ridiculous choices my fucked-up brain keeps making. *I curse it all.* I hobble to the shower and grab my shampoo and conditioner. I bend over the sink and wash my hair continuously until all I can smell is the scent of strawberries. Even when the scent has permeated the air, I wash it one more time. Then I slowly sink to the floor, ignoring the way my hair drips down my back onto my skin.

I don't know how long I've stayed like this. I guess it must have been awhile, because the next thing I know, Zander is wrapping a bathrobe around me and pulling me up. I should be worried that I'm naked. I should be worried that I appear weak and broken. Something about the way he wraps the robe around me and helps me up, feeding my hands and arms through the sleeves, while supporting my weight, tells me I'm safe. Maybe I'm just completely out of it. Could I be in shock? Surely that's the only thing that could explain why I would ever feel safe with a man.

"I was wondering when you were going to let it out, sweetheart."

"I'm so stupid," I whisper, like it's a dirty secret. It might not be a secret, but I definitely feel dirty. I have for so long, nothing will ever make me feel clean again.

"You're just searching," he says applying pressure to my neck so I will hold my head down. Once I do that, he wraps a towel in my hair. Then, he picks me up and carries me out of the bathroom. I should argue, I should insist he put me down. I don't. I lay my head against his shoulder and rest, as if I'm boneless. When he places me on the bed, I still don't argue. The time to panic should be when he gets on the bed behind me. *I don't.* He spoons me, gathering my body up close and pulling it back against him. His warmth reaches me, but I still feel so cold. This whole time, I've been crying. I feel like I could cry forever. He places a kiss on the top of my head and doesn't say anything else. He just holds me, letting me cry. Eventually I feel a shift on the bed and then he's reaching me some tissues, before settling back down behind me.

"You're going to make yourself sick, Hellcat," he rumbles, his head is somewhere over top of me. I'm burrowed against his chest, absorbing his heat.

"Nicole could die and it's all my fault," I whisper my biggest fear.

"She's not going to die," he argues.

"You don't know that," I answer, wishing there was some way he could tell me for sure Nicole will be okay. I need to know with a hundred percent certainty that my best friend, the only person besides Ray I've ever cared about in my life, is going to be okay.

"You don't know she's not. Don't borrow trouble, it comes knocking on its own too easily."

I'm mad at him. Mad that he won't tell me she's okay. Mad that he won't give me the words to make the fear inside of me go away. It's not logical, but it's the truth.

"You should leave," I tell him. It's childish considering everything he's done, but if he can't make Nicole better then he's just someone else to witness my guilt.

"Go to sleep Hellcat, tomorrow you can fight me. Tonight let it go and let me take care of you."

We lie like that in silence. Zander holding me close. I should put a stop to it, but there's that feeling again... that sense of... *safety*. Sleep is coming for me, but I can't shut my brain down entirely.

"I only wanted to save her... save her like I wish they had saved me..."

Chapter 10

CRUSHER

SAVE HER, LIKE I *wish they had saved me*....Those words strike something inside of me that refuses to let go. I've replayed them for days. She needed someone to save her and no one did. What does this woman have hidden? Why do I care so much? Why do I need to be the one she reaches out to? I have all these questions and very few answers.

I've been staying at Dani's every night for a week. It's been heaven and hell. She's as prickly as a cactus and I have to handle her with care. At the same time, she makes me laugh. We have a lot in common and every once in a while she lets her guard down and I see this other side to her. It's vulnerable, soft, and sweet. It soothes me. Still, I'm enough of a sadistic jerk to admit I get off when she comes at me with her sharp claws and lethal tongue. There are times I want to grab her and show her exactly what I want her tongue for. I haven't. Fuck, I'm getting blue balls holding back with her. Still, when she lets me see her vulnerable side, and her words come back to me, I hold back.

If something doesn't give soon, I'm not going to be able to control myself much longer. *Every night* she crawls into bed. *Every night* she rubs that deliciously perfect ass against my crotch and my dick weeps with need. I've been a walking hard-on since that first night. After a week of no relief, you would think my cock would get the damn message. *It hasn't.*

Today has been the worse yet. All day Dani has been prancing around the house in these barely there shorts and a black tank top and the bitch doesn't even have a bra on. Does she know what she's doing to me? Fuck, she probably does. It's almost time for her to crawl in our bed. If I don't blow off some steam then I'm not going to be able to lie next to her without my head spinning in circles and smoke coming out of my ears. I'll need to be locked up in a padded cell.

With that in mind, I jump in the shower and do something I haven't done since I was a horny teenager. I take matters into my own hands. As the water beats down on my back, I lean against the shower wall and close my eyes. Immediately Dani's face comes to mind. I know everything about that face now. I know the scar under her chin, the full lips that smile ever-so-slightly when she thinks I can't see. The way the glossy red lipstick she wears makes them shine and seduce with just a glance—all of it comes to mind so easily. Yet, the thing that hits me the hardest are her fucking eyes. *Eyes that set me on fire.* They're deep brown with a hint of yellow. Bottomless pits of feeling, which sparkle at me as if they hold secrets only I should ever know. Nothing in my life has heated me or torn me up like they do.

My tongue slides out against my lip and *goddamn*, I wish it were her lips I could taste. If I keep my eyes closed and concentrate on the water sliding on my skin I can almost convince myself it's her hands, her fingers, tracing my body, touching me slowly and driving me crazy. I reach for her shampoo…strawberries. I never thought of that scent as sexy before, but it is. I pour a generous amount in my palm and then slide my hand over my cock, applying a tight pressure in my grip and get lost in the pleasure. I remember the feel of her ass, so firm and rounded to perfection raking against my cock and brushing against my balls, begging me to fuck it. For the last week all I've thought about is digging my hands into her sides, pulling her hard against me and riding that ass until I explode. Damn, she'd be so tight there, she'd come close to choking my cock. I picture it in my mind. Me bending her over and fucking her ass, my balls slapping against her pussy, one fist wound tight in her hair as I order her to play with her clit. My other hand would be full of her breast, kneading and pulling on those taut nipples, bringing her just enough pain so her muscles would squeeze me even more.

I jerk my cock harder and faster, in rhythm with the fucking I'm giving Dani in my mind. My balls tighten and my heart is thudding heavily in my chest. I'm so damn close. I imagine her calling my name out as she shatters into a million pieces and I can't stop her name falling from my lips as I come. It feels good for the space of a minute, maybe two and then I hate the fact that my cock isn't inside of her. I lean against the shower door, wishing she was with me.

It's then I see her body shadowed through the frosted glass. She's outside the shower watching.

"You could come in if you want, Hellcat. It'd be a lot more enjoyable than staying out there."

"I...uh... thought I would brush my teeth before we go to bed," she stutters and it's damn cute and just another piece of the mystery.

She can be such a hard-ass away from here. The boys at the club have nicknamed her Ice, because they swear her pussy would freeze a man's dick. They don't see the side of her I do, and that's fucking fine with me. *I don't want them to.* I want to save all of her sides for me and me alone. I don't want those horny bastards anywhere near her. Which hasn't been an issue because, Nicole got out of the hospital yesterday and Dani still refuses to go to the club. They talk every day and Nic has tried and tried to reach Dani and ease her guilt. I don't think it's working, but I know the fact that Nic isn't blaming her outright in front of the club, is making things easier for Dani.

You could say the devil made me do it, but I open the door and let her see me. My dick should be good after just coming, but the instant I lay eyes on her, it begins to harden. She's got on a long white t-shirt... fuck it's my t-shirt. Her hair is pulled back in a pony-tail on her head and she doesn't have a trace of makeup. It's official, this is how I like her best. *Jesus.*

"Crusher, you're naked...."

"Say my name."

"What....I just..."

"I am not Crusher to you. Say my name, Hellcat."

She watches me closely, her eyes dart down to my dick and then back up to my face. There's heat in hers. She blushes. Another piece to the mystery that is Dani. I feel like I just keep unraveling them.

"Zander..."

Why does it feel like I won a fucking war when she says my name? Her eyes go back to my cock and stay there. She's killing me.

"Come here, Hellcat,"

"I don't think that would be a good idea..."

"I think it's the best one I've ever had. Now get your ass over here."

I wait to see what she does. I'm convinced she'll turn and run. I've not pushed anything between us this last week, but hell everyone has a breaking point. *I've reached mine.*

When she takes a step towards me, stands in front of me and looks up at me with those beautiful eyes, that's when I tumble. I don't do relationships. I don't even chase after women. Dani made me break that second rule and right here, right now with her looking at me as if I might destroy her, but she still does it? I *fall* completely for this woman. There is no rhyme or reason. There hasn't even been a great build-up. *It just happens.* She owns me in ways she'll never know, because I'll never tell her. The only thing she needs to know is that she is, mine.

I reach out and run my fingers through her hair, letting the dark curls weave around them, then I look into her eyes.

"Tonight you're mine, Hellcat."

My voice is hoarse and full of need, but I notice from the look on her face she's pulling away because of panic. Before she can run away, I use the hold I have on her hair and pull her in closer to me.

"Zander...you're all wet...I..."

"I'm about to make you just as wet, sweetheart. *Just. As. Wet.*" I whisper each word as if it was its own sentence, right before my lips touch hers. I forge into her mouth intent on conquering it. After a week of thinking of nothing else but getting inside this woman, I don't have time to make it pretty, all I can show her is my need.

Chapter 11

DANI

O H GOD, OH *God, oh God, oh God, Oh God. What am I doing?* The refrain plays over and over in my head.

"….now get your ass over here."

That should make me run. I should tear out of the house and not look back. Instead I'm walking towards him. *Can I do this?* I want to. *Oh God, I want to!* Acknowledging that alone, scares the hell out of me.

I'm scared…no, check that. I'm terrified. I'm still trying to figure out what I'm doing and then…*he kisses me.* It's not like our previous kiss. It's unlike any kiss I've ever had before. I didn't even know kisses like this existed. He takes over my mouth. His hand is pulling my hair and pulling me into him. My body is not my own, it's frozen. I can't move, so when he pulls, I fall against him. His body is wet and warm to the touch, my hands rest on his stomach and he continues owning my mouth. I'm lost in the soft feel of his skin beneath my fingers, the taste of him, and the way his tongue completely devours me. I'm lost in the moment and it feels…great. *What have I been afraid of?*

His hands move down to my thighs. The pads of his fingers are rough and calloused and they tease against my skin, sending goose bumps down my spine. He breaks away for a minute and looks at me. I have always wondered what they meant in books when they said someone had obsidian eyes, but now I can see it—dark, mysterious and sexy as hell.

This last week has been torture. It's been so long since my body has even had an interest in a man that I've spent each day wondering what I'm doing. I want the day to hurry and end, all so that I have an excuse to get in bed with Zander and let him hold me. When his arms go around me, I don't worry. I don't panic. I don't do anything, but lie here and listen to him breathe, taking in his scent, his touch and feel at *peace*.

Still, it's been building—this feeling to be closer to him, this need to touch him, taste him and see if he can make me feel normal. *Is he someone I can trust?* He's giving up so much to stay here and take care of me. They captured Irish and really any threat there might have been to me, is gone. Still, he insists on staying here to keep me safe.

When I'm in his arms…I forget the past and all the reasons I shouldn't want to get close to a man and I remember that I'm a woman and I have… *needs*. Zander awakens those needs. He has since I first laid eyes on him, but it's worse since we've been living together. *I'm tired of fighting it.* I'm curious to know if it could be…good…

So, I'm standing in front of a naked Zander, his hands on my thighs, his fingers brushing underneath the rim of his t-shirt I'm wearing, and he's looking at me as if I'm his next meal. I'm nervous, I'm scared, but I want him to consume me too. For once, I want to let go and experience…*to feel.*

"You're sure, Hellcat?" He asks.

"Not really," I answer honestly and his sigh echoes in the room. He starts to pull away. "But, I want to try…" I add to stop him.

His hand comes up to the side of my head and he massages his fingers into my hair and keeps this intense stare-down aimed at me.

"Time for truth, Hellcat. What are you hiding behind those beautiful eyes?"

"I don't want to think about the past. Not right now, Zander. Not with you."

"Will you tell me someday?" He asks.

My stomach sinks. "This was a mistake," I tell him, feeling let down.

"Don't do that, sweetheart. Don't run, not now. I just need to know that someday you'll be able to trust me with those damn secrets that haunt you."

I take a deep breath. His words turn over in my brain. They mingle with the want, need and fear…lots of fear.

"Before I got shot, we barely had a conversation, Zander. I don't want to even think about my past. For once in my life I want to know what it feels like to have a man between my legs that I don't hate. You have a reputation for being the Savage MC stud. The one who satisfies and makes them beg for more. Tonight, I just want to see what makes all the girls throw caution to the wind for a man and not regret it. So if that's not you…*forget it.*"

I've said too much. I always do when my anger and fear mix, but I don't want this from him. I want him to take. I was trying to shore up the courage to offer and not fuck it up with all the other shit that always stays in my head. I turn away from him, taking this as just another sign that I'm not a normal woman. *I never will be.* I get to the bedroom, pulling clothes out of my dresser. Tonight is not going to be a sleep night. I'll go study the dancers or something. It's time I wake back up to reality. This past week with Zander made me forget who I am.

I slide my jeans on, button them and then try to remember where Nailer left Nic's car keys when he dropped off a few days ago. I keep Zander's shirt on. Screw him. I'm claiming it. When I go to leave the room I realize Zander is standing in front of the door, a white towel swung low on his hips.

"Come here, Hellcat."

"I think the time for that is gone, I'm heading out to Pussy's."

"What the fuck for?"

I wonder what he would do if told him the truth? Fuck it, tonight seems to be the night for truth.

"I go to study the dancers."

"The dancers? Is that it, you like chicks too? Cause sweetheart, I'm okay..."

"God, how did I forget you are an asshole? I go to study the dancers, so I can be better."

"I don't think you should be dancing."

"I don't actually care what you think. Anyways, I'm heading out. I'll talk to you later, Zander."

"Why does it matter if you dance better?" He asks, and this time the tone of his voice changes. I don't know what it is, but it makes me feel like he really wants to know and apparently tonight I'm in the mood to just tell everything—almost.

"Because, my body is all I have to depend on. If I'm good at dancing and make sure I stay in shape, then I'll be able to take care of myself wherever I have to go."

He frowns, like he doesn't like my answers, but then why would he? He doesn't know who I am.

"Is that why you starve yourself all the time and drink that damn tea shit that stinks to high heaven?"

I shrug, "It's called a cleanse. It keeps my metabolism up, and I don't starve."

"Hellcat, you have so many twists and turns you make me dizzy."

"Don't worry about it Stud, not like it matters. I'll talk to you later," I say feeling defeated now. I got up the courage to take the plunge and it didn't happen. Now, I just feel stupid, and I need to get away from him.

"I accept your terms," he says just as I begin to push through him to leave the room.

My hands freeze on his chest and I look up at him.

"My terms?"

"Yeah. You don't want the past brought up. You want to use my dick, I say absolutely. I just have one question. You answer it, and we'll get this party started."

I take a step away from him, wondering exactly what he's got on his mind now.

"What's the question? I already told you, I'm not discussing my past."

"I get it, but what I have to ask you is very important on how we proceed here."

His answer confuses me, but I'm curious and I still....want... him.

"Okay shoot, but I'm not promising to answer."

I thought that would make him smile, it doesn't. He looks totally serious and asks the one question, that I kind of hoped he would never ask.

"You said you have never had a man between your legs you didn't ha...."

"I told you I'm not talking about this," I interrupt him.

He puts his hands up before I continue and moves so that he is completely blocking the door. Blocking any hope of escape.

"I'm not asking for details, sweetheart. I'm asking you to tell me one thing and one thing only."

I have this horrible feeling in the pit of my stomach. I feel exposed—like I've given too much away. I can't take it back now, it's too late. I let my guard down and all I can hope is that it doesn't come back around and bite me in the ass.

"Go ahead and ask me then."

"Have you ever had an orgasm?"

I don't want to answer. *I don't.* I also can't forget how sweet he's been this week. How he's taken care of me, how he's been watching out for me, protecting me and most of all…*how he makes me feel.*

"I don't see how this…"

"It makes every fucking difference in the world. So I'm going to ask you one more time Hellcat, and you're going to answer."

"Has a man ever made you come?"

I drop my gaze and stare down at my feet. My toenail polish is chipped. I should fix that before I go out…

"Hellcat, eyes. Give me those eyes. Has a man ever made you come?"

"I…no. There are you happy now? *Jesus.* If using a man for sex is this difficult, I have no idea why women don't just remain virgins."

He gives me a kind of cocky half smile and the little lines at the corner of his eyes crinkle. I get that damn feeling in my stomach that he's been giving me all week. *Damn it.*

"I'll show you why in a minute. Now, I have one more question."

"Oh no. No way Stud, you said one question and that's what I agreed to. *One question.*"

"That question, necessitated the next."

"Necessitated? Jesus Zander,"

"Have you ever made yourself orgasm, Hellcat?"

My heart stops. There's a question I wasn't expecting. If I

tell him the truth will he see how truly pathetic I am? Shit.

"No, and that's all you're getting. Do not bother asking me why, Zander or so help me I will take that lamp you're standing beside and bang it over the side of your head."

He doesn't say anything in return. Instead he walks to the bed, turns the covers down and turns back around to look at me.

"Get up here on the bed, Hellcat," he orders and his voice has that rough, gravely tone he used when he said my name in the shower… when he… God, he got himself off and mine was the name he had on his lips. That has to mean something right? *Shit. What am I doing?*

Chapter 12

CRUSHER

"COME HERE, HELLCAT."

"Zander, I don't..."

"Dani? I'm not repeating myself again. *Come here.*" I order her. It's probably the completely wrong way to handle her—hell, to handle this entire situation. Yet, it's who I am and I can't change, even for her. *She's the one.* I feel it in my bones. I need her to accept me, because I'm going nowhere. I'm here for the long haul with this woman.

I watch as those big beautiful eyes fill with panic. I'm going to kill the son of a bitch who did this to her and when I do, I'm going to do it painfully and slowly. There's a moment when I think she's going to run screaming out of the room. Then, I see resolve flash in her eyes.

"I'd like to point out, you did in fact just repeat yourself," she says in that sassy little tone she gets, even though fear is making her voice shake, I smile. She walks to me, looking anywhere but my face.

"You make me weak, what can I say?" I tell her and I'm not just talking about right now.

She looks down at our feet, still not looking up at me. I want this, I want her, but she's going to have to give me certain signs.

"Strip."

That gets her attention. She looks up at me like I've lost my mind. Hell, the last week of touching her, having her so close and doing nothing but sleep, I probably have.

"What?" She questions.

"Strip."

"Zander, this is not..."

"Damn, I had you pegged wrong, Hellcat," I tell her, hating that I have to do it this way. Sometimes you gotta do, what you gotta do.

"What does that mean?"

"I thought you had fire, Hellcat. I gotta say I'm more than a little disappointed."

She looks at me and then, just like I knew she would, her eyes shoot fire at me. She whips my shirt over her head and throws it at me. It takes all I have not to grin. God she's beautiful. I let the shirt fall to the ground and wait.

When I don't give her the reaction she's wanting, she unbuttons her pants and pushes them down her hips before kicking them at me. With her leg hurt, they barely lift off the ground. I can tell that annoys her by the way she lets out an angry snort. Her breath blows her bangs up and she's so damn cute in that moment. Then, I take her in. She has on this sea green and black lace bra with matching panties, and is so fucking sexy my dick is as hard as steel. At the same time, the childish look on her face makes me want to turn her over and tan her ass.

"Are you happy now?" She huffs. Damn, it's like she's daring me to slap that ass.

"Depends on if you have the guts to finish what we've started, Hellcat. It just depends," I answer, doing my best to sound bored.

She gets on the bed. She's got her hand draped over her

breasts, trying to keep me from seeing anything, which considering she goes out half-naked most of the time, is confusing as hell and just another reason she keeps me on my toes. Dani is such a contradiction. On the surface you would think she was this badass, and then when you look closer… she's so innocent and scared to show me her body. I'm going to do everything I can to make this good for her—to make this all about her. I'm going to have blue balls after this shit, but I need her to know that she is special. That I'm not what she thinks—not by a fucking long shot. I climb on the bed beside her and start by wrapping my arm around her and pulling her to me so her head rests on my shoulder and I can breathe in the scent of strawberries on her hair. It soothes me. It gives me a sense of belonging. I've never had that in life—not even with Melly.

"Zander, I know I've not had good experiences with this, but I don't think this is how you have sex."

"Hush, Hellcat. We'll get there."

"You're a very confusing man," She mumbles.

I kiss the top of her head and let my fingers stroke her side, gently and slowly each pass up and down I get closer to the rim of her panties. I can feel the small jerks in her body with each pass and the way her body tenses up. She likes what I'm doing, but the fear is still there. It hurts me, for her. No woman should have this fear about sex. Is this why she hasn't had an orgasm? What kind of assholes has she been inviting into her bed that they haven't made sure she was with them for the whole ride?

An image of that fucker Beast comes to mind and I beat it down. I'm going to kick that man's ass. It's just a matter of time. This is his loss, if he couldn't appreciate Dani when he had his chance, he's even more stupid than he looks. I lean down to whisper in her ear at the same time my hand pushes down into her underwear. Her body goes tight, but she doesn't stop me.

"Rest easy, Hellcat. I'm just going to make you feel good right now. This is all about you. I'll do nothing you don't want, sweetheart."

"But..."

I slide my fingers over the top of her pussy. She's waxed clean, not a surprise considering she dances in little more than a G-string, but I still wonder what she would look like with a small patch of hair there...I want to see it someday. I put my finger on the slippery little hood on her clit and use another finger to brush it... and then pinch lightly. I slowly move my fingers up and down the valley of her pussy, teasing and caressing all around her clit but never touching it—concentrating mainly just on the hood. Her hips begin moving back and forth in a little broken circle and she lets out a whimper to let me know she likes what I'm doing. I decide to reward her and pinch the hood harder this time and add a little more pressure to my strokes.

"I'm going to own this pussy, Hellcat. You're already getting so wet for me and I haven't even started yet. Do you like this, baby? Do you like it when I touch you like this?" I ask her while I pinch the covering over her clit hard, harder than I had.

"Zander... I...I need..."

I let my index finger move along the inside of the lips of her pussy, getting as close to that throbbing little clit as I can get, but still not giving her the relief she really needs.

"What sweetheart? What do you need?" I ask grazing her clit finally, but just for a second and then I go back to repeating the pattern all over again.

"I...oh God, do that again."

"What's that? What did I do? Was it this?" I ask, my lips close to her ear, I lick the inner shell and then suck the lobe into my mouth and bite down.

I push down on her clit, applying pressure hard, until I hear her gasp and her hip thrusts up to meet me. I slide my finger unto her clit over and over before pushing in again. Each time her clit pulses, harder. I can feel the jerking hammer of it with each caress. Liquid heat meets my fingers as I continue my onslaught on her pussy always ending on a pinch sometimes light, sometimes harder before petting her again and repeating.

"Zander, that feels… what are you doing? That feels…"

Her need has amped up, her hips are moving and she's tightening up against my hand trying to ride my fingers. I can't let that continue, I need to make this last longer. I shift so I can see what I'm doing. I stop all movement and she cries out in frustration and looks down at me.

"Take off your bra, Hellcat. Take it off and let me see you tease your nipples."

"Zander…I…"

I take my hands and rip her underwear on one side and push it out of my way. I watch her as the sound of ripping fabric fills the room and mingles with our ragged breathing.

"Do it," I order. Her tongue comes out to dance on her lips as her eyes watch me closely. There's fear and worse…shame in those eyes. I take one hand and pull the lips of her pussy back and then slap against it with my other hand. "I said do it, don't make me repeat myself again, Hellcat."

Shock registers on her face and her body becomes inflexible, but then sensation must have hit her because she tries to capture my hand between her legs to ride it. I imprison one leg in my hold, not letting her. Finally, she gives up and her fingers dance over the hard nipples that are poking through her bra.

Cute. She's cute. I give her that. I spank her wet pussy again.

"Without the bra, sweetheart. You know what I want. Give it to me and I'll make sure you're rewarded."

She sits up enough to undo the clasp on the back of her bra and then slides it off her body. Her arm goes around immediately to try and hide her tits from me. It's annoying but I'll bring her out of that. I'm going to fuck those babies and soon.

"Lick your fingers, Hellcat."

She looks at me like I'm insane. I sigh and pull away like I'm going to stop giving her pleasure. There's not a chance in hell at this point, but she doesn't know that.

She quickly sucks on her fingers and she doesn't mean it that way—I can tell, but it's sexier than hell. Fuck, just watching her, has me throbbing. She moves her fingers down to her nipples and begins rubbing them. Her eyes lock on mine and the need in them humbles me. I'll be the first to make her orgasm. I'll be the first to bring her this pleasure. I'm going to own her entire body, but I'm starting with her pussy. It will be mine and from this moment on, not one damned mother fucker is getting anywhere near it.

I've somehow managed to keep the towel around me, not wanting to scare her, but I know it's about to go too far and very soon I'm going to be in that pussy. I hope I have her so far gone by then that she doesn't get freaked out. I don't know what's happened to her, but I know it's enough that I need to treat her like a frightened virgin. Trouble is, I haven't actually fucked a virgin, so I'm using pure gut instinct here.

"Pinch your nipples at the same time, Hellcat. Pinch them and pull them at the same time."

I thought she would question me, or even refuse to do it, but she surprises the hell out of me by doing as I tell her to. I move my fingers back and forth now, petting her pussy because she minded me so well. I use the tip of my finger to push against her hole, sliding inside of her just a bit, before pulling back out. I do this repeatedly, slowly—never rushing. She keeps thrusting up, but I don't falter, only allowing my finger to enter the tiniest fraction.

"Zander!"

"What is it you want, Hellcat? You want me to finger fuck your pussy, sweetheart?" I growl. She's stopped playing with her breasts. Now her hands have grabbed the rails on the headboard and she holding onto them while her body keeps twisting up to try and find what it needs, what I'm not allowing it to have. I should reprimand her, but seeing her so lost in pleasure with no more than what I'm doing, stops me.

Instead, I decide to reward her. I thrust one finger in completely and then another while using my thumb to press down on that hard little button that keeps calling my name. I pick up the speed of my thrusts now, using my fingers to completely own her hot cunt. Mine. I'm the first to give her this and I'm going to be the motherfucking last.

"Yes…Fuck! Zander… please."

When the word please leaves her lips, I smile. Her head is thrown back and she has no idea what I'm about to give her. I pull the damn towel off and throw it on the ground. My cock is dying to slide inside her, and it will, but not yet. Not until I have her completely at my mercy. With that one thought in my mind, I keep thrusting my fingers in and out, but now I add my tongue on the hard nub of her clit, flicking it playfully a few turns before I suck it completely in my mouth. Her juice slides against my fingers, her soaked pussy overfilled. I release her clit with a pop and then slide my tongue down the channel of her pussy, moaning at the sweet, creamy taste of her. I barely have time to savor it before she calls out my name and comes hard against my fingers. I growl, because that was too soon. I sit up and her whine of protest doesn't go unheard, but I'm already way ahead of her. I grab her hips and pull her up so her pussy is at my face and then I dive in. My tongue replaces my fingers, but I also use my lips, my teeth, and hell anything else I can, to torture and drink her down. She twists and turns, trying to get away, when my tongue slides back and forth along her clit, lashing it before sliding back inside. I nibble and suck on every tasty inch I can find as she begins to flood me with more of her sweet cum. Her second orgasm is more intense, her body is shaking, her cry is louder and her body is thrusting against my face. I let her ride it out on my tongue slowly licking her until she calms. I ease her body back down once her cries of pleasure die down into whimpers.

While she's recovering, I reach over into the nightstand drawer and grab one of the condoms I stored in there a few days ago. Not to sound cocky, but I knew this was going to happen, I just had no idea when. I slide the rubber over my aching cock, damn thing is so ready to blow I'm surprised the latex fits. I position myself and look down at her.

"Dani sweetheart, look at me." She moans, her body literally shaking with the small bursts of pleasure from her second release. "Dani, now."

She looks up at me. Our eyes meet. This is it. Fuck, this is finally it.

Chapter 13

DANI

I'M IN A haze traveling somewhere far away and I feel completely weightless. It's his voice that calls me back. Zander. I search him out and fight my way to him. The look on his face is intense, white hot and full of need...for me.... he wants...me...

"Dani, now," he says and for the first time since I invented her, I feel like Dani. Our eyes lock.

"Don't take your eyes off of me, sweetheart. I want to see your face every second I'm inside of you. You hear me?"

My heart kicks up in fear. It's been so good to this point...can I trust him to take it further? Will it be okay? I bite my lip and nod, giving him my yes. I don't want this to end, in fact, I want it again and again. He's like a drug and I damn sure want to be addicted. He takes his cock and rubs it back and forth against my opening. The slick sound of us together is loud even over my uneven breathing. I never realized that being with someone would feel like this. Instinctively, I know it's because I'm with Zander and that's why it feels this way. There's something about him that called to me from day one. That thought should scare me. Maybe it's post orgasmic stupidity, but I'm not scared. I think I'm even starting to trust Zander.

That's my last thought before he thrusts into me. Oh hell.

He's…big… but I'm so wet he goes in easily, it's just he makes me feel…stretched. That feeling only intensifies when he pushes my legs back so they bend and lay against my stomach. Unfortunately, that's also the time when memories try to weigh in. Michael's face becomes superimposed on Zander's, and instantly my body snaps out of its' sex-induced haze. Zander is leaning over the top of me and I feel exposed. The panic starts.

"Hellcat. Stop. Look at me. Who am I?"

"Zander…" I say, trying to hold onto his voice.

"That's right, sweetheart. Now wrap your legs around me and hold on and I'll take you on a quick ride."

I try to breathe through it, letting his voice push the panic back. I don't want Michael to ruin this. I can't let that happen, he's already taken too much from me. I wrap my legs around him, and he takes his hands and pulls them higher up, so the heels of my feet are digging into the cheeks of his ass. He sinks deeper inside of me and his face is next to mine. Our lips are just a breath away from each other. His eyes are closed and he doesn't move. I'm afraid I've done something wrong. I start to ask him when he slowly opens them.

"You feel so fucking good, Hellcat. Mark this down sweetheart, you can use my dick any fucking time you want."

His words make me smile. Which seems an odd thing. Smiling…while having sex…with a man I like…

"So you're giving me permission to use you for sex?"

"Abso-fucking-lutely."

"You might be crazy, Zander," I tell him, but his name comes out broken, because he finally starts moving and I can feel him slide out and then slowly slide back in.

"Shut up, Hellcat and kiss me. Tell me how you like your taste on my lips."

His words excite me. I'm feeling something I don't think

I've felt since before I lost my mom…happiness. Then his lips are on mine, I taste myself and it mingles with his own unique flavor and it makes me hungry for more.

"Thrust up to meet me, Hellcat and grind that juicy little body into me. Do it," he growls in my ear when we break apart to breathe. I follow his directions, while he kisses down the side of my neck, using his teeth to lightly graze and nibble the same path. Our speed picks up and I feel my release rising. It's bigger, more intense than the other two and I have a moment of fear. It's too late to turn back though. My release slams into me with the force of a tidal wave. My nails dig into Zander's back and I know I'm leaving marks, I just can't help it. I hear him groan out with his own orgasm. If this is what sex is, it's no wonder Nicole is so crazy over Dragon.

"Damn Hellcat," he whispers into my neck, then he slowly pulls out of me and lays on his side.

I watch as he disposes of the condom and I would have thought I'd feel weird, but I don't. I think I'm mindless and boneless. He throws it in the waste basket by the bed and comes back to me. He angles it so my head is on his chest and he's holding me close. He pulls the sheet over us, which I'm glad for. I had actually forgotten I was lying here naked.

I search for words to say to him and my brain comes up empty. My eyes start to go heavy and I want to fight it, but I can't seem to beat it back.

"Zander…" I whisper knowing I'm going to be asleep soon.

I feel a brush of his lips at my temple and then he whispers the sweetest words I've ever known.

"Rest, sweetheart. I'll be here keeping you safe. Let it go and rest."

Safe.

That word echoes as sleep claims me and the damnedest thing happens.

I believe him.

Chapter 14

CRUSHER

I'M IN DEEP shit. As I watch Dani look over her shoulder at me leaving the shower, that's all I can think. It's been three weeks. Three weeks since I've sunk inside of her. Three weeks since I've had a taste of her and I still want her every fucking minute of every fucking day. She's changed. We laugh. We play, and even more than those two. We enjoy being around each other. She cracks me the hell up and she's like a giant kid sometimes and I love every fucking minute of it. This morning I have to head out to the club, Dragon wants me and Bull with him when he questions Irish again. I dread it. I fucking dread it more than anything I've ever faced. Still, I know it needs to be done. We need to know everything we can about why Irish betrayed us and who he was working with. That doesn't mean getting the information is fun. Dani and I talked about it last night. She knows I'm dreading today and though she may not agree with what I or the club is doing at least she seems to accept it more. Her way of showing her support is surprising me in the shower and begging me to fuck her. Color me happy. She's got me sewn up, and she doesn't even know it. She still has it in her head we're just using each other for sex. Fuck buddies. The woman is clueless. She's not getting away from me—not now. As she gives me that sweet smile over her shoulder and steps out of the shower I realize I'm going to have to move this up a little. I can't have her thinking she is free to find another man's cock. Oh-hell-no. I'd kill the mother fucker. I can't ask for all of it at once. She'd run and run fast. Still, I need her to give me something more... It's stupid. I should be patient. I'm not and never have been and with Dani I'm finding those words even truer.

I turn the shower off and grab a towel. I dry quickly, throwing the towel on the floor and follow her into the bedroom. When I get there, she's searching in the dresser for clothes. I come up behind her, pulling her towel off and throwing it on the ground. Skin against skin...better Dani's skin against mine. Heaven.

She tenses up at first, but then relaxes back into my arms. She gives off a happy sigh when my hands cup her breasts and I start kissing on her neck. My dick, which had just fucked her into oblivion, is already stirring in interest. Yeah, I'm in deep shit.

"I told you I don't like it when you sneak up on me, Cowboy."

"Seeing you bent over like that, I lost my mind," I respond my fingers plucking at her nipples smiling at the way they harden and stand at attention with just my first touch.

"Zander, there's no way you can be horny again so soon. You just wore me out in the shower," she says her voice taking on that husky, needy tone that makes my cock ache.

I take hold of my cock, rubbing it against her ass and letting it slide in the cleft of her ass, the head teasing her opening. Someday. She pushes back against my cock and my balls tighten. Someday soon.

"I wore you out, sweetheart?" I ask, making sure I continue worrying one of her nipples while playing with her ass too.

"Yes..."

She gasps as I push just a little harder against her ass. Shit why didn't I put some lube in that drawer when I stocked it with condoms. I'll make sure I take care of that today.

"Well if you're so tired... you could suck on my cock.

Her body tenses and she pulls away. "We should get going. You have to be at the club and I need to check in at work and see when they're putting me back on rotation."

"Whoa, Hellcat, I think I liked where we were headed before better. We got time."

"I got stuff I need to get done," she says, not looking at me and getting dressed. Damn I guess playtime is over.

"Okay sweetheart, fine. We'll pick this up later." I cave, slapping her ass just as she pulls up these pale pink panties that don't do a damn thing to make my cock deflate. "Why don't you meet me at the club later tonight? Freak is claiming Nikki as his old lady. There's a big party planned. We'll eat and visit a bit, before coming back here."

She finishes buttoning up her jeans, turns and looks at me and I can tell by the look on her face, I'm not going to like what she says next.

"I don't want to come by the club, I told you. I don't belong there."

Yeah, I was right, I don't like it.

"You sure as hell do," I argue, ready to have it out, because it's time we clear this shit up.

She's running a brush through her hair and her eyes seek out mine through the mirror.

"Zander, the men there hate me and I just don't belong with..."

"The fuck you don't. You're my woman and the men will get over it, they just don't know you."

"Your woman?"

"We've been fucking like bunnies and I've been in your bed every night for a month. I don't see how that could have escaped your notice, Hellcat." I grumble, getting pissed off now. I grab my jeans and pull them on. If I'm going to fight, I'll be damned if I'm doing it with my dick swinging in the cold.

"We made a deal…"

"What does that mean?" I have to ask, because honestly I am at a complete loss. The damn woman has given me whiplash here.

"That means when we made this bargain, we agreed it wasn't serious. *It is just sex.*

"I think it's pretty clear we've gone beyond that Hellcat, and I'm doing my best to take us to the…"

"I don't especially like where you were leading," Dani says and starts putting on that damn red lipstick.

My cock pushes against the zipper of my jeans, at the thought of her sucking me and leaving a ring of lipstick behind. Jesus. I shake my head to clear it. I lean down and kiss the top of her head and breathe her in. My hand caresses her skin and I stare at her in the mirror.

"Sweetheart, I know you have issues about the club, I'm not pushing you on them. I just want you to think about meeting me. I want to show you off," I whisper, trying another tact.

Her hand comes up and grazes my five o'clock shadow and she quietly sighs.

"This is more than just a bargain over my dick, Dani. Give me that if nothing else."

Her eyes stay on mine in the mirror, "It is."

Two small words and they literally rock my world. I wanted them, I just wasn't sure she'd give them.

"So, you will think about it, yeah?"

She nods a small half nod. It's something.

"How about I let you selfishly use my cock again before we head out."

"Do you take Viagra?"

I am busy pulling her back to the bed when her words make me do a double take.

"What in the hell are you talking about? Junior here doesn't need anything but you to be ready to party."

"Junior?"

"My dick? My hammer, my sword, my bologna pony, my one-eyed snake, my anaconda, my anal-impaler…"

"Anal-impaler?"

"Oh yeah, Hellcat, don't worry. I'll show you that side of him later on. Tonight in fact, I'm more than willing."

She shakes her head, but she's laughing.

"I think it'd be better for your rep if you try not to refer to your cock as junior."

"You think?"

"It's short changing the little guy."

"Little? Ouch that hurts, Hellcat," I tell her, picking her up and throwing her on the bed in retaliation. She squeals out as she sails the small distance and flops on the mattress.

"Maybe I'm mistaken. I mean it's been a whole twenty minutes. Perhaps I've forgotten his mighty, ferocious proportions," she says giggling.

I stand at the foot of the bed, watching her laugh and that feeling of being where I belong hits me again.

"Well then, unbutton those pants and prepare to be amazed," I grin.

She does as I ask, and her eyes take on that glazed, aroused look I've come to recognize and love. I shed my own clothes.

Once I'm naked, she starts pushing her pants down and I immediately help her, praying she's already wet, because I can't wait to get back inside of her. Relief hits me when I find her soaked and more than ready for my dick. I lay on my back and pull her on top of me, holding her until she guides me inside. I've noticed this is her favorite position and I'm all about pleasing my woman. She slides down on my cock and I watch her face, hypnotized by the pleasure that reflects back at me.

"Zander," she moans as my cock stretches her.

"Yeah, Hellcat?" I ask, grabbing her hips and helping her to grind against me, once I sink all the way in.

"I was completely wrong. I'm overwhelmed by the size and girth of Junior."

I grin. "Damn straight, now show him how sorry you are for underestimating his awesomeness."

"I'll see what I can do."

Then she picks up the speed of her ride and I can do nothing but lose myself a little more.

I'm in deep shit.

Chapter 15

DANI

I'M IN THE kitchen, having just fed Zander a late breakfast and by that I mean he had me on the kitchen table. When I hear the door close announcing Zander has finally taken off to the club. The man is insatiable and he makes me crave him so easily, I honestly don't know what to think about it. He could become an addiction and sadly, I think I'm already way too attached. Before, all I could think about doing was leaving and going to Mexico—getting away from Michael, Dragon and his crew. Am I blinded because finally I know what it feels like to find pleasure in a man's arms? Maybe, but I'm more scared it's Zander himself. He's fun to be around. One of my favorite things to do lately has been just cuddling on the sofa with him watching old movies. Zander watches old movies, and when I say old, I mean John Wayne westerns. Still, I like it and they are fast becoming my favorite too. I've also, not even had a drink, other than a beer every once in a while. I still take my meds, but really only at night to help knock me out. I've learned the hard way, dreams are something I do not want to have.

Maybe Nicole is right and I need to breathe. Really, Michael would never think of finding a shipping heiress in the backwoods of Kentucky surrounded by bikers. Maybe I can finally let my guard down a little. Zander wants me to go to the club though and I'm not ready for that. I know it upsets him. I hate that. I hate it. He called me his woman...that terrifies me, but thrills me too. If he knew my past I know that would change, but the fact that the thought even crosses his mind now...It makes me want to cave.

If I go to the club he'll see how different I am from the others. He'll recognize all the things Michael saw and then this...whatever it is, will be over. I need it, if only for a little while longer. It's the closest I've ever been to happy. It also feels good to not take as much meds and shit. Maybe since I'm doing better with Zander around, it would be a good time to go back into that therapy group Nicole is always trying to drag me to. Zander makes me stronger, maybe I can get strong enough to stand on my own. I sigh and then jump up to sit on the counter. I grab my cell and call Nicole, maybe I can get her to go out with me. I could use a night with just the two of us. I miss her.

"Hey Dani," she answers on the third ring.

"Hey yourself, you sound tired, are you overdoing it?" I ask her, worried. It seems so weird not having her around and close by.

"Nah, Dragon won't allow it. If anything he's driving me crazy. Damn man thinks I should do nothing but lay in bed all day."

"Well Nic, I mean you did almost kick the bucket. It's probably a good idea if you took it easy and just laid around," I say feeling stupid. I mean she'd been home a week, but of course she should be recuperating. I shouldn't have even thought to ask her. It's a reflex with me, I know. For so long it's just been the two of us, so it's hard for my brain to adapt that we are growing...apart. The mere thought makes me begin to panic. God, I need to stop that. Normal people do not panic at the drop of a hat. They don't hold onto their best friend afraid of losing them. I want to slap myself and scream and...shit.

"Don't you start on me to! I'm not even doing that much. I'm organizing a party tonight for Freak and Nikki, he's claiming her as his. The boys and Twinkies are the ones doing all the actual work, but you would think I was out there moving the damned tables! He's driving me crazy, Dani."

I smile, I can't help it. "You love it."

She gets quiet and then when she does answer, her voice is softer and happier.

"It is good. I've never had anyone worry about me...besides you I mean."

Guilt hits me and I know me confronting her about Dragon is not what she meant, but it is there regardless.

"I really am sorry Nic, I was stupid. If I could go back...I would...you know?"

"I told you to let it go. We survived and I know you wouldn't have me hurt in a million years. Just from now on, talk to me about this shit and let's act together please, not fly off, jump first and question later?"

"Yeah, I fucked up," I say and the truth of that twists in my stomach—talk about understatement of the century.

"Yeah, you did," she responds, though the tone of her voice is sweet and I know she's not condemning me—even if I deserve it. "Dragon is good to me, Dani. He loves me and takes care of me. I wouldn't want to live without him."

I listen to her. I'm more than a little jealous. She sounds so happy and secure. What would that be like?

"So, I guess the next party at the club, claiming a woman will be yours and Dragon's?"

"Oh girl, I think we're way past that," she laughs. "Dragon won't let me out of the damn room unless I have the jacket on he had made for me. He wants the world to know I'm his."

"You know, that sounds kind of barbaric. Having anyone speak of you as their property." I say, because she told me about the leather vest that said Property of Dragon on the back of it.

"These bikers live in a different world. Besides, I like it. A man in this world doesn't claim a woman unless he plans on keeping her. It's a big deal and a huge step for them, because let's face it, these boys don't need a woman. They have women jumping in their beds left and right. For them to want to tie themselves to one woman? That's all about pride and respect for the women they care about."

I listen to her words and Zander's face pops in my mind. He wanted me there tonight. He said I was his woman. He wanted to show me off. My heart speeds up. I bite my nails as I listen to everything she says and in my mind relate it to me and Zander. Is that what he thinks about us? After just a month really? Is that even possible?

"I thought Nikki and Freak hadn't known each other that long?"

Nicole laughs, "Girl please! Don't you remember how Dragon took over my life from day one? Moss doesn't grow under these boys' feet."

I think about it. Honestly, it's true. They really haven't been together that long. If I am important to Zander…if he really means that I'm his woman…maybe…I mean I could swing by for thirty minutes or so, right? I could make it that long without doing something stupid. I hear Michael's voice in my head telling me how pathetic and idiotic I am… I tap it down. I definitely need to go to a meeting. It's time I start trying to make a life for myself. Michael thinks I'm dead. Zander doesn't need to know.

"I...I might drop by the club tonight, after my meeting..." I tell her, and I can hear the nerves in my voice. When Nicole answers, I can tell she hears them too.

"I'd love that, and it'll be okay I promise. Dragon will behave."

She thinks I'm worried about the club's reaction to me, since the shooting. Truth is, they've all pretty much made me aware of how they feel about me. I kind of agree with them, so I'm okay with it. Just the thought of being around so many men...I've never allowed that to happen. Add that in with being around crowds...that's a recipe for a panic attack. If I go to a meeting first? Could I do it? Or would a meeting and the memories it brings up make it worse? Shit.

"You still there, Dani?"

"Yeah, just thinking. I'm...going to try and go to a meeting."

"That's good honey, you want me to go with you?"

"Nah, Dragon would flip if you try and go out." I don't mention with me, but I think that's pretty clear. "I'll swing by when I'm done."

"I'm proud of you Dani, I know it's hard."

She does know. She just has no idea how hard, but then again she doesn't know the entire story. She never will.

"Talk to you later, bitch. Take care of yourself and listen to Dragon, take it easy. I need you healthy, please?"

"Will do, mommy. Can't wait to see you."

"Later, woman," I say hanging up. I stare at my phone for a few more minutes, wondering if I'm doing the right thing. I'm probably deluding myself. With my history I don't think I could hope for a normal life, but if I could have Zander...could continue the last month...Maybe if I can manage to stay in therapy and do better I might be able to keep him...longer.

That thought is what pushes me to get moving. I will do this. I will clean up and go to a meeting and even set up more. I'll drop by the party and make Zander happy. I will do this. I can do this.

Chapter 16

CRUSHER

I DON'T WANT to be here. This damn party is dragging I texted Dani, but she's not answering. I was really hoping she'd show up tonight. It kind of pisses me off that she's not willing to be here. I look around the party and Nicole is sitting in Dragon's lap, Nikki is sitting in Freak's, Hawk and some of the other boys have Twinkies. Frog is talking to some blonde, I can't remember seeing around here before. Bull has Bambi in his lap and you can tell they're not far off from finding a room. Shit everyone is paired off but me. Trouble is, I don't want what is here for the taking. The past few weeks with Dani have been the best in my life. I want more of it—more of her. I can't force her though and I sure as hell ain't going to chase a bitch to give her my dick.

I'm being a jerk. Truth is, I'm two small steps away from being drunk. Today was fucked up. We ended a life today. We ended the life of a brother today. Yes, the brother was a traitor, he fucked us over. Yes, he was a waste of air, but still a party for any reason seems the wrong thing to do tonight. I keep remembering his eyes when he told us to go fuck ourselves. Eyes of a man I fought alongside of for years, eyes of a man I thought of as blood...hating and mocking me—all of us. That's bitter shit. So the fact that Dani isn't here, is just icing on top of the fucking cake.

I take another swig and sigh heavily. Fuck it, I should just get out of here. Hop on my bike and head out somewhere maybe find some strange...

"What's up, Bro? You doing okay after today?" Gunner interrupts my thoughts, as he sits down at my table.

"Fucked up day," I answer taking another drink—this time emptying the glass, save for the ice, which is a waste of space, but for some reason Nailer thinks I drink on the rocks. I've never corrected him. Shit. I feel like I'm on the rocks, so I guess it fits.

"Amen," Gunner says looking out over the crew. "All the brothers seem to be getting their dick sewn up. I guess you'll be next."

"Don't see that happening," I answer honestly. I mean I can't even get her to come here to the party. I guess I was taking whatever this is between us to mean more than it did. I feel like a damned pussy. Shit, I'm acting like one.

"Really? You and that Dani chick seem pretty fucking tight. You're there every night."

The man is starting to piss me off. Nosey-ass fucker.

"It's a job. I'm there until Dragon calls me off of it." Lie. Dragon told me I could come back to the club after Irish was questioned the second time. I'm there because I want to be.

"Damn though man it's been a month, and well after today the shit is finished. I mean, hell you're there all the time. No down time, that's kind of shitty. Plus, that's a long time to go without pussy—especially for you and I know you ain't getting shit from the Ice Maiden."

There's that fucking nickname again. Some people are just fuckin' clueless. There's not a damn thing cold about Dani. I love everything about that woman...except for the fucking fact she doesn't want anything from me but my dick.

"I didn't say I wasn't getting laid," I answer and wish I could take the words back. I'm holding another glass of whiskey, that I don't even remember pouring, watching the amber liquid swirl around. Yeah, I'm pretty fucking drunk, there's no two steps away from it now.

"Fuck! You made it in with the Ice Maiden? Damn you are the King of Pussy. I bow to you, man. I didn't think they'd make a dick around here she'd look at. Though I guess threesomes are her thing if you go by that night at the movies and we all know that's your specialty."

Specialty? He makes me sound like a damned porn star. Worse, I don't want to be reminded of that night. I don't want to remember that she chose to leave that night with another man…fuck two men, when I asked her not too. Hell, I really have been deluding myself. What the fuck have I been thinking? She even told me she was just using me for my dick. I finish the rest of my new drink in one long swallow.

"You need to share man! Hook a brother up. I don't care to tag team her. Hell, I'd love to tap that. Damn, I'd love to have her mouth wrapped around my cock."

His words, just twenty minutes before, would have got his ass knocked out. Hell, I would have done it even ten minutes before. Now? Now, I remember she's not here. I remember that she asked to use my cock and my cock only. I remember she chose that bastard in Skull's crew over me and finally I remember I'm speaking out of my ass, that she won't suck my damned cock. So, what I say next is pure bullshit and I don't mean a bit of it. I shouldn't even say it—but I do.

"Yeah, she's good. Sucks me like I'm a Popsicle on an Arizona summer day. Best head I've ever had."

"Hell, I knew it. She likes threesomes, you need to let me join you guys sometimes. Freak is out of commission now.

You need a new partner."

I want to laugh. He knows shit about Nikki and Freak. I shrug, "Sure I'm about finished with her. You know me, got to have variety. I'll ask her about it before I move on though."

The lie hurts me to say. It lays flat in my stomach and feels like led.

"Fuckin' A! I'm about to go party with Lips, want to join in?"

"Nah man, I'm about partied out. Think I'm gonna crash in my old room tonight."

"Want me to send you a Twinkie?"

"Nah, Dani wore my ass out before the party. I'm good."

He slaps me on the back and leaves. I stare at the empty glass, sliding it back and forth between my hands, listening to the sound of it scraping on the table and the ice rattling inside. I can hear it even over the noise in the room. Perhaps it was that, or the fact I am drunk, or hell maybe even a mixture of both that make it so I don't hear Dani. I can't really say.

"Hey lover," she purrs from behind me, her breath hitting my neck, her voice sweet in my ear.

At first I think I'm dreaming, like I've conjured her up in my imagination and I'm so damn drunk I just think she's here. Then I feel her hand slide down my chest. I lean back against her letting my hand go up around her neck and pull her down to me. I bury my face in the side of her neck and breathe her in. Fuck. She's here. I want to yell at the top of my lungs. Fuck yeah, this means I'm getting to her.

"I missed you, Hellcat," I tell her and goddamn it's true. I've never missed a woman before in my life, but this one and Melly.

"I heard. You want to party with Guns, Cowboy?"

Oh fuck! Hell no I don't want to party with Gunner! Shit,

did she hear that and want it? Is that what this is about? I'm not down. Fuck, no. Not Dani. She. Is. Mine.

"Not tonight, sweetheart," I growl. Not ever, I add silently.

"No?" She asks me, biting on my neck while her hands go down to my pants working on the zipper and button. Holy shit, does she mean to fuck me here in the club, with the party going on? I mean, okay it happens with Twinkies, but I never thought Dani would be into that. I'm not sure how I feel about it, but I'm getting hard at the thought. Still, I don't want my brothers seeing me fuck my woman. She's not some Twinkie or a hanger-on and she sure isn't a whore to be used and forgotten.

"Hellcat, let's move this into my room or better yet we can go home…"

She bites my neck again and it's harder than normal, but the sting of pain feels good.

"But Zander, I want to suck you. I want to suck you hard. Don't you want that?"

"Yeah, sweetheart, you know I do but…" I stop as she moves around to the side of me. She's undone my pants now and my cock is hard. The head stands at attention begging her for more. Oh fuck, I guess we're going to do this. I'm not about to pass this up. Still, I try one more time before she has a chance to get down on her knees. "We should save this for a few minutes," I whisper, though it can be heard because the room is dead silent now. "We can take it to my room Hellcat, so I can thank you properly."

"But Zander, I'm on fire for you. I need to suck you…hard." She says, one hand squeezes my cock and strokes it.

"You are? Even with everyone watching, sweetheart? If you're okay with it then suck me, I'm dying for those full red lips.

"I'm more than okay with this, Cowboy. I'm too hot to wait. Don't you ever get so horny you have to have it? So hot you feel like you're on fire, Zander?"

"Fuck. You got me there now, Hellcat." I answer, because she's stroking me so firmly and it's fucking hot having others watch her pleasure me. Hell, my balls are heated up and ready to blow. This is going to be over almost as soon as she sucks me into that damned mouth.

"Really Zander? Are you hot?"

"On fire," I growl. "Get down here and let me feel that damned mouth."

"Will that cool you down, Cowboy?" She asks, leaning down into my ear. My eyes go to her breasts, her cleavage on display and I know I'm going to titty-fuck her tonight too.

"Yeah..." I'm already lost, imagining my cock thrusting between those breasts and spraying cum all over her face.

"Are you hot as a summer day in Arizona, Zander?" She asks and I pull my eyes away from her breasts to look at her. Her voice sounds different this time. My head is foggy and there's something...not quite right.

"You got me on fire for you Hellcat, you know that."

"Good, then I think I should cool you down," she says.

I smile. Finally.

Then I feel cold all over my cock and look down to see she's poured the ice from my glass in my lap and all over my exposed dick.

"Well damn! Look there! I cooled you down too much, because it seems you have a case of whiskey dick, Cowboy," she says and then pours the rest of the bottle of whiskey on me.

I jump up as she empties the last of the bottle on my dick.

I'm busy trying to get the ice out from around my balls and abused rod, all while cussing. I really should have been paying more attention, because then I would have noticed she's holding a rather large, black, overnight bag in one hand. She swings it hard at me. It slams me in the face, and I fall to the floor. My head smashes against the wood flooring and it's a damn good hit, because that, combined with the alcohol I've consumed, almost blacks me out. The world goes gray, but I manage to hold on when I hear her yell to Nicole.

"Nic? I'm going to go spend some time with Ray and Paul. Call me if you need me."

Then she takes the empty bottle of Jack and throws it hard against my alcohol-drenched cock.

"Since you're getting bored, Crusher," she says sneering my club name, "Move your fucking shit out of my house while I'm gone."

With that she stomps out and even in my drunken misery, I have to say she looks fucking phenomenal. In the same thought, I realize I've lost any chance I ever had with her. *Fuck.*

Chapter 17

DANI

"I'M FINE NICOLE, I promise. It's been good. Paul and Ray have been taking great care of me," I say into the phone, looking out the small window of Ray's condo that I've been staying in.

"You need to come home Dani, I miss you."

"I miss you too, more than you know. I've needed this though, it's been good for me and I'm finally going to therapy regularly. You'd be proud of me. I'm almost like a real girl now," I joke.

Still it's true. My month here with Ray and Paul has been good. It's a month in which I've pulled myself together more. I've been going through therapy for survivors and that's what I am. I'm not a victim. I am a survivor. I survived violence. Period. It's developed into my daily mantra. I'm a survivor. I've let my past rule me for too long. I thought I deserved what Michael dished out. It doesn't make sense, but that's how I felt inside. I still have my moments, but I'm a lot better. I can't spend my life like I have. I could have gotten Nicole killed. No matter what she or anyone says, that's on me and I need to make changes. I have to make changes.

"Are you coming home?" Nicole asks and I want to say that my home isn't there. Then again, my home isn't here either. I have a lot to figure out. I may be hiding from my past, but Ray, Paul, and my sponsor are all right. I can't let my past choke out whatever future I can make for myself.

"Maybe. What's been going on there?"

"Not a lot. We have a new girl staying with us Caroline. She's sweet."

"Sweet like a Twinkie?" I ask before I can stop myself.

"Nah, Carrie isn't a Twinkie. She's someone from Dancer's past. Dragon said she has something to do with why he's in jail. I think Dancer was defending her or something. I don't know, Dragon's not said a lot. You know, club business and all that."

"Sometimes it's better not to know," I answer. Dancer is a Savage member that has been in jail for the last couple of years. Whatever his past is, it's probably not good and I think Dragon is smart for trying to protect Nicole.

"Maybe, but it is annoying to be the only one out of the loop. I feel like I'm the only one with my head buried in the sand around here."

"Well knowing that crew, there's some that have their heads in their ass, so at least you're not them," I answer, thinking of Zander.

Nicole snorts, "I'm not arguing. I'm glad you caught Crusher lying. You don't need to go there, you were smart to shoot him down. He does ask about you though."

"Do you tell him I've died and he can see me when he gets to hell?"

"I told him the truth."

"Well that's boring," I respond.

"I told him you moved to Texas to live with two men who love you and treat you like a queen."

I smile, but just like always, when I think of Zander, my heart hurts. Nicole has no idea just how much I did give him. I can't bring myself to tell her. My time with Zander is just that, mine. It's something I can't share with anyone, not even Ray. I'm not sure how you can grow to need someone in the short span that Zander and I spent together, but somehow it happened. It doesn't matter though. I've been gone a month and there hasn't been a word from him. I know it's not like we were a real couple, but if I had meant anything to him, I'm sure I would have heard from him. Then again, if I was important to him he wouldn't have been talking to Gunner and saying those things anyway. Nothing about that night showed any depth of feeling, and nothing since. Dragon would never let Nicole leave him without trying to win her back. That's something else I've realized in the last month. There is real love out there. Paul and Ray have it. I've seen it. They care about each other. I've never seen that. Dad married my Mom to get access to her fortune. He used me to get out of debt with Michael and .... Michael is just pure evil. Nicole is right. I should have never thought of Dragon like that. He's not. Dragon is another thing I have to address in my life, which is why I'm calling.

"Hey, Nic? Do you think I could talk to Dragon?"

"Dani…I…"

"Please? It's kind of important.

"I don't have a good feeling about this," she grumbles.

"Thanks."

"Hang on," she sighs.

I wait another few minutes. I'm about to hang up, figuring Dragon took the phone and is just ignoring it. I couldn't really blame him.

"Shoot," his gravelly voice, comes over the receiver.

"I," shit what did I want to say again? My hands have a cold clammy sweat covering them. "Hey, Dragon."

"D."

That's it, just my initial, and no how are you, or how have you been…it's another sign that this call, though needed is not welcomed. Nothing about me will probably be welcomed by Dragon.

"I uh…"

"Spit it out D, I've got shit to do." He grumbles and I can hear Nicole in the background censuring him.

"I wanted to apologize," I say weakly, because it is weak. There's nothing I can say that can make up for what happened and what I almost did.

"You almost got my woman killed. Not exactly something you can fix. If you were a man I would have killed you for what you did to Nicole," Dragon says coldly and his words go through me.

"Dragon! Hand me that damn phone. We've had this out and I can't believe you right now!" I hear Nicole in the background, yelling. I swallow and forge ahead.

"I get that. You don't know me, but I had good reason to worry about you, and I'm not sorry I tried to keep Nicole from making a mistake. I'm just sorry that I went about it like I did. You weren't who you appeared to be…" Lame, but it's the best I can do without telling him who he was in my brain at the time, and he doesn't get that. He can't.

His silence greets me.

"So, I'll just let you go. I just wanted to let you know I was sorry and I won't question Nicole again. You love her and you'll protect her. That's enough. Some men…a lot of men aren't like that. Nicole deserves that. She hasn't had it and…"

"D?" Dragon interrupts my rambling, thank God.

"Yeah?"

"You should come home. Nicole misses you."

"I kind of messed up," I say and I think only part of me is

talking about what happened with Nicole. Zander. I should have never gone there.

"You plan on doing it again?" Dragon asks.

"No," I answer and silently add on both counts.

"Then get your ass home, you make Nicole happy. I want her happy."

"I get that," I reply, not really giving him an answer.

"And, D?"

"Yeah?" I asked feeling a little lighter and more surprised at the invitation to come home. Is Kentucky my home?

"We don't hurt women, ever. You feel me?"

"I...well..."

"I'm saying you're safe here, D and I'll be cool as long as you don't pull that shit again.

"I'll think about it." I answer, wondering if I will ever really be safe again.

"Fair enough," he says and the phone goes dead. Guess Dragon ain't one for goodbyes.

I hang up and take a deep breath. I'm feeling at loose ends. Paul had work tonight. He's a bartender at a local club. Ray is working there too, as he does every night. He's the bouncer. He's also convinced I should go there tonight. I'm not. He'll probably win though, because I have no desire to sit home alone.

"You about ready, Kitten?"

I look up to find Ray standing in the door way. He's literally gorgeous. He's got eyes so blue you'd swear the sun was behind them making them shine. This perfect angular face that shows off his five o'clock shadow perfectly. His body shows that there is a reason he is a fitness trainer. His arms are muscles galore, abs that make women and men drool, and finally there's his laid back, don't fuck with me, but I'm the guy next door attitude. Ray has it all, including a heart that is so giving I think he must be from another planet, because they just don't make people like that here on Earth.

"I really don't think this is a good idea."

"That's your problem, you think too much," Ray says looking like a giant kid.

I shake my head and pull myself off the bed. I'm ready as I'll ever be. When I make it to my bedroom door, Paul pulls me into his arms and holds me close and kisses the top of my head. I'm not exactly short, but Paul towers over me. It doesn't intimidate me though, I feel…safe. The only other time I've felt that way in my life has been with Zander, and doesn't that just suck.

An hour later I'm standing by an old cement column in the corner of a busy bar, listening to music and watching the dancers. It's not my cup of tea. Some man is whaling on a juke box about a woman's sundress and how he's going through withdrawals over her. I refuse to think of Zander. This is probably why I never listen to country music. It's damn depressing. I'm still nursing the same rum and coke that Paul sent over when we got here an hour ago. I don't really drink a lot these days. I've learned that drinking might numb me, but in the long run it makes the nightmares worse.

"Seems like I'm always chasing you, Hell Cat. One of these days, I may just get tired of that."

My body freezes. My heart races. It's been a month, why now? More importantly, how? I don't ask. I still my reaction, as best I can. I don't need to show him any weakness.

"No one asked you to, Crusher. I think you just can't take a hint."

"I can baby, I absolutely can."

"Then why are you here?"

"I missed you," he says and it's said in a quiet voice, but there's...feeling in it.

"I doubt that. I'm sure you and Gun found a new play toy before I even crossed the state line," I say bitterly, because I am bitter.

"I was a fucking ass."

I still haven't turned around to talk to him. I'm afraid. I kind of hate him for that too.

"You won't hear an argument from me," I respond, taking a drink. Zander's arm comes around and takes the glass away from me. I still can't turn around to see what he's doing.

I think I'm frozen, afraid to move. If I do, will he really be there? If I do, will I see the truth in his eyes, that I was just a lay and I was right...I meant nothing to him?

"Hellcat, we need to fix this, I've missed you and I think you've missed me too."

"We barely had any time together, and we were just fuck-buddies."

"I think it was more than that."

"No, it really wasn't, Cowboy. I'm not even sure why you made the trip." Or how you found out where I am.

"Because your lips might be saying no, but your body is saying something completely different."

"I think you're delusional, Zander."

My heart is beating hard against my chest. It should freak me out that Zander is here—that he found me. I know Nic would have never told him. We agreed a long time ago to never tell anyone where Ray lived. So, I should be worried about being tracked here, instead I feel this small ball of hope inside because Zander came to find me. He moves closer to me and I feel like I don't have any control of my body when he gets this close. I do my best to calm my heart. I don't want to betray what his closeness really does to me. It's not easy. Especially when his body pushes against my ass and I can feel his hard erection brush against me. A minute later the heat of his breath fans my bare shoulders.

His hands loosely hold my hips, while I try to look out over the crowd in the bar and find Paul or Ray. Someone to save me, because I know if Zander is involved I can't save myself. I feel the tips of his thumbs at the top of my blue jeans, brushing the skin exposed between it and where my tank top begins. My brain is screaming danger, because that's what Zander is. He is danger with a capital 'D.'

"That right there is what I mean. When those thick, beautiful, fucking lips of yours say my name, all I can think about is you whispering it against my cock, right before I grab your hair, plunge inside and fuck your mouth like it's meant to be fucked."

His words flow down my spine and they lodge deep. If I close my eyes, I can see him doing that same thing and me...the woman who has hated sex...suddenly craves being weak with a man. What the fuck is he doing to me? Can he hear how my breath catches and becomes ragged? Shit is he looking over my shoulder and noticing how hard my nipples are right now?

"You have a strange fascination with my mouth," I tried to make that sound bored. I failed.

My body feels like it's on the edge of a cliff and I'm scared to death of what will happen if I jump. Zander is not safe. I can't control Zander. No longer than we were together, when he said those things at the club...he hurt me. He hurt me deeper than anyone had—not physically, but emotionally and with my past that's an accomplishment. I've made so many bad decisions, what happens if he's just another one? I'm leaving to go back to Kentucky soon. Would it be stupid to give in? Wouldn't it be wiser to keep my distance? I've never wanted a man before Zander. Never. What happens if I pretend just once like I'm a normal woman without a fucked up head, without a past that is going to get me killed someday? What happens if I give in and pretend?

"Hellcat, you have no idea, but I could show you, baby. I could show you a hundred different ways and I'd make damn sure you enjoy every…fucking…one," he says drawing my attention back to our conversation.

His last three words are paused and hoarse sounding. They are timed and in tune to the way his hand comes around and nudges my chin, so I look over my shoulder at him. He finishes his reply against my mouth and I open for his kiss without thought.

I drink in his taste. God, I've missed him.

Chapter 18

CRUSHER

IT HAS TAKEN a month of scoping out Nicole's cell phone, and following leads from the greyhound station to find Dani. The bitch knows how to hide her tracks. The surveillance videos at the bus stop don't even look like her. She hides her hair under a hat, she wears big, loose clothing and she never, not once, looks at a security camera. It's like she instinctively knows where they are. That says a lot and what it says doesn't make me happy. My woman has some deep, dark shit to tell me about and we'll get there. Right now, I'm too overwhelmed with finally having her in my arms. I had almost given up hope it would happen. I thought it was over when I didn't hear from her after that first week she left. The silence was deafening. Still, I couldn't fully give up and now I'm here with her.

It's been so long since I've had her in my arms, so long since I could take in her scent, touch her, breathe her in and just hold her. I can't let her get away from me again. She turns completely in my arms, our lips never fully breaking apart. Then, my arms are full of her, my mouth is full of her tongue, my hands are full of her ass, and I use that to pull her hard against me—so tight even air can't get between us. God, I've missed her.

Eventually, we're forced to break apart to give our lungs

oxygen. We pull away from each other's lips slowly. That's when I get it. Those eyes. The eyes that have haunted me the last few weeks, look up at me. They're dark, intense and liquid with emotion. I need this woman. I need that look on her face every fucking day.

"I've missed you, Hellcat," I tell her before I can stop myself. Her forehead crinkles and I know she's thinking about what she should say or do to stop this. It won't work. There's no stopping this and no matter what she says, I can tell she wants this as much as I do. I press my lips against the crease on her brow and just continue holding her.

"What you did was wrong."

I don't argue…I can't argue.

"I am not a Twinkie! I won't be shared with your crew, Zander. I won't be talked about with your crew."

"I was a drunken, fucked-up, fool, Hellcat. I didn't mean the shit my mouth was spewing. It won't happen again."

"I don't think we should happen, I mean it was only supposed to be for sex anyway and…"

I imprison her chin in my hands and pull enough until she looks up at me.

"I. Was. A. Fool. Gunner said something that pissed my whiskey-soaked brain off and I said shit without even meaning it. I don't think of you like that, Dani. I told you, you are mine. Mine, Hellcat and I sure as fuck ain't sharing you with no-fucking body." I lay it bare. I owe her this. I just hope I get through to her. When she doesn't respond I say again, "You're mine, Hellcat."

"And who are you exactly?" A man asks from behind Dani. I look up at him and take him in. Overgrown muscles, a too pretty face and much too cocky. He needs to step back from my woman immediately. I move my hand up to Dani's side and pull her into my side and facing the asshole. He's not getting near her.

"What's it to you?" I ask, ready to take him down.

"Zander…"

"I asked you a question, pretty boy. Is there some reason you're interrupting me and my girl?"

"Your girl?"

"Ra…" I squeeze Dani, before she can say anything. I got this. The sooner I take care of him the sooner I get her and hell I need to get her, and soon.

"That's right. My girl."

"Weird she hasn't mentioned you in the month she's been living with me."

Heat hits me and anger fills my body. What the fuck? What the ever-loving fuck? She left me and moved in with some Arnold Schwarzenegger wanna-be, with a pretty face. I look at Dani and she's staring at the other guy and she looks like she could spit fire at him, so I relax, marginally.

"You're not helping, Ray," she says, and I sneer. Ray, pussy-ass sounding name.

"Not trying to help Kitten, just wondering why you're making out with some man in the middle of the bar."

Kitten? Fuck that shit, right there.

"Who the hell is this Ray, Hellcat and explain fast before I end his ass right here."

'Ray' looks away from Dani and back to me. He takes me in and that's fine. I want him to, because I'm about to beat his ass down. He needs to see the motherfucker that is about to make him bloody.

"Jesus, you said Nicole got mixed up and attached herself to a biker Kitten, you didn't say you had done the same thing."

Hand to God, if this motherfucker doesn't stop calling my

woman Kitten I'm going to make sure he doesn't have a voice to use. That way he won't be able to say anything ever again. That's probably the thing to do really because his voice is annoying as hell.

"I'm not mixed up with a biker, Zander and I are..."

"Fucking like rabbits," I interject before she can say anything that might piss me off even a tenth more than I already am.

She lands a hard elbow into my side and I grunt, pulling away to rub the spot her blow landed.

"What the fuck is that for?"

"Because you're pissing me off!" She says.

"Well join the fucking crowd. It doesn't quite fill me with rainbows and little pink ponies to find out my woman has been living with another man."

"I haven't been...little pink ponies?" She stops mid-sentence to ask, looking exasperated, and sexy as hell.

"Yeah those damn..."

"I know what they are, I'm just...I have no words."

"So this is the guy you've been mooning over for the last month?" I look up to see yet another pretty boy standing in front of us, although this one has way-less muscles and is shorter—more Dani's size than me or the terminator-wanna-be.

"Jesus, Nic told me you were living with two men, I guess I should have listened," I grumble taking my hand away from her and raking it over my face and then massaging the tension in my neck. How the fuck do I handle this? I need to take her ass back home and tan her hide. Hell, maybe I should lock her in my room until the only cock she can ever think about is mine. That idea definitely has merit. I look up when I hear a table being scooted beside us. Hellcat has another bottle in her hand and she's aiming it at my head. Arnold has his arms around her and is pulling her away from me. Now, I should be grateful, but I kind of want to rip his arms off his body and beat him to death with them.

"What the hell you coming after me for? You're the one sleeping with two men! After you yanked my cock out in the middle my club, woke Junior up to play and then poured an expensive bottle of Jack on it and leaving my heart broken." Okay, by this time I'm poking her like she was an angry bear more than anything else. It's fucking fun to watch her and I'm a sadistic S.O.B.

The twins, and I mean that in the form of the bad Arnold and Danny Devito movie from way back when, freeze and look at me like I have three heads and then back at Dani (who tries to fly at me again), and then they do the strangest thing. The tall dude kisses Dani on top of the head and whispers something in her ear. The smaller one, hugs her and then they look at me. I expected shit to be thrown so I could finally beat them down. Instead I get an invitation.

"Come on up to the bar and we'll get you a drink on the house," the smaller one says.

I turn to look at Dani, trying to figure out what her mood is, and where her head is at when she just shrugs and walks towards the bar. I look at her buddies and they basically do the same, except Arnold slaps me hard, a little too hard, on the back and we follow her. At least I'm not the only one chasing after her, but I am going to make sure I'm the only son of a bitch who catches her. Ever.

Chapter 19

DANI

I WANT TO kill Zander for being such an idiot and I'm pissed off that yet again he's insinuating I'm sleeping with two men. I would have thought he knew me better by now. It is one thing that I lead others to believe that's who I am, but he should know better. I'm trying my best to get away from Ray so I can brain the big, dumb-ass Cowboy up the side of his head with this bottle. Him or Paul (I can't see who) takes the bottle away and then Ray kisses the top of my head. He bends down to whisper in my ear and I go still. Still. It's all I can be when I take in his words.

"Damn Kitten, when you leap, you go all in. Welcome to the land of the living, Doll-face."

Once I'm still Ray lets me go. My urge to kill Zander is over though. Instead I let Ray's words settle inside of me. He's not wrong. When Zander is around I am...alive. I'm usually frustrated and wanting to kill and scream like a banshee—but I am alive. Never once, not once since getting close to Zander, (and really before that) have I been afraid of him hurting me physically. In fact, I'm so comfortable with that knowledge that I strike out at him, without the usual sick fear that comes when I'm around a man—any man. That is...extraordinary. It says...so much. Then, I concentrate on Ray's other words. When I decide to jump... Shit! I've already jumped. I'm so deep into whatever this is with Zander that no matter what happens, he's going to take a piece of me. That is stupid. That is monumentally stupid. I don't have many pieces left, certainly not enough to be giving them away. It's too late and just thinking of the consequences robs me of my voice. So, all I can do is shrug at Zander and walk towards the bar. I need to regroup.

APPARENTLY A FEW drinks and lame jokes is all it takes to make men best friends because Zander, Ray and Paul have all been joking and laughing, so much that they're annoying the hell out of me.

"Don't you have a job here or something?" I remind Ray, because I want to talk with Zander, or at least I think I do. It would be nice to at least have that option. He looks at me and that smirk he is wearing, annoys me. He knows what he is doing.

"I am working Kitten, I'm on a break."

"It's been an awful long break," I mutter into my drink.

"She's right, Crusher. We'll talk tomorrow I figure." He turns back to me before Zander responds, "I take it you're going home with him and not Paul and me?"

"I don't…"

"Yeah, I got her," Crusher says interrupting my denial.

"Good job. I'll probably stay with Ray then until clean-up is done. It'll be late so we may stay in the office apartment in the back. Since you have company and all," Paul adds, being about as subtle as a Mack truck.

"Jesus, why not just say Dani, we're getting lost so you can get your brains screwed out by the hot cowboy-biker," I mutter and apparently not too quietly because Crusher laughs—loudly, Ray and Paul do too.

"Paul and I are going to get lost so you can get your brains screwed out by the hot biker. Is that better, Kitten?"

"Oh loads," I answer sarcastically. I ignore them all. When they leave, I continue ignoring Zander. Out of the corner of my eye I watch him stand up. He's hovering over me waiting for a reaction. I don't give him one. Apparently he can't appreciate that he's being ignored because instead of letting me continue, he sighs heavily (and loudly), then picks me up in his arms and starts walking out of the bar. Now I could complain and whine, but I don't want to. I've wanted to be in Zander's arms and alone with him since that kiss. So, I just lay against him and enjoy the feel of him holding me. In fact, it's so nice, I decide to play.

I use my hand to pull his shirt up out of his jeans and slide my hands against the warm skin of his stomach. I push until the shirt is wadded up under his arms and then I slide my tongue against his nipple, flicking it before sucking it hard into my mouth with a groan. I've missed his taste.

Zander grunts softly. "Are you horny, Hellcat?"

I smile, biting down on his nipple. My man isn't one for sweet words and seduction. My man. I like that. He can be mine, at least for a while. Surely the universe owes me that? I use my hands wrapped around him to pull his head down to me.

"I've missed you," I whisper into this ear.

"Have you, sweetheart?"

"Yes, I've even dreamed about you," I confess, using my nails to lightly rake down his stomach, grazing his nipples. God, surely we'll be at his car soon.

"What was I doing in these dreams?" He growls, as I pinch

his nipple, and bite down on the lobe of his ear at the same time.

"Fucking me," I answer, knowing my words are getting to him and intending on making sure I drive him crazy. Somewhere in the back of my mind I marvel that I can be this free with Zander, even after he was such an ass. I'll think about that tomorrow, tonight I want to be laid a lot. Is it my imagination or did the speed of Zander's steps pick up? Not my imagination, I think because a second later we're standing at his truck. He drops me gently to the ground so I'm standing. I lean against the side of the truck bed, and then his lips are on mine and he's claiming my mouth. I don't know how long we stand there kissing. I do know when we break away I have to heave oxygen into my system. His hands go to my waist and he's undoing my belt. I should tell him no. We're outside and though we're mostly hidden by his truck and the car beside us, it's still out in the open. I don't. Instead, I unlatch his belt and go for the button and zipper next. I want…no, I need him inside of me.

"How was I fucking you, sweetheart? Tell me." He orders, his voice deep and laced with need. I'm so wet and aroused that I don't even argue when he pulls my tank top off and I'm standing outside with nothing covering my breasts but a white lace bra. He drapes my tank over the side of his truck and then pushes my pants down off my hips.

For a minute, my nerves get me. Then, I take in the look in his eyes and the need dripping off of him. That's for me. Me. So I push it away and concentrate only on the here and now and Zander.

"You were eating my pussy, making me come over and over."

"Does my woman like it when I eat out her sweet, little

cunt?"

"God, yes."

"That's good to know, but I'm not going to eat you out right now. Do you know why, Hellcat?" He says, and his coarse words stall me. I can't do anything but shake my head no.

He reaches down and finishes what I started with his pants. Pushing them off his hips, I notice he's not wearing underwear. Zander always goes commando and I don't think I truly appreciated that fact until just now. He takes his large, swollen cock into his hand and starts stroking it. My eyes are glued to his movements. I watch him slowly and firmly stroke his cock, moving slowly back and forth. The head of his cock is slick, wet, and glistens under the yellow beam of the outside light that illuminates the parking lot.

"I asked you a question. Answer me, do you know why?"

I couldn't tear my eyes off his cock if I wanted to. My mouth is dry and I'm dying to touch him. So I reach out my hand to do just that. "No..."

Zander doesn't let me touch him though. He grabs my hand and uses it to spin me around so I'm pressed against the side of the truck. My hands grip the top of the bed and I hiss at the cold metal feel against my stomach and breasts. His hands roughly pull my underwear down. He pushes against me, his cock slipping in my ass and pushing against the entrance, but not actually going in. His hand comes around and fingers push inside my pussy. I gasp at the intrusion and tighten my inner muscles against them, trying to ride.

"I didn't eat out this sweet fucking cunt because it's been too damn long since I've been inside of you and I'm going to fuck you and fuck you hard to make up for that. Right here, where anyone can see us. Right here, because I'm so fucking hard I can't wait and you're going to love every minute of it aren't you, Hellcat?" His gravelly voice whispers against my ear, so smoky and thick it's like I can feel the words pour over me. I'm lost in this man.

"Yes," I tell him, because there can be no other answer.

"Yes, what?" He growls as his fingers slip from me. Before I can mourn their loss, he pulls at my hips and positions me and then slides into me. It's fucking brilliant. My hands tighten on the truck, wadding the black tank underneath them, and I hiss at his hard intrusion.

"Fuck me!" I growl out, frustrated when he refuses to move.

That must have been the magic words because he begins sliding in and out of me, I thrust back against him, trying to meet him and drive him in deeper. He's slamming me hard, so deep inside of me that I can taste him. My orgasm is building, I can feel it start and I want it, I need it and that's when I see him. There's a guy two cars away watching us. I can't make a lot out. He's hidden in the shadows, but I can see him reach down to his pants and take his dick out. My heart picks up a beat. I swallow. Oh shit.

"Zander..." I squeak. Stopping the way I grind back against him, so I don't meet his thrusts.

Zander slaps my ass and pulls me back into him and it feels like he's gone deeper than he ever has before. I can't stop myself from clenching his cock hard and angling so he rakes the sides of my walls as he withdraws.

"Zander, we're being watched," I gasp but I don't break our stride this time, I can't. It feels too good.

Zander thrusts back in and holds still, slamming me against the side of the truck and pushing against me so tight he doesn't allow me room to move. I look over my shoulder up at him and see he's watching the other guy stroke his cock and then he looks down at me with a cocky grin, that I've seen probably a hundred times, but never as devilish as it is right now in this moment.

"Then let's give him a show," he says and my heart stalls. He can't mean...

"Umm...I don't want..."

That's when he begins thrusting in and out of me again and his hand comes around to play with my clit at the same time. Oh God! The dual sensations wash through me and Zander knows exactly where to touch me to set me off. The muscles in my pussy start to quake and my stomach clenches with the release building inside of me.

"Look, Hellcat. See what you do? Just the sight of you getting fucked makes him so hard he has to stroke himself. He's getting ready to come everywhere just because you're taking my dick."

"But, Zander..." I question, still not sure. I'm excited and I feel guilty for feeling that way. The truth is I do like it, but I don't think I should.

"Hush, sweetheart and come for me. He can't see you and he's never going to have you. You're mine and when he explodes all over himself just from watching you getting fucked? I'm going to fill your pussy so full of cum it'll be leaking out of you for a fucking week."

I bite my lip, still not a hundred percent sure. Then, Zander is fucking me harder and pinching my clit and demanding I take his cock. I watch the stranger's hand move up and down over his cock, going faster and faster. Our eyes lock as my orgasm hits and I scream out Zander's name, the guy's hand is covered in his own release. A second later I feel Zander explode inside of me and a second orgasm hits me when his finger pushes into my ass. I feel so full, so stretched and I think I might black out as wave after wave crashes into me. When I'm finished, Zander is wrapped around me, His cock has slipped out but I still feel him pressed against me. I can feel the sticky wet liquid sliding down my legs and I should feel embarrassed, I don't. I look over my shoulder at Zander.

"I can't believe we just did that," I say and my voice hurts, confirming that the screams I gave just minutes before were loud.

Zander grins that damn cocky grin again, and I can't be upset. After the orgasms I've just had, he should feel cocky. Hell, I feel cocky.

"We're just getting started Hellcat, we're just getting started." He says and then kisses me hard.

When we break apart, I look around to see and the guy is gone. Thank God. That would have been embarrassing. It's hard to believe that before Zander I never really had consensual sex and now…now I'm having sex in front of strangers. What is he turning me into?

Dani. A small voice whispers from inside of me and I smile. I like being Dani.

Chapter 20

CRUSHER

WE'RE LYING IN bed hours later and I'm holding Dani in my arms. Finally, after a month of feeling unsatisfied, it's like having a five course meal after being stranded on an island and barely surviving. Her head is on my chest, she has one arm wrapped around my waist and I have her hand close to my face inspecting the delicate bones of her wrist, the light dusting of freckles that dot her arm. My finger traces a light brown beauty mark just under the bone in her wrist. I bring it up to my lips and kiss it for no other reason than I can. When I look down at her she is watching me closely. There's a look of such longing on her face. It makes me want to promise her anything in the world she wants and then bust my ass to make sure she'll get it.

"What are you thinking, Hellcat?"

"Why do you call me Hellcat?"

"It fits you," I tell her, only giving her half the truth.

She strains up to bury her face in my neck and breathes in against my skin.

"Are you sniffing me?"

"You smell good," she mumbles, her lips placing small kisses against my skin.

I want this. I want more of this. I want this forever. I'm not letting her get away. Her fate is sealed. It was before this, but in this moment with the softness she's showing me and the peace I feel? It's cemented.

"I've missed the hell out of you, Hellcat."

I feel her lips stretch into a smile against my neck—which is good. I want to give her more smiles.

"Sure you did, Cowboy."

"Don't do that, Dani," I chastise her, pulling away so she is forced to look at me.

"Do what?" She asks genuinely confused.

"Treat me—treat us like we're just fucking. We're not. I know that and you know that."

"Zander…"

"Admit it, Dani. Give me the words."

"I…maybe? I don't know. If it's not just fucking, what are we?"

Disappointment hits my gut hard, but I shake it off. Dani wasn't what she appeared to be at first and still she's let me in. Hell, even after my monumental fuck-up she let me back in. I need to hold on to my patience a little longer.

"I don't know how to make this any clearer to you. You're mine." I tell her, hoping it finally gets through to her.

"I'm not sure I can handle being a man's property."

So much for patience. "Too damn bad."

She pulls up so the upper half of her body is stretched above mine. Which is okay—more than okay. The sheet falls away and pools at her hips. It's a damn good show and she's so put out with me that she doesn't seem to notice.

"What is that?" She asks and I have to force myself not to stare at her breasts. "Why do men think they can own a woman? What in your DNA makes you think that you can have a person as property and do with them whatever you want? What the fuck is it?"

Whoa, there's a lot there to digest, but along with the anger in her eyes I see something else, and what I see is fear, I need to rid her of that before she can accept my claim.

"It goes both ways, Hellcat. I belong to you too."

"I...wait...What?"

"I said I'm yours too."

"What does that mean?"

"Just what I said. I'm yours."

"As in...all mine?"

I fake a heavy sigh and slide down in the bed further, flopping my hands out on each side. "Do with me what you will, oh Mistress."

I look up at her and wink. She kind of half smiles, but she's looking at me more intently than I imagined she would.

"Seriously, Zander."

I bring my hand up along her jawline, rubbing my thumb along the bone and take a breath.

"Did Nicole explain to you what claiming someone was in the club?"

"Well, yeah, but that's them. They're a couple and well we're..."

"We're what?" I say trying my best not to get exasperated at her.

"You know what I mean, they've been together for a..."

"Damn it woman, how long do you think Dragon and Nicole were together, before he claimed her?"

That seems to make her stop and think, so I press my advantage.

"How long have we been together, Dani? "And I can tell you right now, you can count the month you've been gone because my dick hasn't gone near another woman since the moment I got a taste of you."

"I...you're serious?"

"As a heart attack."

"There are things about me, things you don't know...and Zander, it's not that I don't want to tell you...I just don't think I'm ready to tell...anyone."

"Hell...," I stop when she puts her finger to my lips.

"I've been working on it the last month, honest...and I'm not saying this to hurt you, Zander. That's the last thing I ever want to do, but I'm not sure I can...I mean I'm not sure I'm ready for more than just this...I'm not sure I'm ready for us." She sighs and it sounds like the weight of the world is on her shoulders. "And I know..." she whispers like it's a dirty little secret, she doesn't want to admit. "I know that I'm not ready for others to know there is an 'us'."

I let her words sit with me a moment. There are different ways I could react to what she's telling me, but she's trying I can tell that and I have seen enough signs to know I need to go slowly here. Still, I need a few things made clear.

"Do you plan on fucking other men while we're sleeping together?" She jerks back like I slapped her.

"Of course not, but..."

"Do you want to keep going with whatever this is between us?"

"Yes," she whispers, answering me eagerly and her tone is full of pleasure.

"Then we'll do this on the down low, just the two of us." She smiles and I feel the need to clarify my answer. "Just until you work it out in your head Hellcat that the two of us are meant to be together."

She thinks about it and must agree because she gets this devious little smile on her face and leans down to whisper in my ear, "We have a few hours to play before Ray and Paul make it back."

"Is that so?" I ask, as her hand slides down under the cover.

"Oh yeah."

"What would you like to do?" I ask.

"You," she answers simply and there's this happiness in her eyes.

"I don't know Hellcat, I'm pretty tired."

"Sorry Cowboy, but as my property, you must agree to my demands."

"Is that so?" I ask on a groan because she wraps my already hard cock in her hands.

"Afraid so, Zander. I don't make the rules, I just enforce them."

"Well if there's no other choice," I say lifting her up to straddle me. "But, since I'm so tired, maybe you could do all the work."

And just like that, she guides me inside of her and lowers herself down on my shaft. Heaven. Warm, soft, wet, sweet Heaven. *Dani.*

Chapter 21

DANI

TWO MONTHS I'VE been home. Two months that Zander and I have been hiding whatever we are. Two months that have flown by and even I will admit that it's good. That being with Zander is good. He's getting frustrated with me. He's tired of keeping us a secret. He's right. I totally agree with him, it's just anytime I get close to confessing to Nicole that I'm seeing Zander, I chicken out. What if by bringing it out into the open I jinx it? What if that's the very thing that ends it? I don't want to lose him. I don't think I'll survive losing him. It scares the hell out of me to admit that because no matter how I try to convince myself otherwise, the devil will come calling.

The club has been changing since I came back. There was this darkness over it since Irish's betrayal. It affected every member in some form or another. I know it's hurt Zander. He doesn't talk about it, but he's having nightmares. He won't even tell me what the nightmares are about, but on the nights he stays at the house, he rarely sleeps more than a couple of hours. Since I have my own nightmares, I completely understand.

Then there are nights like tonight. I try to avoid nights like tonight. I couldn't this time. The club is celebrating Carrot Top's birthday. Carrie is the girl Nicole said the club was protecting because of Dancer. Don't get me wrong, I like her.

She's sweet, if not a little too innocent. That's not the reason I have issues with her. No, I have issues because she gravitates towards Zander. At first it didn't bother me, but then she started calling him Alexander and he lets her...

She's everything he should have. Sweet, innocent, untouched by the darkness that's in this world. Someone that could love him wholly and freely. She's everything I've never been. She's everything I've never had the chance to be. She's sitting with my man, Bull, Freak and Nikki, Nicole and Dragon and they're laughing. They're happy. She's accepted. She hasn't fucked up. They don't resent her. They look out for her, they care about her...they gave her a sweet nickname and not because they think she doesn't have a heart...Yeah, I really should have avoided tonight.

"What's up Ice? You want to dance?" I look up to find Gun standing by the bar. I shake my head. The man gets an A for effort.

"I thought we agreed you should give up trying?" I ask turning my attention back to my rum and coke, which these days has a lot more coke and very little rum—of course if tonight keeps going this way, that might change.

"Nah, eventually I figure you'll give in," he says sitting down.

"Have a seat," I say sarcastically, but not really being a bitch. Truth is I like Gun. If he'd quit trying to get in my pants, I'd probably talk to him more than anyone.

"Thank you, don't mind if I do."

"Why aren't you over there eating cake and doing birthday shit?" I ask talking about the big table Zander and the others are sitting and laughing at. I don't turn around to see it, because it kind of...hurts.

"Not my scene," he says taking a pull off a beer that Six

puts down for him.

"What is your scene?" I ask not really interested, but Zander's laughter rings out and it hits my stomach and pains me. I made this situation and I'm jealous. God, I am so screwed up.

"You got nothing to worry about you know," he says instead of answering my question.

"What are you talking about?"

"Crush, he's all tied up over you babe, you got nothing to worry about."

"I think you should probably quit after that drink, Gun. You're not making a bit of sense."

"He's worried about Red, he thinks of her like a little sister. She's a lot like Melly and he's worried because Dance comes back next week."

His words hit me in the face. Melly? My first instinct is to ask him all about this Melly, but I can't. That would give away more than I should.

"I figured Dance coming back would be good? I thought Nic said him and Carrie were family."

"She made a bad decision and Dance got in the crossfire because of it. It's the reason he's been in the can for the last two years."

It seems me and Carrot Top have more in common than I imagined. I thought I was the sole heir to the throne of bad decisions. Guess I have some work to do to keep the title. So, fuck it, let's add one more into the list.

"So, who's Melly?" I ask, my vision filled with the drink I've barely touched.

Gun laughs, and pulls my attention to him. He's holding out his hand.

"C'mon Ice, if you want that story, I get something out of it. Dance with me."

"I don't dance," I grumble, but let him pull me off the barstool.

"Sure you don't, I guess Pussy's just hired you because of your sweet disposition."

"I never realized you were such a sarcastic ass, Gun. Besides, in case you haven't noticed, Pussy's hasn't let me dance since I got out of the hospital—all I seem good enough for these days is waiting tables."

"Yeah well, you didn't think Crush was going to let his woman dance for other men, did you?"

"Motherfucker! I knew it." Gun laughs as we reach the dance floor, which is really just a corner of the club that's covered in old, scratched parquet flooring. The rest of the boy's club has concrete floors. He pulls me in way too close and when I try to put space between us, he pokes me in the ribs, causing me to yell out. "What was that for?"

"Loosen up Ice, I know when I'm out of the running."

"Yeah well, I heard all too well what you wanted to be in the running for," I grumble as we start slow dancing to a song I can't even place, and could care less about.

"Hey, I'm a man and you're a hot piece of ass," he responds.

"You're such a sweet talker Gun. Really, with lines like that I'm surprised there isn't a gang of women behind you, just waiting for their turn," I tell him, rolling my eyes.

His hand moves down to my ass and he squeezes.

"If you want to keep your hand, how about you move it up to my back?" I warn him. He laughs, but does as I ask. When he makes no move to talk, I sigh—loudly. "Hello? Melly?"

He laughs, and I know right then he was waiting for me to push it. Asshole.

"Melly is a girl Crush grew up with. He was in love with

her. Young love, you know?"

"As in you never forget your first," I say, while inside my heart feels like it's in a vice grip. Fuck. "Yeah, I'm familiar."

"Who knows, they were both kids though. Crush tried to save her and couldn't. He blames himself."

"How did she die?"

"Her own father shot her and then turned the gun on himself. Crush was the first to find her," Gun says with distaste and who could blame him? Even as jealousy hits me, my heart breaks for this unknown girl.

"He told you all of this?" I ask him, not even noticing we're now dancing on our second song.

"He had nightmares about her in the service, broke down and told me and Freak about it one night while he was drunk, some ghosts don't let go."

Fuck, don't I know that better than anyone?

"Why are you telling me?"

"Because, you can be a hard bitch, but I see that same haunted look in you. Just thought it'd be good if you knew Crush gets it."

Jesus, men are clueless. He doesn't even realize he's ripped me to shreds. I look at my hand and the way it lightly trembles on his shoulder and know I need to get out of here and soon. I've not had an attack since Zander came and got me, but I can feel this one coming and it's going to be bad.

"Can you take me home?" I ask, because I know I can't drive. There's just no way.

"I can get Crush to…"

"No!" I yell before I can stop myself. "I mean I don't want to bother him, I just…I really need to get out of here."

"Sure, Ice. Come on." He takes my hand and leads me off the dance floor.

I follow him like a robot. I feel like I've taken a knife to the gut and since that's happened before, I'm all too familiar with the feeling. Trouble is, this one hurts more than the real knife ever did. As we leave the club, I don't look at the table Zander is sitting at. I don't look at anything but the back of Gun's cut, stumbling behind him and wondering if I will survive. The nightmares Zander's been having? Were they really about this Melly? Does he see the same darkness that Gunner sees? Is he trying to save me because he couldn't save Melly? The woman he loved, the first woman he loved? Heat surges through me, heating my face. I feel like such a fool. I knew it was too good to be true that someone like Zander could want to be with me, for me—love me for me...

When we get back to the house, Gun insists on going inside and making sure everything is okay. After he inspects every room he comes back down. I've already downed some meds. I'm sitting on the couch and trying desperately not to cry until he leaves. I don't know why the possibility that Zander is only with me to try and fix what he couldn't with someone else hurts... so deeply. I know I'm probably not even acting logical. Then again, I've never been logical. All I know right now is my world is upside down, because with Zander I wanted one thing. I wanted a piece of something good. Something that was all mine. Something that had nothing to do with anything or anyone else, just me.

I'm so broken and lost in my own misery that I don't even realize I'm already crying until Gun comes and sits beside me and pulls me into his arms. The echoes of my cries can be heard in the quiet room. Gun says nothing, he just holds me. Turns out that's exactly what I needed because I just let it all out. I cry for everything I've lost over the years, everything that's been done. I cry for everything I want and everything I'll never have. I cry for me. I grieve for me and then when I've finished, I cry for one other person. I cry for Melly, for a girl who should have had everything wonderful in the world including the best man I've ever known in my life. The girl whose life was stolen from her by a bastard just like Michael. I hope they get to meet each other in hell someday.

Chapter 22

CRUSHER

I'M FUCKING PISSED. I pull up in my woman's driveway to see Gun's bike in the driveway. When I watched the two of them leave I wanted to beat the shit out of him. I didn't. I stayed where I was. Dragon wanted a meeting after the party with me, Bull and Dance. So, I had to stick around. In four fucking hours, Gun never returned and now I find him here. He is not moving in on my woman. No fucking way. That shit ain't going to fly. I jump off my bike and make a bee line for the house. When I come through the kitchen, I can see Dani asleep on the couch with her head in Gun's lap. He's sitting there watching TV, combing his fingers through Dani's hair and I see mother fuckin' red.

I don't even think about it. I charge in and grab him by the upper arm and haul him off the couch. Now, Gun and I are close to the same size but I'm pissed and I catch him unaware. I can see out of the corner of my eye that Dani almost gets pulled off the couch with him, but she stops herself. I can't stop to think of her just yet. I have Gun up and my fist plowed into the side of his face before he can get his feet under him. He sways back against a chair, but damn it. He doesn't fall. He comes at me and lands a pretty solid hit into my stomach, but I bring my knee up, grabbing the back of his head and slamming him into it. This time he falls on the floor, blood spurting from his nose and I feel immense satisfaction until a remote control slaps me hard across the side of the face before falling to the ground.

Dani threw the remote control at me and she's standing in front of the couch breathing fire at me. She gives me a look that could kill a lesser man and then goes to Gun's side.

"What the fuck do you think you're doing?" She growls going down to inspect Gun's nose. She yanks her t-shirt over her head and now only has on a sports bra thing that she uses to work out in. Again, I must say, fuck no!

"What the hell are you doing? Put your motherfucking shirt back on. Wasn't it enough you were hanging all over each other when I got here?"

She pushes the bottom of her shirt against Gun's nose. Asshole that he is, he just sits there and watches me.

"You have completely lost your damned mind, Zander. What the fuck gives you the right to storm in here and start throwing punches at anyone?"

"Well hell, could it be that my woman had her motherfucking head in another man's lap?"

"So? It's not like I was sucking on his cock! I was sleeping!"

"You shouldn't be sleeping on any fucking part of another man's body! Besides I know you weren't giving him head, that'd be a fucking miracle."

She freezes and I know I've gone too far. In the last couple of months I've done everything, but get down on my hands and knees and beg her to take my cock like that. Still, I shouldn't have said that shit, especially in front of Gun.

"I can't believe you right now," she says her voice quiet, but hard at the same time.

"Yeah well, excuse me if I get pissed off when I see my

woman getting close to another man."

"Did you see me snatching Carrot by her hair and dragging her away from you?" She asks going into the kitchen. I give Gun another hateful look and this time the motherfucker looks entirely too cocky.

"What the hell you looking at?" I growl at him.

"Another one bites the dust," he says cryptically and I don't have time to figure it out because, I'm busy trying to decipher Dani's words.

"Why would you grab Carrot? I ask, thoroughly confused.

"Gee I don't know, maybe because she keeps hanging all over what is supposed to be mine. Always with those big eyes saying Alexander this and Alexander that. It's pretty damned pathetic."

"Are you jealous?" I ask in amazement. That was apparently the wrong thing to ask because a kitchen bowl comes sailing at my face. I dodge to the side just in time. The bowl was metal and falls against an end table with a loud clang. Gunner walks around me and hands Dani her shirt. She takes a sandwich bag filled with ice and wraps it in a kitchen towel putting it gently against his nose with a hiss, and bites her lip. She's so concerned about him that I want to hit the son of a bitch again. Gunner has been hurt worse from throwing punches in the ring we keep when one of us wants to let off steam. So when the son of a bitch wiggles his eyebrows I make a note to kick his ass, when he can't hide behind my woman. "Answer me, woman! Are you jealous?"

"Fuck you, Zander." She growls, stomping out of the kitchen heading towards our bedroom.

I follow her, stopping beside Gunner to throw a fucking elbow into his side. "Get the fuck out of here before I kick your ass so hard they'll find pieces of you on Highway 80 for the next fucking twenty years." His laughter echoes behind me as I go find Dani.

"Shouldn't have tried to keep you two a secret, Crush Man."

"Fuck off."

I slam our bedroom door against the wall when I come in. She's searching through her closet and comes out with one of my faded t-shirts. It's the one I let her sleep in, when I allow her to wear clothes to our bed. Which honestly, isn't very damn often. Hell, even if I do, I always end up taking it off her in the middle of the night. I'm getting hard just thinking about it, and I need to have this out with her. Damn woman has me so messed up over her, I don't know if I'm coming or going.

"Answer me, Dani. Are you jealous of Carrie?"

"See? That right there!"

"What?" I ask, completely clueless.

She goes into the bathroom for a second, coming back out without her jeans on and rubbing that face cream between her hands she always puts on her face before we crash. She stands in front of the mirror, rubbing her face and all I can think is, she is everything I have ever wanted. *Everything.*

"Carrie! See?"

"Woman, you need to start making more sense!"

She turns to me then, drying her hands on a towel she finds on the dresser.

"You call her Carrie! No one else does! Not one of them! They all call her Red, but not you, no way! You call her Carrie!"

"It's her name!"

"And she's sweet! She's so damned sweet she makes my teeth hurt."

I fall back on the bed, letting my elbows prop me up. I'm pretty sure I'm going to be here for a while. "Is there a problem with Carrie being sweet?"

"She calls you Alexander! You call her Carrie!"

"Sweet fucking mother of Hell! That's our names!"

"Do you hear anyone else using them? No! Just you two! And she zeros in on you, no matter where we are or who is around! She sees you and it's like a heat seeking missile or something. Bam! Zander's here! Cue Carrie!"

"What the hell do you want from me? Do you want me to hurt her, just so you will feel better? Is that it?"

"No! She's who you deserve!"

With those words, I'm not finding this so funny anymore. "What the fuck are you talking about, Hellcat?"

"She's sweet, and kind, and good. She's beautiful, innocent, and everything you should have!"

I look at her like she's insane. Does she not look in the mirror? Does she not realize how she is with me when we're alone?

"She's also in love with Dance," I try reasoning with her first, because other than fucking a woman or eating her pussy, I haven't really dealt with this drama bullshit.

"That's just because you don't press it. If you did, the minute you had sex, she'd be yours."

The way she says that, grates my nerves.

"You know Hellcat, I am more than just a cock."

"I know that!"

"It sure doesn't sound like it," I grunt falling back on the bed. Jesus this relationship stuff is for the birds.

"I just meant with her you'd have someone who isn't scarred and broken. She doesn't know the ugly in the world. You could make her happy. She'd love you, and give you babies and the life you deserve."

"Jesus, you got all this from her calling me by my first

name?"

She's got these big tears in her eyes and my gut twists yet again. I really need to kill the motherfucker who hurt her.

"You should go, Zander. This isn't working."

"The hell it isn't!" I growl. "Get over here now, Dani," I order.

"Zander…"

"Now, Dani. Don't make me come to you, get your uptight, high maintenance, drama filled ass over here, now." She doesn't move. I stare her down. "Now."

She frowns, but it's more with sadness and confusion than anger. With a broken, dejected noise she walks towards me. When she gets close enough, I reach out and grab her hand and pull her down on top of me. I slide my hands up under the t-shirt, my dick instantly hardening at the feel of her soft skin, so heated to my touch. I pull her until our faces are mere inches apart.

"Quit trying to give me away, Dani. I'm not going anywhere. I'm yours."

"You deserve someone better…"

I sigh and hold her tight and roll over, bracing my weight. She's now on the bottom and I'm on top of her. "You do realize there's a very good chance you could be pregnant?"

"Zander…"

"I mean it, we've been fucking nonstop and I haven't used protection since that first time. Unless you're on the pill?"

"I'm not, but…"

"So it's entirely possible."

"No…I can't have children, Zander."

The words are whispered like a dirty secret and that haunted look I see in her eyes grabs me. I've seen it before, but it's never been more blatant than it is right now. I lean down to kiss her forehead, wishing only to comfort her.

"Doctors have been wrong before, Hellcat."

"Not this time," she whispers avoiding my eyes.

"Nonsense, you just didn't have the right man before, we'll prove the doctors…"

"You can't fix what's not there anymore, Zander."

"What are you saying?"

"Have you noticed that we've had sex almost every night and you never had to worry about me having periods or anything?" She says looking at the wall, and still not at me. Her voice sounds…dead.

"That's just another reason we should…"

"You still don't understand," she whispers and this time her eyes turn and seek mine and the look of pure agony in them rips me wide open. A part of me wishes she would look away again, the pain is that intense. She pulls away so she can roll to her back. I turn on my side so I can see her, connect with her. I want her to know she's not alone. Her hand has a fine tremble in it as she reaches her stomach. It moves across her womb in a slow, stumbling movement. "I forgot. It was just once. I hadn't slept and I was so tired…"

"Hellcat, you don't have to tell me this," I tell her, because her voice is getting so weak, so lost. My breath stops in my throat. She doesn't hear me. I can tell. Her eyes are focused on the ceiling and she's lost in thought. I don't know what's coming, but I know it's bad. I place my hand over hers, hoping she absorbs some of my heat, that maybe I can reach her, and pull her out of whatever hell she's fallen into.

"I was sick. It's not an excuse, but I had a high fever and the salad Michael allowed me to eat wouldn't stay down. I was so weak. I was cramping, but I thought…I thought it was because I hadn't ate anything, except the salad. I only meant to lie on the floor for a little bit. Just long enough to rest. I was so dizzy. When I woke up, there was blood. There was so much more than there should have been…I must have slept. It was dark outside. Michael would be home any minute and I had to clean it up. He didn't like…nothing could be dirty. I cleaned. It was clean, I swear. It was, it sparkled, just like he always wanted."

"I'm sure it was. You did good, Hellcat," I tell her, because fuck I don't have any other words. I don't know what to say.

"No, I forgot…"

"What did you forget?" I ask, afraid to know.

"I left the bloody cleaning cloth in the trash. I knew better. There were protocols, rules I needed to follow. I was so tired, Zander…so tired."

"I know sweetheart, I know. Tell me what happened next, Dani."

She turns to me then and she's looking at me like I should know what happened. I think I do, but I need to hear it from her lips. I need to hear her hell and then I need to spend the rest of my life, dragging her far away from it.

"Michael said if I couldn't remember to clean up after myself, he'd fix it so I'd never have to worry about it again," she says, her hand gripping her stomach so tight under my hand, I get afraid she is going to hurt herself. I move down to kiss her hand slowly, so not to startle her. I pull her fingers from her stomach."

Fuck, no.

"What did he do, Dani?"

"He cut…he…there was a knife…he was so mad. I should have known better. I was stupid. So stupid," she whispers crying. The tears are silent, there are no loud sobs. I think if there was, I could handle them better. No, these are just long silent tear drops falling from her eyes and her eyes are full of grief.

"I'm sorry baby, I'm so sorry. I pull her hand up and kiss her stomach, the skin there is smooth. There are two little small scars. One on the edge of her belly-button, and the other underneath it.

"Did they arrest him, sweetheart?" I ask, knowing that they must have, but needing assurance. I'm going to have Freak start hunting this motherfucker down—tonight.

"No, Michael sat on the board of the hospital. It's amazing what money can do," she whispers. "Besides he had them convinced I did it, because I didn't want the baby."

"Baby?" I ask my heart coming to a stop before painfully starting again. There was so much more than there should have been. Her words come back to me. Shit! She had miscarried and then the fucking son of a bitch…I couldn't even think of the words. I couldn't.

"I hated her father, Zander. I did…but I would have wanted my baby. I would have loved her…"

That's when the silent tears break over into full sobs. I kiss her stomach and then lay beside her, and gather her in my arms letting her cry. Hell I want to join her. I brush her hair over and over with my hand, letting my fingers sift through the dark waves. Each tear she sheds breaks me a little more.

I was going to find this Michael and kill him. Then bring him back just to kill him again, over and over.

Motherfucker, I was going to kill him so many times his corpse will rot before I am finished.

Chapter 23

DANI

I'VE HEARD OF the morning after regrets, but I've never allowed myself to have them. I'm having them now—although probably not the same kind that everyone talks about. I can't believe I told Zander all of that last night. Why? Why would I do that? I've never told another person that, not even Nicole.

I wake up alone in bed. I panic at first. Maybe I gave too much away and Zander cut his losses. I've kind of been expecting that, so it wouldn't be a surprise. Then I hear noises coming from downstairs. Happiness and fear swamp me at the same time. I have to fight the urge to pull the covers over my head and pretend nothing happened last night. I've run away enough though. So I force myself up and run to brush my teeth and clean up a little.

In the bathroom the strangest sensation hits me. I see Zander's toothbrush next to mine. It's silly and shouldn't mean anything, but as I touch it. I feel warm—happy. I'm still grinning as I finish brushing my teeth and sliding on a clean pair of panties over Zander's t-shirt. I run a brush through my hair and just pull it up in a ponytail. Then, I make my way downstairs.

Zander is standing at the stove…cooking. He's wearing his jeans and nothing else. I might be slightly twisted, but the sight of him barefoot in my kitchen I find...sexy.

"I thought the woman was supposed to cook," I say because I feel awkward staring at him with my tongue hanging out and nothing to say.

"Sweetheart, you're a hell of a woman, but you can't cook worth shit."

I smile, because really he's not lying. I never had to cook. Michael had personal chefs and Nicole was freaking Betty Crocker. I do have one secret, I wonder what he would say if I told him I could mix any drink known to man and make some that he's never heard of that would knock his socks off? Probably nothing it's not a great talent, I suppose.

"Is it manly for a biker to cook?"

"When it's me? Definitely."

He has a point because when he turns to the side and winks at me I look down that delicious tatted chest, over those washboard abs, and finally to the 'v' indentions on his side and notice the button on his pants is left undone, I'm instantly aroused—weak in the knees even.

"Hellcat, if you don't get that look off your face we're not going to be having breakfast anytime soon."

"What are we having?"

"Bacon and eggs," he replies turning back around.

"Well, I'd be alright with waiting then..." I answer him.

He turns around and looks at me and his eyes rake over me intently. Then he pushes the skillet he's working with off the burner and turns it off. He wipes his hand on a dish towel before throwing it on the kitchen table I'm standing beside.

"Are you sure you up for it, Hellcat? You had a bad night last night."

I feel heat hit my face. I don't really want to talk about it, but I force myself to not back down.

"I miss you," I answer honestly.

His rough, callused fingertip brushes along the side of my face. The scratchy feeling, combined with the heated look in his eyes sets my pulse to racing.

"God, you're beautiful."

His gruff voice dances over me and when he's looking at me like that, I believe it—or at least believe he feels that way.

"Does this mean we're going to have bacon and eggs later?" I ask, dying to have him inside of me again. He's a drug and I'm completely addicted.

"Undress for me, Hellcat."

He tells me, standing back with his ankles crossed, his arms are folded and he's leaning back against the stove. He looks every inch the cocky male that I should run from, but instead I'm completely captured by this man. I have a moment of nerves before I lift his shirt up and throw it on the floor, leaving me standing in nothing but a pair of purple boy-cut panties.

"Those too, Dani."

I swallow nervously, but peel them down and kick them next to the shirt. He walks towards me. He reminds me of a jungle cat on the prowl. My heart kicks up, because I know I'm the one he is stalking.

"Do you know what upset me the most about last night, Hellcat?" He asks. One of his hands starts along my ribs and travels down to my hip. His other hand is playing with the ends of my hair and he uses a finger to trace along my collarbone.

"What?" I ask, and my voice comes out breathless, my knees feel weak and I feel these tiny electrical charges zapping all over my body, leaving goosebumps in its wake.

"That you would think I would choose Carrie over you. Hell picking anyone over you would be stupid. Do you think

I'm a stupid man, Hellcat?"

One finger slowly trails under the swell of my breast and I hiss at the excitement churning inside of me.

"She'd be a better choice for you," I answer honestly.

He pinches my nipple hard and I gasp from the sting of pain. I should hate it, but I feel moisture gather between my legs.

"Do you think I'm a stupid man, Hellcat?" He asks again.

"I'm broken, Zander," I finally tell him with complete honesty.

He leans down and sucks my nipple into his mouth, teasing it with his tongue. My hands come up to hold his head, my fingers tighten in his dark mane. He releases it and the popping sound blends with my moan of pleasure. He slowly begins kissing down my stomach, sliding to his knees in front of me. He places small, sweet kisses on my waist and stomach, his tongue following the path. When he comes to my belly button his tongue flicks in and out of it before biting into the delicate skin. My knees threaten to buckle. His hands grab my hips and he looks up at me, his eyes look like pools of dark ink—intense...all consuming.

"Why are there no scars, sweetheart?" It wasn't what I expected and I feel the urge to shrink back inside myself. I fight it off. I can do this.

"It's amazing what the right doctors and money can do."

His eyes hold mine, but he doesn't reply. I'm so focused on watching his face and on waiting for his reply that I didn't expect his fingers to push inside of me and I gasp at the welcomed shock.

"My Hellcat is already wet for me."

"Zander," I moan as he pushes against my leg to make me widen my stance.

"You didn't answer me earlier. Do you think I'm stupid?"

As he asks the question, at least two of his fingers are moving slowly in and out of me and his other hand is spreading my pussy open for him. The cool breeze of the ceiling fan hits my sensitive skin and combines with his hot breath and the chill spreads through my system and I moan from the excitement building inside. Zander pulls me in and weaves a spell around me. He makes me someone I don't even recognize, but someone I want to keep being...His.

He flattens his tongue out against my pussy and licks me, just once. He finishes by flicking his tongue on my clit and thrusting his fingers hard inside of me.

"So good, Zander. God, you're so good."

In response he sucks my throbbing clit into his mouth and traps it between his teeth and then bites.

I jump at the unexpected pain. I start to complain, but he soothes it with his tongue. He stops his fingers though, and I moan at the loss.

"You didn't answer, Hellcat. Do you think I'm stupid?"

I look at him confused. I feel like if he doesn't continue soon I'm going to combust.

"No..."

"Who did I claim, Dani?"

"Me..."

"Good girl," he says getting up. I want to beg him not to stop, but I'm so drugged with desire and confusion, I can do nothing but watch him.

He sits down at the table, pulling his chair back. He looks at me expectantly.

"What...?" I ask, because he keeps looking at me like I should be doing something.

"Get up on the table and give me breakfast woman," he

orders.

"Me...On the table?"

"I'm going to spread you out on this table. I'm going to eat your sweet little pussy until you fuck my face so hard you come all over it. I'm not going to stop until you admit that you're mine and realize that I don't want any other woman, but you."

"Zander," I try to interrupt, but he doesn't let me.

"And finally, I'm going to give you my dick and fuck you hard. I'm not going to stop until you understand once and for all that the only fucking reason you're not wearing my cut and my name is because you're the one not ready and after hearing about your past—I get that. Still, you gave me your body and you're giving me more. So, I can wait, because I know what I want—I got what I want, right here. Now get your fucking ass on this table and give me my breakfast."

His words hit me. I mean they hit me. Everything that he says, all that he says, pierces me and lodges deep inside. It hits in spots that have been so empty, so raw and alone for so long, I thought they were dead. I have what I want, right here. How is it that seven words can rock the foundation of your whole world, but make you feel like you could fly at the same time? I love this man. I've only loved four people in my entire life; my mom, Nic, Ray and now...Zander. I love him. It scares me, it terrifies me, but his words give me courage. Courage, because I know he means them and I trust him. I trust him completely.

So, even though my legs are shaking I walk to him. I slide up on the kitchen table and sit in front of him.

"Lay back, Hellcat," he orders, making no effort to move. His voice brusque and demanding.

I do as he tells me, bringing my knees up and bracing the bottoms of my feet on the table. I hear a chair scrape against the floor and then his hands are pulling my legs up on his shoulders. I barely have time to adjust before his face pushes against my pussy and he starts tasting, licking and eating me as if he were a dying man and I was the only thing that could save his life.

It's an apt analogy, because he *is* saving me…one broken piece at a time.

I love him.

Chapter 24

CRUSHER

"Hellcat?" I whisper, as I sneak into her room. It's after three a.m. and I'm fucking killed. So much has been going on at the club in the last six months. It feels like I never look up. Dancer came home and though that was a good thing, he's got some heavy shit on his shoulders and he's still having trouble adapting. He and Carrie are expecting a baby and that seems to have helped. What hasn't helped was the club finally discovering who was behind paying Irish and Twist. The trail led us straight to the father of the man Dancer killed.

Fucker almost took me, Dance, Carrie and Bull out before we got him, but we managed to survive and get the motherfucker. Bull was hurt pretty bad, he's a tough son of a bitch, though. He had to be, to survive having his brain bashed in and then being stuck in an explosion. It's left him with a lot of problems, but I know he'll come out of it.

The constant uproar and danger was wearing the club down, but it was also the one thing that convinced Dani to move into the clubhouse full time. Which was damn good, because Dragon is keeping me so fucking busy, if she didn't live here I'd hardly get to see her. I need that woman more than air at this point. I'm completely, lost in her. The only thing giving us any trouble is that she's still hiding the fact that we're together. It's pissing me off. She has this idea in her head that Dragon would forbid it and it would cause me trouble in the club. I told her I didn't give a fuck and she was wrong, but she panics. She's not ready to tell Nicole yet either. That's going to have to change soon. Gunner and Freak already know about it and I'm pretty sure Dragon and the others suspect it. Kind of hard not to, when we fuck anywhere and everywhere we get a chance. My woman is adventurous, hot, needy and always ready. The only thing I can't seem to talk her into is giving me her mouth. She hasn't told me a lot about her past, but I know her problems with it begins and ends there. I'm patient. I can wait, and honestly if I never get that from her, with everything else she gives me, I don't give a fuck.

I go over to the bed and she's asleep, a better man wouldn't wake her. I'm a bastard though and I need her. I strip down quickly and slide into bed behind her. She wiggles that naked ass of hers against my dick and I nearly moan out loud.

"I told you not to get in bed with me this late. My boyfriend will be home any minute," she whispers and I smile at the joy I hear in her voice. I did that. I bring her joy. She's completely different with me than she is with everyone else.

"How long do you think we have before he shows up?" I ask, playing along.

"How long do you think it will take you to make me come?" She asks barely able to hide her giggle.

"One minute," I answer, only slightly exaggerating. Over the months we've been together, I've memorized her. I know the sensitive spots and the ones that bring her the most pleasure by heart. Fuck, I dream of them. I'm pretty sure I could make her detonate in under three minutes. Good thing I'm not that stupid. I love bringing her along slowly, torturing her until her need overwhelms her.

She lets out this big sigh and I hear the laughter in her

voice. "It's not bad enough you short change 'Junior'. Now you're trying to become a minute man. I feel it only fair to warn you that women like men that last a long time."

"I haven't noticed you complaining," I tell her pulling her back against me, so I can hold her tight.

"I didn't want to hurt your feelings."

"How thoughtful of you," I say sarcastically, burying my face in her neck and breathing in her scent.

"I try. You doing okay? Did you get everything squared away?" She asks and I kiss her neck, tasting the slightly salty skin there, wanting more.

"Yeah babe, it was a quick run. Dragon wanted to make sure we were back for the party tomorrow," I answer. Me, Dragon, Six and Gun all went to Gadsden, Alabama. We needed to personally oversee a shipment of guns that the parent chapter of Savage MC was sending through our state and up to Ohio. We've had so much trouble lately that this was one thing we could not have a fuck-up with. That shit is getting embarrassing and makes our club look weak. We can't afford more and risk the parent chapter wading into our local business. Luckily tonight's shipment went well, since Dragon was dying to get back. There's a party tomorrow to celebrate their upcoming wedding and the fact that Nicole is pregnant. Which brings me back to what I want to talk to Dani about.

"I think we need to announce that you and I are a couple tomorrow."

Her whole body tenses up, "No."

It's one word, but hearing it so adamant even after all this time, pisses me off. I mean hell, I'm starting to feel like the dirty secret she's embarrassed of and hides.

"Dani…"

"No. It's Dragon and Nicole's big day. That's not the right

time to tell the club about us, Zander."

"Half the club already fucking knows. It'd be better if Dragon and Nicole heard it from us, instead of others," I argue but honestly, it's the same argument I've been using since that day in her kitchen months and months ago. I don't understand and I'm getting fucking tired. I love this woman, but I'm not sure I want to continue with a woman who can't even admit to people she wants me.

"Only Gunner and Freak know. Will you let this go? I told you I'm not ready, Zander."

I shouldn't have brought this up tonight. I'm tired and worn out and I should have just gone to sleep and let it be. Trouble is, I've been away from Dani for two nights. I missed the fucking hell out of her and for some reason I thought us being apart even for two damn days might make her realize that it's time we make it official. I had myself convinced she would be ready and the fact that she's not sits bitter in my gut.

"I'm starting to think you're never going to be ready, Hellcat."

"I will, it's just. There's things I'm dealing with, things I need to make sure are over before I close the door on the past," she says and her voice is small and hurting. Any other time I would cave, but her words just piss me off all the more.

"Fine, then tell me what the fuck is in your past."

"I've told you..."

"No, you tell me bits and pieces that leave me stumbling around in the dark."

"I've told you more than I've ever told anyone," she defends, her voice full of panic.

"Bullshit! I've spent over six months searching for this motherfucker, Michael Smith. I've searched in Texas, and any state close to Kentucky. Hell, I've searched in fucking Italy because you mentioned your mom had family there. Give me something, Hellcat. Jesus."

The vibe in the room has changed. If I wasn't so upset, I would have noticed it. Trouble is my anger is amped up and my frustration is so big that I don't—until it's too late.

Dani reaches over and turns the bedside light on. Her face is pale, her eyes haunted and the tears in them aren't what finally gut-punches me. No, that would be the stark fear that is coming off of her in waves.

"You…you've been searching for…you've been trying to find Michael?"

"Of course I have. Do you think I'm going to let that motherfucker live after the hell he put you through. I'm going cut a piece out of him every day for a month before I finally end the motherfucker."

"I…you…why didn't you tell me this? Zander, you can't find Michael."

"I fucking will. Mark that down, Hellcat. I will find him and drag his ass to Kentucky," I tell her completely serious.

She jumps out of bed, and the fear coming from her is so large you can almost smell it in the room. She goes to her closet, pulls out a pair of jeans and begins putting them on.

"What the fuck are you doing? Do you know what time it is? Get back in this bed, Dani."

"I can't believe you. I let you in. I trusted you and you go behind my back and do this? Do you have any idea what would happen if Michael knew where I was? I barely got away last time! Are you trying to get me killed? To get Nicole killed? Do you have any idea what you've done?"

"Fuck no I don't, because you won't tell me shit! So tell me so I can end this sorry son of a bitch once and for all and stop my woman living in fear all the time!"

She yanks my shirt off and throws it at me, slides on a blue t-shirt of hers, and then finishes turning, staring at me. Her face is a combination of fear, anger and…fuck I've seen that face. I know that face. She's going to run. Just like Melly, she'll run and I won't be able to save her. Only this time it will destroy me. I loved Mel, I did in a sweet and young love kind of way. We would have been happy, but Dani…fuck she owns me.

"I told you shit. I told you it didn't matter. I told you I got away and asked you to leave it alone. You told me you would. You lied, Zander! I trusted you. I gave myself to you! You're the first man I've ever willingly given myself to and you lied! You have no idea…none. My God! If Michael knows someone is searching for him, it's just a matter of time. You'll have killed the only people in the world I care about."

"Damn it, stop being a drama queen! He's one fucking man! I got this shit. You just need to trust me."

"Drama queen? That man you're trying to bring back to Kentucky, bring back to me is evil."

"I can be too, especially when a son of a bitch is messing with someone I love!"

She stops and I think, finally. Finally I've gotten through to her.

"What you've done could kill the only people I've ever loved. Nicole and Ray are all I have in the world. You could have killed them. Hell what you did still might."

Her words slice me open in a way no blade ever could.

"You have me, damn it!"

She looks at me with tears pouring down her face.

"I don't want you."

"What the hell, damn it, Dani!"

"Get out!"

"I'm not going…"

"Get the fuck out. I wanted to find out about sex. I wanted no strings. I wanted your dick—not you! That's why I kept us a secret! I thought we were just having fun. This is not fun anymore. I don't want you in my life. Get the fuck out!"

I thought we were just having fun. I wanted your dick—not you…

Well hell, I don't need a brick house to fall on me. Or shit maybe I did, because it sure feels like something has slammed on my chest and is not allowing me to breathe. I leave with a slam of the door. Fuck this, ain't no pussy worth this shit.

Chapter 25

DANI

IT'S JUST BEEN a few days and I ache for him. I crave him. I'm on day three of hell. Living here at the club and seeing Zander every day, but not talking to him, not touching him or even having his smile when we pass, is destroying me. I regretted the shit I said to him the minute I did it. I just couldn't stop. The thought that Zander was out there trying to find Michael, chills me to the bone. If Michael knew where I was, he wouldn't rest until he killed Zander. He wouldn't stand for any man touching what he deemed his property. Hell he killed the gardener for just smiling at me once. He bragged for a week on how he made it appear the man had accidentally locked himself in the greenhouse and the propane heater had a malfunction causing carbon monoxide to build up. He would torture Zander just to get to me, because he would know it would hurt me.

Zander thinks he and the club can handle Michael. He has no idea how powerful Michael is. He doesn't know who Michael has in his back pocket or the shit he has on government officials that assure he's not going to get caught. He thinks Michael is a fuck-up who gets his rocks off on beating women. If he knew the truth? There would be no controlling Zander on avenging me. Or even worse Michael would do just like he had done with the doctors and the police. He would tell

Zander about my hospital stay in Rose Hill and convince him I was insane. He would convince Zander that he was the wronged husband trying to heal the crazy woman. I've seen him do it over and over. I couldn't handle that look in Zander's eyes. It would destroy me.

Michael can't be stopped. The fact that he had me admitted into a psychiatric facility so easily, just because I refused to marry him, showed me that. It made me fall in line—well, after being locked up for a month. Had I known the brutal hell that awaited me on the outside, I would have gladly spent the rest of my days behind the gray walls and steel bars of Rose Hill. Besides, everything that Michael has gotten away with since then, shows me he's invincible. From the murders, to the cops in his back pocket, to the doctors who sided with him along with the lawyers and court judges—with all those on his side, there's nothing Zander could do to Michael. Trying would either put him behind bars like Dancer, or get him killed. I can't risk either. I love him.

I need to move. I can't go back to the house because Carrot Top and Dancer have moved in there. I should go back to Ray and Paul's. I have a room there, they want me. I can't bring myself to move away from Zander. At least not yet. The thought of not seeing him every day, at least from a distance brings a panic more intense than any I've ever had.

I'm out back of the main Savage MC Compound, where they usually have the parties and bonfires. I'm sitting on an old picnic table thumbing through the rental adds in the local London newspaper. My heart's not in it. It's just not. I'm about to highlight a listing that's downtown next to the restaurant that Nic and I like to eat at a lot, when a large hand swipes the paper away.

"What the fuck is this?"

Zander.

"It's a newspaper, Captain Obvious."

"You aren't fucking leaving, Dani."

"There's no reason for me to stay here anymore, Phoenix has been caught." I tell him, referring to the man who tried to get revenge on Dancer and the rest of the crew. "In fact, all the Savage Brothers' drama has quieted down. Nicole is growing fat and planning a wedding, Carrie is growing fat and playing house with Dancer. All is right with the world. It's time I strike out on my own."

"You don't think I'm reason enough for you to stay here?"

Yes! My heart cries. I ignore it, for a question I need to know the answer to. "Did you stop looking for Michael, yet?"

Silence.

I nod in response. "Then no, you aren't enough," I lie.

"So it's all your way or no way, Hellcat?"

"On this? Yeah it is."

"If I agree? If I give up and accept your terms and stay away from searching this Michael out? What do I get?"

"What do you want?" I ask, my heart hammering in my chest.

"You."

"You had me."

"Without restrictions. No more sneaking, no more hiding that you're mine. You take my claim, you wear my jacket and you fucking wear my name."

Again, my heart screams yes. Then, I remember that Michael is out there and I remember what he could do to Zander and I…panic. I want to. Would it be safe? Michael would never look for me in the midst of a motorcycle club. It wouldn't ever occur to him that the woman he once knew would do that. Would it be fair to Zander?

"I'm...scared," I whisper quietly, because ultimately it all boils down to that.

"Have I ever done anything Hellcat, to make you think you should fear me?"

"I need to go slowly, Zander. I have to..."

"I have to have more than we did before."

My stomach knots up. I understand, but it doesn't make it any easier.

"I liked what we had before..."

His hand pulls my chin up so my eyes meet his. I will never get over the fact that this man could easily be a Greek god. His dark eyes pull me in and they refuse to let me go.

"Hellcat, give in."

"Why are you making this all or nothing?"

"Because woman, I love you. Do you not fucking get that?"

It's the second time he's said it really. The first time, I didn't allow myself time to think on it. This time I try to let the words sink in.

"You promise me, Zander. If I tell you more about me...about why I'm this way...you'll stop seeking out Michael. You'll help me move forward and give me time?"

"As long as you really try, then abso-fucking-lutely, Hellcat."

"I love you..." I whisper, because I feel like he should know.

"Hellcat," his voice drops down to a whisper. It's thick and full of emotion, but I push ahead before I can second guess myself.

"I warned you I am broken, Zander. I can't give you what you want. At least not right now."

"What are you gaining by keeping us secret, Hellcat? Tell

me."

I think about his question—really think about it. It might not make sense, but I'm protecting him. If people don't know, if it's not common knowledge, then if the devil finds me Zander won't be a target.

"Safety," I tell him. He looks confused. He doesn't get it, I can tell from the look in his eyes.

"This back and forth, push and pull needs to stop between us."

I don't know what to say to that, so I just stay quiet.

"If I agree to this shit? If I give you a little more time, you're going to tell me about your past. You're going to trust me and you are going to accept my claim eventually. Let me hear those words out of that damned mouth of yours."

Just agreeing to this is causing my heart to stutter and a cold, clammy sweat to pop out over my body. "If you promise to leave Michael alone, then yes," I qualify.

"And you'll be in my bed tonight?"

I don't even have to think about that answer, "Definitely."

"Then we have a deal, Hellcat."

Chapter 26

CRUSHER

I'M LYING THROUGH my fucking teeth, but if it gets my woman back in my bed, if it gets me the names I need to end the son of a bitch who hurt her and most of all gets her to the point where she will finally accept my claim, then I will lie. Fuck, the truth is, after a few days and nights without her, I'd do almost anything.

"Isn't it kind of early to go to bed?" She asks as we make it back to my room. I lock the door with a lazy smile.

"If we were going to bed, maybe."

She turns and looks at me and I can tell she's nervous, but she's also excited. She wants this.

"Hellcat, I should warn you, this won't be my finest hour, because I want you too damn much to make it last," I say while stripping.

"The fact that you're saying it will last an hour proves you're wrong," she says taking her clothes off too.

Any other time I'd undress her, but I am dying here. I've spent the last two nights without her and fuck me, I need her. When I look up, she's finishing taking off her panties and bra. She's beautiful. I've always known it, but right now it's driven home what a lucky bastard I am. Dani and I have so much back and forth arguing, then fucking and then arguing some more, sometimes I give myself whiplash. The truth is I don't know shit about relationships and Dani's so messed up from her fucker of an ex that I doubt it could be any different, but even with all the conflict—it's better than anything I've ever had. It's better than anything I've ever imagined.

I take her in my arms and instantly that empty spot that has haunted me the last few nights, is gone. She links her hands behind my neck and pulls my head down to her lips. Her warm skin is pressed against mine, but it's still not close enough. I don't think it ever will be.

"I've missed you, Zander," she whispers, her sweet lips grazing my five o'clock shadow, her teeth nibbling the same path.

"God I have you too, baby. Climb up here on the bed and let me love you," I demand anxious to get inside of her.

"I…I don't want that," she says pulling back slightly and disappointment swamps me.

"Hellcat, I know you…"

"Sit down on the bed, Zander," her quiet plea has me catching my breath. I've always been the type to demand what I want in the bedroom, but right now I can think of nothing I'd rather do than obey Dani. I don't know what she has in mind, but I'm anxious to find out.

I turn so my back is to the bed. I keep one of her hands in mine and my eyes on her, I back up the few steps it takes until my legs hit the mattress. I sit down. Slowly she lowers down in front of me on her knees. I don't know how it's possible but two emotions war with each other immediately. First and foremost is the urge to scream yes at the top of my lungs. Then guilt because I know she's scared of this. I don't know why, but I do know whatever the story is behind it, will be bad.

"Dani, sweetheart, you don't have to do this," I tell her and I end my sentence on a groan as she takes my cock in her warm hand and strokes it once.

"I want to do this, Zander. I might be a little unsure, but I've been imagining giving you this for weeks. I want to make you happy. I want to give you pleasure."

"My sweet, Hellcat," I whisper, bending down to kiss her. "I love that you want that, but it shouldn't be all about me. Anything we do together should bring us both pleasure. If it doesn't then we shouldn't do it."

"But…how?" She asks confused and I'm not exactly sure what she's asking, but I go with it.

"How about you just play a little and if you don't like it you climb up on my dick and ride me? I ask and when she still looks nervous, I add, "Anytime Hellcat, you never have to do anything here. I want you, just you and anyway I can get you." I tell her, trying to reassure her. Then, I wait to see what happens.

Her hand reaches down first to cup my balls. I want to moan out loud at the way she gently massages them, as if she is testing their weight. Her hand comes up and wraps around my cock and pumps it up, and then slowly down.

"Before you, Zander…do you know I thought a man's penis was ugly? I would have been happy never seeing another one in my life," she says stroking me one more time.

"They all are except for Junior, Hellcat. Not even worth your time." I tell her trying to joke, but the words come out in a moan because she places a chaste kiss against the head of my dick.

She rubs her lips together. I know she tastes me, because my cock is weeping for her. I hold my breath wondering what will happen next. I don't have a long wait. She runs her tongue over my head again, gathering more fluid and bringing it into her mouth. I watch her tongue move and become hypnotized with the movements. I'm so lost that I'm completely unprepared for the way her mouth slides down over the head. I want her to go further. It takes all I have, not to grab her by the hair and push her farther down on me. I catch my hands half way there and divert them to her tits. I don't want to scare her. Her nipples are hard and begging for attention. I roll them between my thumb and index fingers, teasing them. Her mouth slides down a little more on my shaft and I tug on her nipples as a reward, before going back to playing with them gently. One of her hands is still massaging my balls and it feels so good I could honestly come from just this alone. That won't happen though, because she slides further down my cock nearly taking my entire length into her mouth. Heaven—motherfucking heaven.

I groan out loud from the combination of the soft, wet hot haven of her mouth and the way her tongue is caressing my length. She holds still and looks up at me with her eyes. My hand shakes like a fucking school boy as I move her hair out of the way. I've been a man whore. I love women and I love fucking, but I don't think I've seen anything sexier in my life than the sight of Dani on her knees in front of me, her mouth full of my cock, her eyes dark with need and my hands full of her breasts.

"It feels good, Hellcat," I'm lying because it's so fucking more than good. I'm not sure there are words invented to describe it. "Suck me, baby. Suck my dick hard, please?" I add, holding her breasts completely in my hands and squeezing them repeatedly, loving the way they contract and expand in my hands.

Dani's eyes close and she sucks hard. She works my cock with her mouth while using her hand to stroke me at the same time. If I allowed myself I would have already shot my load.

Someday soon, I plan on coming this way. Just not today. I move my hands under her arms lift her up. She reluctantly lets go of my cock with a popping noise. She stands up on her own and looks down at me in confusion.

"What? Why did you stop me? Was I doing it wrong?"

"Hellcat, listen to me. Nothing you give me will ever be wrong."

"Then what..."

"I need the taste of your pussy on my tongue."

"Right now? But I was enjoying sucking on you. I wasn't done," she says almost in a pout and I grin. It will take us a while to get there, but this woman is perfect for me.

"That's good because you're going to keep doing it," I answer, and then I lie back on the bed. "Climb up here and sit on my face, Hellcat. I'm about to show you why sixty-nine is the best fucking number ever made."

She looks unsure, but crawls up on the bed and straddles my face.

"That's it baby, now lie down against me and take my cock back in that beautiful mouth of yours, while I make you feel good."

It takes her a few minutes to get settled, but she stretches out and slowly my cock slides back into that hot little mouth. I moan out my pleasure against her pussy. I use my tongue to delve into her hole and then back out to flick that hard little clit over and over, lashing it. I push my finger into her ass and use my other hand to push her deep into me, encouraging her to ride my face. Her pussy tastes so sweet and tangy and I know it's a taste that I will need every day for the rest of my life.

We work together, as if we've been fucking together our entire life. She's devouring my cock while I'm trying to do the same with her juicy little cunt. Her essence is sliding along her legs and bathing my face. Her clit is so hard it quivers every time I run my tongue over it. When she starts rotating her hips against my face, clenching so fucking hard she could smother me and riding me faster and faster—I know we're close to the end. That's good because my balls are so full, I'm about to lose it. I use her own wetness, by gathering it on my fingers and then sliding them into her tight little ass. I begin fucking her ass hard with two fingers, doing my best to keep her pussy hard against my mouth, and eating her out like a starving man. She's taken the entire length of my shaft in her mouth. I tongue fuck her over and over in tandem with my fingers, using my free hand to grind her back and forth on my face. She has all of my cock and sucking it so hard, I'm surprised she's not choking on it. Then she groans, the sound vibrating against my dick and her pussy spasms and I know she's done. She comes all over my face. I drink her in, continuing to fuck her harder and harder, not allowing her to come down. As her second orgasm begins on the heels of her last one I lose it. My cum jets into her mouth. I hear her grunt and her mouth slides up letting cool air hit my dick. I jerk and quiver in her hand, as she continues sucking on my head, swallowing me down.

Eventually we clean up in the shower, go another round while we're there, and then slide back under the covers. I'm holding her close, enjoying having her in my arms. Feeling at peace with the world in general right now. It's early, barely dusk, but I'm not moving the rest of the night. About the only thing I plan on doing tonight is fucking my woman again.

"Wow," she says after curling into my side and laying her head on my shoulder. I bend down and kiss the top of her head, my fingers again finding their way into her hair, which is slightly damp from our shower.

"You can say that again," I whisper, nuzzling her soft hair

and placing yet another kiss, before lying back and staring up at the ceiling.

"I wish I had met you six years ago," she says sometime later. Her voice sounding sad.

"We've got each other now."

"I would have been better for you six years ago. Six years ago, I wasn't broken, I wasn't afraid, I could have loved you with a whole heart."

I study her words, dissect them.

"Is that when you met Michael?"

"I was so young and stupid. Graduating high school and thought I knew everything. Michael was older, good-looking, charismatic, rich, all those things you read in books that make the perfect man."

I knock down the jealousy inside of me at her words. It's not the time. Still, it will give me another reason to kill the motherfucker.

"I think that's my biggest guilt, the thing that sticks with me the most..." Her voice is weak and full of distaste.

"What's that, Hellcat?"

"The fact that in the beginning, I wanted his attention. I enjoyed being around him. I wanted his touch."

"That changed?"

"There was something off about him, something that didn't feel good about him. I didn't notice it at first. At first I was totally lost in my first taste of young love. I had men after me before because of my dad's money, but Michael had his own. So, his interest had to be just in me, you know?"

I don't say anything. She's talking freely and my mind is busy making notes. Finding new layers to Dani that I didn't know existed. Her fingers are tracing one of the tattoos on my chest, so I just continue stroking her hair and listening, afraid to bring her out of the place she seems to have slipped into.

"Slowly though, things started happening that set off alarm bells."

So much for remaining quiet. When she doesn't continue I urge her on, "Like what?" I have to have this information.

"Kissing me a little too rough, grabbing me when he was upset and leaving bruises. Things he would later apologize for. He would send me flowers or diamonds to make up. Until that one day."

"What happened then?"

"It was innocent really. I was waiting for Michael at his home. He had his driver pick me up and told me to make myself at home, that he would be home late. He was stuck in Manhattan at the office."

Manhattan? Drivers?

"He told me to bring my swim suit because we were going to fly to Rio for the weekend. I didn't really want to go, Daddy insisted. I think he was planning even then, but I didn't know it at the time."

"Planning what?"

"Marrying me off so his company would merge with Michael's. He had ideas of becoming the biggest shipping conglomerate in the world or at least the Eastern seaboard."

My mind is reeling at the information. Holy fuck. I had no idea.

"Since working late to Michael always meant really late and that meant not going to Rio, I decided to swim. I did my usual laps and laid in the chaise. I must have fell asleep…"

"What happened then?"

"When I woke up the gardener was standing over me. It scared me at first. He was Michael's age, not as good-looking, but he had these beautiful blue eyes that shined. He was sweet.

We talked about the flowers he was growing in the greenhouse. I fixed him a sandwich and we were still talking when Michael came home."

"What happened then?" I asked when she got quiet.

"I learned my lesson," she said and something about the way she said it made me not question her further.

"Why do you call me Hellcat?"

"Because you're a pussy with claws," I answer her easily.

"Gee, Zander that's romantic."

"But when I make you purr, it's so good I just know I'd brave the fires of hell to have more."

"That's slightly better."

"I try."

"I should be sleepy," she mumbles placing a kiss on my shoulder.

"You're not?"

"Nope, not even a little bit," she says and then gasps as I lift her on top of me.

"What are you doing?"

"Helping you get sleepy, Hellcat," I tell her as I hold my cock and let her lower down on me. I watch my cock slowly disappear inside of her and can't imagine a better feeling in the world. Her moan sounds like one of agreement.

Later that night while she's sleeping I get out of bed and make my way to Freak's office. It's an attached room in the club. It's bigger than the other members have, but then it is where the security feeds are kept, the businesses we own are monitored and whatever the hell else Freak does that is over my damned head.

"Hey what's up, man?" He asks when I enter the room.

"I got a bigger lead on that Michael I had you searching for."

"Well that's good because I can't find a Michael Smith that fits any of the details you gave me."

"Yeah well, that's because his last name isn't Smith."

"Well fuck, Crush man, I can't perform miracles. You have to get me the right information here."

"I don't have a last name but I have more details."

Freak sighs, but gets a pen. "Go ahead, give it to me."

"His name is Michael, asshole is loaded. He runs a large shipping business and it's based in New York, possibly Manhattan."

"Fuck me."

"See what you come up with okay?"

"Yeah, okay I got some shit I'm working on for Dragon that comes first, but I'll get to it tomorrow at the latest."

"Good enough, just keep this between us, okay?"

"Does this mean more shit is headed towards the club?"

"This is personal, that's all you need to know."

"Whatever. Talk to you later."

"You got it," I tell him, closing the door. I know I promised Dani, but I am going to kill this motherfucker and get rid of the ghosts I see in her eyes. She may get mad, but in the end she'll thank me. I'm sure of it.

Chapter 27

MICHAEL

"**D**O YOU HAVE an update for me, Donald?" I ask while going through the files my secretary put on my desk. I have an important business meeting in the next thirty-minutes and I really don't have time to fool with my fucking cunt of a wife. Still, if the lead from Kentucky turns out to be solid, then I will act upon it. No woman makes a fool out of me, especially not Melinda.

"Yes sir, the person or persons questioning and looking into your business history was in fact traced back to the Savage Brothers Motorcycle Club, in London, Kentucky."

"Interesting. And Melinda?"

"It is her sir, she seems to be staying here with that girl you didn't like from her college. Nicole Wentworth. Nicole is marrying the leader of this club. Melinda doesn't seem to be part of them, though she goes by the name Dani Smith now."

"Any other information?" I ask as the pencil in my hand snaps in two.

"No sir, I have started surveillance, per your order."

"Give me two days to get things in motion and then approach her with a meeting place and time. I will text you the information and Donald, I want pictures."

"They have already been uploaded to your personal phone, sir. Do you really think she will capitulate easily?"

"No, I'm counting on it being a fight. You and I both know how much fun that can be when it comes to Melinda."

"Yes sir, we do. I shall report in tonight."

"See that you do," I order, hitting the button and turning off the speakerphone.

I recline back in the seat as I think about the information I just received. Finally, after all this time I am literally days away from having Melinda in my grasp again. I'm going to kill her. It will be easy enough, since the world already thinks she is dead. First, I will make it hurt. I've always known she was alive, but I'll be the first to admit that the bitch covered her tracks well. I discovered the orderly's part in all of this to begin with. I should have had the employees taking care of my wife vetted better. Turned out he was the cousin to a former play toy. In gratitude for him helping my wife to escape, he died rather tragically in an automobile accident. People really should check their brakes on their vehicles before heading up to the mountains to ski.

I've been searching ever since, but the trail began and ended with the orderly. I did have Nicole watched for a month or so after Melinda's escape, but she appeared to be clean so I gave up that avenue. It is my fault I suppose. I should have had Nicole watched continuously. Oh well, you live and you learn. I have them both in my sight now and I think I should make the lovely Nicole suffer just as much as Melinda. Perhaps I shall make her give up her husband to be. After all, she stole my wife—it seems only fair.

I pick up my discarded cell phone and relax again pulling up the images that Donald sent me. I thumb through them slowly, taking every small change that Melinda has had over the years. The change in her hair color is annoying. She'll have to fix that. It's her natural color now, you can tell, but that is not what I like, now is it? When she dyes it, it will be with red hair, I decide. The pictures catch her, sitting outside on a picnic table, standing beside some men at an ambulance, and various other things. What catches my eye the most is the dancing. It appears my Melinda has been making a living taking her clothes off for strangers. I always knew she was a little whore, but the fact that she has turned her back so completely on her family name is sad. Her father warned me that her mother didn't exactly have good breeding, merely money. You get what you deserve, I suppose. I will make sure Melinda knows she cannot get away from me, and I will make her pay. Then, I will end her once and for all. I can't have her coming back from the dead. It took me too long to finally get my hands on her inheritance. I'm not about to give that up.

I click the button on my office phone to activate the intercom. My secretary voice rings out through the speaker.

"Yes, sir?"

"I need you to find some properties for sale in London, Kentucky."

"Kentucky, sir?" She asks, disbelief thick in her voice.

"Yes, I'm looking specifically for old abandoned factories, buildings with large square footage. I need it out of town or in a less crowded area."

"I'll get right on it, sir."

"Good. Also, the meetings today and the next three days can't be rearranged, however start clearing my calendar for the next three weeks."

"Three weeks, sir?"

"I believe that's what I said? Perhaps your time would be better spent doing as I say and not questioning me."

"Yes, sir. Anything else?"

"When you have the information I have requested, I think

it's time for a lesson in questioning your master, don't you, Ms. Caldwell?"

There's a moment of silence, before her voice comes back over the speaker.

"Yes, sir."

"Good, please come prepared by bringing the flogger I prefer, do not disappoint me by bringing the smaller one."

"Yes, sir. I understand."

I can hear the tremor of fear in her voice. It makes my dick throb. The best thing about my secretary is that she will take everything I give her because she needs the job. My specialty is finding the weak and exploiting them to my advantage. Ms. Caldwell's mother is in an expensive rehabilitation center after strokes have left her completely paralyzed. Bad for her, but very lucky for me. Very lucky indeed.

Chapter 28

CRUSHER

FUCK, LIFE IS good. When you wake up every morning and those are the first words you think, you know it's going to be a good damn day. Or, at least that's what you expect. Some days it doesn't work out that way. Still, waking up next to Dani, her taste still on my lips, my arms full of her and her 'I love you, Zander' being the first thing I hear, has a way of filling a man with hope. I've got that every morning for a solid month and it's been the fucking best month of my life. I've had it good with Dani before, but now we have less walls between us. She's even starting to show me more affection around the club. She's slowly coming out of her shell. She's still very careful what she lets slide in front of Dragon and Nicole, but I know eventually we'll get there.

I'm not a hopeful man. I'm a man who shoots straight from the hip, doesn't expect much, but is satisfied with the way life is. At least, I was until Dani. Having her, makes everything better and it makes it seem like anything is possible. She fills an emptiness that's been inside of me since losing Melly.

"What are you doing today, sweetheart?"

"More wedding stuff, I guess. Yuck."

"Not a fan of weddings?"

"Hell no," she says, kissing on the side of my neck. I don't know if it's because Dani discovered sex recently, or if it's just the way the two of us are going to be with each other, but we fuck so often my balls are staying sore and I don't even give a damn. Apparently, neither does Junior, because he's already standing at attention.

"Does this mean, you're going to make me live in sin the rest of my life?" I ask as my hand slides in between her ass cheeks. She pushes against my hand, showing me that she wants more and fuck, I'm ready to give it to her. I've slowly been getting her used to being fucked in the ass. First with my fingers and most recently I made her wear a plug in her ass all day. She was so fucking horny and wet by the end of the day, I wasn't sure my cock would survive.

"By living in sin, does that mean you're going to fuck me every day?" she asks her tongue sliding along my nipple, her ass thrusting back against my hand.

"Fuck, yeah."

"Then, yes please," she says, sucking my nipple into her mouth with a hungry moan.

I'm ready to get her on her hands and knees and fuck her hard and long, when a knock at the door makes me freeze. Dani continues teasing my nipples while her hand moves down to stroke my cock.

"Yeah?" I holler out, grunting as Dani moves those lips down my stomach.

"Hey, man? We need to talk," Freak calls out just as Dani takes my cock into her mouth.

I lean up on my arms to watch her mouth slide down on my shaft and her eyes stay on mine the entire time. So fucking hot. God, I'm a lucky S.O.B.

"Yeah, man, I'll catch up with you later," I tell Freak. Dani lets go of my cock slowly and this time sucks one of my balls in her mouth, using her tongue to caress it.

"Man, it's kind of important. I got that information on that Michael you asked about. You won't believe who this motherfucker is."

Dani freezes and her eyes lock with mine and three things hit me at once. One, the sheer look of terror on my woman's face. Two, the way it slowly merges into anger and even through the hate in her eyes, I see something worse. Betrayal. She thinks I betrayed her. I feel her fist slam down on my balls. I grab my crotch in reaction, cussing like a motherfucker, as the pain slams into me. It's one thing to get hit in the balls. It's another fucking thing to get hit in them when you are close to shooting your load. Son of a bitch! My boys may never recover.

"You promised! You fucking promised me!" She yells, sliding off the bed and going to the drawer she cleaned out for her clothes. She's pulling on some cut off blue jeans, her boobs completely bare, and if I didn't feel like my jewels are permanently out of commission, it would have been sexier than hell, except for the tears.

"Hellcat, I had to find him. I needed to make sure I kept you safe. I can't do that by burying my head in the sand."

"Trust me, you said. I've claimed you, you said. I'll never hurt you, you said! You're a motherfucking, son of a bitching, cock sucking liar!"

"Now wait just a fucking minute here," I growl jumping up. I'm fumbling with my pants putting them on and wince at the sting of pain my boys feel as I move them around. Fuck, couldn't I have picked a quiet, meek woman who didn't give me shit? "I am none of those things, damn it!"

"I can vouch that he doesn't suck cock," Freak says, as Dani pulls the door open while pulling her t-shirt down. Damn it! She needed to put on a mother-fucking bra!

She grabs the papers from Freak and turns to look at me.

"You promised that you wouldn't do this!"

"It had to be done! We have to deal with this shit."

"No! We don't. We don't have to deal with the fallout here. I do!"

"You're mine, that makes us a team and we'll deal with shit together, Dani! Stop trying to do all this shit on your own. You've been doing that for way too fucking long and we've seen the cluster-fuck that happens when you do!"

Fuck. I shouldn't have said that. I know it was wrong. I knew it the minute I said it and I know it even more when she blanches like I slapped the hell out of her.

"You have no fucking idea what you've done, Zander. I do. I've lived it. It's not us that will have to deal with the fallout, it's me. I'll be the one he will come after. Me and all the ones I love."

"You said you loved me that means the bastard will come after me and I want him to, I got this, Hellcat. Have faith in me."

"I did. You betrayed it," she says and her voice is full of pain now, the anger gone.

"Hellcat, let's talk about this."

"The time to talk would have been before you betrayed me," she says pushing Freak out of the way and leaving the room.

Freak looks up at me and he has a look on his face I do not like.

"What?" I bark, my heart hurting, my balls sore and my head spinning. I didn't want Dani to find out like this. I needed time to break this to her. Fuck.

"She might have a point," he said sitting in a chair and looking at me with a look of blame, which pisses me off.

"You telling me if this was Nikki, you wouldn't have done

the same?"

"I don't know, what I do know is I would have talked to my woman about it."

"Dani doesn't act rational, if I'd told her, she would have made me promise not to."

"That seemed to work out well for her the last time."

"Fuck you, motherfucker. I know you, you would have done the exact same thing that I did. Now quit acting like you know every fucking thing and tell me what the hell I need to know. I need that info, then I need to go get my woman and calm her ass down, all because you couldn't shut the fuck up and let me get my dick sucked," I'm pissed. I'm more than pissed, but even though I'm directing the anger at Freak, it's me I'm pissed at. I should have thought this through more. Dani trusted me and this had to gut her. I should have handled this shit better.

"How the fuck was I to know you were in here getting your Johnson sucked. Fuck, how was I to even know she was the bitch this was about. You just said it was personal. I did this as a favor for your fucking ass."

He's right and I should man up. I'm not about to though, too much shit to deal with right now and Freak is at the bottom of that list.

"Tell me what I need to know," I growl, sitting on the bed and rubbing my poor, abused balls. I'm going to make Dani kiss them better. Well, after her ass calms down. Right now I'm not letting her anywhere near them.

"It's not good, man. Your Michael is Michael Kavanagh."

"So?" I ask, totally clueless.

"The shipping god? Tycoon? High rolling mofo who has the U.S. exporting and importing wrapped up?"

Fuck.

"So, what's his connection with Dani?" I ask, needing to know.

"No, idea. He was married to a Melinda Marinetti, sole heir to the Marinetti dynasty. Reports say that Melinda was hounded by mental breakdowns and it was a rocky marriage. She died in a house fire five years ago. Police believe it was suicide."

"So where does Dani come in the picture?"

"No idea, unless she was this man's mistress or something. Rumors are he has a lot of those."

That doesn't ring true with the story that Dani was telling me. I'm going to have to talk to her and hopefully after I calm her down, she will see this is really the best way to deal with the situation.

"Re-print that shit off. I'll drop by and get it after I see to my woman."

"Does Dragon know you've claimed her?"

"No, but he will," Dani just needs to get it in her head first."

"Don't put it off too long."

I nod, because he's right. I should confess everything to Drag and come clean. I can't yet though. Especially since Dani may never want to speak to me again.

"First, I need to calm down my woman," I answer honestly.

"Good luck with that."

"I'm going to need it," I tell him leaving the room, and preparing for war. A war I will win, because Dani is not getting away from me.

Chapter 29

DANI

I HAVE SO many emotions running through me at once, I don't know what they are. Mad, hurt, anger, and betrayal all top the list. You could take your pick really. I couldn't go back to the club yesterday, not after learning what Zander did. I needed time away to think. Trouble is I feel like the walls are closing in on me. It might be possible that Michael doesn't know someone is running a check on him or gathering information. Possible, but not very damned likely. Which means, Michael will be checking out the Savage Brothers MC, he'll be checking out Dragon. He'll find out that Dragon is marrying Nicole…and from the name Nicole everything else will click into place. It's not a matter of if it will happen, it's a matter of when. So I need to plan.

When the fuck did Freak start running Zander's information requests? Was it after my big mouth gave Zander details? Or hell, even before that? How long of a head start do I have on Michael?

I spent last night in a small mom and pop motel three counties over. I knew if I stayed anywhere in London, or even in Skull's territory that Zander would find me. I can't handle that—not right now. I need some time. Zander is so convinced he can handle Michael, maybe he can? I don't know. Maybe I am short changing my man. What I do know is that I have seen up close and personal what happens when Michael is unhappy. If anything happened to Zander, Nicole, Ray or Paul, I wouldn't be able to go on. The risk is too great. I have to protect them. I need to contact Ray, because I'm going to need new papers sent to me. I'll have to strike out on my own. There will be no safety net and I'll be on my own this time. Nicole has a life. I'm not sure how I'll cope not being a part of her life. I'll miss the birth of her baby. I'll miss so much. The thought hurts me, but I tap it down. My life has never been about getting what I want. I shouldn't have allowed myself to forget that.

My decision made, I pick up the phone and dial.

"Hey kitten," Ray's voice almost makes me smile.

"Hey Ray, I umm…would it be possible for you to get me some new papers."

My question is greeted with a moment of silence and it's thick. He knows there would be only one reason I'm asking.

"Is this phone secure?"

"Yeah I picked up a burner."

His sigh is loud and I can't stop the tear that falls. It was a call both of us hoped I would never have to make.

"How'd he find out, honey?"

"Zander thought he'd get revenge on what was done to me," I said lamely.

"Idiot," Ray groans.

I swallow, not really liking that. "He loves me," I defend lamely.

"He's trying to get you killed," Ray growls.

"He doesn't know Michael. He thought he was protecting me."

The silence stretches again.

"You love him."

"I love him," I answer honestly. "I love him more than anything in the world. Enough that I have to protect him, Ray. I can't let Michael touch him."

"Do you want to see if he's right? Maybe he can handle Michael? He has fighting power behind him at least."

I think it over. I have all the faith in the world in Zander. Even though he lied to me, after I got over my initial panic, I understood. He wants to make life better for me, he wants to protect me and take away the shadows. He wants to save me. I get it. What I have with Zander is the first real adult relationship I've ever had. At the same time, I don't think Zander understands who he is dealing with.

"I may try to stay. I want to be in Nic's wedding and I'd love to see her baby."

"Yeah, I can't believe she's knocked up."

"So sweet, Ray," I tell him sarcastically.

"Paul says that all the time, especially when he's got his lips wrapped around..."

"Spare me please," I laugh. "Can you get me the papers? I need to be able to leave quickly, just in case. You still have the bank account info, right?"

"Yeah I got it, Kitten. I'll have them made up today and overnight them to the safe address you gave me when you first moved."

"Thanks Ray-Ray, as always I owe you more than I could ever repay you."

"Anything for you. Take care of you and always check in. It's our deal."

"It's our deal," I tell him, hanging up.

I stare at my phone for a little bit, before I start packing up. It's early, like really early, four a.m. to be exact, but I knew I needed to call Ray in Texas, because it would be three there and he'd just be getting in from work. I have Nic's car. She gave it to me to use. Still, I use my old clunker for the most part. Nic's car reminds me too much of my old life. I left it in the parking lot at the Club. I need to go back and collect it and check on Nicole and get ready for that damn fitting we have this evening.

IT'S ALMOST EIGHT by the time I pull into the parking lot. I stopped and had breakfast. I looked around some shops for a few items to pack in case I had to make a fast getaway. I picked up an extra burner phone to give to Nicole. I couldn't give her my number if I left. If I did that Zander would find me easily. Also, Michael would be able to use her against me. Actually he still might, but I'm doing everything I can in my power to prevent it. The rest I will have to trust Dragon to handle. If I leave, Nicole will tell him and he can protect her. He'll have to protect her.

I park Nic's car and grab my oversized purse and the bags I collected shopping today and hop out. I store them in the trunk of my car. I need to have Nailer go through my vehicle and make sure it's ready to travel. Again, Nic's car is the more logical choice, but my old junky car is the last thing Michael would expect to find me in. Maybe it's time to dye my hair again. Not blonde or red…never those again. Pink? Blue? Those ideas hold merit. There's a club hanger-on Tami that comes by with those colors. Frog and Hawk joke they pick her to tag-team all the time because they want to taste the rainbow.

There's a white envelope on my windshield when I reach my car. My first thought is that Zander left it. It even makes me kind of smile. I need to talk with him about boundaries and promises, but I don't want to give up what we have. I hope I never have to. He is all I want.

I throw my stuff in the car, relock the doors and then grab the note. I frown. My name is written on the outside, but it's not Zander's writing. I open it and there's a feeling of unease slowly filtering through my system. I am just not one for surprises. As I pull it out, my heart immediately begins to pound. My hands begin shaking.

A clipping from a period in my life that I've spent a lifetime trying to forget.

'Society darling, Melinda Marinetti to marry Michael Kavanagh.'

I read the headline and my stomach churns in fear. Times up. Somehow I convinced myself I was overreacting, that Michael wouldn't notice the inquiries Zander and Freak made. I won't be able to stay now. The tears gather in my eyes and I do my best to hold them back. Not here—not out in the open for anyone to see. For all I know, Michael is watching even now. So, I dig deep and find the Dani that I invented, the one who captured Zander's attention. I wad the paper up in my hands. It takes all I have not to run inside, to the safety of the club. I hold my pace slow and steady. I'm thankful I took the time to wear my pointed stilettos and designer jeans. My makeup is even done perfectly—including my bright red lipstick, and my hair sleek and pulled up high on my head in a ponytail. The click of my shoes on the worn concrete help me to count with each step and I concentrate on my breathing, until I'm out of sight.

The front room of the club is empty, so from there I half walk, half jog to Nicole and Dragon's room. I hope Dragon is gone by now, he usually is, but I don't have the best of luck—I think that much is clear.

"Nic! You up?" I ask in a panic, my voice probably too loud. I knock on the door with more force than necessary, but damn I need her. Just being in her presence helps.

"Come on in," she calls out.

"Dani, please don't give me shit about the dresses again. I gave in and let you have…"

"Nic, please."

My voice is thick with fear. I can't stop it. I haven't had a panic attack since I started therapy, but I can feel one now, trying to take hold of me.

"What?" She asks, and tries to say Michael's name because she knows only one thing would put me into the state that I am.

I can't let the name leave her lips. I push the wadded up picture at her, partly to divert her, but mostly I need it out of my hands. It feels as if it is burning me. She takes the paper and presses it against her leg to try and get the wrinkles out.

"Where did you get this?" She asks and I hate that her voice has panic in it too. Maybe I shouldn't have shown her.

"My car."

"Maybe you left it…" She spends the next few minutes trying to convince me that I just forgot I had it. What she doesn't realize is that Ray helped me burn everything that would ever remind me of Michael. I needed it all gone. She finally stops arguing and crushes the paper up in her hand. She looks at me with tears in her eyes. We both know what this means, even if we don't want to know.

"You do not have to leave! Right here is the safest place for you! Dragon and the boys will protect you!"

I drop down beside her on the bed. I can't stop the tears that are falling. It feels like I'm making the hardest decision in my life… and maybe I am. We argue some more, Nic wanting me to trust the club, me listing the reasons I can't. They're not completely truthful. The main reason is I need to protect her and I need to protect Zander. That is my only concern. All she's doing is making me long for something that can't be. Finally, I shut her down with the one truth that even she can't deny.

"Nic, Michael won't rest until he has killed every member of the Savage Brothers and he'll make sure it is painful," I tell her.

"Dragon can handle him…we have to tell him," she says, but even I can tell her arguing is weakening. "Dani, I'm getting married in two weeks!" She finally says, when all we manage to do with the other topics is go in circles.

I try to reassure her, but the two of us just end up crying. It hurts me that I have laid this on her. Nicole has always been my rock, she always manages to take some of my burdens, making my load lighter. She always does her best to help hold people she cares about together.

"We'll figure this out…" she says finally. Sometimes there just aren't words to help.

Chapter 30

CRUSHER

DRAGON PUT ME on babysitting duty, which normally I would hate. Not so now, because I get to remain close to Dani. She's not going to make it easy though. When they all pile into the Tahoe I'm driving, she makes sure to get in back with Nicole, Carrie and Lips. Nikki piles in beside me and I find myself hoping like hell she doesn't mention the night Freak and I shared her. It was before Dani and I ever got together and I shouldn't feel a bit of fucking guilt over it. Yet, for some reason sitting in this car beside Nikki feels wrong. I want my woman beside me. As the girls finally get settled and buckled in, my phone vibrates with a text message. Freak. I can't deal with him right now. He's trying to convince me to talk with Dragon about this Michael guy and I probably should. The truth is I just don't want too. I want to handle this. I want to be the one to take care of my woman, make it so she is safe—not just today but every day. So I ignore the message.

I drive them into town peeking through the rearview mirror at Dani. I catch her staring at me a few times. She doesn't respond when I wink at her. The next time I catch her eyes, I mouth the words I love you. I wanted some kind of reaction from her this time. I don't get it. All I can see is sadness so apparent it pains me. I need to fix this and soon. I can't let this fester between us. What Dani and I have is too fucking good to let it go sour.

I drop them off at the door of the bridal shop.

"Aren't you going in, Crush?" Nikki asks, and son of a bitch, I don't like the way her eyes look me up and down. I should, because she's a hell of a woman. But I don't. My dick is owned by the brunette spitfire currently ignoring me and sliding out of the vehicle. Once Dani exits, she slams the door and I wonder how it stays on its hinges.

"Hell no, I ain't setting foot in that store. My dick would become permanently limp if I spent much time in there. I'll be here waiting on you girls."

"Well we can't have that, can we?" she winks and laughs at me. My eyes catch Dani's and that uncomfortable feeling, only increases.

Shit this relationship stuff might be the death of me. I need to turn Dani over my knees and spank her ass for running once again. I don't because I know this is all my fault. I should kill Freak instead. At the thought of Freak, I remember his message. I pull out my phone and call him.

"Bout fucking time," he grumbles.

"What's up?" I ask, my eyes following Dani as she walks into the store. She's looking so fucking hot in those high-as-fuck shoes of hers and her fucking lipstick. If I wasn't trying to get her to forgive me, I'd push her up against the wall and make sure that every fucker around knew who's dick she was taking tonight and every fucking night.

"Up? I just fucking lied to my fucking brothers for you, you son of a bitch and I fucking know you ignored my message!"

My back goes straight as his words register, "What the fuck are you talking about?"

"Surveillance showed someone snooping around Dani's car

last night. I didn't mention what you had me digging into because if Dragon knows you suspected something and didn't tell him, he'd shoot us both in the nut-sack for not telling him. You need to get your ass in gear and fix this soon, Crush. Cause, I'm telling you man, if you don't tell Dragon, I'm going to."

My head goes down and I lean against the building. Fucking-hell. "Are you sure this has anything to do with what we've been looking into? Maybe it's just an obsessed fan, pissed because she's not dancing now?" I'm grasping, I know I am, but there's no point in jumping the gun too soon.

"Drag and the boys suggested that, but he put a fucking lojack on her car. It's not the cheap kind either, so I think we both know what we're dealing with here, Crush."

"Fuck. I'm stuck in town with the women. I'll be there as soon as I get done. I need to see the footage and then I'll talk to Dragon. Can you sit on it until then?"

Silence greets my question and I know I'm putting Freak in a twisted mess here. I'm asking a lot of him. Thing is, Freak and I are closer than the other brothers, and I know when push comes to shove we have each other's backs. I just don't like asking this of him.

"You get today man, and then I'm going to have to talk to Dragon. There's just too much shit that could go bad. I warned you this Kavanagh wasn't a fucker to be messed with."

"Yeah, I got it. Thanks, man. Let me know if anything else comes up. I want to stay close to Dani, just in case."

"Yeah sure, but get your ass in here when you get your bitch settled."

I hang up feeling like lead is sitting in my gut. I look through the glass doors of the bridal shop and Dani is up on a pedestal in a pink dress, but it's different from the others. It is cool...frosted and I love it on her. She's standing there with a small smile on her face, touching the dress with those sweet, soft hands of hers that make me beg and I make a vow. A damned vow that I will keep her safe and end this fucker Michael once and for all. Not only that, but when it's all done...I want Dani in a dress, with a smile on her face saying I do. I'm marrying that woman. I'm claiming her in every fucking way imaginable and no one is standing in my way—especially some cocksucker in New York that gets his rocks off by hurting women.

Dani looks up and our eyes lock. Hers are haunted and I want to be the man that takes the ghosts away. I put my hand on the glass, palm open and fingers spread. I want her to know that I am her man. She studies me for a minute, and she looks so hurt, lost, alone, one of them or hell maybe all three. Then she gives me a half smile. It doesn't reach her eyes, it doesn't overshadow the ghosts. I need to try harder, especially since, I'm the motherfucker who put the sadness there this time.

Yeah, I definitely need to do better.

Chapter 31

DANI

JUST AS I figured, trying on bridesmaids dresses blows chunks. It also seems to go on forever. I'd rather be anywhere but here. My mind is busy trying to figure out what the hell I'm going to do. My heart is hurting and I'm trying to resist the urge to take the non-prescribed type medication that used to help me. I haven't needed to touch the shit since I went to Ray's. I've always had Zander beside me at night when the panic attacks threaten to hit. Now with that damn note on my windshield, it feels like a panic attack is just around the corner. I need my head clear for this. I need to make sure Nicole and Zander are safe. So, I can't be weak. I can't. But my hands are shaking, my head is pounding and I really just want to crawl in a bed and sleep. Michael almost destroyed me once before. If he gets his hands on me again, I won't survive. Then again, he's not going to let me live. I know it. The world thinks I'm dead. Michael has the green-light to do whatever he wants to me and he will. I know he will.

I can't sit in this fancy ass store a minute longer. We've all had our fittings done except Nikki and if I hear one more time how she's had my man's cock in her I'm going to blow a gasket. When Lips joins her that's it. That's just it. Jesus! I know the man isn't a choir boy, but I don't want to hear about him giving it to women I like.

"I need a drink!" I call out, standing up and needing to get the fuck out of here.

Nikki and Lips are going on how they'd join me, but their men need them blah, blah, blah. If their men need them so much, they need to make sure they're too busy to get around my man's cock! If they join me I'd probably scratch and claw their eyeballs out like the jealous bitch I am right now. This is what Zander has made me into. Will he go back to fucking them when I'm no longer in the picture? Shit. I don't want to leave him. I don't want to let go of him. The thought of him belonging to another woman besides me, feels like it's ripping me apart from the inside out. It's a deeper hurt than any I've ever had and when I feel tears sting my eyes and the breath in my lungs lodges in my throat, I know I need to get a grip.

"I'm out of here!" I yell out to everyone, not bothering to turn around, and doing my best not to sprint to the damn door, to get free. When I make it outside, I breathe deep. My eyes are closed and I keep picturing Zander with Nikki and Lips, giving them the smile that should be mine. I know I'm not being logical. I know whatever he did with them was before we slept together, but it doesn't fucking matter right now.

"Hold up, Dani!" Nicole calls out and I turn to watch her come out of the shop. I stop, but only because it's Nicole. I really want to take off running. She's insisting on going with me, even when I try to discourage her by lying and saying I'm going to a bar. There's no way I can afford to get drunk right now. I finally give in when she threatens to order chocolate milk at a bar. She'd do it too, it's one of the reasons I love her. So, we head off to Weaver's a local restaurant in town that's supposed to have been here since the town was first created or some shit like that. I don't know, I just know the food is good.

"Any more notes?"

I knew this was a mistake, she just confirms it with her first question. "No," I answer praying that will be the end of it. It's not. We go back and forth over me telling Dragon and I know that I'm putting her in a hard spot. I absolutely am, but I can't. Dragon and his men go head long to protect the ones they care about. This means Zander would jump in with both feet and take off running. I believe that, because I know he loves me. Dragon might not care that much for me, but he does Nicole and if he thought for one second that someone was threatening his woman or his child, he'd go in, guns blazing. Michael operates outside the law, much like the Savage MC, but (and this is a very big but) he owns the police. When I say he owns them, I'm not talking about the cops in a local town or surrounding areas, I'm talking, judges, senators, representatives and every office in between. Hell, he's even been invited to dinners at the freaking White House. I've tried fighting this and I know. I'm going to do everything in my power to deflect Michael away from the ones that I love and if that fails I've left a packet of detailed information that goes to Dragon if I die. In it is every crooked politician and the information Michael holds on them all, along with detailed information on Michael. I've held it to myself all this time, thinking that I might could use it to bargain with those on a higher food chain, if Michael ever found me again. Me surviving is no longer my goal, I'm going to die and truthfully if Michael gets his hands on me again I'd rather die. My goal is only making sure that those I love are kept out of this. I can't give the info to Zander. If something happens to me, he won't control himself. He'll act first and then think. Dragon will be more methodical. Doing this, giving Dragon the one card I have against the devil…it's all I can do.

The arguing with Nic and I continues back and forth and

my guilt from the whole shooting with Tiny gets involved and I'm glad I haven't ate. I feel like I want to hurl. Nicole will never understand how much I regret that day. She can't. She doesn't know what happened with Ms. Martens. She doesn't have my memories. She doesn't have visions of someone she likes being tortured. Not to mention, that she was tortured in much the same manner as Dragon was doing to one of his on. Sure I understand why, now—maybe I did even then. Still...the past and the present meshed together and I just reacted, wanting to keep my best friend safe.

"Afternoon, ladies," a voice says from my side.

A voice, I never wanted to hear again in my life. A voice that haunts me almost as much as Michael's does. I count backwards in my head and steady my breathing, deliberately lowering it. I can't show fear, I can't let him see weakness. I slowly lower my hands to my lap and turn to face Michael's lapdog. I hate the son of a bitch and it would make me the happiest woman in the world to do nothing more than kill him slowly. I guess Dragon and I aren't so unalike after all.

I do my best to appear like I barely give him a second notice. I try extra hard to make it appear I don't even know who he is. I give what I hope is a tiring sigh, then respond. "Not interested buddy, move along."

"Really, Mrs. Kavanagh, I assumed you would be most interested in what I have to say."

"Sorry, you have the wrong person, buddy," Nic answers, reaching under the table to grab my hand. I am pretty sure I cut off her circulation, squeezing it in answer. She and Donald go back and forth and it's enough to let me know that Michael has indeed been checking out the Savage MC. The reality of that settles into my stomach. The only bright spot is that by sending Donald here first to give me a warning, means Michael is unsure of how to proceed around the Savage crew. I will have to use that to my advantage. Maybe I will be able to stay around a little longer.

"...I have a message for you, Melinda. It's from your husband," Donald says dragging me back to the conversation at hand. Hearing Michael being referred to as my husband throws me for a loop. It causes my facade to slip.

"I...I don't...."

"Save it, we both know that you would be lying. Mr. Kavanagh will be in town next week. He will expect you at this address on the day and time listed. Do not disappoint him," he says putting a piece of paper on the table.

Next week. I have one more week here. Well no, not really. If I want to try and get away I need to leave soon. So really, I have mere days to say my goodbyes. Days to memorize everything about Zander and try to take a lifetime of memories with me to wherever I end up or into the next life, because I know that's the only outcomes available to me. The thought that I have to leave Zander, that I won't be allowed to love him and take care of him, grow old with him....the fact that I can't even give him the daughters and sons he deserves all flood me at once. So when I turn back to Donald, it is not fear I feel. It is anger. It is rage. It is hate.

"You can tell Mr. Kavanagh to go fuck himself—preferably with a sawed-off shotgun and the safety in the off position."

"I can see hiding in the hills with a bunch of uneducated Neanderthals has had an unfortunate effect on you, Mrs. Kavanagh. A shame but, hopefully, not an irrevocable change."

"Being around real people has had a fucking great effect on me, douche bag. Why don't you get the fuck out of here so I can enjoy my dinner? I got to tell you, your stink is starting to affect my appetite," I respond and yes, I'm trying to channel

Zander and sound like him. I'm rather proud of myself really.

"Really, Mrs. Kavanagh, I do hope you remember who you are, before you meet with your husband."

I flip him off with both hands, it feels like the only thing to do.

"I would suggest you remember your station, before coming to your husband."

"I would suggest you go to hell."

"Do not make Mr. Kavanagh come and get you. Rest assured your punishment will be much worse if you do. You have brought enough disgrace upon the Kavanagh name."

I stay quiet until he's out of sight.

"I'm going to have to leave, Nic."

She nods, but immediately tries to tell me how she can help. We go back and forth, but I finally end it, distracting her.

"....Here comes Crusher. Let's just let it go for now. You get back to Dragon."

"What about you? Where are you going?" She asks.

"Think I'll head down to the Den and find someone to scratch an itch," I lie with an easy smile.

"If you want company tonight Hellcat, I'm free."

"Hellcat?"

"It seems to fit," he shrugs.

I get up from the table, part of me remembering the conversation we had before. Little does he know, I could never handle dragging him into hell with me.

"I don't think so, stud."

"Baby, I could scratch your itch so well, you'd purr for days."

"From what I hear, your scratcher has been around so much, it's liable to cause an itch a girl needs medicine for."

"Didn't realize I was dealing with Queen Elizabeth," he

replies confusing me.

"What the hell are you talking about, Crusher?" She asks.

"The virgin queen?"

Asshole. Suddenly this little conversation doesn't feel like an inside joke. It hurts, because in every way that should count Zander had my virginity. So, I decide to hit him with my new found knowledge of his extracurricular activities. "Long way from a virgin baby, I just don't happen to want Nikki and Lips' sloppy seconds."

"I could make sure you liked it."

"Bigger men than you have tried and failed—and I do mean bigger," I tell him before walking away.

"See? Pussy with claws. Hellcat," Crusher yells back and I flip him off, then continue walking away.

Chapter 32

CRUSHER

SHE'S SLIPPING AWAY from me. I'm in a fucked up mess, I've yet to tell Dragon shit about Michael. Freak is pissed off at me, I'm doing everything I can to try and figure out how Michael and Dani are connected and where the fucker might strike and all I can think is, she's slipping away from me. I know it—I can feel it. On the surface you would think I am getting everything I want. Dani's not hiding the fact that she's sleeping with me anymore. She's on me like white on rice lately. I've fucked her everywhere imaginable and every way imaginable. We've fucked against walls, on my bike, in the car, in the movies, I've got her off in the club while we watched the others dance or play cards—seriously you name it and we have done it. Hell, I even fucked her on the table in the church room the other night.

So you would think I'd be a happy motherfucker, with sore balls and a worn out dick. Well two of those are true, but I am far from happy, because Dani is preparing to run. I can't allow that and it's making me crazy. I need her to trust me, to be open with me. Of course she was doing that and I jumped the gun and fucked it all up, obviously I'm an idiot.

We're all at the beach now at Twin Rocks picnic shelter. Dragon had this idea that the club needed to spend some time together. I agreed because I get my woman in a bathing suit and I'm not a fool. She's in my arms and we're playing in the water while Drag and Dance grill and the other girls are taking in the sun. Bull is off talking to the other brothers and Freak is shooting me looks. I feel a tinge of guilt every time he does. I'm going to have to deal with shit and soon. Not today though. Today I need to make sure that I give Dani every reason to hang on to us.

"You're so fucking beautiful you make me hurt," I tell her. We're sitting in the water, just on the edge. It splashes against my sides as the waves push into the bank. Dani is in my lap her arms hanging loosely behind my neck, her eyes looking down at me and her legs wrapped around my waist. Her hair is wet and pulled from her face and she's smiling…at me. If I could have this for the rest of my life, I'd be a happy motherfucker. How often have I thought this lately? It just keeps getting truer every day.

She tilts her head to the side and looks at me, like she's trying to figure out life's biggest mystery.

"Beauty fades, Zander. It can be changed or altered, it can even be fixed. You should have seen my stomach before Dr. Bradens got a hold of me."

I bend down and place a small kiss on her stomach. "It wouldn't matter to me what you look like. You'd still be beautiful, never forget that, Hellcat."

She takes a deep breath and then looks over the beach, before her eyes come back to mine. "I'm thinking the fact that we're fucking is no longer a secret."

"Thank, fuck. I want the world to know."

She leans down and places a light kiss on my lips, but I can't let it stop at that. I slide my tongue into her mouth and deepen the kiss. It's long, it's slow and it's sweet. "I love you, Hellcat," I whisper against her lips.

"I love you too, Zander."

Our foreheads touch and we stay like that and I wish I could freeze the moment forever, because it is that perfect.

Then...all hell breaks loose.

Gunfire rings out repeatedly. The sand around us pings with either the casings or the real fucking bullets, I have no way of knowing and I'm not about to stop and look. I instantly flip Dani and me over, so I can lay on top of her. I don't have a fucking thing for cover, but me and I'm glad that I'm so much bigger than her so I can hide her body. She's whimpering underneath me and I kiss her ear, keeping my head down and trying not to move.

"Let me up, Zander. God don't do this, you need to go take cover," she cries and I move just enough so I can kiss one of her eyes. There's sand on her eyelid, but her salty tears mingle and hurt me.

"Shhh...sweetheart. My brothers have this. It's going to be okay. Just hold still a few more minutes."

Just like that it ends. The ringing of the shots stop and the sound of a vehicle peeling out from the parking lot above can be heard. I get up and pull Dani up carefully. I rake the excess sand off her body, and check her over for marks. Satisfied that she's okay, I pull her close to me and walk towards Dragon. He's checking over his woman and issuing orders at the same time. He looks at me and Dance and orders us to go with him. I want to scream, fuck no. I need to be close to my woman. I can't.

"Freak. You keep close to Dani for me?"

Freak is mad, I see it all over his face, but he agrees. I think I've run out of time to come clean to my brothers. I look down at Dani and kiss her again, but quickly and with just a small taste of her mouth.

"I'll be back Hellcat, stay safe."

"Don't get hurt, Zander. Please? I couldn't handle it if something happened to you."

"I'll be fine. You just be waiting when I get back. I love you Melly."

I thought she would kiss me again, she doesn't she pulls away from me and turns toward Gunner and Freak. I know she's blaming herself for this. It pisses me off. I can't get into it right now though. I have to go with my brothers.

IT'S LATE BY the time we get back and my ass is dragging. Drag and I managed to capture one of the motherfuckers and he sang like a fucking canary. Which was good and bad. I had to tell Dragon I knew about Dani and Michael and parts of what I already knew. To say my brother was unhappy was a freaking understatement. All I want is to crawl into bed, hold my woman and grab a couple of hours sleep before I face tomorrow. That's the only plan I have. Until I open the door to Dani's room and see she's not there. We've been sleeping in her room most every night, but maybe tonight she wanted to wait for me in mine. I take off to my room and I start to feel fear when it is empty too, but that's not what causes the feeling to bloom into a full blown panic. No, that would be the envelope on my pillow. The name Zander, written on the outside of it in Dani's handwriting.

I sit down on the side of the bed, my body feeling like lead. My fucking hands shake when I rip it open and pull the two page folded note out.

Zander,

I figure if you're reading this you already know I'm gone. I wanted to stay. Today at the beach, I actually thought about it. I can't though, that's a dream and I definitely don't live in a dream world.

I asked you not to contact Michael, because I know him in ways you never could understand. I've been married to him for over six years now as Melinda Marinetti. Though we only stayed together one year, Michael won't ever willingly let me go. I only escaped the first time by changing my name and hiding. If he gets a hold of me again, he'll kill me this time. I'm actually okay with that. If I was brave perhaps I would actually beat him to the punch. I find I can't though.

As odd as it sounds I want to live. I want to take the memories of you and the love you've shown me and live. You made me truly feel like Dani, a woman who could handle life and anything thrown at her. I will always be Dani now and that makes me happy. This way a part of me will always belong to you.

What you need to understand, is this is not your fault. This was set into motion before you even knew who I was and I can't let my mistakes, my past hurt you in anyway. I'm no longer a scared seventeen year old child. I'm an adult. It's time I stop hiding and leaning on Ray and Nicole for help and live whatever life I have, for however long I have left.

I love you, Zander and I know you'll be upset by this. Please understand, I wanted to stay and I really thought about it. Then today when you called me Melly, I realized, I can't. I'm not the woman for you. Memories of you will help me survive my past, but you have to be free to find the woman who will make you put your past behind—make you put Melly in the past where she belongs.

Gun told me about Melly, I know how it must haunt you, but everyone has a road to follow in this life. You can't be responsible for all the wrong turns others take. It's enough you made me grateful for my wrong turns because I got to love you, if only for a little while.

Be happy, Cowboy.

Love,

Your Hellcat.

Melly...My mind goes back to when I told Dani goodbye.

"I'll be fine. You just be waiting when I get back. I love you, Melly."

Fuck! I called her Melly! Why? I don't think of her as Melly. I never have. Melly was from a different time. Melly was a time when I was a boy trying to be a man. It was puppy love and nothing like what I feel for Dani. Was it because of the danger? Or because I knew Dani was thinking of leaving? I can't be sure and I'm not even sure it matters now. I caused her to leave. Tears sting my eyes as I bring her letter up to my face and breathe in the scent of her from it. When I think of my woman out there alone with a maniac I set on her heels after her, my heart stops. When I imagine how she must have felt to be called another woman's name...

Fuck. I let the tears fall. There's no shame in them. I did this. I caused this. Now I just have to figure out some fucking way to fix it all.

Chapter 33

MICHAEL

I SIT BACK against the leather in my limo watching the small screen before me as Melinda comes out of the Savage Clubhouse. She's got a travel bag over her shoulder and holding a jacket in one hand. I suppose she really does think she's getting away from me. It never ceases to amaze me how stupid women are. Does she really think I'm about to let her get away?

I knew having those stupid hillbillies fire on her friends, would cause her to run. If there is one thing I can always count on with Melinda it's that she always sacrifices for the people she cares about. It's how I got her to say I do, after all. She would have never agreed to it even after trapping her, if I hadn't threatened her precious Nicole. I'll get them both this time though. I've decided it's time I play with Nicole's life much like she has played with mine. We'll see how she likes it. I never did like the bitch, but she'll be fun to torture in front of Melinda.

I watch as Melinda gets into the ugliest car I've ever seen in my life. With all the money she stole from me you would think the least she would do is drive something decent. That is her problem though, she is short-sighted. She never sees the bigger picture. To this day she still believes her father was broke, and I saved him. She has no idea his money was what I needed to stay solvent. It's also the reason Melinda must die in Kentucky. I am getting married soon and my new intended comes complete with political reach and bank accounts that will do quite nicely. It's a good thing too, because the woman is so horribly homely. Of course that's good in one way. I can do anything I want with her and she's just thankful.

I watch until Melinda pulls out of the compound, and then I turn off the screen. Donald had men splice into the camera feed at the compound so I can monitor things. Melinda, who apparently now prefers to be called Dani, is much too stupid to realize that Donald will be tailing her every move. Too bad time is short, if not I would let her run for a day. It'd be so fun to let her think she got away, only to watch the hope drain from her eyes when she realizes she hasn't.

I pick up a discarded manila folder Donald handed me earlier. In it are all the bios of the members of the Savage Brother's MC as well as their allies and women. I thumb through it till I find a picture of Melinda—now apparently known as Dani Smith. Not much in there other than her best friend Nicole Wentworth. She grew up in the small town of Blade, Kentucky apparently. Ironic since I shall kill her with a blade. She strips for a living and has a lousy credit rating. It's such a far cry from the person she was born as, the person I married…I could almost applaud at how deep she went undercover. She's wasted too much of my time though. I need to wrap this up and head back to New York and pretend to be the happy, doting fiancé of one Miss Rebecca Barters, heir to Barters Industries and Holdings, which includes the billion dollar coffee product shipped straight out of Columbia. I have plans for that business.

I pick up Melinda's picture and frown. She really is quite beautiful. I must ruin that before I am finished with her too. I pick up a letter opener off the small console in front of my seat. I use it to stab the picture and pin it to the seat beside me. The sharp file stabs through the picture and coincidentally right between the eyes of Melinda's likeness.

I pick up my cell with a cold smile, already anticipating my revenge.

"Donald, intercept my runaway wife before she can leave the city. Bring her to the building we've purchased. I shall deal with her further from there."

"Excellent. I shall see you soon. I'm about to board my plane."

I hang up my cell, sticking it in my pocket and slide out of my limo, leaving Melinda's picture behind me. This will be the last time I chase after that fucking bitch. In fact this will be the last time anyone chases after her.

That thought cheers me as I board my private jet headed for some Podunk town in Kentucky.

Chapter 34

CRUSHER

I'VE TORN THE place apart looking for Dani. She's gone. My heart hurts and I'm running around like a crazy man. I've asked everyone I can find if they've seen her. It's driving me crazy. I know she's not been real popular at the club, but Jesus Christ! We've just been fired at in our own territory! We're on lockdown here! I'm pissed, no I'm beyond fucking pissed.

"What the fuck do you mean you don't know where she is?" I growl as Bull delivers the news.

"Just that. I brought her home, she said she was tired and was going to lay down. So, I let her."

"Jesus you didn't think watching over the women meant you needed to put guards at the fucking doors? Or hell, the gate itself?"

"You know what, Crush? If you got a problem I guess you should take it up with Freak, since he's the one Dragon put in charge of security and shit."

"Fuck you. Dragon told you to take care of the women."

"And I did, I brought them to the fucking compound and that's where the security comes into place. I'm fucking tired of you and the other brothers coming to me when shit hits the fan, like I have a damned thing to do with it. I haven't been in control of security or knowing what the fuck is going on here, since my accident."

"You're the fucking Enforcer here! You know to watch over the women!"

Bull stands up and leans in on me and gives me a hateful look, "I did what I fucking was told to do. I told the women to stay in until you guys got back. It's not my fault you can't keep the pussy you're banging in line. It's also not my fault if there weren't guards posted out front, or at the door because, and this is the last fucking time I'm saying it, I wasn't the one told to do that fucking shit. So I'm sitting here watching a woman I care about and women who actually listen when I tell them do something. You got a problem take it up with Dragon, or that fucking cunt you're sticking your dick in every night, or better yet, why don't you take it up with Freak, since you and him seem to be able to keep shit to yourselves! So what if it puts the rest of us in danger!"

I don't even think, I plow my fist hard into his face. The club has been going easy with Bull since his injury. Fuck that shit. I've had it. He falls back on the table it turns on its side and dumps him on the floor. He lays there wiping the blood off his lip, staring up at me. The club members around us were already pretty quiet watching us, but now you can hear a pin drop.

"Fuck you motherfucker, you lay off my woman. She's mine and by God you will give her the respect she deserves in this fucking club."

"You need to start thinking with your head and I'm not talking about the one on your dick," he responds, making no move to get up.

"And you need to stop feeling fucking sorry for yourself and get your head out of your ass and help your brothers. We fucking helped you when you needed us," I growl and stomp off, time to find Dragon.

"Does your woman know where Dani is?" I ask right outside of Dragon's door—my anger still at a head from dealing with Bull. Not to mention, every minute that Dani is gone my gut clenches. I am feeling like she's playing into Michael's hands and I'm blaming myself.

"Nicole is sleeping fucker, step back into the main room and we'll talk," Dragon tells me as he closes the door to his room.

"Fuck, that. I need to find Dani. Does your woman know where she is or not?"

"You need to step the fuck back, man. I told you Nicole is sleeping. She cried herself to sleep and by God she's going to rest. You feel me?"

I rake my hands through my hair, and follow Dragon back the way I just come. "You don't understand Drag, this bastard will hurt her."

"You knew about this shit?"

"I knew she was running. Didn't know what from, until all this shit went down. She left me a note, a fucking note!" That's kind of a lie, but I need Dragon to help me here, the rest of the fucking shit I'll deal with after I get my woman back.

We walk past Bull who is standing now and gives me a fuck you look, as we pass.

"Something you want to tell me, brother?" Dragon asks when we make it into his office. The other members, including Bull, join us and close the door.

"She's mine, Dragon. I've got to find her and you can either help me or get the fuck out of my way," I tell him. I know I'm out of line, but with every minute that passes I don't give a damn.

We go back and forth and I'm tired of it. When I point out to him that if it was Nicole instead of Dani involved he'd react differently. I guess he had enough. He grabs me and slams my back hard against the wall. I don't fight him. I know I've fucked up. I've fucked up for everyone involved. "You need to calm your ass and sit the fuck down."

"Nicole is involved, motherfucker. Now you need to listen to me. Step. The. Fuck. Down. Do not cause me more shit, because all that will do is slow us down."

"I will find her, Dragon."

He goes on some more, but I ignore it. I need to plan out my next move, because it's becoming apparent I'm on my own when it comes to protecting my woman. When Dragon brings up the guy we captured I turn my attention back to him.

"Where's our guest?"

"Frog's sitting on him at the shed," Hawk speaks up.

"Call Frog, tell him to let the son of a bitch go."

No. Fucking. Way. He can't let our only lead go! What the fuck is he thinking? "The fuck you will, that might be the only lead we have back to Dani!" I yell before I can stop myself.

"Crush, man, I'm not telling your ass again," Dragon says, and honestly he keeps talking, but all I can hear is the incessant need to find Dani, in my head.

"We need to work him over and find out exactly what they know about Dani. We can get this Michael's whereabouts from him that way. None of this cat and mouse shit," I argue.

"Get the fuck out!" Drag orders. The room goes silent.

"Damn it, Drag! We have to…"

"You're not hearing me motherfucker, I said, get the fuck out. I can't deal with your shit right now. You are out of this until you manage to get your head out of your ass, untie the knot in your balls, and listen to sense."

"Drag!"

"Get out, motherfucker! Now."

I look at my brother and I want to literally rip him apart right now. Fine. I'm on my own. I prefer it that way. Fuck him. I guess when it's my woman it's not important. I'll save her my-own-damn-self. Fuck them all.

Chapter 35

DANI

MY HEAD IS a mess. When the man you love calls you by another woman's name. That shit hurts. When it's the name of his first love, it fucking hurts worse. Was he just with me to try and save me when he couldn't save her? I can't help but think that's the case. It doesn't matter in the big picture, because I know Michael is behind the shooting and once that happened, it was all too clear that I couldn't stay. Zander could have died trying to protect me, and Nicole and Carrie are both pregnant with their whole lives ahead of them. I can't stay, and more than that Zander needs to find a woman to love that he doesn't have to save. He deserves it.

I caught Bull in the bathroom. I know what he does in there. I don't think the others have caught on yet, but I've done it for a long ass time. He's taking away the pain with pills. I hope he finds his way out of the hole. It's a fucking dark place to be and the urge never goes away. Like right now, I'm sitting in an old ratty-ass motel room on the Kentucky and Missouri border, trying to keep my head straight and figure out what the hell my next move is, when all I really want to do is self-medicate, and get lost in a bottle.

I should probably take the meds the doctor prescribed, but right now I'm afraid to. I can't afford not to be alert. I want to call Nic or Ray, but I can't, at least not yet. I need to be far away before I even attempt it. I would love to call Zander. Just so I can hear his voice, even though I know I shouldn't.

I decide I should at least get some food. It would be smarter to run through a drive through, but I think if I sit alone in this hotel room that the urge to call Zander will win, either that or I'll start drinking. So, I leave and search out an all-night diner. I find one just over the Missouri state line. It's deserted except for a waitress and a cook, but it looks clean and I haven't had anything to eat today, so I go for it.

"What'll it be?" The waitress asks. She's actually wearing a pink uniform like something off of an old TV show, her tired red hair is pulled up on top of her head and she has on a dark red apron. She's holding an ordering pad, but no menu I guess she figures I don't need one.

"Coffee and can I get a toasted turkey sandwich? On wheat?" I ask, because without a menu, I'm kind of flying in the dark here. It must have been okay because she nods and goes back into the kitchen. I look around for a bathroom and decide to go freshen up.

I look in the mirror and barely recognize the woman staring back at me. She's worn, tired…she looks so damned tired. I get lost in the reflection trying to remember what I looked like before Michael came into my life. I find that I can't remember, and that makes me want to cry. Would Zander have liked Melinda? The Melinda I was before Michael had me in his sights, obviously. Or would he not have been attracted to me at all then, because I didn't need fixing? Why I'm even worried about it, escapes me. Whatever the answer, it doesn't change the outcome.

When I make it back to my table, the diner is empty and pretty damn quiet. I guess they decided to take a break since it was deserted? Having worked as a waitress before, I can understand that. My sandwich and coffee are sitting at the bar and the smell makes my stomach growl in hunger. It looks good, or it's just the fact that I'm starved, but I dig in. As good as the sandwich is, the same can't be said for the coffee, it's bitter and has a nasty after taste, and it's kind of what I'd imagine drinking cardboard is like. Still, I finish it off because I'm so tired and honestly, taste is an afterthought at this point. I just need something to help me stay awake.

"Hello, Melinda."

My hands freeze on my food as I look up at Donald. Fuck.

"They let any kind of vermin in this place I guess." I tell him trying to figure out how to get the small pistol I have in a holster on the inside of my jacket. It seems so much easier in the movies.

"You would know, my dear. Let's get up now, I have orders to bring you to your husband and it's getting late."

"I'm not going back," I tell him, turning to the side so he might not realize I'm trying to reach behind my back.

"Oh but you are."

"We're not alone, I'll scream and raise such a fit the others will call the cops in no time," I tell him ignoring the voice that says that cops are useless.

"That would be kind of hard, since the waitress and the cook are dead."

"Fuck..." I whisper, before I can stop myself.

"Perhaps later, now either you come quietly to my car or I'll pick you up and carry you out of here. Either way is good. The stuff I put in your coffee should already be making you sleepy. I do hope I didn't put too much, it's hard to judge really."

As he talks, I already know he's right, because the room is getting blurry and I'm so tired. My arms feel like they are weighted down, they are so heavy. He's going to get me. The thought terrifies me enough that I can fight it and get my hand on my gun. I make a quick decision to shoot him instead of me. My hands are shaking from fear and the weight of the weapon, but I pull it out and aim at his crotch. Honestly, I dream of shooting his and Michael's dick off. I try to steady the gun and shoot but I can't seem to get my fingers to work, to squeeze the trigger. I scream out at myself as Donald grabs the gun. He wrestles it out of my hands and then slams the butt of it against my head. Blackness envelopes me and all I can think is, I hope I don't wake up this time.

Chapter 36

CRUSHER

I SOMEHOW CONVINCE Frog to leave me in charge of the fucker we captured. I realize I've gone way too far to come back, but in truth I don't care. I will do whatever it takes to save my woman. I know I was stupid and made her doubt that, but I have never thought of Dani as Melly. Melissa and I were kids, and it was a different lifetime. It was young love and it ended heartbreakingly. I mourn the loss of her life every fucking single day, but I don't mourn it out of some great love.

Dani and my love for her are all consuming. Honestly, it just hit me this last freaking month. Before she was an obsession, but the last month that we've been messing around back and forth…I've come to realize that she is everything I could ever want. When she smiles or laughs, I get a feeling of peace that I have never had in my entire life. She flipped her lid over the fact that I had sex with Nikki and Lips. It didn't even matter that it happened before the two of us got together. That's when I realized that she was feeling the same way. When she began whispering that she loved me? I drank that in, and I drank it in deep. If she dies, I won't mourn her. Hell no. I'll make sure I join her. It's just that fucking simple.

When I get into the room where the fucker is being held, I get pissed all over again. He's barely been worked over. I've seen Drag in action, so I know when he's gone easy on a motherfucker and the fact that he did this time, pisses me off. I know he blames Dani for what happened to Nicole, but Jesus this is just fucking wrong. It also cements my decision. I'm essentially going rogue here. I'm ignoring a direct order from my president and I'm putting the good of one over my club. I feel betrayed too, though. I don't think they left me with any other choice.

I stir up fear in him for a little while and then sit down. I reach in my shirt pocket, under my vest and pull out my smokes. I put them on a table and then light one, inhaling deep. I let the nicotine calm me and center me. I don't smoke often, but then again it's not every day your woman is in the hands of some sick fucker and you can't find her.

I've got this ass-wipe thinking I'm going to burn his balls off. He's not really talking, so I guess the possibility is still on the table. I got my name because I used to be able to crush just about anything with my bare hands. Right now if I didn't have to keep him alive, I'd crush his head off his neck, it would stop all the whining he's doing. Instead, I pick up my knife. I'll cut his skin in small strips until he gives me the information I need. If that doesn't work then, and only then will I touch his fucking balls. I'm sure those fuckers stink, plus he looks like the kind of coward that's going to piss himself.

IT TAKES ME about an hour to get some information I can use. Still, it's a long shot. While I was burning off fingerprints and pulling his teeth, anything that might be used for identification purposes, the fucker finally let it slip who hired him. It wasn't Kavanagh, but the guy set up a meeting area out at the old tobacco barn on Route 11. It's not much, but it's the first glimmer of hope I have. I quickly ended the mother fucker and buried him on an old hiking trail. It's not far away from Savage MC land and if Dragon finds out he's going to be all kinds of fucking pissed at me, but I don't have the time to be neat. Every minute that Dani is gone is another one that Kavanagh might find her and fuck….to be honest I think he already has her. I can't even think about what might happen to her.

I decide to head back to the club. I can give them the information I have and get some back-up. I'm going to need help. I don't know what kind of fire power Kavanagh has and I'm not about to fuck up what might be my only chance to save Dani. When I get there Nicole is crying and everyone is gathered around, and for a minute I think Dani has already been killed. I can't breathe. It's like someone has my heart in their hand and they're squeezing it so tight that the pain is debilitating.

"They have Dani, Dragon. He's demanding I…he was torturing her. He has Dani, Dragon." Nicole says, her words disjointed and full of pain. My world stops.

"Where Nicole?" Dragon questions.

"The old abandoned Laurel Elementary School. Dragon, we have to save her. She's in bad shape."

"What kind of fucking shape?" I ask, because I can't stop myself. I see the look Dragon gives me and the pity in his eyes, but I don't give a fuck.

"He…they beat her. She, oh God, I've never seen someone hurt that bad before. He'll kill her if we don't get her."

I've heard enough. They can all stand around and talk if they want to. I tear out of there heading straight for the old school.

I make it in record time and way ahead of my brothers, but the place is empty. There's no sign of the fucker anywhere and worse, there's no sign of Dani. I comb through the place and I find a corner covered in blood about the time the rest of the crew show up.

"Son of a bitch!" I growl when I see the huge amount of blood. She's so small. How can she withstand so much blood loss? I close my eyes and remember that day on the beach when she smiled and kissed me. I hear her whisper, I love you Zander and it's all I can do to keep standing. I turn on my brother. "I knew by you fucking around it would end up screwing us in the ass. Now we have no idea where the hell Dani is!"

Dragon doesn't react with words, he swings and uppercuts me under the chin. I wasn't expecting it, so I fall back on the ground. I want to get up and go a few rounds with him. Dragon is a mean motherfucker, but then so am I and it just might make me feel better to pound him. I don't though. I know I'm in the wrong here, but goddamn it I need him to help me get my woman back.

"Motherfucker! That is not what screwed us in the ass!" Dragon yells, and squats down to look at me. He's vibrating with anger. He can join the club. "What screwed us in the ass, dick-weed, was you overruling my fucking orders. Tell me, where the fuck is my prisoner today, Crush? What the fuck did you do with him?" When I don't answer him he grabs me by the hair on my head and pulls me up to stand with him. "Where the fuck is my prisoner, Crush?"

I think about not answering, but in the end I'm honest with him—or at least mostly honest. "I did what you wouldn't."

"Yeah, and what was that, brother?"

"I interrogated the ass-wipe," I say easily, half hoping Dragon will start whaling on me and give me an excuse to hit back.

"Gee, wonder why I didn't think of that. Tell me Crush, did you find out one more damn piece of information?"

I should be honest here, I need his help, but I'm tired of Dragon being a sanctimonious asshole. If this was Nicole missing he'd be going fucking crazier than I am. So, I don't tell him shit. I'll do it on my own.

"Do you know why that is dick-head? It's because he didn't fucking know anything!" He growls. "Did you set him free, at least, and have someone follow him?"

Here is where guilt hits, because I really should have done better with this part, if nothing else. Still, it is what it is. "There wasn't anything left to set free," I tell him.

As lies go, this one is the least of my worries.

Chapter 37

DANI

I DON'T KNOW how long I've been out. When I come to, all I know is that I'm staring at the face of the devil himself. I also notice my hands are tied. My feet are free, but that doesn't help me get the knife I have hidden under my jacket.

"We meet again, dear wife. You look pretty good for a dead woman."

"It's amazing what escaping life with a fucking asshole will do for you," I answer. I get a kick to the stomach in thanks for my sarcasm. Since I'm expecting a lot more, I suck it up. "Nice to know you're still the same bastard you've always been," I grunt, because it's hard to catch my breath.

"Aw, my Melinda how I've missed you, but I don't remember you being quite so outspoken before. It will be fun breaking you. I shall have to do it quick though, since you can't live much longer. You see dear wife, I'm getting married next week."

"My condolences to your fiancé."

"Melinda, you sound almost...jealous," he says and he bends down to the floor where I'm sitting, bending down so his face is mere inches from mine. Inside my heart is hammering and I'm a nervous wreck. I've been afraid before. I was married to the devil himself, so I've been deep into fear. So deep that my body felt frozen, but right now I have to acknowledge that it's over. I'm dying.... I'm dying tonight. Within that certainty there is freedom. There's nothing more that Michael can do to me than he doesn't already have planned. He's going to take it all from me. He's going to kill me. So, when he bends his face down towards me, I look at him. I really look at him. He once had features a teenage girl found dashing and debonair. Now, they fall flat and I only see the ugly. Eyes that once looked dark and mysterious are now hidden behind designer shades and seriously, we're in an old deserted building. The lighting in here sucks. Why on Earth would you wear sunglasses? I don't need to see his eyes to know that they're soulless.

"Jealous? You have to be kidding me," I tell him, my stomach churning with the need to vomit.

"It's okay Melinda, I can give you a pity fuck for old time's sake," he says moving in. He grabs my hair and gathers it in a tight hold, pulling my face closer to him and his lips are so close to mine that I am enveloped by his sickening scent. "I do remember what a wild girl you are, maybe I'll let Donald join in. One last hurrah before you die, this doesn't have to be a completely unpleasant experience."

It takes everything I am and everything I have inside of me, not to close my eyes and get lost in the nightmarish memories he triggers. Instead, I beat them back down and give Michael my best fuck-you look and spit in his face. His face goes stony hard and I know I'm going to pay for that. I watch as he reaches into the pocket of his suit-coat and takes out a white handkerchief. He uses it to wipe off his face. Once that's done, he takes his sunglasses off, carefully folds them and places them in his now empty suit-pocket. He then takes the handkerchief, and even though I try to scoot back and get away from him, he grabs me by my hair, jerks my head back hard, and slams it into the concrete wall behind me.

The pain from the blow radiates through my entire body. I feel like I'm in a tunnel and I'm having trouble getting the room to come back into focus. There's a roar in my ears and I'm doing the best I can to shake it off. Before I can, he's stuffing the handkerchief into my mouth. I gag and choke, but he makes sure the entire thing goes in my mouth.

"There, I forgot how fucking annoying your voice was," he says, standing up.

"I believe it's time for lesson number one, Donald," he says and the sick pleasure in his voice is heavy in the air.

I push back further against the wall. I know it's useless. I have nowhere to go even if there is some space between us—still, I do it. It must be some fight or flight reflex. It's the absolute wrong thing to do. Now I'm against the cold, hard cinderblock with nowhere to go, and Donald and Michael are standing in front of me. They are the two most vile and disgustingly evil men I have ever known in my life. If I could talk, I would scream, yell, berate, and curse… anything to make me feel better and to feel less…helpless. I pull on the bindings on my wrists and there's a little give. I pull and tug harder and harder, hoping with everything in me to get them free.

That's when I see it. The shiny steel pipe that Donald is holding and that is why being against the wall is a bad thing. There is nothing to cushion me when my body absorbs the blow. It comes hard and the breeze from the swing reaches me first, sending chills from the cool air over my body. Then the pipe connects with my knees. As blows go, it could have been worse. There are much worse places to be hit than in your knees. I've had them all, so I know. Yet, the force is so strong and the pipe is so heavy that it doesn't land with a thud. No, it cracks into the bone and pain radiates immediately. Tears gather in my eyes and spring free. I hate giving them tears, but there's nothing I can do.

I've barely recovered from the first blow when another one follows it. This one is higher up on my legs, just above the knees. He's trying to break my legs. I see it in their smiles, in the sinister way they look down at me, knowing they will get everything from me. I vow then when I die, I will find a way to reach around them and drag them down into fucking hell with me. Michael reaches down and grabs my head, pulling out the handkerchief he leers at me.

"Are you ready to be nicer, Melinda? Surely you'd rather this go easier on you? At least die with the dignity you never possessed in life."

"Fuck…You…"

I'm gasping and the tears clog my throat, but he looks at me strangely. I think my reply surprises him. I count that as a moral victory. The pain in my body is so intense there are black dots floating in my eyes and I truly want to pass out.

"Melinda, you are even more stupid than I gave you credit for," Michael says resignedly, stuffing the handkerchief back in my mouth.

Another hit by the pipe, this one lands against my stomach and my body feels like it's being split in two from the blow. I don't get to recover, before there's another and then another. Four repeated hits in the same area and I'm close to losing consciousness. I think the last two went higher than I first realized, because my breathing is ragged. Broken ribs? Maybe…I can't be sure. Donald grabs my foot and pulls me roughly down to the ground. I lie there in misery. I can't do anything else. Then I see the knife in Michael's hands. A moment later I feel the cold metal of the blade dance under my stomach. I'm waiting for the red hot fire of the blade slicing into my skin. I don't get that. I can't be happy about it though, because I feel the chill of air hit my skin as the blade slices through my shirt and bra.

It's my worst nightmare come true. Lying on the cold floor, my body exposed to the two men that have violated me, haunted me...destroyed me. Michael puts the blade flat against my face and slides it down my forehead and further to my nose and my chin.

"It's time for the fun to really begin, Melinda. If you tell me where my money is, I might do you a favor and end you before there's too much pain."

I close my eyes and try to pretend I'm somewhere else. It's impossible with the pain. I can do nothing but cry and scream against the gag, as the knife slices into my stomach. I almost lose it at the white-hot agony that comes with the slicing of Michael's blade against my skin. It's familiar, but new and more intense than I remember. Perhaps time had soften the memories after all, I'm not sure, all I know, is that with the second...or maybe it was the third....it all goes hazy. I feel Michael cut from the bottom of my ribcage, down my stomach, and darkness swallows me. I welcome it.

I can't be sure of what happens next. Which is good and bad. I could have sworn I heard Nicole crying and for the space of a minute, I thought I might have been rescued. Then I feel the far-off dull pain of someone kicking my stomach and the stretching of the cuts on my stomach. I hear crying and it sounds so mournful, so sad. I want to reach out and hug the person for the pain they must be enduring. Then I wonder...if maybe I'm the one who is crying? I hope I don't give him that...I hope it's not me.

I FEEL LIKE I'm disconnected from my body. The pain is intense, but it's almost as if I'm above it all looking down. I keep going in and out of consciousness, so I'm not sure how long Michael has had me. I don't know why I've held on. Maybe I really am stupid like Michael says. Surely a smart person would have already given up and died. I don't want to live, I'm pretty much done and yet, somehow my body refuses to let go.

I'm being moved. I can hear voices over the pounding in my head. For a brief moment, I thought I felt the warmth of the sun on my body. I'm not sure. I can't open my eyes, their swollen shut. I don't exactly remember when that happened, I just remember the repeated blows from Michael. I'm burning up…fever…infection…the thoughts are jumbled in my head, but I know that's what it is. I've lost blood, but nowhere near enough. Michael is a master at going to the limits of what a body can withstand. Still, he wants me dead, so this beating, this punishment is so far beyond anything he's ever done before.

I hear the slam of a door and then we start moving. A car…I'm not in a seat though. I'm pretty sure they've thrown me in the trunk. There's a moment when they go over something that jars the car and I bounce, causing even more pain than when they moved me. Railroad tracks. I let the hum of the car take over in my head and try to…die. It doesn't happen. Breathing is getting harder though. Each breath is painful and shallower than the last. Is this a sign that it will all be over soon?

Eventually, the vehicle comes to a stop. I can hear the soft thud of doors closing. At least I figure that's what they are, because the car rocks after the sound each time. Above me I hear the trunk lid opening.

My left arm is broken and useless, also the hand itself feels…different. The sleeve of my jacket has been split and there's a large cut in the skin there. My right arm still seems to be working, but I hold it close to my stomach. I want them to believe it is as useless as the left. I also want them to believe I am completely out of it.

If Michael thinks I am unconscious, then I might be able to store up enough energy to use the knife I still have in my jacket. They've cut off the rest of my clothes. I don't know why they left my jacket. Perhaps I have pure dumb luck? Maybe God decided he needed to answer one of my prayers after all and this is His way. I probably am going to hell soon. I don't see me making it to the pearly gates, but if I do, I intend on filing a grievance against the whole prayer selection process.

Someone is lifting me and the shift of my bones is so sudden that the pain is blinding. My head is hanging down and straining my neck, the pounding in my head, along with the pain from the rest of me is so all consuming that I almost black out. I can't let that happen.

I'm tossed down on the ground with a thud. I wait. It seems all I've been doing is waiting my whole life. Waiting for Michael to kill me, waiting for someone to rescue me, waiting to feel normal, waiting to feel alive, and waiting to die. That has been my life. Here in this moment I've come full circle. Only, this time I know that I can't wait anymore. I can't. I can't wait for someone else to give me, my death. I can't wait for a rescue. It ends here.

I hear talking off to my right. I can't make out the words over the drumming pain. It doesn't matter anyway. My hand pushes under my jacket to the inside pocket. It takes time, I don't know how long exactly, but enough time to get my fingers and hand to cooperate and find the handle. My hands are covered in blood and the handle keeps slipping out of my grasp. Finally, I get it positioned just right and pull it out of the pocket and lay it under my breast. I do my best to work and try and get my thumb to hit the release button for the blade. I can't find it, and I can't see. I have no strength, so I have no idea if I will even be able to push it in. I want to scream at how useless it all seems. I try...I try...and I try. I just can't seem to get it.

Then, I hear Michael's voice, "Is she dead yet?"

"She's not cold, though I don't see how the bitch could still be breathing," Donald answers.

"She's like a fucking cockroach, that's how," I hear Michael answer and desperation swamps me.

With renewed strength, I push until I feel the spring snap and the blade unfold. It is Crusher's hunting knife. I saw it before I left and had to take it. I had hoped to use it on Michael, but since that opportunity didn't present itself, I have to do what I can.

I want to yell at Michael and give him a great big, fuck you. I can't. I'm too weak and they might stop me before I can carry this out. All I can do is be satisfied with the fact that I am ending this. Me—not Michael. I'm taking the only thing from him that I can—his pleasure in taking my life.

I should have done it long ago. I just didn't want to accept that it was my only choice. I'm glad I didn't. If I had, I would have never met Zander. I would have never got to love him and somehow that is worth all the pain. I do wish I could see his face again, or hear his voice one more time, but perhaps its better this way.

With that thought, I summon up what strength I have left and plunge the knife into my chest. I was aiming for my heart. I don't think it made it. My hands are shaky and so weak that I know instantly it didn't do the ultimate damage, but I can feel the blood leaving my body and know it was enough.

"Fuck!" I hear someone growl and I could almost smile. It's not physically possible even if I wasn't tumbling into the darkness.

Chapter 38

CRUSHER

I'M LIVING ON fumes. I look like some motherfucking junkie. I can't even remember the last time I ate or did any of the things that you normally do to prepare for the day. I don't even care. I've been casing out this motherfucking barn for two days. With each hour that passes it feels like a piece of my soul is being chipped away. The woman I love could be dying, hell maybe she's already dead, and I'm sitting in the weeds, twiddling my goddamn thumbs and waiting. I try not to imagine what they're doing to her, but I'm failing. Each thing that comes to my mind is more horrific than the other and my own imagination is slowly driving me crazy.

I just pulled to the end of an old, forgotten road that leads to the barn. I went home last night. I didn't want to, but I needed to refuel and see if there were any new leads at the club. It's been two days and I can't afford to waste more time. I need something to do. I need to find Dani. The problem is, I don't have any more info and not a fucking source to find more. None. I pour a cup of coffee out of a thermos and watch as my hands shake. Jesus. I have to grip the thermos cup with both hands.

I know I'm fucked up. I know I haven't been acting rationally. I keep asking myself would it have been different if I had talked to Dragon. Would he have listened when I told him that

Kavanagh's patsy did give me more information? Would Dragon admit he was wrong? The shit I've done...I don't even recognize myself. I don't know how I knew that Dani hadn't got away. I just did. Sometimes her face would come to mind, and then I would think of my mom and the fucking shit she put up with and then Melly...and that horrible night when I found Melly with her brains blown out, lying on the floor beside that sick fucker of a father she had and I'd lose it.

It seems my life has been spent surrounded by women that needed my help and my failure, to protect them. I couldn't save my mom. I couldn't save Melly. I had vowed to protect Hellcat and I honestly thought I could and yet I fucked that up too. Would Dani have still ran if I hadn't called her Melly? Would it have made a difference if I explained about Melly? If I had talked with her? I don't know and all these questions and mistakes I keep making are weighing hard on me. I just need to find Dani, find her and get her home. Then, I can spend the rest of my days trying to prove to her that she's all I'll ever need in the world.

I slide out of the truck and trudge through the briars and weeds until I can see the old tobacco barn in the distance. My heart speeds up and skips before hammering in my chest...hard. There are cars out front. Three to be exact and one is a fucking Mercedes Benz. My first urge is to run in there with guns blazing. I can't risk it. If Dani is in there, then I need to make sure she's out of harm's way. I can't think of her being anything but alive. I just can't.

I slowly make my way to the barn, trying to be as quiet as I can. I have my gun ready, but I'd rather not let them know I'm around. I noticed a giant crack between the wood on the far side of the structure the other day, and I make that my goal. I get there and can literally taste the adrenaline pumping in my system. Please let Dani be okay, please let Dani....

All thoughts cease as I look through the crack. I want to scream. I want to put my gun in and shoot every fucker in there. I can't. I need to do this smart. I have to, but what I see breaks me. Dani is lying broken in a corner. She's unrecognizable. I'm not even sure I'd even realize she was a person, if not for the long dark hair that is knotted and caked with dirt and...blood. Her face is mostly hidden but what I see is swollen and bruised so badly that you can't even make out her features. Then, I hear the men off to the side talking.

"I planted the bomb in Dragon's vehicle. It'll go off when he takes it out of park."

"It didn't go off earlier today," the guy I recognize as Michael says, slapping him on the back of the head.

"Ow," he says grabbing his head. "It wasn't supposed to. It set the system up, it'll go off when the gearshift is moved from park now. You said you wanted them both to pay, Boss."

Fuck. I need to get a call out to Dragon and warn him. I can't take the time to do it now though. Doing so, would risk being found and not being able to help Dani. I pray I get through before it's too late. It twists in my gut that I'm choosing Dani over my brothers, but it doesn't stop me.

The men talk for a little longer, then Michael and one of the others leave. It takes all I have to let him go. I push up against the barn as they go out the front entrance. I peek around the corner to see them get in a sleek black Mercedes. When they drive off, I take a breath of relief. Before going in and getting my woman, I try and call Dragon. I want to give it enough time to make sure Michael doesn't come back.

Dragon's phone rings twice.

"Yeah motherfucker, want to tell me where you've been?"

"Drag, listen quick, man."

"Where in the fuck are you? Do you know what went down today?"

Dragon's voice is faint at best. The line is full of distortion and noise and I have to strain to hear him.

"Do not use the cages today!"

"What are you saying asshole, I can barely hear you?"

"Man, listen the cars are rigged to blow. I got Dani now, but you really..."

"You got Dani? Fuck, man your signal sucks. Where'd you find her? We'll..."

"Listen, Dragon! I can't talk. You got to hear me. The cars, especially yours—don't use them today. Don't use any of them, get Freak to..."

The call drops.

Fuck! I try several times to reconnect and keep getting a Call Failed message.

I have to worry about Dani, I don't have time to spare.

I go to the front of the barn, take a breath to steady myself, and draw my gun. Then, I kick the door open, firing while searching for the fucker that Michael left behind. I train my gun on him and then shoot until the hammer clicks and nothing happens. I watch as his body falls to the ground, then reload my gun in case the others come back.

I go to Dani and get down on my knees, checking her out. The sight of her hurts. It was bad from a distance, but it's much worse up close. She has to be dead. No one could survive this kind of beating, especially a woman as small as Dani. I should have gotten here sooner. My hand trembles as I move it to her neck, which is colored with...rope burns? Did they strangle her? I try to move her hair, but it's so caked with mud and... shit, it's soaked in her blood. I slide my fingers to her throat trying to find a pulse.

I find nothing.

"Oh fuck, Hellcat, don't do this to me. You've got to survive, to punish this S.O.B."

I go down flat on my ass, feeling the hurt and pain seep into my system. I let another woman down; I was too late...again. I reach out for her hand, I need to hold it, if only for a minute. Her beautiful hand that I've felt slide over my body countless times, is now almost as unrecognizable as her face. Her fingers have been broken and they're swollen and distorted, bending in ways I'm not sure can ever be straightened. Then I notice she has no small finger. It has been cut right at the base of the hand. The wound is open, angry, and infected. Motherfucker.

I scream out in denial, as I pull her broken body over to my lap and I hold her hand in mine. I feel as if I'm dying inside. My eyes close as the tears fall. I close them to try and stop the flow, but it does no good. I see her, her face as she's laughing at me, her eyes when she needs me, the look on her face as I'm sliding inside of her, and finally my favorite memory. The memory from the day at the beach when she kissed me in front of everyone and gave me a look of trust. Trust she misplaced...because I failed her.

"I'll get him, Hellcat. I'll get him and make him pay."

I kiss her forehead in goodbye and slide her off my lap. I notice a hunting knife on the ground. Something about it is familiar, but I push it away. I need to get her out of here. My woman deserves to be at rest in the sunshine. When I get revenge on these motherfuckers, I know in my heart I'm going to join her. We didn't have much in this life, but the next...the next I will make it my mission that she knows nothing but joy. I'm preparing to get her out of here, when I hear it... It's faint, very faint, but I latch onto it immediately.

"Zander," her voice whispers, it's disjointed and full of pain.

"Oh fuck, sweetheart, you are hanging on. That's my Hellcat. I knew you had balls of steel. Let's get you home."

It takes me awhile to get her out of there because every movement causes her pain and I can't risk them discovering us.

"Hang on a little longer, Hellcat. Just a little longer and I'll have you at the hospital."

"No."

It was one syllable but the terror in her hoarse, whispered voice spoke volumes.

"Hellcat."

"Married. He'll…please, Zander."

Married. My Hellcat doesn't know it, but she's going to be a widow pretty fucking soon. I call Doc and arrange to have him meet us at the club. Then I try constantly to call Dragon. Each time the call goes unanswered and I'm asked to leave a message, my gut clinches. Fuck. I hope I wasn't too late. That's when I notice it. I don't know how I didn't before, maybe it was because her injuries are so damn extensive that I could look for weeks and not find them all. I don't know, but there is a large stabbing wound in the middle of her chest. Thankfully, it's nowhere near her heart, but there's so much blood.

Hospital it is. I reach over and grab an old shirt that is lying in the passenger floorboard and push it into the wound. I wince because I know that fucker can't be clean, but it's all I can do for now. My foot presses harder on the accelerator, but inside I feel like time is running out.

Chapter 39

BULL

WE'RE ALL AT the hospital. It's a fucking mess. Dragon's car blew up at the wedding. There was nothing left of him or Frog...nothing. My brothers are gone. Nicole is a basket case. I helped get her settled and the Doc gave her something to make her sleep. I posted Freak and Hawk outside her door and ordered them not to let her leave or let anyone in. Then Doc told us about Crusher and Dani and the rest of us came here. It's bad...really fucking bad. I don't think I've ever seen any motherfucker in this shape—let alone a woman. How she's still breathing is beyond me.

I'm trying to keep my head today, because I know I'm going to be needed. Still, I'm having these fucking tremors in my arm and it feels like a hot poker is being jabbed in my eyes. These goddamn headaches won't let up. They're coming more often and it's to the point that they are constant now. My vision is blurry as hell in my left eye. The attack that day at Dancer's did more damage than I've told any of them. Fuck, the pain is crippling at times. I started popping pills like candy to just function. That's no longer cutting it, which is why I'm here—in a fucking medical supply closet, talking to Nurse Melissa Anne Allen. She's getting me some stronger pain meds. I could get them through the pipeline at the club, but not without my brothers finding out. I don't need fucking nursemaids.

So I found my own route. Nurse Allen here showed up at a couple of club parties and after giving her my cock a few times, she seemed eager enough to help me, as long as she gets to keep coming to the parties.

"Do you have the stuff? I ask sounding bone-deep tired and I am....in more ways than one.

"Sure do baby, I got all you need to make you feel so fucking good you will be flying."

"Let me see it," I growl, wanting to get the fuck away.

"No way, I want a ride on that stallion you got between your legs. Been thinking about it all day," she says, already pulling the blue uniform shirt over her head.

"Jesus, 'Lissa, I just gave you my cock this morning. I'm here for my brother. His old lady is in bad shape. It's not the time to be fucking you."

"It's not the time to be getting shit to make you high, but I don't see that stopping you. Come on! It can be a quickie, I'm on duty anyway."

Fuck it. I grab her by the back of the neck and push her over the small desk, with her ass facing me. Any other woman might have second thoughts, but not her. She helps me by sliding her pants down over her ass.

"This is going to be hard and fast," I tell her and that's the only warning she gets. I undo my pants just enough to get my dick out.

"Just how I like it, baby," she purrs.

I fish around in my pocket for a condom and quickly glove up. Then, I lean over her looking at the small shelf. I push shit out of the way, ignoring how it falls to the ground. I grab a large white bottle with purple writing that says lubricating jelly.

"What's this shit for?" I ask squeezing the cold gel out in

my hand.

"We use it for probes and things like ultrasounds," she says gasping because her hand is already working her clit.

I use my free hand to slide the gel all over my latex covered cock. If I was a better fucking man I'd make sure that ass had lube. I'm not. I haven't been a good fucking man for a while. No one has noticed and I'm fast approaching the point where I don't give a fuck.

Once my cock is covered enough, I grab her hips and slap her fucking ass hard. She gasps.

"Well get ready to be probed by my cock then."

She laughs and turns to the side watching me. She moves her hands over her breasts and squeezes them until the skin goes white.

I push her back around to the position I need. "Pull these fucking ass cheeks apart if you want my dick, you're going to take it up the ass like the dirty little slut you are," I demand.

She does as I order and her hips are bucking back against me, eager for the reaming I'm about to give her. When she pulls those cheeks apart, exposing the pretty pink rosette of her ass, I rub the head of my dick over it a few times, watching at how the clear lube, slickens up so it's nice and wet and waiting for me. I position my hand over her mouth. 'Lissa is a screamer and while normally I dig that shit, I'm not about to be discovered in a supply closet, with my pants down and pills in my pocket.

"Bite down on my hand to keep quiet and we'll get this ride done."

As romance goes, it's shit, but this isn't about hearts and flowers. I plunge into her ass hard and her teeth bite into my hand and I growl at the flash of pain. I fuck her harder in retaliation. I'm pounding her hard. Hell my balls spank against her pussy with each thrust and she's so wet I can feel it, even with the brief contact. Her ass is so fucking tight she's strangling my cock. I push my hand down on her back, flattening her against the desk and causing her ass to thrust out even more. That slight movement causes those tight anal walls to flutter around my cock and I know I'm about to fucking blow.

"If you want to come with me like a good little whore you better start fingering that pussy, 'Lissa."

She groans against my hand, but wastes no time in doing as instructed. I keep pounding her ass until I feel the heat run through my balls and feel them tighten, as my cum begins to gather. I slide out of her ass, whip the condom off and finish by jerking my load on her back and watching it run down her ass.

"Now you can smell like a dirty little slut who needs a spanking the rest of the day. I bet those doctors like working next to you smelling my jiz all over you." I tell her taking my hand away. I wince. Damn, she made me bleed. I turn to the small sink in the corner, I take one of the rough paper towels and roughly clean off my cock and throw it on the floor. Then I wash off my hands.

'Lissa comes up behind me and runs her hands over my bare ass. I jerk away enough to pull up my pants. "No more, I need to get out and be with my brother."

"Yeah, if they're still out there," she says cleaning herself in the sink as I turn away.

"Why, what do you mean?"

"She coded before I even met you here. They were working to try and bring her back."

"You didn't think to tell me?" I growl, opening the pill bottle and swallowing two down.

"I didn't figure you cared. You said you hated her the other night at the club, remember? Besides I know you wanted those pills, that is more important to you," she shrugs.

I freeze. Fuck. I want to argue, but I can't. She's completely right. I would have left to get the pills regardless if I had known or not.

"Later, 'Lissa."

"Party this weekend at the club, right?" She asks, and I grunt. "Great I'll see you then!" I guess she takes my grunt as agreement.

I go outside walking in the direction I left my brothers. As I take a few more steps I hear an announcement over the intercom.

"Code Blue emergency trauma. Code Blue."

Fuck.

Chapter 40

CRUSHER

I SLAM MY fist into the wall, because I have nothing else to hit. They took her away from me almost an hour ago. They wheeled her through the metal doors on a gurney and wouldn't let me stay by her side. She looked so pale, her skin almost having a blue tint. I spent the first thirty minutes answering questions the doctors asked, talking to the police, calling in markers all over the fucking county to keep this shit quiet, and locking it all down. The last twenty minutes I've been pacing back and forth waiting for someone, anyone to tell me what's going on with my fucking woman.

Bull showed up with a few of the brothers, but honestly I wish they hadn't. There was an explosion at the church. Hell, I had even forgotten that Dragon was getting married today. I lost him today, him and Frog and the weight of that is so heavy on my shoulders right now, I don't even have words. I should have tried to get a hold of him sooner... I should have kept trying. I should have told him I had a lead on Dani. Would he have postponed the wedding to save Dani? I got two of my brothers killed. The shame and grief of that suffocates me. The hardest part though is the guilt of knowing that if I could go back and change it? I wouldn't. I couldn't risk delaying another minute to get to Dani. Fuck! As it is, it might be too late.

"Any news, man?" Bull asks. I didn't even notice he was

behind me. I'm rubbing my hand from pounding the cement wall and trying not to think about life without my woman. I wasn't lying. It may take me a little bit to kill Michael, but once that's done I will join her.

"None," I answer, my voice full of frustration.

"Shit."

"Pretty much. What happened to your hand?" I ask him when I notice a thin half-ring of blood on the skin between the thumb and index finger.

He looks down at his hand, staring at it before shrugging and stuffing it into his pants pocket.

"Who knows, at least I'm not pounding walls in with…"

"Mr. Dawson?" The nurse asks from behind me. I jerk around and walk straight to her.

"Dani?"

"Your wife is hanging on, sir. She's being prepped for emergency surgery right now, her spleen is ruptured, and has been for at least a couple days now. We wanted to wait until she was stable. She coded once, but seems to be holding her on now. Her injuries are extensive, but right now the spleen is first and foremost on our list."

"Can I…I need to see her before she goes into surgery."

"Sir, that's really not encouraged and she's unconscious right now. Why don't you have a seat and I'll make sure…"

"I need to see my wife," I demand again, interrupting her.

She frowns at me, and then nods her head. "I'll talk to the doctor, as soon as he gives the ok, you can see her."

"Thank you," I say and I mean it. I think if I have to go any longer without seeing Dani's face and reassuring myself that she was in fact still alive, they'd be sending the men in white coats down here to haul me away.

She leaves and my pacing starts again. In just a minute she

comes back and leads me through a small corridor into a completely white and metal room. There are machines beeping and Hellcat is hooked up to wires and monitors and she looks so frail...so lifeless. I go to her side. They've set her arm and her fingers are wrapped too. The wound on her chest has been stitched and she's been cleaned, honestly though her face is still so swollen that it's hard for me to believe this is my woman. Then I notice something that is horrific to me, even over everything else. Her hair has been cut...no not cut...sheered.

Maybe the nurse noticed my face, I don't know, but she answers the unspoken question.

"Sorry sir, it was best to expedite and try to get her clean for surgery. She had some rather large lacerations on the side and back of her head. It was the easiest solution. It will grow back."

My hand reaches out to touch the baby blue cap like thing they have over her head.

"I love you, Hellcat. You fight and hold on for me and I'll be here. I'll be here waiting for you."

The words seem hollow and empty. I should have something important to say, something that will make her fight her way back to me. I can't think of one damn thing. As they wheel her out of the room, it feels like I have no reason left to breathe. I know it's a feeling I will become achingly familiar with if Dani doesn't survive.

"I'm here waiting for you, Hellcat. I'm right here. I'll wait on you forever."

As she's taken from my sight, I realize that I am completely telling the truth. I'll wait for her for the rest of my days and then some.

I start praying. I don't know if it will help, but it sure can't hurt.

Chapter 41

DANI

I'M SO TIRED. It feels like my eyes have cement blocks on them they're so heavy. It's all I can do to open them. When I look around and see the hospital room, terror instantly hits me. I look around frantically, knowing Michael will be there. That's when I see him...Zander. He's in a large recliner beside my bed. His hair is tossed every which way on his head, his face looks haggard, and there's beard growth on his face that he's never had before. He's wearing jeans and a white t-shirt. He doesn't even have on his cut. His feet are kicked out on a stool. He's snoring and it makes me want to smile, but that would require too much movement and the pain right now is way too intense. I look over at the door and Freak is standing there by the door, arms folded and looking every inch the bad boy biker he is. I lick my lips and try to find my voice. It hurts to breathe, so I'm figuring talking is going to be worse.

"Freak..." The sound is hoarse, dry and squeaky all rolled in together.

He immediately looks over at me, "Hey, babe."

"What are you doing?" I ask wincing at the effort it takes to make a whole sentence.

"Standing guard so Crush will sleep before he keels over."

My eyes go automatically back to Zander and my heart flutters with a warmth inside of me.

"Standing guard?" I ask.

"That bastard is still out there. We protect family babe, always."

My breath lodges in my throat and I'm not sure what it is but it warms me from the inside out. Family?

"I'll let you talk alone with Crush and relieve Hawk, he's out front."

"Three of you?"

"Six, we've got Torch and some of Skull's crew watching the entrances to the hospital. That bastard won't get a hold of you again." He closes the door as he leaves and I think about all that he just said. It's a lot to take in.

"Stop it right now, Hellcat."

I look up to find Zander pulled up close to the bed, his elbows are on the mattress and he's staring intently at me. His eyes look so tired and yet they glow with emotion.

"Hi..."

"Hey, sweetheart." He says leaning up to kiss my forehead. Even that slight touch hurts, but I ignore it and just breathe in his scent.

"How long have I been out?"

"Not long honey, you're a survivor. You fought your way back hard, and you need to stop what you're doing."

"Stop?" I ask, feeling his hand slide along the side of my face.

"Worrying about getting others involved. We got this Hellcat, and it's not just you involved now. The club has a score to settle with Michael and it's the kind that only his head on a fucking platter will solve."

"Score?" I ask, confused. I know Freak said I was family, but this seems...

"Dragon, honey. Michael had his vehicle rigged to blow.

He and Frog didn't survive," Crusher tells me and I don't understand…there's so much sadness in his expression and then it hits me that Dragon and Frog…they…oh God, they died. I gasp and suck in a breath, because I feel like I'm drowning in the pain that causes it, along with the pain of knowing Michael killed someone else I cared about, punches me hard in the stomach causing tears to run from my eyes. Not Dragon! He and Nicole are supposed to be married. They have a baby on the way and Frog…he was so young and I don't think he even got a taste of life…or love. My heart is hammering against my chest and I can't seem to recover enough to catch my breath.

"Nic…Zander, Nic? The baby?" I ask, not able to form a complete sentence or thought. My mind is going in a million different directions.

"They're okay, sweetheart. Nic's having a hard time adjusting, but she'll be okay."

"I…oh God Zander, this is all my fault. This was why I left. I can't let more people die for me."

"Stop it, Hellcat. That fucker is a mean son of a bitch who has needed to be killed from the day he drew his first breath. You can't take his actions on your shoulders. We'll handle him. You just need to concentrate on getting better."

Logically, I understand his words. I just can't bring myself to feel blameless. The bodies in my past keep piling up and for no other reason than they wanted to help or protect me. When is it going to end? My hand goes up to my chest. I don't feel anything by my heart, so move it up till I find it, way too high to hit the heart and not even close to where it needed to be. Michael is right. I am pathetic.

"That one scared us the most. It was deep. You lost a lot of blood from it. It's good I found you when I did," he says and my hand freezes on the rough skin.

"You shouldn't have saved me, Zander."

He doesn't respond and I'm too lost in my thoughts to realize that he's upset. I close my eyes as the tears fall. Poor Nic.

"Look at me, Hellcat."

I can't bring myself to, even when he uses the command in his voice that I normally wouldn't argue with.

"Hellcat, now."

"I did it," I whisper to him softly, because I'm ashamed. I don't really want him to hear me. I'm ashamed that I was weak. I'm ashamed I didn't manage to do it. I'm ashamed for being in this situation. I'm sick with regret that me living took the life of two men...two really good men...two men who were loved and had a life of happiness ahead of them.

"You didn't do shit, Hellcat. It was that fucker, Mich...."

"I stabbed myself, Zander. I wanted to die. I wanted to take that from him. I couldn't even manage to do that. I'm weak and my weakness...killed..." I can't even finish the thought. I killed Dragon... "You should have let me die. It would have been better if you did."

Zander gently pulls my face towards him. He's leaning over top of me and his eyes are full of emotion.

"You need to shut that fucking shit up right now, Hellcat. You need to listen to me. You are the strongest woman I have ever met in my life. The shit you must have lived through, the shit you just lived through? That would destroy someone weak. There wouldn't be anything but pieces left of them. You are fucking amazing and if I have to tell you that every day for the rest of our lives together, I will. So just cut that shit out about being weak and how it would have been better if you were dead. Hand to God Hellcat, if I was in a world where you weren't breathing, I'd follow you wherever the fuck you went, because you're it. You're it for me."

"Zander, please just stop. We both know the real reason you even look my way and I'm too tired to pretend otherwise."

Zander sighs and sits back down holding my hand. I look down at our joined hands and find another reminder as to why I'm not good enough for him. My hand is bandaged up, but even in the bandages you see that I no longer have a pinky finger. It's one more thing that Michael has taken from me and one more thing that Zander shouldn't have to worry about. He needs a whole woman, one who can give him babies and be there for him in ways I'm too broken to manage.

"Enlighten me, Hellcat. Go ahead and tell me what the fuck is the real reason I need you."

"You couldn't save Melly, so you want to try and save me. It's okay I get it, and I could even live with being her substitute, but you deserve better. Somewhere you'll find a…"

"A woman who drives me completely fucking crazy," he growls. I look up at him then, he's angry. "What does it take to make you shut your damned pie-hole and listen to me?"

"Zander…"

"Don't you Zander me, it's time you listen to me, Hellcat and you better fucking listen. I watched my mom get shit on and be my old man's punching bag for years. I couldn't save her and that sucked, but I was a damn kid. Melly was a beautiful, sweet, innocent girl that the world slowly destroyed. I wanted to save her, she wouldn't let me and it was because we were both still kids. I would have loved her. I would have taken care of her and been happy. You're right. You're abso-fucking-lutely right."

"Zander, I don't want to hear about…"

"You, Dani or Melinda or whoever the fuck you are…"

"Dani," I growl because I hate Melinda, I never want to be Melinda.

"You, do not make me happy—not even a little bit."

His words hurt me and I feel like he just slapped me across the face.

"You make me screaming mad, confused, weak, aggravated, crazy, and horny as fucking hell..."

"Listen..."

"And completely fucking whole, for the first time in my life."

I freeze right before I tell him to shut up. "I... uh what did you say?"

"I said you make me whole, Hellcat. When I'm with you, I feel at ease, relaxed, and peaceful, even when you make me want to scream. I've never had that in my fucking life, but most of all Hellcat, you make me feel... alive. I need you, Hellcat. I need you more than any man has never needed a woman in his life. You aren't a substitute for anyone, sweetheart. You are my fucking world."

"Zander..."

"My fucking world, Dani..." He whispers leaning so close his face comes to mine and holds me prisoner in his gaze. "I love you."

"Zander..."

"I love you," he says again and his lips are so close I can feel his breath on my skin, almost taste him on my lips.

"Zander..."

"I love you," he says again, his fingers lightly brush against the side of my neck as he holds my face in place.

"Will you let me finish now?"

"Not if you're going to say more fucked-up crazy shit," he answers.

"I love you," I tell him and I know my eyes are wet with tears.

"I give you permission to say that every fucking day for the rest of our lives, Hellcat."

"I'll see what I can do," I tell him and he places a small kiss against my lips.

Chapter 42

CRUSHER

I'VE GOT MY woman back at the club. She's slowly healing, but doesn't really venture out of our room. People make her nervous, especially if there is more than one or two. It's been a few days since her release and she's still a mess. To me, she is the most beautiful woman I have ever laid eyes on. I can't believe the courage this woman possesses. I wasn't lying to her that day in the hospital, others would have caved long ago. Hell, I'm not even sure I have what it takes to fight for as long as she has.

Nicole finally came by and visited Dani yesterday, but it didn't go well. I understand that she is mourning the loss of Dragon, but she tore into my woman and made yet another fucking hole in her heart. I wish I could magically make it all better…for Dani, for Nicole, for all of us…this place is so fucking depressing since Dragon died, it seems unreal.

Today is Dragon's funeral. Freak has been doing some digging and put a few feelers out. The club is preparing for Michael to attack. I haven't told Dani. It would just make her feel worse. She's in no shape to venture out anyways. I'm going to make sure she's never alone. Freak wouldn't tell me how he knew that fucker was planning an attack, but he said it was reliable. So fuck, I know it's coming today. Another thing pissing me the fuck off, is that Skull is hanging around and staying close to Nicole. He's like a dog in heat. Dancer seems to be allowing that shit too. I know as club VP, I should probably step in and get him the fuck off the grounds, but I got my hands full. I don't see why Bull and Dancer can't step up. Still, I've decided after the attack today, that fucker and his whole crew need to be scarce on Savage land.

Fucking hell, I guess if you get down to it, I'm probably the club President now. We haven't had a formal meeting though and honestly I can't assume leadership. I betrayed my brother. Maybe if I had handled things differently, Dragon would still be breathing. That's a fucking hard truth to face. So, Drag's death is on my shoulders—no one else.

A brother I served with, Diesel, is in for Dragon's funeral. He keeps hitting me up to help him with his crew. He just lost an old lady. I've told him how fucked up I've been doing things concerning Dani and for some reason he respects it. Says he wished he had done more to save his woman Sheila. It's fucked up, but I'm considering it. Dani and I need a change.

I have checked in with Freak and the others and there's firepower lined up at all the entrances and hidden throughout the parking area. Bull has fixed it so the gates will remain open, while the riders go out and then he'll circle back. It'll appear we've been lax and that will set it up for Michael to make his move. Then the men from Diesel's crew, a few from Skull's and Bull, Nailer and Six will attack back. I'll be coming out at the end, to finish off Michael. I get that. That is mine. I'm going to drain the life out of that sorry motherfucker with my bare hands. The other brothers didn't argue. It wouldn't have mattered if they had. Dancer is in charge of protecting the women outside and I'm putting Hawk in charge of keeping Dani safe.

It's the perfect plan, but with each minute that passes I feel as if I'm crawling out of my skin.

"Zander, you're killing me. Go to the funeral, Dragon would want you there," Dani says interrupting my thoughts.

"Nah, sweetheart, I'm good," I answer brushing hair out of her face. She's lying in bed, and looking at the new e-reader I got her. I was a stupid-fuck, because she can't hold it and turn the pages right now, but she just looks at it, telling me no one had ever given her anything before, except Nicole and Ray for Christmas. Birthdays they usually just took her out and that's wrong. I'm going to give her the world if I can manage it.

"You're making me nervous, Zander and since I'm going stir crazy in this bed, that's saying something."

"I'm sorry Hellcat, just a little out of sorts today that's all."

"Out of sorts? Sometimes you are so weird," she grumbles laying back on the bed with a huff.

"Good thing you like weird," I smirk.

"Ehh...I'm just with you because of Junior."

"And Junior, thanks God for that, every damn day."

Dani rolls her eyes and I wink at her. When we're like this, just the two of us, everything seems fine—at least on the surface. She has new demons now and they circle around her at night. She's not sleeping and she seems untouchable at times. Still, I know she's trying, and there's not much more I can do. I've talked to her about therapy. Dancer is attending weekly meetings with some shrink and he says Dani needs to see her. Dani won't talk about it right now, and I don't want to push her, but after Michael is gone...if things don't get better, I'm going to have to do more than push.

"You look tired Zander, you should rest."

I take her hand and hold it in the palm of mine and kiss the back of her knuckles. She tries to pull her hand away, because it's the one with the missing finger, I don't let her. I kiss it and hold it against my face, letting her know I see nothing different, she's still beautiful.

"Look who's talking."

"A fine pair we are…"

She stops and we look out the window, when we hear the gunfire outside. It looks like we've reached show time. I stand up quickly and kiss her forehead.

"Stay put, Hellcat, I'm about to go make you a widow and I need you to stay here and be safe."

"What? Zander, you can't…"

"Don't argue with me, Hellcat. I got shit to handle and I don't want to be distracted worrying if you're doing what I told you to do, or not."

"What I'm told? Zander! I don't have to…"

"Shut it, sweetheart. We'll talk when I get this shit done."

I close the door, giving Hawk the okay. I draw my gun and head out to make my woman a widow.

I make it outside and slowly move from the door. Gunfire has slowed and I mostly get to see the aftermath. It pisses me off, for this one I wanted to be in the thick of it. Taking care of Dani, was more important though. As I round the corner I see him, Michael. He's been shot in the legs. That's the orders I gave. I want this fucker alive. I'm going to make him eat his own goddamn dick before I end his sorry fucking miserable life. In fact, I'm so engrossed in planning my revenge that I completely miss the fact that somehow my woman got away from Hawk and is standing at my side.

"Hello, Michael," she says. Her voice is surprisingly strong, but motherfucker I'm going to beat her ass.

Chapter 43

DANI

"HELLCAT, I THOUGHT I told you to keep your ass in bed, and stay safe," Zander growls while kicking the gun that Michael had dropped farther away.

"You did, I ignored you."

I think if it was possible steam would be coming out of his ears. It's cute but I can't think about Zander right now. I know he's upset, but I needed to be the one to do this. I owe Hawk, for stepping back when I told him I needed to be the one to send Michael to hell...not to mention he gave me his pistol to do it with and helped me outside, since walking is still a major fucking undertaking. I wanted a larger gun, I don't know much about them really, but bigger is always better I'd imagine, but he said I couldn't withstand the kick of bigger. He's probably right, but it still makes me sad.

"Damn it Hellcat, you're not in any shape to be out here..."

"This fucker is mine," Dragon says. I look up to see him standing in front of me. Michael is the only thing between us. My heart fills with warmth to see him there, even if I don't understand it. Still, Michael didn't beat him and sure as hell didn't rape him, so I ignore him. Zander however, doesn't.

"Dragon? What the fuck...How the hell are you standing here?" He asks, his voice full of shock.

I tune them out, I have other things on my mind. I stumble walking closer to Michael and Zander is right there holding my arm. I hate that I need help, but I'd rather lean on Zander than fall on my ass. Still, for this next part, I pull away.

"Do you know what I hated most about being married to you, Michael?" I'm being so calm… it feels wrong. I should be cussing or screaming or beating the shit out of him. Maybe the beating has done something to me after all? I feel…so calm and fuck, maybe even happy. When he doesn't answer I shoot his dick. Unfortunately, I miss and it goes wide and to the right catching his thigh. Still at the sight of the blood that funny feeling increases. Definitely happiness.

"You stupid cunt! You don't have the brains enough to finish me off. You were always weak! You should count yourself lucky that I…" he ends in a scream and I look over to see Zander has shot the fist that Michael had been shaking at me. I notice he used a smaller gun too and the wound he made is bad and bloody, but not so bad he'll die right away. So, I guess small guns have their place. Still…

"Zander, this is my job," I grumble, not really upset, but still I wanted to do this on my own.

"He was pissing me off. It was either stop him or kill him completely, I should be rewarded, Hellcat."

I shake my head, but I smile. Yeah…happiness… it's a great fucking feeling.

"Oh will you quit whining?" I growl at Michael when he keeps holding his hand and shit…is he crying? I didn't do that shit when I was being beat.

"Melinda, we should talk about things. I can," Michael starts and I have to stop him. His voice annoys the fuck out of me.

I shoot him again, this time I wanted to shoot him in the

head. I really hate the name Melinda, but it goes wide with the kick of the pistol. I thought I only hit the cement he's lying on because there's dust, but when it clears he's bleeding from his ear. Good enough I suppose.

"I hated your smell," I say when it becomes apparent that he's not going to respond. I would smell you everywhere around the house. I'd bleach the place down and still your smell would be there. I can't even describe it. You were like something I couldn't get rid of, that was slowly rotting away…"

"The clap?" Zander asks.

"And I…" I stop to look at Zander… "What?" Seriously, the man is nuts.

"The clap? Ole' Michael here reminds me of something like that. Rot your dick off and impossible to get rid of."

"They make medicine for the clap, Zander."

"Yeah they do for Michael too," He says and shoots him in the dick and sadly his shot doesn't go wide. Michael screams and cries like a little baby.

I hold my head down. "I wanted to do that," I pout.

"You were taking too long, now I didn't kill him but if you don't do it soon, I'm going to."

"Zander!"

He shoots him in the other hand.

"Fine! Jesus you're impossible," I growl upset that he's making this go way too fast.

"We own the police here Hellcat, but there will still be too much to contain. Not to mention, you're taking too fucking long and about to fall over," he explains, and then he makes it all better… "Plus this whining piece of shit is taking up too much of our air. He doesn't deserve to get anything from you sweetheart, except a load of lead."

I look up at him and smile. Well as much as I can, because it fucking hurts.

"Michael?"

He doesn't answer and Zander's heavy sigh is almost comical.

"Michael," I begin again. "Consider this payback for the gardener who was a nice guy, who had family and loved ones." I shoot him in the stomach. Michael is starting to look blue and his voice is getting weaker. I probably should hurry this along. "This is for Ms. Martens," I tell him, shooting him in the stomach again.

"Hellcat…" Zander warns.

"This is for all the other people you hurt," I shoot again at the opposite leg and hit somewhere along the thigh. Zander of course sighs again.

"This is for raping me," I whisper, and I hate that some tears escape with that confession. I shoot him in the area of his dick again. Michael isn't doing anything by this time. I don't know if he's alive or dead, but I can't stop. "This is for letting Donald rape me," I say again, crying harder now, and that just pisses me off. "This is for making me hate myself," I shoot him in the head. I don't stop until the hammer of the gun clicks and bullets won't come. "Let me have your gun!" I growl at Zander, dropping the gun I had to the ground.

"Hellcat, honey…"

"Give me your damn gun!"

"Hellcat," he starts again.

"Zander!"

"Jesus, I am going to tan your ass when you get better woman," he grumbles handing me the pistol he's been using.

"This is for making me hurt…for making me run…for causing me to get my friends mixed up in any of this…for hurting Nicole and Dragon…for killing Frog…" I add all I can think of until Zander's pistol is out of bullets. I would have demanded another gun and kept going, but Zander picks me up and takes me to Hawk.

"Take her back to her room and this time do what I fucking tell you and keep her there," he growls. He's mad, but even so he kisses my face gently and whispers into my ear, "I'm so fucking proud of you, Hellcat."

Then I'm in Hawk's arms and going back inside. I can hear Zander growl at Dragon, but I let it go. He can handle his own shit. I'm suddenly very tired.

Chapter 44

CRUSHER

MY WOMAN HAS motherfucking balls of steel. Jesus. She fucking amazes me. Even with all the shit going on I couldn't be more proud of her. I knew she was special from the first moment I saw her, but fuck, I had no idea.

I'm on lock down, per Dragon's orders. I haven't told Dani. I don't want her worrying. With Michael gone, she's going through some shit. She's not really talking to me about it, and that shit needs to stop. I'm fully expecting to have my patch taken and voted out of the club. The branding of the tat is going to hurt like a motherfucker, I'm okay with it. If I had to go back I'd do it all again.

Besides, the fact that Dragon felt it was okay to fake his own fucking death and tell the President of other clubs and not let his VP, or his Enforcer know speaks volume about the shape of this fucking club. It's not completely Dragon's fault, Bull and I are responsible too, but I'm still fucked up about it. The more I talk to Diesel, the more I am sure that a change of setting would be good for Dani and me. Diesel and I were just as tight back in the day as I was with Dragon. I respect him and I'm pretty sure it'd be a good move.

"What are you thinking so hard about, Cowboy?" Dani asks.

"I'm thinking how motherfucking lucky I am to have you,"

I tell her and it's the truth.

"Yeah, I'm a real catch," she sighs holding her hand up, the one with the missing finger, to look at it.

"You are, Hellcat. You're everything and more than I could have imagined."

She shakes her head no, but squeezes my hand.

"Have you talked with Dragon? Is Nicole okay?"

Nicole went into early labor the day of the funeral. She was too early in the pregnancy and the baby had some major problems, but the little guy is a fighter and gets to come home soon. Nicole has led my brother on a major fucking twisted trip. It's been so bad between her and Dragon that even my woman took Dragon aside and gave him advice. I never thought, I'd see that. Still after a couple of weeks it looks like they've found their way back together.

"Yeah baby, the doctors even think Dom can come home soon," I tell her.

She smiles, "That's good."

"What do you think about going on a trip with me when you're able?" I ask her because before I make a final decision I need to know. I'm doing nothing without my woman from here on out.

"A trip?"

"Yeah, sweetheart. I'm thinking a change of scenery would do you good. Diesel asked me to come help him out at his club and I'm thinking about it. I think Tennessee would be good for the both of us."

"Tennessee?"

"Yeah baby, we could rent a house on the water, I think you'd like it." I watch her face closely. I don't want to do anything she's not a hundred percent on board with.

"Zander, I'm pretty messed up. I don't think…I'm not sure

I'm ready for…I mean, I love you, I do. But, there's just…"

I put my fingers on her lips. I know where she's going, and I just can't let her go there. She will heal. I will get her there. It's just going to take time.

"Do you want me?"

"Well, of course, but…"

"Then we take each day together. No promises, no pressure," it kills me, but I understand. She looks sad, but doesn't argue. I start to say more when there's a knock on the door, I let it go and get up to answer the door.

When Bull, Dragon and Dancer are all at the door, I know the time has come.

"We need to talk," Drag says, looking around me at Dani lying in the bed.

"Yeah, okay. Can I say goodbye to my woman first?" I ask quietly, because I don't want Dani to know what's going on exactly.

Dragon nods and I close the door, and walk back to the bed.

"Hellcat, I got some club business going on. I'll try and hurry back. You can text me though, okay?"

"Is everything okay?"

"It's perfect and when I get back we're Tennessee bound… sound good?"

"If you're sure…" she says hesitantly, and I think she sees that I'm holding stuff back but she nods. I give her a kiss. It's not as passionate as I want, but still sliding my tongue inside to taste her, soothes me. I'll handle this and get back to my woman soon.

I close the door behind me and look at my brothers.

"You called me out," Dragon says and his face is remote, but I think I see a flicker of something there that lets me know my brother hates this fucking shit as much as I do.

"I did," I can't deny it and I wouldn't.

"It can't go unanswered. Out back in the yard, meet me in ten. I win, you get the cooler for a couple days while I arrange the vote. You win, you get the President patch."

Fuck, and I say fuck for two reasons. I told Dani to text me and if I get the cooler, I'm not going to have a cell phone and even if I do, there's no signal. Secondly, I may strike at Dragon because I'm pissed at the way he did stuff, but I'm the one who fucked up here, so I'm not gonna even try to win. Dragon is President of this club and even if I don't like how he did things with Michael, it was brilliant, proving he is a leader. I'm not. I don't even want to be.

"See you in ten," I say resignedly, because fuck, this is going to hurt.

Chapter 45

DANI

"How are you feeling?" I look up to see Nicole standing at the door.

I was hoping it was Zander. I haven't heard from him in two days. I wanted to ask the others, but they don't really talk to me and I don't want to make myself look stupid by asking for a man who might not want me anymore. He's not even answered my texts.

"Bored," I answer, turning my attention back to Nicole as she comes in and closes the door. "How's Dom?"

"He's good, really good. I was hoping we could talk for a little bit, if you're not too tired."

Things are stilted between me and Nicole now. She held me responsible for Dragon's death and I understand. I hold myself responsible too. I want to fix it, but I don't really know how. I'm hoping time manages to do it.

"Nah, I'm bored out of my mind. I'm thinking about going outside and walking a little bit. I need to feel the sunshine on my face."

"Zander wouldn't like you overdoing it. You've healed a lot, but you were in bad shape."

"Yeah well, I haven't heard from Zander, so I'm not sure that matters now."

"I uh…You don't know?" She asks, her voice sounding

surprised.

"Zander is under lockdown by the club. They're having a vote today to decide on kicking him out of the club," she answers.

"But...he and Dragon are like brothers...that doesn't make any sense."

"He called Dragon out, and I guess they had to go all he-man over it. There's protocol and rules that can't be broken."

She says that last part imitating Dragon's voice and I could almost laugh if I wasn't so worried.

"Where is Zander?"

"How the fuck do I know? Some place called the cooler. They're getting ready for church now though, so I imagine he'll be there with the rest of the morons," she answers sounding as frustrated as I'm feeling.

"I need to go there," I tell her, already heading towards the door.

"Women aren't allowed in church, Dani."

"If it was Dragon being voted on, would you just sit by and wait?"

"Fuck, we're going to church aren't we? If my ass gets paddled and I can't sit down next week, I'm coming after you bitch," she grumbles, but when I look up she's smiling.

"I love you Nic, I know I'm a fuck-up and I'm trying to get better, but I love you," I tell her because I need her to know that.

"I got you, girl. I'm sorry too, I've been a bitch to you since the bomb and everything else. I shouldn't have been. We made decisions together and you had valid reasons for trying to keep the club out of it. It'll work out."

Something clicks inside at her words.

"Badass Bitches for life," I smile repeating a forgotten

motto from our school days.

"Ride or die even," she adds and we hug. Then she lets me lean on her as we walk to our first and probably last ever, church meeting.

WE GET INTO the church room quietly. It seems too easy and when Nicole winks at me, I'm pretty sure she somehow cleared it with Hawk or one of the others first.

"Do you have nothing to say for yourself?" Dragon is asking Zander.

"Bastard had my old lady, I handled shit that needed to be done. I got Dani back and I'd do it a fucking hundred times over. If that gets me booted from the club then what-the-fuck-ever," Zander answers and my heart stutters at what he just put out there in front of all of his brothers. Brothers who admittedly have warmed towards me, but for the most part view me as an outsider.

"You defied direct orders, and put the club in jeopardy. You put a woman before your brothers, and you had the fucking balls to call me out in front of others. I should strip you of club colors right here and close the fucking vote. The end."

"She's not a woman, she is my old lady," he says once again, telling the world it's me he chooses. Me. Even more than that…he sounds…proud. Do I make Zander proud? Despite my past? Despite the things Michael did to me?

"She hasn't agreed to that shit, so that makes her a woman," Dragon answers and I feel ashamed because I think back to the last conversation that Zander and I had. I should have just told him right then that he was it for me.

"Bullshit. I claim her. My woman needed me. I did nothing more or nothing less than you would've done," Zander responds and I know I can't handle anymore. I'm his woman and it's time I stop being afraid of what that means. If he can put me before everything and be proud of that then I need to work harder to be the woman he deserves.

"He's right," I say and I wish my voice sounded stronger. I have trouble being around crowds and a room full of angry men isn't exactly fun times for me.

"What's that, Hellcat?" Zander asks. He gets up and comes to me, his voice full of emotion and love is shining in his eyes. Love...for me...It warms me. The emptiness and dark I've been feeling...part of it heals with that look. Zander loves me. I'm not a substitute. I'm his.

The reality of that hits me and I stumble, but I catch myself. The last thing I want to do is fall and ruin this. I hold steady and look my man in the eyes. My man.

"I admit that I'm yours. I was yours then. I...I..." The enormity of what I'm doing here hits me. I'm giving myself to another man. I'm doing it with...joy. I look around at all the men staring at me and I can't tell what they're thinking. Do they find me lacking? Do they think I'm not good enough for their brother?

"Say it, Hellcat. Say it," Zander says and the emotion in his voice is so thick, I push forward again.

"I'm yours Zander and I definitely claim you as mine."

Zander kisses me on the forehead and wraps his arms around me. I hear his intake of breath and then he whispers to me, "That's my angel."

I can't stop the tears that fall. I don't even try. I'm finally in the arms of the man I was meant for all along. I'm where I belong...where I've always belonged.

"Go on back to our room, I'll check on you when I'm done," Zander tells me and I don't want to leave him alone to face this vote. I want to be here for him.

"But...,"

"I'm proud of you Hellcat, don't worry. I'll do what I need to do and then I'll come to you."

I try to give him a smile and turn to leave. I'm kind of ashamed of the mess I've caused him. He deserves better.

"Hellcat? My woman doesn't look down. Remember?" I stiffen my back and smile. He's proud of me. I'm his.

"I won't forget," and I'm talking about more than just looking down.

"That's my girl."

"Just get your shit done, Zander, and quit busting my ass."

Chapter 46

CRUSHER

IT'S BEEN A month. Dani and I have been in Tennessee with Diesel's crew and he's urging me to stay on, as his second in command. I'm pretty sure I'm going to. I love Drag and the boys, but honestly I need a fucking change. My woman fits in here. She's happy. The other old ladies have welcomed her completely. There's only one dark spot. Dani hasn't given herself to me. She's healed now. Still has some problems and pain, but for the most part she's healed. I've done everything, but right out ask. I've tried to be respectful, but motherfucker my balls are going blue here.

She's bent over our bed, making it and smoothing out wrinkles. She's got on some cute little hot-ass shorts and a red t-shirt that says badass bitch on it. My eyes are glued to the way the fringe on her shorts plays and caresses the mound of her ass cheek, almost letting me see the curve and my patience snaps.

"Are you ever going to let me fuck you again?"

She straightens slowly and turns to me. Her hair has grown back out some, it's now almost to the top of her neck. The bruises have left her face and there's nothing but one very small scar under her chin. She still wears that damn dark red lip stick that instantly makes my cock hard. Under the thin strap of her top you can see her new tattoo. She thought the scar where she tried to take her own life was ugly. I thought it was beautiful. I had her get a tattoo over it and she agreed, she even allowed me to pick what I wanted. I think she thought I would choose my name. Don't get me wrong, I fully intend too. Still, I wanted the one word that summed up what that scar was all about. So in flowing letters covered in barb wire and roses the word Courage brands my woman. That's my woman. That's my woman to a fucking T...

"Excuse me?"

"I didn't stutter Hellcat, I asked if you're ever going to let me fuck you again."

"Zander, I've been...I mean... You want to have sex?" She asks finally and Jesus what kind of question is that to ask a man?

"Are you fucking kidding me? Junior is slowly dying and withering away, Hellcat. I'm dying to get back inside you."

"I'm scarred up pretty bad, Zander."

"You're fucking gorgeous."

"I...Shit, Zander you might not...I mean, I might not..."

"Strip, Dani."

"Zander..."

I walk to her then. She's nervous. Motherfucker! How could I have been so stupid? I turn her so her back is to me and then pull her shirt over her head. I don't give her time to question anything. I unlatch her bra and throw it on the ground with her shirt. I pull her back against me. My arm sliding across her warm breasts, as I kiss the side of her neck.

"Zander...I'm scared."

"I got you," I answer, sliding my other hand around to undo her shorts.

"I'm lost," she says. "I can't even find myself," but even as she says it her lips are turning to mine, and her hand comes up to pull my head down to her.

I don't let her pull me in until my eyes find hers.

"Then hold on Hellcat, because I got you and I'm not letting you go. Believe in that," I tell her.

I see a smile slide onto her lips and that's when I claim them. I drink in her taste like the man I am. A man who has been starving for over a fucking month for his woman. I push her shorts and underwear down to her knees, before I even break the kiss.

"This is going to go fast, Hellcat," I tell her and I'm mourning it. It's her first time making love since the attack. A better man would be slow and soft with her. He would make her see how fucking beautiful she is. I promise I'll give her that soon, I just think it's beyond me at this point.

"Take me…take me just like this…"

Now, I'm not a foolish man that would ever turn down a plea like that, but something in her tone makes me stop and realize I was worried about going too fast for a reason. I can't take her like this. I need her to look in my eyes when I love her. I need her to see the truth, that to me she is the most beautiful person on the face of the Earth.

For that reason and that reason alone, I pull back.

"Step out of your clothes Hellcat and get on the bed," I order.

"Zander…"

"Do it now, Dani. It's time I show you the fucking man you've tied yourself too."

"Jesus, we've been together for a while now. I think I know," she grumbles, but she does as I order.

I take my clothes off, without saying anything else. Her eyes never leave me though and the hunger on her face is all I need to know. I'm doing the right thing.

"Do you want my cock?"

"God, yes."

I stroke myself watching her closely. She's lying on the bed naked and motherfucker, a weaker man would come right then.

"Spread your legs, Dani. Let me see my pussy."

She swallows nervously but does as I tell her to. She's got a neatly trimmed pussy now, letting that soft brown hair cover her mound. The sight of it fucking turns me on.

"Do you know how fucking beautiful you are, Dani?"

"Zander…"

"You're every fucking wet dream I've ever had in my life."

"Zander…"

"Except for one thing…"

She freezes, looking up at me. Her hand automatically goes to her stomach and I shake my head. I know it worries her. I see how she looks at me when she's around Diesel's baby boy, Ryan.

"I'm a selfish son of a bitch, Hellcat. I don't want to share your fucking body with anyone—not even our child. We can adopt. You'd be a wonderful mother and I'd be proud to have kids with you, but that fucking body of yours is mine."

She tilts her head to the side and looks at me, like she's having trouble believing me, "You want to adopt a child…with me?"

"In a fucking heartbeat. What part of, I'm in this forever, are you not grasping, Hellcat?"

"I love you," she whispers and those long thick eyelashes of hers are wet with tears that want to fall.

"I love you." I answer with a smile. "Now do you want to guess what one thing keeps bothering me, Dani?"

She swallows, but nods her head in a yes. At the same time her hand comes up to the scar on her chest. I shake my head.

"Don't even think it, that scar is fucking beautiful. When I look at it, I'm reminded of what a strong woman I have. Of the courage she possesses and how fucking amazing she is. The kind of woman who survives. That's the kind of woman a man holds onto—the kind of woman a man raises a family with, the kind of woman a man grows old with."

The tears slowly slide down her cheeks now, but she's smiling so I figure it's okay.

"So what is it you don't like?" She asks, her voice thick with emotion and love. I can literally hear the love.

"I've never watched you make yourself come," I tell her with a cocky-ass smile and really, who wouldn't be cocky with all that I have.

"I...what do you want me to do?"

"Have you ever made your sweet little pussy come?"

"When we..."

"No, sweetheart, without me."

She blushes and my body feels as if electricity is running through it. I will never get enough of this woman.

"Show me, Dani."

I expect her to tell me no, and honestly I'm too far gone to push her if she does. She surprises me yet again though, and I should be getting used to that by now. I watch as her hands move over her breasts and down to her stomach, slowly they trail down to the part that has me mesmerized at the moment. The soft hair shielding her is wet and glistens, beckoning me.

"Pull your legs up towards your chest and plant those heels on the bed. Show me what's mine, Dani," my voice is hoarse with need.

She does it and I watch those pretty fingers dance along the lips of her pussy.

"You're so wet for me, aren't you, sweetheart?"

"Yes," she whispers.

"Do you want my cock?"

"God, yes. I've been dying to have your cock back inside of me."

Her honesty pleases me.

"Spread that juicy cunt open for me and let me watch you tease that throbbing little clit of yours, baby."

I watch her slide her fingers over that hard, swollen nub. She's so wet the liquid shines up at me and I have to have her. Fuck, I need to make it last longer, but I just…can't. I bend down and pull her hands up and lock both her wrists in one of my hands.

"I'm sorry baby, but I just can't wait."

"Thank, God. Hurry Zander, fuck me. Please," she growls in my ear.

I hold the head of my cock against her opening and look her in the eyes.

"No more doubts, Dani. You're mine. You've always been mine."

"No more doubts, Zander. I'm yours."

With her words ringing in my ears, I slide inside—sinking all the way in. Once there I don't move while I catch my breath.

"Every time you're inside of me, it just gets better," she says, her words echoing my thoughts.

I kiss her, because there are no words that I can give to say what I want to. Then I release her wrists and pull back so just my tip is inside her. I'm on my knees now, and I lift her ass and pull her down on my cock, watching as I disappear out of sight. Fucking phenomenal. I repeat that several times, enjoying the feel, the angle, and the way my dick scrapes against the walls of her pussy. It slowly drives Dani crazy as she starts lifting her body up higher, bracing herself on her elbows. She's doing her best to thrust herself back and forth, but I have my hands on her ass and I'm doing the work here. I'm the one allowing her to have, what I choose to give her.

"Zander!" She growls and I can't help but smile.

"What's wrong, baby?" I ask, slowing my thrusts and tilting my hips to the side so that it hits her differently with each slow glide.

"I need you to stop torturing me and give me your dick, please..." she says, and she does in fact sound desperate.

I support her with only one hand and take my free one to move my finger against the swollen lips of her pussy. My thumb searches and finds the hard distended nub of her clit. It pulsates and I smile as I push hard against it and then let up, petting the pretty button in reward. Her hips jerk up, elongating the reach of my cock inside of her. I take over controlling everything and enjoy the show, never speeding up my movements as my fingers dig into her thighs. It makes me feel every inch the conqueror and possessor of her and her body.

Her head is thrashing back and forth and her whimpers have become unintelligible.

"Do you get it yet, Dani? Do you get that you're mine? That I'm never fucking letting you go?"

She doesn't respond, well other than a moan when my cock thrusts back inside. This time however, I don't withdraw. I stay lodged completely inside of her and adjust her legs so they wrap around my back and then I stretch back over her body, my eyes seeking hers. Her hands come up to my face, touching me softly. So fucking softly they almost feel as if she's praising me. I can't remember another woman ever touching me with such gentleness. Her dark eyes shining with emotion and it's all directed at me.

"I love you, Zander. As long as you are with me, I am where I belong."

Her words touch places in me that I didn't even realize were raw, and they heal. I should give her sweet words now, but they're all jumbled up in my brain. All I can think is…mine.

My voice is hoarse with emotion and love, so much fucking love for this woman I know that she's sunk so deep inside that she's more than a piece of me. She's all of me. She owns every inch of me and I wouldn't want it any other way.

"Hold on, Hellcat. Hold on tight and never let go," I order and with every lunge inside of her it pushes her up on the mattress. Her heels lock against my ass, as she takes my body into hers over and over. Her nails bite into my back and I hiss at the sweet sting of pain.

"Give it to me, Zander. I'll hold on, I'll always hold on to you, Cowboy. Always."

I take her promise and we finish our ride together—just as it should be.

Epilogue

DANI

Two weeks later

"HELLCAT! WHERE ARE YOU?" I hear Zander yell, as the screen door to the house we've been staying in slams. We've been living in the house that the Savage Brothers' owned on the lake. It's been a good place. It has felt like home, but today we're moving out. I'm nervous, but I know that with Zander, any place will be great. We bought a home on Cherokee Lake and it's beautiful. It's everything I have ever wanted. It's on the water with a large deck for club gatherings or just me and Zander relaxing in the evening. It's homey, and it feels…peaceful.

Zander decided to stay on as Diesel's Vice President. I'm not sure what made him decide to leave Dragon and his crew, but when he asked what I thought, I left the decision completely up to him. All I could give him was the truth—I'd be okay no matter where we ended up as long as we were together.

Diesel has been having personal problems. He had an old lady who died a few months ago and left him with a little boy. The sweetest little boy I've ever met in my life. From all accounts, his mother sucked, but it makes me sad that the little guy will never get the chance to know his mother's love. Diesel asked Zander to come in and help watch over the club, while he devoted more time to his son, Ryan. I think it's good. Zander likes the men and I'm even fitting in with the other old ladies, especially Brenda, Copper's old lady. She's not Nic, but we have bonded. Life here is just…good. Really good.

"In here, Cowboy," I yell back packing up the last of our clothes in the suitcases. I smile as arms come around me, I straighten up and feel Zander push up against me. He burrows into the side of my neck and I tilt to the side to give him more room, my hands resting on his.

"I missed you," he whispers, biting on my neck and I know he's leaving another mark. He says he feels the need to mark me every day so I never forget who I belong to.

That will never happen, but I like looking in the mirror and seeing the small bruises from his loving. I wear them proudly.

"You've only been gone an hour, Zander," I tell him on a sigh, as he sucks the lobe of my ear into his mouth, his warm breath sends delicious chill bumps over my skin.

"Hellcat, I miss you the minute you leave my arms," he grumbles and I can't argue, because I feel the same. "Are you ready to roll?" He asks.

"Ready as I'll ever be. Are you sure this is what you want, Cowboy?"

"I've never been surer of anything in my life. This is it, Hellcat. This is where we're supposed to be."

"Did you talk to Dragon?" I ask him, because that's the only misgiving I have. Dragon, Dancer and Bull are Zander's family, the only ones he's ever claimed as family. He loves them. So, having him decide to just leave them makes me nervous.

"Yeah, sweetheart. Quit worrying everything is good. We're meeting them in Vegas in two weeks for the wedding."

"Nicole still has no idea?" I ask, turning around to hug him close.

"Nope, so don't be giving it away next time you and her have those two-hour long conversations."

"Hey, I don't get to see her so we have to have our weekly catch up chats."

His rough fingers brush the side of my face, his thumb brushing back and forth at the top of my cheekbone. "Sweetheart? Are you going to be okay with this? I don't want to take you away from Nic. If you want to stay in Kentucky…"

I stop him with the touch of my fingers against his lips. I laugh as he instantly sucks them into his mouth. I frown for just a second as I catch a glimpse at the missing pinky. Most days I don't notice it and it doesn't bother me. Zander has made it clear it doesn't bother him. I shake it off. It's just one more shadow of the past that I fight from time to time. Zander is my tomorrow—my future. I don't know what the future holds, but I know that we're together in it and as long as I have that…I have everything…

"Hellcat?"

I shake off my thoughts and smile up at him.

"I love you, Alexander Dawson."

"Ugh, that name," he jokes. He's happy. You can see it all over him. I make him *happy*.

"It's beautiful," I argue shaking my head at him. "The point is, you are my future. I have Nic, I'll always have her. You though aren't my family, you're everything to me. You are the one person in this life I couldn't survive without. I'm good as long as you're with me."

"Then let's get to our new home. We have a lot of work to do."

"Work? Zander the house was completely done and our

furniture was moved in two days ago! We can't work, the club is coming over tomorrow. I need a day to relax."

"Sorry Hellcat, but you don't get that today. I'm on a mission."

"A mission? Already? Are you going out of town?"

"Nope. I'm going to fuck my woman in every room of our new home. Then I'm going to eat her sweet little snatch outside under the stars by the water until she begs me to stop."

Heat and electricity run through my body at his words.

"Well what are you waiting for, Cowboy? I ask him grabbing a suitcase, which he takes out of my hand, while grabbing the other one. I let him get away with it. I've learned with Zander to just let the he-man tendencies take over—they usually lead to really good places.

"You just want me for my dick," he grumbles walking out of our old bedroom.

"Well that and your tongue…" I joke.

"I'll show you my tongue, damn it."

"I'm counting on it Cowboy, I'm counting on it."

The End

Hope you enjoyed the new installment of the Savage Brothers MC. Turn the page for a sneak peek of the next installment due out at the end of the year, Trusting Bull. As well as a sample of some of my favorite authors!

TRUSTING BULL

By: Jordan Marie

Chapter 1

SKYE

I LOOK AT the man on my exam table. I shouldn't be attracted to him. I mean he's good looking, so he would catch any woman's eye. He's tall and has arm porn that would make any woman weak in the knees. He's got an aura of danger about him and a bad boy vibe that goes on for miles. That's not why I shouldn't be interested in him though. No, that reason is pretty much summed up in one sentence.

"You have gonorrhea, Mr. Kane."

"That's not fucking possible."

"I'm afraid it is, the good news, is that despite your lapse in judgment, it is curable. However, I would suggest we test you for other sexually transmitted diseases including HIV."

"I don't fucking have AIDS lady."

I frown at his reply. It's not the first time I've dealt with a belligerent patient, but after working for thirty-six hours straight, I'm just not in the mood.

"Mr. Kane, have you or have you not been having sex?"

"Yes *doctor*, but I always wrap my shit up. So I'm telling you, your goddamn diagnosis is wrong. Now how about you get your ass out there and find me someone who knows what the fuck they are doing around here."

I hold my head down and let out a big breath. I rub the tension headache behind starting at my temple. I really should have tried to do my residency in New York. I stupidly thought the small town atmosphere of London, Kentucky was what I wanted.

I'd like to say my next actions are because I am tired, or the fact that I'm on my period. I'd also like to think it is because of this patient's crappy attitude. Still, I know the truth. The truth is Mr. Kane hit a sore spot. I'm vain enough to admit it. His words too closely relate to the chewing out the chief resident gave me this morning. The reason I was hauled onto the carpet wasn't my fault, but a mistake by a nurse. Yet, since the resident in question is busy banging said nurse, I got the fall out. So, with Mr. Kane's words, I can't hold back. I don't even try. *I snap.*

"I do know what I'm doing. I absolutely know, Mr. Kane. The fact that you've had sex with someone who has gonorrhea, upped your chances of getting the disease. Now if you did in fact *wrap it up*, then possibly you didn't when you gave or received oral sex. Perhaps you had one night of drunken sex and forgot to *wrap your shit up*, as you so colorfully stated. I do not know how or with whom you transmitted the disease. What I do know is you have in fact got gonorrhea, or more commonly referred to as the clap, if that helps. So what's going to happen, Mr. Kane, is simple. You can keep a civil tongue in that pretty boy head of yours when speaking to me and be thankful that you do just have gonorrhea, or you can leave. Now, I will warn you, if you choose to leave that foul discharge that you've kept hidden that keeps leaking out of your penis, will only get worse. That burning sensation you have when you urinate, will only increase. Those swollen glands along your neck, will only get worse. What I suggest you do instead Mr. Kane, is step up."

He looks at me strangely. I can't say as I blame him. In

fact, had my chief resident walked in during my speech, I would be in major hot water. However, he didn't and I'm tired, plus Mr. Kane is the last patient that stands before me and a much needed three days off. So instead of practicing caution, I forge ahead.

"Pretty boy?" He asks. "Did you just call me a pretty boy?"

"I told you to step up. Take your medicine like a grown man, without belittling those of us who are trying to ensure you receive quality medical care. Take tests to confirm you don't have something worse and finally, make a list of your sexual partners and find out where you contracted the disease and make sure they get treated so that the cycle ends."

"You just called me pretty boy," he repeats and I try not to blush.

That was probably going a step too far. Well, in actuality, the entire speech was going too far. If he files a complaint, I am most likely through here. I'm not sure I care at this point.

"Mr. Kane, honestly it's late. I'll have the nurse come in and give you a shot and I'll need you to follow up with your family physician..."

"Your eyes sparkle when you're mad."

"I really...what did you say?"

"I said, your eyes sparkle, when you're mad," he repeats.

"Are you seriously...you're *hitting* on me?"

"Is that so hard to believe?" He asks leaning back in the chair and I think maybe I've lost it. It's definitely past time for me to go home.

"Considering I just told you that you have a venereal disease and the fact that I am your doctor, oddly enough Mr. Kane I do find it hard to believe."

"I don't happen to believe you, but even if what you say is true, I take the meds you give then I'm good right?"

I'm at a loss. I choose to ignore the part about him hitting on me. Hopefully after tonight, I won't see him again. So, I concentrate instead on the only thing that matters.

"Providing you make sure the woman or women you have been having sexual relations with are treated, then yes."

"Sexual relations? C'mon Doc, let's call what it is. Fucking."

At his explicit words, I feel heat creep into my face and it annoys me. I'm not a prude for god sake, it's just this is not the type of conversation I would choose to have with a patient.

"Regardless of what you call it, you need to contact them and find the source."

"You're talking get a list of names of everywhere I've stuck my dick? Hell, I can't remember that, Doc. It's impossible."

"The symptoms have a limited gestation period, so really the last three weeks to be..."

"That's impossible," he says again interrupting me and this takes me back. *Seriously?*

"You can't remember who you've had sex with in the last *three* weeks?"

He shrugs, "Not really, no."

"Of course you can't," I mumble, without meaning too. What was my original thoughts on this man? Yeah, I'm definitely *not* attracted now. "Regardless Mr. Kane, that is for you and your doctor to discuss. I will of course give you a shot of antibiotics tonight. Your primary care physician can further treat you when you follow up."

"Excuse me Dr. Walker, I heard my boyfriend was here. Oh Bull honey are you okay? I told you, you should see a doctor about that cold. How about I take you to my place and make you some soup and..."

I'm frozen as the whore of St. Lutheran Hospital walks

through the door—otherwise known as Nurse Melissa Allen. The very nurse who caused me to get my ass chewed out earlier tonight. Of course she's this guy's girlfriend. *Of course.* The only bright spot I can find in this scenario is that perhaps Melissa has also passed along the gift of love to Dr. Eldrdige. It couldn't happen to a nicer guy really.

"I take it you two know each other?" I sarcastically add since she's about to smother him in her breasts. To his credit Mr. Kane pulls away from her and looks more annoyed than anything.

"We've been dating for the last three months," Melissa pipes up proudly.

"Odd, I thought you were dating Dr. Eldridge," I say marking the medication orders down in the chart, and ready to get out of there.

"We're not exclusive," Nurse Allen says.

"We're not dating, we're fucking," Mr. Kane says, almost at the same exact time.

"I see. Well then, I'm sorry Nurse Allen but you probably should be tested for gonorrhea and in fact you might should ask Dr. Eldrdige to also."

She gasps and steps back like I slapped her. *Oh if only I could.*

"What did you say?"

"It would appear your boyfriend…"

"We're not dating we're fucking," Mr. Kane interjects and I want to laugh when Melissa shoots him a dirty look.

"It would appear Mr. Kane has contracted the STD. For your safety you should also be tested. I can order it done now if you'd like?" I say and I try to keep the glee out of my voice. I would *love* to have the hospital tech to run the tests. It would be so much fun to watch it filter through the hospital grapevine.

"That's not necessary, there's no way that I have the clap! And if you mention this to anyone I will make sure that your supervisor…"

"Shut it, Melissa. I think I want you tested," Mr. Kane interjects.

"I will not," she counters.

"You will if you want to step foot back in the club."

Really this could almost be fascinating if I had any sleep. I haven't and I desperately hate being anywhere near Nurse Allen. So I decide to extricate myself from the situation.

"Well, you two can discuss this later. I'll have one of the nurses come in to give you your shot, Mr. Kane and to discharge you. Please make sure you follow up with your doctor."

"Oh I will. Don't you worry about that," he says and he seems to be smiling a lot for a man who has just been face with the diagnosis that he has an STD. Then again, if women like Melissa is who he dates and since he can't remember their names three weeks later, perhaps it is.

I close the door and take a deep breath. Dr. Torres is already being handed charts. I'm officially off duty. *Hallelujah!*

For an extra Treat for you readers I have a sample of three of my favorite authors!

Sapphire Knight treats us with: Exposed
Honey Palomino tantalizes us with: Remember Me
Kathryn Kelly teases us with: Misled

EXPOSED

By: Sapphire Knight

Chapter 1

CAIN

6 Months Ago...

*F*UCK, I'M HUNG-OVER. *I have to quit doing this to myself. The shower helped a little. Now for a shot of Jack and some aspirin, that'll make this fucking pounding chill out.* I make my way out of my room and down the hall to the bar area. I look around and take in the bar of the clubhouse. *Man this place is trashed.* There are empty beer bottles and full ashtrays layed all over every surface. The shiny bar is the only clean piece of furniture in the room. It calls to me like a becon. I walk towards it and kick trash and looks like a few pair of panties out of the way.

"Yo Cain, you beat that pussy up last night man?" I look over and see 2 Piece sitting in the corner of the room in a booth.

"Damn man I didn't see you. Yea, I hit that shit then sent her ass packin. Why? You hit it after me?" I grab a glass and a lemon from the bar and make my way over to him. He's already got a bottle of Jack in front of him. *Guess he had the same idea.*

"Fuck no, man, I had that crazy red head stripper that was grindin on my shit all night. Not bad pussy either." He says and takes a big gulp of Jack. I sit down across from him and pour me a double. *Just enough for me to chase this shit outta my head but not make me wanna puke.*

"You chasing the beast too brother? My fuckin head is killin me today." I take a drink and suck on my lemon.

"Yep. You a nasty fucker eatin that shit after a nice sip of whiskey." He looks at my lemon with distaste and I chuckle a little. They don't believe me when I always tell them that lemon has Vitamin C and helps you bounce back quicker. They all give me shit for it, but whatever, I'm always feeling better quicker than they do. I finish my whiskey and stand up. I stretch my muscles out. *Shit I'm sore all over.*

"I'm out man, I'll be back later." I chin nod at 2 Piece and walk towards the door.

"Later brother, don't forget you fight tonight." *Fuck. I did forget.*

"Yea, I'll be ready."

"You better be fucker, if I lose my money bettin on your ass, Imma kick it after you're done."

"Haha your ass should be payin me for winnin you that mother fuckin money!" I salute and make my way out. 2 Piece is cool as fuck, he's one of the first brothers I got close to when I started to come around the club. I open the door and the heat hits me like a punch to the gut. *Hotter than a nice piece of ass today.* I make my way to my girl.

"Hey pretty girl, you ready to go for a ride?" The guys give me shit for talking to my bike, but I've heard a few of them talk to theirs too. They just like giving me shit since I'm one of the youngest in the club. I've fought my ass off this year for my bike. She's a 2014 Harley Davidson Custom Iron 883 with Hard Candy custom paint black and all black trim. My custom bike isn't really made for long rides but I can always use my old bike if I need too. I take my small shammy towel out and lightly dust her off. I climb on and kick my kickstand up and start her up. The rumble vibrates through my muscles and it's a feeling of comfort like a nice home cooked meal. *Yea, like I've had one of those recently. Speaking of food, I need to get my ass to H.E.B. before all the church freaks show up.* I check my watch, 11:30. I may just make it before they swarm the grocery store.

I pull into the H.E.B. parking lot and thankfully they don't look busy yet. Sundays after 12p.m. everyone seems to leave church and come straight here, it's like a ritual of something. Then I have to deal with their judging eyes. The holier than thou seem to think I'm a menace because of my tattooed covered arms, hands, and neck. I always wear clean clothes but it doesn't matter when I have my cut on. I'm automatically a hellion. I may be a brawler, in a motorcycle club, enjoy partying and ride a bike, but I've known some way worse people then myself. *If any of you fucks had half a clue what bad really is, I'd look like a fuckin Saint.*

The air conditioning hits me and it's like a drink of cool, refreshing water. *Christ it's a hot Texas day today. I'm thinking that run up north might be a good idea right now after all.* I only go on long runs when they need my strength. I usually help the Club Enforcer with his duties. It's relaxing to weed out the fucks that need persuaded, found, killed, etc… I never said I am a good guy just that I have met worse.

I hate shopping. This is why the brothers have their regular fucks go to the store for them. I'm too picky for that shit. I like what I like and don't need some piece of ass getting whatever she feels like. Men's body wash—Old spice sport, Toothpaste—Aqua fresh, Mouthwash—Colgate spearmint, Garnier hair goop for my fauxhawk. Bitches don't know that shit, and I don't want any of 'em to either. I better pick up some grub and Gatorade while I'm here too. Granola bars, Nutra Grain bars, Honey Buns, red Gatorade and some chicken strips for my lunch-check.

I make my way up towards the check-out aisles. I'm passing by the orange juice when I see the sexiest ass on a woman I think I've ever seen. I start to check out the rest of the package. *Bitch is bangin'* long straight black hair down her back, tattoos all over, hourglass figure. *Baby has some thighs I could seriously see wrapped around my face.* She's got the curves you grab onto from behind while you slam into her. She's tall but still short to my 6'1" self. *Please have a good face, please have a good face, please.*

"Hey sweet cakes, want me to get that juice for ya?" She's reaching for the top shelf, but the juice is pushed back too far for her. She turns to face me and I'm hit with some icy blue eyes in almond shaped eyes. I swear my dick convulses when I see her face, even if she is scowling. Her expression quickly changes to surprised. *There's only one person I've seen with those eyes before.* I blink and she comes into focus. *Holy fuck, she's grown up. London Layla Traverson, my school age crush. Boy she was a sweet one when we were in school. I still remember the only time I ever got to hold her close. Her best friend's mom had just died and London was a mess too. I was so happy I got to hold her, but I don't know if she even realized it was me that day.* Those beautiful blue eyes blink up at me a few times and I smirk. *You aren't the only one who's changed.*

"Hey hot stuff, that'd be great." She says sassily and winks at me. *Oh sweet cakes, you have no clue what you just did. I'm gonna get a taste of you this time.* I rest one hand on her hip as I reach past her and grab the juice. I squeeze my fingers a little and I hear her suck in her breath. *That's right baby.* I hand her the juice and grin my panty dropper grin down at her. *Works every time.*

"Thank you, what a true gentleman." She hits me back with a little smirk.

"Baby they're ain't nothin gentle about me." I reach out and tuck a piece of her silky black hair behind her ear. She chuckles a little and shakes her head like I just told her something cute.

"See ya around BABY." She says the baby part sarcastically and starts to walk off. *Grrrr I'm so gonna smack that ass when I get her on all four's.*

"Wait a sec, you left without asking for my number." She turns back and rolls her eyes at me.

"Why would I give you my number if you call me baby? Real original. Clearly I'm not like every "baby" out there. I'm colorful, at least try a little harder next time." She starts to walk to the front to a cash register. *Well fuck, apparently she's grown into a ball buster too. That's too bad; she used to be so sweet in school. Then again the last time I saw her I was in 7th grade. It's been what like 10 years?* She was a year younger than me but I used to go to her math class and help some of the students with math questions they had. She would always smile real sweet and ask me to help her. I thought she might have a little crush on me but I was shy back then. I ended up moving away. Well my dad went to jail so I didn't have a place to live anymore. I guess you call that "Moving."

I check out and head to the bike. I guess I had less shit then London because she comes walking out as I'm stuffing my purchases in my big backpack. She's parked one row over and there isn't many people here yet so the lot's pretty empty.

"Hey Layla!" I holler at her and she looks around the parking lot before her eye's come to rest on mine. She looks at me puzzled, probably wondering how I know her middle name.

"The only other thing I've ever called "Baby" is my bike. So take it as a huge compliment, sugar tits." I start my bike and rev the engine. She says something but I can't hear her over my pipes. I give her a two finger salute and drive out of the parking lot.

I keep checking my mirrors and London is right behind

me. Not too close or anything, but enough so I can tell it's her. *She can't live out here unless she lives' out of town.* The compound is outside Georgetown about 20 minutes to the east. *Maybe she's in school up at College Station?* I make my turn to the compound— *bye baby, glad I got to see you grown.* I give the sign to the prospect at the gate. *Shit what's his name again? I'm supposed to pay attention if he's doin ok so I can eventually vote him in. Ah fuck it, I'll ask Ares later.* He's the Enforcer and knows everything about everybody.

I park and shut off my bike as I'm climbing off; a car parks next to me. I look up *Shit he let London through the gate?!* She climbs out of her little silver Honda Civic.

"Hey!"

"What's up?" *Maybe she decided to give me her number after all.* She rounds the front of her car and comes to stand in front of me.

"Why did you call me Layla?" She has her forehead scrunched up and she looks adorable.

"It's your name right?" I ask her seriously. I know it used to drive her crazy when people would call her Layla because someone would always end up singing the song with it.

"Yo Cain! You just comin back from town?" I look over and Ares is walking towards me. Ares is a big motherfucker, I'm talking 6'6" and built like a brick house.

"Yea man, just hit up H.E.B. why?" I check him over, he doesn't seem to be pissed about anything. Yet I'm one of the few he actually let's see him get pissed. He likes to blank out on anyone else if something bothers him.

"Nothin bro, just need some smokes. I'll ride in, get some gas too." He gives me a chin lift and sits on his bike.

"I thought you quit man? Your ass is gonna get Cancer with all the road fumes!" Yes I am conscious about health, I may not make great decisions but I do try to take care of myself when I'm not partying. The only time I touch any drugs is before I brawl. Hence my name: "Cain." I like a little cocaine before my fight, it helps get me hyped up and ready to rip a fucker apart.

"When did you grow a pussy? I left my momma a long time ago, but if you wanna do some dishes go on in and let Candy know. She'll be happy to let you help her clean up."

"Fuck you man, we both know my dick's bigger than yours! Don't say I didn't worn your ass, when you're hacking up like an old fucker." He starts laughing and flips me off at the dick comment. We've both fucked bitches out in the bar so he knows my dick is bigger. I turn back to London, *shit I got sidetracked.*

"Your name's Cain?"

"Yea sweet cheeks. Why'd you follow me? You know you're in the lion's den coming onto the compound." She gives me a little smile and shrugs her shoulders.

"It's ok darlin' I'm not scared of cat's." *Oh man, this chick is pretty fuckin perfect!* I can't help it I bust out laughing. She's in the middle of a biker compound and she's calling us a bunch of cats. If she only knew. The prospect looks at me and I give him a chin lift so he knows she's ok. Doesn't matter the douche shouldn't have let her through the gate in the first place.

"So how did you know my name?" She smiles at me but looks curious now. *I've got her interested. I bet Layla was the last thing she expected to come out of my mouth.*

"Well we went to school together but I'm guessin you don't remember me?"

"Trust me Cain, I would remember you if we went to school together. I'm pretty sure I would have rode on the back of your bike a few times if you had." She gives me a cocky grin. *Yea I bet you were the fuckin cat's meow to all those boys not knowing how to handle someone like you.*

"Ah no, when I was in school I didn't have my bikes or my car. I think the last time I saw those icy blue eyes I was in 7th grade. You were always a cute little thing, but I must say I'm really appreciating this grown up version of you a lot more." She looks towards the sky like she's thinking really hard.

"I know a few boys who moved around that time, but I never knew a Cain. Did I ever talk to you?"

"Yea actually you used to ask me to help you with your math, I don't know why though. You were really smart, it was almost like you were just fuckin with me." Her eye's light up and she looks me over slowely from head to toe.

"I can take my clothes off if you wanna get a better look?"

"Were you this cocky back then? Cause I'd definitely remember you. The boy I remember always asking for help, I was in 6th grade and he moved, and his name was not Cain."

"I know sweet cheeks, my name is Brandon Meeks. I go by Cain now." Her eyes bug out and she looks at me from head to toe again. Just to be a bastard I reach back and start to pull the back of my shirt off at the nape of my neck.

"Eeek! What are you doing?" she yells.

"I told you I'd take them off so you can get a better look." I give her my panty dropper again and she returns it with her own sexy smile.

"Oh you're a bad, bad boy. Your straight trouble now aren't you?" I throw my shirt in my back pack and wink at her.

"I don't know what your talkin bout, I'm over here sweatin like a sinner in church, just tryin to cool off. What about you? You wanna take yours off and cool down too?" She beams a wide smile at me.

"Oh My God! You are bad! You were so sweet and shy back then!"

"Yea and you were short and didn't have a juicy ass either. I see time's been good to you though." She just smiles wide and shakes her head as I try to get into her pants.

"I gotta go Brandon, it's so awesome to see you though."

"All right London, give me your number so we can keep in touch this time, yea? And it's just Cain."

"Alright Cain, type your number in my phone." I grab it and enter my digits then quickly press the call button, in case she tries to sneak off without giving me hers. My phone vibrates and I hands hers back.

"Safe drive and text me sometime." I lean down and kiss her right on the lips. It was chaste but she clearly was not expecting me to just go right in. I'm not a pussy, I'll eat some, but I won't be one.

"Have a good one, oh and Cain? It's not baby." She says as she's getting into her car. I walk around to her window and she rolls it down. I lean on the car and put my face close to hers.

"Your only baby because I think you're as sexy as my bike. I told you, she's the only other one I've ever called baby before." I kiss her on the lips quickly again and walk towards the door to the club. *Yea she'll be back or text me.*

Available now:

Secrets (A Russkaya Mafiya Novel)
Book 1 Tate and Emily's Story

Exposed (A Russkaya Mafiya/Oath Keepers MC)
Book 2 London, Cain and Cameron's Story

Relinquish (A Russkaya Mafiya/Oath Keepers MC)
Book 3 Avery and 2 Piece's Story

Corrupted (A Russkaya Mafiya Novel)
Book 4 Viktor and Elaina's Story

Coming soon:

Friction (An Oath Keepers MC Novel)
Twist's Story

Forsaken Control (An Oath Keepers MC Novel) Ares Story

*Unwanted Sacrifices (*A Russkaya Mafiya Novel) Nikoli's Story

Unexpected Forfeit (A Ground and Pound Novel)

Stay up to date with Sapphire:

Email:

authorsapphireknight@yahoo.com

Website:

authorsapphireknig.wix.com/authorsapphireknight

Facebook:

www.facebook.com/AuthorSapphireKnight

REMEMBER ME

Gods of Chaos MC

By: Honey Palomino

Chapter One

RYDER

*We're not called the
Gods of Chaos for nothing.*

THE GLARE OF the streetlights hit the chrome on my bike as I turned off the freeway and onto the unpaved road that led to my clubhouse. Dirt flew up on both sides of my thick tires. My headlight cast shadows of the tall, towering pine trees of the Tillamook Forest across the road; the only thing lighting my way through the heavy darkness of the woods. Five curvy miles later, I was separated from all civilization, and the familiar peacefulness washed over me.

I was home. I was right where I belonged. I might have outgrown all the partying a little over the years, but it was all I had ever known. That life out there? Away from the clubhouse? I didn't belong there. I never had, and I never would.

As I roared up to the rundown cabin, the never-ending party was at its peak. Deafeningly loud music poured from the open doors and windows, and a glowing amber light spilled onto the dirty bikes parked out front. Each person that trailed in and out of the door had a drink in their hand and most had a smile on their face. The women all had a wiggle in their step, as they sashayed past leather-clad, drunken hell-raisers, flirtatiously batting their eyes and swinging their voluptuous hips.

The sun had set, and just like it did every night, the wildness began seeping out into the darkness at the God of Chaos MC Clubhouse like a slithering, evil snake.

IN THE CORNER of the parking lot, a circle had formed around Riot and Slade, two of the Gods. They were in their usual fighting stance, playing a game they both seemed to enjoy immensely, for whatever perverted reason. Both shirtless, their dirty jeans and boots were the only protection that stood between their flesh and the ground, or each other's fists.

Slade was bleeding through his grin, while Riot danced around him, trying to get another hit in before Slade knocked him out. Slade always won. I didn't bother to keep watching, because it always played out the same way. Slade would knock him out, then pick him up and take him inside and pour whiskey down his throat till he shook it off and they laughed about it into the early morning hours. They were both more than a little crazy, but I loved them.

Near the window to the right of the front door, I saw Zander, my VP. His old lady, Valerie, was on her knees, servicing him with a vigor that almost made me envious. I laughed when he caught my eye and winked at me as I pulled off my helmet and parked my bike. He gave me a thumbs up as I strode past him, shaking my head with a smile as he buried his hands in his old lady's black curls and looked up at the shining stars sprinkled in the sky above us.

The sound of breaking glass and a string of words that would have made a sailor blush echoed out the window on the other side of the front door.

As I approached the door, I ducked just in time to miss the flying beer bottle that escaped from the doorway, followed by Thorn, our prospect, – one hand gripping his girlfriend Tiff's ass, and the other outstretched and reaching for a wall to steady them both on. His hand missed by two inches, and they both tumbled to the ground in front of me, their tongues still firmly tangled together.

I stepped over them, picked up the surprisingly still intact beer bottle, and headed towards the bar to find a fresh one for myself.

This place was hardly what any normal person would consider peaceful. But that was just it. It wasn't normal.

And my brothers here? The outliers? The fringe of society? The partiers? The survivors? They weren't normal, either.

All we knew was chaos. The only way we knew how to live was on the edge.

We were born in it. We were raised in it.

It defines our very existence in this world.

Hell, every day we continue to create it, just by being alive.

We're the Gods of Chaos.

And we love every fucking chaotic second of it.

Chapter Two

GRACE

DO YOU EVER wish you could change the channel on your past? Give yourself a whole new identity, and lay down the unfortunate baggage you were assigned to carry into your future?

You do your best to leave it behind, but the memories stay with you. Indelible. Unforgettable. Unforgivable.

The best thing you can do is carry on and figure out how to cope when the memories sneak up on you unexpectedly. I should know. I've tried everything to forget. I've turned my back on the places, the people, the pain. But it's always there. Lingering, like a disease.

You can't pick where you came from.

But, eventually, when you get old enough, you can choose where you're headed.

And that's what I did. As soon as I could, I left all the dysfunction of my family behind, and I ran towards my future.

Unfortunately, it stays with you, and you quickly learn you can't forget it, no matter how much you try. If I couldn't forget, as much as I wanted to, I could use the past and everything I survived to make a new life of my own, and hopefully save some others in the process.

My name is Grace. Grace Evans. I used to be Grace Faith Taylor. But I escaped that life, and changed my name. Unlike a lot of people with similar histories, I was able to get out alive.

The key to surviving was simply leaving. As long as I wasn't around my family, I was safe. It was the opposite of how it was supposed to be. I didn't have a normal home.

Now that I was out, now that I was an adult, I set out to turn it around.

I survived hell, and I knew there were others still living in it, and a lot of them had it even worse than what I went through.

MY GOAL BECAME to get them all out, one by one, if that's what it took. No matter how long, or how hard or dangerous it became, it was worth it if I saved just one girl from one more day of suffering.

I grew up, I told my story, and I put my abusers away. The trial was torture, but I got what I wanted. Ten years each. I did my best to put it all behind me after that.

I changed my name to give myself a little distance, a little autonomy.

Then, I worked my ass off until I got into the exact position I needed to be in to do what I had decided I was put here on this Earth to do.

Stop the madness. Stop the abuse of women and children by predatory monsters that wanted only to use them up and spit them out. To do so, I became a monster myself. A one woman army fighting day and night, living and breathing my mission until I *was* the mission.

There was no personal life. There was just my life. And all the others I planned on saving along the way.

I was determined to let nothing get in my way, and so far, nothing had.

Not until now. Now, I had a problem. An obstacle.

And it was standing over me, watching the blood stream

out of my mouth with a joy so evil that it was oozing from him. The thick, heavy strike of his leather boot on my ribs pushed me back six inches in the dirt and my eyes began to blur as the flesh around them began to swell from the impact from his fists moments ago.

One by one, the stars in the sky disappeared, as did his voice, and I lay there motionless, staring into the immense blackness as it engulfed me completely.

From far away, I could hear his evil laughter echoing in my mind until it slowly morphed into a loud, overwhelming vibration that rang throughout my entire body. The trees towering over me, the rocks that lay on the ground beside my lifeless body – the very sky itself – began to vibrate violently and for so long that I finally melted into it, drifting off with the sensation, becoming one with the shaking, until all the pain was gone and I slept the most peaceful sleep I had ever slept in my entire life.

Chapter Three

RYDER

I AWOKE TO the sounds of crickets chirping outside my window, and a tongue twirling warmly around the shaft of my hard cock. Groaning, I reached down and sank my fingers into Cherry's copper curls and sank my cock deeper into her skillful mouth. Tiff's perky breasts pressed into my side as she squirmed against me, her soft body wrapping itself around me in the darkness.

After hours of sinking myself into both of them after returning to the clubhouse, I had drifted off to sleep. But, as usual, the girls were insatiable, only allowing me a brief time to rest before they were begging for more. And by begging, I mean taking. Asleep or not, you'd be hard-pressed to find any man that could resist the hardening of his cock in the presence of these two.

They knew exactly what I liked, and how I liked it. They also knew what I didn't like. And that was the most important skill of all.

I was all business. Don't get me wrong, I was more than happy to get serious between the sheets, or against the wall, or up against a tree in the middle of the woods, but once it was over, I had no time for messy feelings or clingy women. I wasn't old man material. I never had been, and I never would be.

Cherry and Tiff knew that, even if Cherry tried to get a little possessive sometimes. Every now and then, I'd have to remind her of the limits of our interactions. And sure, Tiff was technically our prospect Thorn's occasional squeeze, but as the President of the Gods of Chaos MC, I had earned the right to be with any of the club girls I wanted. Unless she was someone's old lady, and there was only one of those around these days. Most of the brothers weren't too interested in making these girls a permanent part of their lives. Sure, they might take a liking to one or two, but they were rarely attached to anyone in particular. So, I borrowed Tiff every now and then.

I liked the way she tasted. And she reminded me just how much by climbing up and straddling my face at the same time that Cherry smoothly mounted my cock. They rode me simultaneously, deliciously rocking their beautiful pussies against me, their lips and tongues melting together above me. The sound of their moans filled the clubhouse as we worked with a triple goal in mind. Tiff's pussy was like velvet against my tongue, as I fucked into both of them over and over, our bodies meeting in the space between, slamming into each other again and again, harder and faster with every sweet, debaucherous thrust.

Cherry tightened around my cock, her spasming pussy rhythmically pulling me over the edge as I reached up, and grabbing Tiff's hips, I pulled her down towards me and pressed my tongue into her deeper and deeper until she was thrashing above me, the three of us coming together in a symphony of moans and soft screams, our voices echoing into the darkness of the still black night.

We collapsed in a pile of naked limbs on my bed, the girls cooing on either side of me as I caught my breath, our chests rising and falling in the quiet room. This time, the girls drifted off to sleep, and I gently untangled myself, leaving them cuddled together as I snuck off to the shower.

I cherished times like these. Rarely was there anything quiet about the clubhouse. The sounds of the party had faded long ago, and I knew all too well the scene that would greet me when I opened the door that led out of the peaceful privacy of my room and into the chaos of the clubhouse. But every now and then, I was blessed with being awake during those moments in between the chaos.

The peace was comforting.

I showered and dressed quietly, pulling my jeans over my hips, buckling my heavy silver skull belt-buckle, and placing my piece in the gun pocket of my cut. My knife slid smoothly into its leather case on my left hip, and my second knife fit snugly into my black leather harnessed biker boots. I stretched a clean, white t-shirt over my tattooed torso, and shrugged my cut on over my shoulders. I never felt quite right until I had my cut on.

Like I said before, chaos was my life. This vest was a badge of honor, a symbol of respect for everything I chose to do, the very person I chose to be.

It was a part of me just as much as my skin was.

I took one last look at the girls in my bed, looking like angels sleeping with nothing covering them but the pale moonlight streaming in from the window.

Any normal man would not be leaving. Any normal man would not be about to wind his way through the remnants of last night's party, straddle a dangerous machine, and roar straight into the pitch black danger of the night to meet up with a fellow criminal to plan their weekly agenda of crimes. No. Any normal man wouldn't have done any of that.

But, like I said before, there's nothing normal about me.

I walked through spilled beer, side-stepped naked bodies strewn all around, picked up some broken glass, and turned down the stereo behind the bar. When I stepped outside, it felt like only minutes had passed since I had walked in. In truth, it had been several hours, but the night felt young, and as I took a deep breath, letting the cold air fill my lungs, I felt invigorated. Strong.

I pulled on my helmet, started up my bike, and drove slowly, peacefully, down the winding road that would lead me to the main highway that would eventually lead me to the coast, where I was expected in an hour. Plenty of time to go slow and enjoy the stillness of the night.

Unfortunately, that peace was short-lived. As soon as I spotted the headlights, I knew something was wrong. Nobody ever came this far down our road, and if they did, they were on a bike and I knew them well.

At first, I could only make out the shadow of the man. His long, sleek El Camino shimmered in the moonlight like a snake lying behind him, lighting him up. When he turned towards me, I saw the glint of gold in his mouth. Then, I saw the silhouette of his cock in one hand, and a pistol in the other. He froze like a deer in my headlight, to my advantage. Before he could think to take one step towards me, I was on him. As I jumped off my bike, I saw the woman lying at his feet. I saw her bloody face, her skirt hiked up around her hips, her bare legs and feet covered in scratches, and I attacked without any further thought or debate.

Whoever this guy was, he was no good.

I barreled into his chest, knocking him off his feet, his gun skidding through the dirt and resting in the grass ten feet away. Stunned, he stared up at me, locking eyes with me as I grabbed him by the lapels of his filthy white suit jacket. A crumpled pink carnation clung to his front pocket like a dying wish.

"Who the fuck are you?" I asked.

"Fuck you!" A sickly, evil grin spread across his gaunt face.

SWEET ANTICIPATION SPREAD through my veins as I asked one more question before pummeling him.

"Who is she?" I asked, my chin jutting in the direction of the still motionless, bloody woman.

"Just a cunt who deserves what she got." The sick sneer remained on his face until the first contact of my fist. The rest was a blur. I don't know how long I hit him. At least until he stopped moving. A shot in his leg, just in case he decided to come back to while I went to check on the girl.

She had a pulse. Gently, I pulled her long blonde hair away from her face. Her eyes were closed and the swelling was already beginning. My eyes trailed up and down her battered body, and rage swelled inside of me again.

My eyes darted over to the man, and he began moaning softly, barely moving, like a dying piece of roadkill. I rose, my stride unflinching, with more purpose than I had ever felt in my life. My gun was heavy in my hand. My bicep twitched as it went off, my hand holding onto my weapon steadily, with ease, with confident intention.

And then he stopped moving. Suddenly. Easily.

And just like that, the stillness returned. But, while the peacefulness I loved had only been interrupted by a few moments, now, everything was different.

That stillness now came with a price.

I stood over her, staring down at this strange woman, and wondering what the hell I had stumbled upon. Who was she? A hooker? His lover?

I rifled through the El Camino, and found nothing but a

bottle of lube in the glove compartment and a few condoms under the front seat. Two joints were in the ash tray, which I pocketed. No purse, though. I walked over to the dead guy, taking him in briefly before looking through his pockets. I wasn't much on fashion, but even I could tell his suit was cheap by the thin, rough fabric and his shoes, while very shiny, weren't even real leather. His stringy black hair was slicked back away from his ugly, pock-marked face.

I FOUND HIS wallet, with an ID that said he was Franco Javier Corona and had an address in Gresham. Three hundred and fifty-seven dollars in small bills, and two hotel card keys, and not much else. I pocketed the cash, and tucked his wallet back inside his suit jacket.

I looked at the girl again, and shook my head. Something wasn't right. She was too healthy, too pretty to be a hooker. Way too fucking pretty to be the dead guy's girlfriend. Her skin, while bruised and scratched, was smooth and toned, with a perfect bronze sheen to it. Her curvy hips swelled away from a taut, strong core of perfect ab muscles that I could see a flash of because her black tank top was pushed up against the swell of her full breasts. Every hooker I had ever seen was emaciated and ravaged from drugs and other various abuses, and the girl laying in front of me looked as healthy as a prized horse.

A prized, knocked-out, completely unconscious horse.

I realized then I needed to work fast. She would just have to tell me who she was when she woke up. But for now, I needed to get her out of here, and clean up this mess.

I took a step towards her, and my eye caught a slight movement to my left. I looked over in the shadows, and couldn't believe my eyes.

An owl. *The* owl. *No, it couldn't be,* I thought. But he was a dead ringer for the damned owl that had appeared only twice in my past. And just like before, he sat there, staring at me, his huge eyes blinking, calm and noble, looking as if he owned the fucking forest. Could it really be the same one?

If it was, then I knew this was a terrible omen.

The first time he appeared was so long ago, it almost felt like a dream. Twenty years ago and it was the last and only time I had ever loved a woman. I was a naive twenty year old, and I couldn't wait to marry Julie. Young or not, naive or not, I knew she was the one I needed to spend the rest of my life with. We got married on the Oregon coast, both of us wearing black leather and huge smiles. After a year of love-drenched bliss, she died in a senseless car crash coming home from work. The night I lost her, this damn owl showed up as I stampeded through the forest, screaming at the moon in a drunken rage and grief-filled bout of insanity. He sat perched on a rock, his huge golden eyes blinking at me, his eyes filled with what I perceived at the time to be understanding.

THE SECOND TIME was ten years later when my dad died, leaving behind an empty seat at the head of the table at the clubhouse. There was nobody else qualified to fill it, so there I sat, the middle of the night, all alone, listening to my old man's favorite Waylon Jennings record. It was a hot summer night, and the windows were open, the blackness of the forest quiet and inky beyond the window. The owl appeared out of nowhere, landing on the windowsill in a soft, sweeping flap of his feathery wings, scaring the ever-loving shit out of me. We sat there for several long moments, staring each other down in the quiet stillness of the night. Again, he blinked over and over, and my blood went cold when it dawned on me the last time I had seen him was when Julie had died.

And now here he was again. Only this time, he was sitting in the grass, the moonlight falling over his body as he gazed up at me. Something about him was different, but that didn't dawn on me right away. Later, I would realize he looked friendlier, curious almost. Not so serious, perhaps. But tonight, just like before, he filled me with terror just by appearing. So much so that it abruptly jarred me out of my daze and I quickly set into motion.

Gently, I lifted up the girl and placed her in the El Camino. She didn't budge even slightly, worrying me even more. I threw the man's body in the back of the El Camino, thanking him out loud when I saw the tarp already back there, just waiting for the perfect dead body to come along and wrap itself up in it.

"What a thoughtful piece of shit you are," I said to him as I closed the tailgate.

After parking my bike on the side of the road, I hopped in the driver's seat, turning on the ignition. My eyes locked with the owl's once again, who had been silently watching my every move.

"Shit," I muttered to myself.

I started the car and headed down the road back to the clubhouse, watching the owl grow smaller and smaller in the rearview mirror behind me.

MISLED

By: Kathryn Kelly

He deals in a world of violence, sex, drugs, and crudity. As president of the Death Dwellers' Motorcycle Club, Christopher "Outlaw" Caldwell presides over a club in chaos after the death of their longtime president and his mentor, Joseph "Boss" Foy.

Megan Foy runs from her abusive stepfather, hoping for her daddy's intervention to save her and get her terrified mother away before it's too late. Only problem is, she soon discovers her beloved daddy is dead and the man who killed him is the man she's falling in love with.

This is a full-length novel.

Warning: FOR MATURE AUDIENCES ONLY. CONTAINS PHYSICAL ABUSE, VIOLENCE, RAPE, AND EXCESSIVE PROFANITY.

Preface

IN EACH OF us lives good and evil. The conundrum we face as a society is recognizing those we pigeonhole as evil and those we applaud as good. That's the grossest mislabeling in the world, the greatest injustice. Have we not heard of the fable of *The Wolf in Sheep's Clothing*? Do we yet misunderstand how deceptive appearances can be? The sun casting a golden gleam upon us doesn't shield us from the rain. Good and evil are wrapped in illusions we're determined to create.

The man society views as acceptable…you know the one…? He gives up his seat to little old ladies. Attends church. Sings carols with good cheer. Gives a hand out and a help up. That man, too, has evil lurking in the depths of his soul. Perhaps, he's more evil. This man has the ability to charm and smile and manipulate the world to see his goodness. When, in fact, he's the scariest of all.

He's a wife beater and a child molester. He tears down under the pretense of building up.

I know him well.

He's my stepfather.

Chapter 1

"NO! PLEASE. *STOP!*"

The crack of a hand connecting with flesh tore through the tension. Meggie jumped and wrapped her arms around her middle, her sob competing with her mother's pleas. She sat on the edge of her bed, body trembling, praying her mother would survive this latest beating.

Another lick. Dinah wept and Meggie's belly roiled at the tormented sounds.

"Please, Thomas," Dinah cried. "You've got to stop!"

Meggie nodded vigorously. Yes, he had to stop. One of these days he'd kill her mom.

Glass shattered and furniture banged. Dry heaves wracked Meggie at the heavy thud. She knew that sound, knew it meant her mother was careening to the floor. Dinah screamed and Meggie doubled over, sweat popping off her skin, her mother's pain her own.

Surrounded by her white bedroom furniture and pastel green décor, she wondered how her home life was such a nightmare. On the outside, everyone saw the perfect family—a woman, an assistant high school principal, finding happiness in her second marriage with the teddy bear of a middle school math teacher who'd stepped in as a father-figure to the woman's daughter.

Dinah's scream coupled with tearing clothes. Though not in the den, Meggie had seen the situation play out enough to pick out the sounds and their meanings.

"Please," Dinah sobbed. "I don't want to."

She didn't want to have sex, she meant. Meggie bowed her head into her hands, wishing for the strength and fortitude to take it upon herself to kill her stepfather.

"Let's go in the bedroom." Dinah's breath caught around a moan.

Thomas grunted. "I'm fucking you right here. Right out in the open."

Embarrassment competed with Meggie's fear and anger.

Her mother's next sob burned through Meggie and she covered her face.

"Don't. Not in the den. I don't want Meggie to hear."

"Think she's not fucking?"

No. Meggie bit into her wrist, barely feeling the injury but tasting metallic blood.

"No," Dinah echoed through tears. "She's a virgin."

"No. She's not," Thomas sneered. "I should know."

Oh God. Oh God. Oh God. Meggie stared at her bite mark, oozing red, and shook her head in denial.

Silence met Thomas's lie and he took advantage of the stunning insinuation by taunting, "she's been coming on to me for months. I thought it best to keep it in the family."

"Wh-what?"

Meggie wasn't sure if she wanted her mother to believe Thomas or not. Dinah was too broken to attempt to defend her. She hadn't even allowed the police to haul Thomas away, a week ago, when Meggie had called 911. Instead, she'd blamed her injuries on something asinine and stupid. For Meggie's attempt to defend Dinah that night, she'd gotten her bedroom door removed.

"You lying bastard," Dinah screamed.

Meggie drew in a sharp breath, her already aggravated pulse and heart rate throbbing in her ears. She spread her blood over her skin, attempting to refocus.

Thomas yelped and, for a few blessed moments, it sounded as if Dinah asserted herself and inflicted serious damage.

"You fucking bitch!" he snarled. "I'm going to kill you."

"Big Joe is coming for her," Dinah persisted in a wild, unrecognizable tone. "I called him! And I'm going to tell him. I'm going to tell him you've violated his baby. I'm going to tell him and he's going to kill you. He's going to chop your dick off and feed it to pigs."

Meggie cheered at the thought. Her daddy was coming. She'd been trying to reach him for weeks. Left so many messages, it surprised her his voicemail wasn't filled to capacity. She knew how busy he was, so the fact he hadn't answered wasn't real surprising. Sometimes, it took her months to get a response from him. Before, he'd just blaze into town on his bike, the noise of his Harley pipes rumbling in the quiet suburb blocks away. He took a lot of trips, something he called runs.

Ever since Dinah had barred him from visiting at Thomas's insistence, two years ago, Meggie always imagined going on the road with him and his boys.

"You know how hard your fighting makes me, huh, baby?" Thomas crooned.

"Y-yes."

"I'm not letting Megan live with him. When he comes, tell him she's not interested in going with him." He groaned and gasped. "Tell him she doesn't want to see him. Ever again."

Dinah moaned. "Right there, Thomas. Harder."

Meggie's cheeks burned and her stomach churned at Thomas's filthy response. And so the cycle continued, she thought, humiliated. She stretched to her pillow and retrieved the little knife she kept hidden under it. Pressing the sharp blade against her forearm, she sliced down, sucking in a breath at the brief burn and pain. Blood rushed from the wound and her tension and fear seeped away with it. The respite lasted a moment. The satisfaction dwindled in the amount of time it took the pain to recede.

Sniffling, she tightened her mouth and slashed again. Meggie swiped her tears once more and slashed at the wrist she'd bitten.

"Ah, God!" She'd gone deeper than she intended and had to grab the sheet to staunch the flow of blood, the sounds from the den both sickening and infuriating. She wasn't sure if her mother truly liked Thomas's attention or if she just accepted it. In the end, no matter what Thomas said or did, Dinah gave him sex. Meggie didn't want to see her mother as a weak, pathetic woman because it went deeper than that.

Dinah had tried to run in the early days of their marriage. Both times Thomas had found her and beaten her to a bloody pulp before using his fists on Meggie. Her mother had just given up and given in. She knew her mother refused to risk Meggie being hurt again because of her escape attempts.

"Meggie?"

She raised her gaze at the sound of her mother's whimper. Dinah stood in the doorway, her face swollen and bloody, bruises covering her naked body. She clutched the wood molding, trembling.

The sight tore through Meggie and she shoved her knife under the bloody sheet. She stood and swallowed; her chin wobbled. Both she and her mother were wrecks but she couldn't add any stress by allowing her injuries to show. She stepped forward, arms behind her back. "Momma."

Dinah went sprawling and Meggie hurried to the door. Thomas stood inches away, naked, too, and smelling of sweat and alcohol. Unable to stop it, Meggie glared at him, her cheeks burning at the sight of his flaccid penis and hairy testicles. Not that she hadn't seen him nude before but the sight always repulsed her.

The back of his hand shot out. Meggie didn't jump out of reach fast enough. Stars danced in front of her eyes at the slap.

"Please. Not Meggie," Dinah whined, prone on the squeaky clean linoleum.

Thomas kicked Dinah's thigh and she whimpered again. Meggie growled and launched herself at Thomas, buoyed by the thought of her father coming for her, not caring if Thomas beat the crap of her. She'd learned to cover her pain and bruises but she wouldn't have to. She could show each little hurt to her daddy and he'd find a way to make them go away. He'd make *him* go away.

Her fingernails dug into Thomas's cheek and she drew them down, drawing blood just like he drew her mother's blood and sometimes hers. He grabbed her upper arms and slammed her against the wall. Meggie bounced and stumbled onto Dinah, who lay silent and still, but warm, the rise of fall of her back assuring she lived. Thomas yanked Meggie to her feet by her hair. She kicked, connecting with his penis and he dropped to his knees.

Meggie blew out puffs of air, not having much time. Steeped in drunken insanity, Thomas's meanness and strength rivaled a dozen men. She doubted he'd even feel a bullet.

Stupid bull of a man.

Ignoring her pain, she scrambled to her mother and latched onto her hands, pulling her forward. "Come on, Momma. Help me."

She needed to get them to Dinah's bedroom. Just until Thomas drank himself into a stupor and passed out. If she couldn't convince Dinah the wisdom of leaving while Thomas slept off the vodka and bourbon, then, at least, the latest danger would pass. Thomas would be sick for a day and sober for a couple more. Sometimes, he even went a week without drinking. Sober, his hits lacked so much viciousness and murderous intent.

Meggie pulled Dinah another inch and her mother groaned. Thomas roared to his feet. She didn't want to leave her mother but her sense of self-preservation took over. Dropping Dinah's arms, Meggie stumbled toward the nearest door, the half bath right next to her bedroom. His arms encircled her waist. He lifted her off her feet. Meggie screamed, struggling in his arms.

He stepped over Dinah, keeping a firm grip on Meggie, and walked into her bedroom. Reaching her bed, he slammed her down. She sprung up and barreled into him, the maneuver useless. When his hand neared her, somehow she dodged it and, instead, sunk her teeth into the fleshy side.

"Bitch!" he yelled, crashing his fist on the side of her head and her world went black.

MEGGIE ACHED EVERYWHERE—her face, arms, hands, belly, thighs, knees, legs and feet. Even the top of her head and her breasts throbbed. Wincing, she lifted herself on her elbows, the moonlight reflecting on her bare body. Blood and bruises glimmered in a grotesque sheen and she shivered, her skin burning, her insides cold. Whatever sick twist in the universe sent Thomas into their lives wrapped itself tighter and tighter.

Feeling the pain of Thomas's rage sweeping through her body, she understood her mother's decisions. It was the other times. The times when she only listened and witnessed, she resented Dinah's inaction. She sniffled and fell back onto her pillows, tears slipping down her cheeks. The two of them gave bodies of evidence a literal meaning. On them lay a wealth of substantiation Thomas was a violent pig. Then, again, on them a mountain of proof validated Dinah had bad taste in men.

Meggie thought her mother had all types of demons to contend with. While she could always judge Dinah, tell her life happened, she knew so many other factors were in this twisted tale; therefore, her inaction could be overlooked and excusable. Meggie's couldn't.

Dinah didn't fight back. Meggie's sense of outrage overwhelmed her at times and she couldn't help but fight back but there was absolutely no winning with Thomas. Unless they ended up on an outpost in Antarctica, he'd always find them and hurt them. One day, he'd kill them if Meggie didn't do something.

That her mother had done one small thing and telephoned Big Joe was enough. Thomas wasn't going to allow her to leave. No, he wanted to sever all ties between her and her father. But Meggie couldn't allow that to happen. Her father would protect her and rescue Dinah. No matter what else had passed between him and Dinah, he loved Meggie enough that he'd want to see her mother safe.

She swiped the backs of her hands across her cheeks, pain shooting through her at the skim over her welts, bruises and self-inflicted injuries. "Ow!"

The overhead light flipped on and Meggie blinked, the sudden brightness hurting her eyes. She curled her knees into her chest, praying for the ability to disappear. By the time she came to, Dinah and Thomas had been locked in their bedroom. Meggie had dragged herself to her bed, just over an hour ago, taking comfort in her surroundings, which reminded her of happier times. All around her were items she and her mother had chosen when Meggie turned thirteen. A redecorated room had been her birthday present. No expense had been spared, courtesy of her father. Meggie loved Monet and had a replica of *Renoir Painting In His Garden* hanging on her wall. Another wall had a framed print of Minnie Mouse with the words *Explore the Magic Inside*. Pretty lame, she knew, but she really liked Minnie Mouse.

"Girl."

Gritting her teeth, Meggie pretended she didn't hear Thomas, just as she'd zoned out the glare of the light when he'd walked in. Pink roses entwined with green vines were etched on the scalloped headboard on her bed. The footboard wasn't so fancy.

Meggie huddled closer to the wall, searching for her knife but finding the razor blade she'd stashed a week ago.

Thomas's heavy breathing polluted the air and grated on Meggie's nerves. She clenched her teeth, pretending he wasn't there, and raised the front of her gown. Thin silvery lines crisscrossed her outer thighs, mapping all the places she controlled what happened to her body. He was moving around in the room but she didn't care. She knew what was coming, so she pushed his presence out of her head and ran her fingers through her pubic hair. It was so soft, unlike Thomas's. She swallowed, held her breath, and dug the blade into the flesh on her hip, slicing straight, neat and not very deep, moaning at the pressure, the sting. The hurt.

"Scoot over."

She did as instructed, shuddering when he pulled her into his arms and pinched her nipples. She dragged the blade through her upper thigh, the new wounds mingling with the older ones, and the blessed numbness she wanted embracing her. He shoved her nightgown above her waist and bit into her shoulder. She recited the words to *Wrecking Ball* in her head, fisting the blade in her hand, the pain tearing through her just as Thomas inserted his finger…*there.*

"Your ass is made for fucking," he breathed.

Warm blood ran down her hand, joining the dried blood from earlier. He fumbled in his pajamas, his finger going in and out of her.

She remained quiet, still, the song beating through her head, her blood sliding down her skin. The overhead light reflected against her window, but Meggie concentrated and found the prettiness of the night. The clear, velvety brightness of the sky. The…

He shoved his flaccid penis against her and Meggie whimpered, unable to stop it. One day, he'd be sober enough to get a real erection. One day, he'd hurt her rather than just humiliate her. If she didn't act. She trembled, her body a desert of pain and a tundra of shame, layered, hot on top of cold and cold on top of hot.

His hand fluttered across her belly and teased her pubic hair. Cutting her other wrist, Meggie closed her eyes, able to cope and pretend this was a man she *wanted* to make love with. The man who'd love and protect her. He'd listen to Bruno Mars and Miley Cyrus and Adele and Alicia Keys with her. He'd overlook her shame and what she couldn't control and what she willingly did.

God, please. She *would* find that man. She *had* to.

Thomas's fingers squeezed her clitoris and Meggie tensed, his alcohol-laced breath fanning across her cheek. She was as much a coward as her mother. If she had courage, she'd slice Thomas to pieces. She'd kill him with her bare hands, all five feet eleven inches and two-hundred fifty pounds of the mean pig.

"I'm gonna fuck you soon."

Revulsion turned her stomach, competing with all her other emotions and aches. Dinah didn't know how far Thomas had gone with Meggie over the past few months and she worried, if she told her mother, Dinah would be too frightened to do anything about it.

"Your stupid bitch mama refuses to put you on the pill." He licked her ear and snickered, pulling back before slamming against her again. "I bet she will now after I kicked her ass tonight and showed her how I intend to fuck you."

Big, overgrown tyrannosaurus rex. Under the guise of trying to free herself and knowing she couldn't, Meggie jerked her elbow back and thunked his nose. The sharp intake of his breath made the hard slap against her belly he punished her with worth the pain.

He removed his hand from her clit. "Cold, fucking whore. Can't even come when I'm rubbing your pussy."

The scent of alcohol seeped through his pores. His sweat dripped onto her face, mixing with her tears. She wouldn't allow this man to ruin her. Never. She hadn't ever lived anywhere except with her mother, but she had to get to her father. It didn't matter that she'd have to drop out of high school in her senior year. Neither did it matter that her father headed the Death Dwellers' MC. He'd welcome her and he'd get her mother away. She'd call and, if he didn't answer, she'd leave a message and tell him she'd come to him. He didn't have to pick her up.

Thomas grunted then stiffened before shuddering and relaxing his grip on her. A moment later, he yanked her face to the side, almost breaking her neck. He planted his mouth over hers and shoved his tongue past her lips.

Thomas cupped Meggie's sex and squeezed. "I want all that innocence between your legs. Your father will never get you. Never. You're mine."

Though she should've known better, she couldn't help her resistance, which only infuriated Thomas more. He cuffed the side of her head and stars danced in front of her, lulling her to the darkness. She resisted, refusing to give in so completely. If she didn't run away, he'd ruin her and, eventually, kill her. Dinah had married this pig. Meggie hadn't and determination to get away from his sick perversions possessed her.

He leaned in and Meggie spat in his face, then threw her hands over her head to protect herself. He shoved her onto her back, ignoring the cuts she'd done because they were interspersed with bruises he'd caused. He stretched out on top of her and her body screamed in pain. Hatred flowed between them and she almost wished one of them would end it for the other.

But she didn't want to die. Not really. She just wanted to escape and be in control of her body. She wanted someone to love her and shield her. Until she got to her daddy, though, responsibility for her well-being fell on her shoulders. She tried to gulp in air but her lungs struggled for oxygen, Thomas's heavy weight crushing her and placing her well-being in dire jeopardy.

Mama, please, where are you?

Beaten and brutalized and in her bedroom.

Meggie brought her blade to his cheek, furious. Caught off guard, Thomas clutched his cheek and fell to her side. She scrambled over him and off her bed, just managing to evade his grasping hands.

"You little fucking bitch. I'm going to kill you."

Blood dripped from a variety of wounds on her body, so she couldn't hide in the secret cupboard she'd found. A trail of blood would lead him straight to her. Instead, she ran into the bathroom and locked the door.

Meggie rushed to the window over the sink. She kept it unlocked for this reason, learned from almost five years of living with this. Thomas kicked at the door and she shuddered, sorry she hadn't told her father the truth when Dinah first barred him from visiting anymore. He'd asked her.

"Talk to me, Meggie. Is there anything I should know?"

"No, Daddy. I swear, we're fine."

His blue eyes, so like hers, had taken in every last detail of her features, then he'd nodded. He'd seemed old in that instant, tired, and so sad Meggie wanted to cry.

"So your momma just want to cut me out like that? All because the asshole she married don't like me."

"I guess, Daddy," she whispered. The truth lodged in her throat, right on the edge of her lips. Big Joe looked tall and intimidating, his blond hair reminiscent of a Berserker rather than a modern day motorcycle man. If nothing else, he'd take her with him. But, then, she'd have to leave Dinah behind and she couldn't bear to think of her mother being alone with Thomas. "They just told me last night." She mumbled the lie.

Big Joe crouched to her eye level. "You don't lie good, sweetheart."

She lowered her eyelids, embarrassed she'd been caught. Her arms throbbed from her cuts. New ones. Old ones. Partially healed ones. Her long-sleeves hid the wounds from her father, but the guilt of the injuries weighed upon her.

Another moment of silence went by before he turned on his heel and headed for his bike. Before climbing on, he shoved money into Meggie's hands. "Go shopping. Cheer yourself up."

Shopping sounded good. She nodded and embraced him, her world a train of dominoes collapsing at a reckless speed.

"You need me, call. I'm a phone call away. Remember, you're my daughter. No matter what that asshole says to you, don't believe shit. The problem is his, not yours."

Thomas's words weren't the problem. It was his actions.

"If the fucker does anything," Big Joe continued, like he'd seen her thoughts, *"that's when he's going to have real problems. Understand, Megan?"*

That had been the last time she'd seen her father and that conversation haunted her. So much could've been different if she'd spoken up.

Meggie climbed onto the counter and wriggled through the window, feet first. Another exercise borne of desperation. Just as the door crashed open, she landed on the ground outside. Grimacing at the pain, Meggie headed to the clearing behind the house.

"Megan! Where the fuck are you?" The call, through the open window he couldn't fit through, resounded in the quiet night.

She reached her favorite tree, the smell of the spruce and bark and grassy earth calming her, soothing the exhaustion overtaking her. Thomas would pass out soon enough. Meggie just had to bide her time and wait.

Note from Author
&
Links

I hope you enjoyed the story of Crusher and Dani. My readers have expressed mixed feelings on Dani. Through this book she became my favorite heroine to date. She was twisted up inside at a young age and yet she comes out strong and able to love. Some of these scenes were graphic and so hard to write. I'm not sure why I can't do happy-go lucky romance in this series, but it is what it is heh. I have a lot of plans coming up. Besides finishing this series with Bull's story. I am launching a new MC Series with Skull's crew in a new anthology involving Cora Brent who has been one my author stalks since before she created the Gentry Boys and made me fall in love with her forever. I hope you will be on the lookout for it. Skull's crew are definitely interesting. And four members will get their story, including and perhaps the one I'm most anticipating, Beast.

    I couldn't leave this mountain of a book without saying thank you one more time and asking you to stalk me! Well not in the boiled rabbits kind of way, but I truly love talking to readers and finding out their thoughts on my books and well just talking. I'm a talker.

Until next time readers! Much love.

J

Links

Facebook:

www.facebook.com/JordanMarieAuthor

TSU:

www.tsu.co/Jordan_Marie

Pinterest:

www.pinterest.com/jordanmarieauth

Twitter:

twitter.com/Author_JordanM

Goodreads:

www.goodreads.com/author/show/9860469.Jordan_Marie

Newsletter:

http://eepurl.com/barBKv

Webpage:

jordanmarieauthor.com

Playlists

Breaking Dragon Playlist
open.spotify.com/user/12149197675/playlist/1JWfJFpsf4odID9kgVULIV

Saving Dancer Playlist
open.spotify.com/user/12149197675/playlist/1uMJhzmhkKYLeWWW7aBZZX

Loving Nicole Playlist
open.spotify.com/user/12149197675/playlist/1p4Kgn2s29r8ywpOTHWpvr

Claiming Crusher Playlist
open.spotify.com/user/12149197675/playlist/4DW9gRKGd2hEHaJfJOBg4q

Printed in Great Britain
by Amazon.co.uk, Ltd.,
Marston Gate.